"CAN'T YOU UNDERSTAND WHAT THIS MEANS TO ME?"

Sarah begged him, "You can't cheapen this island—my home—in a movie!"

"Cheapen it," Steve repeated slowly. "Is that how you see my work?" His dark eyes glared as his hand snapped out to grasp her wrist like a vise. "Listen, you spoiled little rich— You wouldn't fight me on this if you knew me at all."

"Let go of me," she cried, trying to shake free. "This island is not for public viewing! Some people need privacy, but I guess you can't see that, can you, Mr. Macho Movie Star?"

He flung her arm away, and she saw in his eyes something indefinable...not anger. With an aching heart she murmured, "I—I've hurt you. I'm sorry, Steve."

"Keep your sympathy," he said tightly as he turned away. "The hurt went out of me long ago."

AND NOW...

SUPERROMANCES

Worldwide Library is proud to present a sensational new series of modern love stories— SUPERROMANCES

Written by masters of the genre, these longer, sensuous and dramatic novels are truly in keeping with today's changing life-styles. Full of intriguing conflicts, the heartaches and delights of true love, SUPERROMANCES are absorbing stories— satisfying and sophisticated reading that lovers of romance fiction have long been waiting for.

SUPERROMANCES
Contemporary love stories for the woman of today!

Constance F. Peale

GIVE US FOREVER

A SUPERROMANCE FROM
WORLDWIDE

TORONTO · LONDON · NEW YORK · SYDNEY

Published, May 1982

First printing March 1982

ISBN 0-373-70019-9

CHAPTER ONE

IT WAS RAINING in New York City.

Sarah Mackenzie stood at her office window and peered into the mist, and was able to see only a few lights in the skyscraper opposite. Usually, from her office on the twentieth floor of the building that housed the Duncan-Fairchild Advertising Agency, she could gaze wistfully over midtown Manhattan, and somehow whatever problems she was having with a difficult account were minimized. When it was sunny thousands of windows of countless other structures reflected the tapestry that was New York—a tapestry that included lacy bridges, a vast expanse of water and, in the distance, the proud Statue of Liberty.

But the problem today wasn't a particularly stubborn account, and though she usually enjoyed the rain, the opaque swirl of late-August showers outside did nothing to lighten Sarah's mood. She felt more confined than ever before, and sensing rather than seeing the rush of humanity beneath her, more alone. She found herself suddenly homesick for Samsqua, the island off the coast of Maine that had been her home for twenty years and was often her refuge when New York became too much for her. Her co-workers and friends couldn't understand the sometimes radical shift from self-assured career woman to one who loved the rustic simplicity of her island home, and sometimes neither did Sarah.

She caught her reflection in the rain-dotted window and sighed. *Well, Sarah Mackenzie,* she thought, *are you going to go running back to your island, or do you live up to your New York image and get to work?* Running a hand through her short auburn curls, she tried to take an honest look at herself. She knew she wasn't beautiful in the high-fashion sense of the word, but she was thankful for the prominent cheekbones and clear green eyes—a little too wide set, she thought—that she'd inherited from her mother's side of the family. The Concannons had been sturdy pioneers who'd settled on the island of Samsqua in the early 1800s, and Sarah hoped the same strength of character she saw in her grandmother's face was mirrored in her own.

She turned back to her desk and picked up a paperweight. It was a winter scene embedded in acrylic plastic, and she always expected the snow to start falling when she turned it upside down. The scene on it, one of her sister's first artsy-craftsy works, was supposed to be the snowy wharf at Samsqua. Johanna had made it for Sarah's fourteenth birthday. She'd loved the paperweight from the moment she'd seen it, and later, when she'd left the island, she'd developed an odd attachment to it. She never looked at it without remembering her struggle to pay the rent on her first New York apartment, and the terrible feelings of homesickness and despair she'd experienced then. Such changes she'd been through since that first walk-up flat in a dingy—and dangerous—part of the city! She'd forged her way into the upper ranks of one of New York's best-known ad agencies and her work had paid off. *You've arrived, girl,* she mused. *Don't let them—and yourself—down now.*

At that moment Gail, her tiny wren of a secretary, knocked discreetly and opened the door to Sarah's office. Gail was the most optimistic person Sarah had ever encountered. She was always in a good mood, even when tempers burst into a thousand hot embers and scalding words hung in the air for hours. A petite blonde, she gazed at the world through eyes that seemed as large and blue as the Pacific. She gave Sarah a wry smile and said, "Webb Jackson is on the line, boss. Sorry."

"Gail, I just can't face him now," Sarah groaned. "Can you put him off?"

"It's about his interview tomorrow. You've been promising for weeks."

"I'd better take it, then, I guess." She really did not want to listen to those wisecracks that Jackson's *Women's Wear Daily* readers loved so much. Being interviewed by the brash but somehow likable man was a little like fencing with a master: sometimes you won, but more often you didn't. Still, she usually enjoyed the challenge of pitting her wits against his. And he *was* always fair in print with her; if anything, he glorified her. Warning herself to be careful, she picked up the telephone, feeling a headache coming on.

"Miss Sarah, trying to avoid me, are you? It won't work," he said with laughter in his voice, and she could just see the humor crinkling the corners of his eyes. "Is our interview all set?"

"Yes, Webby," she replied wearily.

"Good. I don't suppose you'll want to talk about the current difficulty with the Madame Celina cosmetics account?"

Difficulty? What...? In a carefully controlled, light tone Sarah said, "What on earth do you mean, Webb?"

"Oh, Sarah, come on!" he replied in mock astonishment. "Everyone up and down the Avenue knows that Harrison Perlmutter's after your hide. Personally I think the man is an ass, even if he *is* the old lady's nephew and in charge of manufacturing. He's really odious, and I don't know how you put up with him."

Sarah tried to sound amused. "Oh, Harrison's all right, really—a stick-in-the-mud, but what else is new?"

"Watch yourself, my pretty one," Webb said. "I wouldn't like to see you get the ax."

"Webby," Sarah asked guardedly, "do you know something that I don't?"

There was a long pause. "Hell, I'm sorry, love. I assumed you knew."

"Knew *what*?"

"I heard this morning that the old dragon's going to haul you onto the carpet. It has something to do, I gather, with the institutionalized approach that you're using in the advertisements."

Sarah laughed, a little of her tension draining away. "As usual, Webb, the rumors are all turned around. Madame Celina's already approved the layouts, and even Harrison's pleased as a pouter pigeon. The institutionalized approach was *his* idea, for heaven's sake. Really, Webb, you shouldn't go around spreading tales," she chided. "You almost gave me a heart attack."

"Okay, you've convinced me. I'm glad for your sake that it was just gossip." He went on lightly, "Now, think of some good 'female executive' quotes for tomorrow. Something about how a poor, underprivileged, forty-thousand-dollar-a-year career girl ekes out a meager living in Manhattan. You know, TV dinners on Fridays, subways instead of cabs—and how, through all the trials and tribulations, she still maintains her Miss Professional Virgin image."

"Look, Webby, I don't know what you mean by that, but if you ever use that term to refer to me in print, I swear I'll sue you! As far as my career goes, yes, I *do* make a lot of money, and earn every penny of it! I've paid my dues in this business. I wasn't given any breaks because I was someone's girl friend or the vice-president's daughter. I've worked like seven men to get where I am. Do you know what that means?'' She drew a long breath, too worked up to stop now. ''Three years without a decent vacation; writing copy at nights and on weekends; making contacts at boring parties; taking clients' insults because I'm a woman working in a man's world; and coming up with original ideas that, at first, everyone thought were outlandish. It was sink or swim with me, and it's paid off.''

''Can I quote you?''

''No, you may *not* quote me! But if you're still around when I'm old and gray, I'll give you an interview that will peel the paint off the entire advertising business!'' She paused and, feeling better for her outburst, summoned a softer tone. ''I'm sorry, Webby. You don't need this any more than I do. It's just the rain that's getting me down. I hate August rain in New York.''

''Why don't we cancel tomorrow's interview, Miss Sarah? Let me take you to dinner tonight. We'll talk off the cuff and I'll do a different sort of piece. You know—about social values. The single-woman approach.''

Did everything have to have an angle, she thought wearily. ''No, Webby, I'm tired. I'm going home to have a fast dinner, then it's to bed. Anything I'd say to you tonight would sound self-sacrificing, and that's not me. I'm just in a mood."

It was true, after all. It was just a mood. But she was worried that the mood wasn't going to go away. She winced as she thought of her outburst. What a way to talk to a columnist! What was wrong with her? Her mind was chaotic—an unusual thing for Sarah Mackenzie, known among her colleagues for her clear thinking and composure.

Webb Jackson laughed softly over the phone. "It's times like these when a big, healthy, strong man with lots of pizzazz would come in handy. Someone with spirit—not like that Schaeffer person you were so involved with earlier this summer."

Here we go again, she thought. *Will people ever forget that?* "Webby, you can be the most exasperating person in the world. If there's one thing in God's world that I do *not* need right now, it's a man. I would fervently like to forget 'that Schaeffer person,' and would advise that you and the rest of this crazy town do the same. Frankly, I can't understand why everyone's so interested in what I do, and with whom."

"Sarah, your friends—if you'd let them *be* friends—only want to see you...settled. You deserve someone better than a louse like Peter Schaeffer—a married louse, in fact."

He really sounded sincere, and although Sarah was becoming contrite she knew she had to steer the conversation away from her private life. She hated people's prying. But she had to admit that she and Peter had made quite a splash around the industry, particularly because they were from different, and competing, agencies. What a fool she'd been, she chided herself for the hundredth time.

As long as she was angry she'd be all right. It was when the hurt settled in again at the thought of Peter's callousness, the way he'd used her, how naive she'd been. . . . That's when she felt humiliation wash over her again and again. And she had to admit her heart had taken a bit of a beating, as well as her pride. Peter had had the kind of boyish charm that set him apart from the jaded businessmen she'd been used to, and she'd fallen for his extraordinary good looks and attentiveness. She'd fancied herself in love and believed it was returned. . . .

Now she *was* angry at herself, for she was close to tears again. Afraid they might overflow, she was about to make an excuse to say goodbye to Jackson when Gail tiptoed into the room and propped a note on her desk: "Boss wants to see you." She gave Sarah a questioning look and shrugged her thin shoulders, then discreetly and quickly left the office.

"Webby, I've got to get off here. See you tomorrow at one." She hung up and rubbed her temples with long slender fingertips that were free of polish, and tried to banish the unpleasant memories Webb's conversation had evoked. Checking her appearance in the mirror on her door, she ran a comb through her shiny auburn curls and blessed the natural wave that allowed her such carefree styling. She added a dash of dark lipstick to accentuate her dramatic coloring, then walked briskly down the long corridor separating her office from Ethan Fairchild's suite. She knocked once and opened the door.

Ethan Fairchild, Sr., was standing with his back to her, looking out over the misty cityscape, much as she herself had been doing a few minutes earlier. He turned slowly, his fine white leonine head downcast and his jaws clamped. It was a pose that suggested all was not right with his world, and when all was not right with Ethan Fairchild, all was not right with the agency.

The living legend of Manhattan's advertising circle had been Sarah's mentor for the past six years, and she credited him with any success she enjoyed. He was patient, supportive and highly intelligent, and he'd also been as kind to Sarah as her own grandfather might have been, had he lived.

He could also be extremely intimidating, she thought—as he was being right now!

"Yes, chief?" *Confidence, Sarah,* she told herself as she approached the massive oak desk.

He looked up, scowling. Obviously he was not playing the grandfather role this time. It was worse than she thought. "You've been on the phone all day," he said irritably. "Jelda Celina has been trying to get through from Milan. She finally reached me on my private wire. All hell's broken loose. Even though the connection was terrible and I didn't get half of the conversation, it has something to do with the *Vogue* ad." He sniffed. "I thought you'd come up with a concept that pleased the old dragon!"

So Webb Jackson was right; the underground was in perfectly good working order! "I thought so, too," Sarah agreed quietly. "As you know, I did two complete presentations. One was the personal approach with *madame*'s photograph and quotes in the ads, and the other was the institutionalized approach, promoting the company itself. Harrison Perlmutter opted for the latter, and *madame* was gung ho."

"Well, she's not gung ho now," Ethan Fairchild snapped. "You're the only one who can do anything with her; she trusts you." He sighed, his eyes dark with worry. "She's flying back from Milan today and she wants to see you at nine o'clock sharp tomorrow morning. Do the absolute best you can, Sarah. The politics involved in this account are very subtle, and you may have to mask your personal feelings." His face softened, and he suddenly became the grandfatherly figure. "I don't have to tell you how to handle the matter, my dear. Just remember it's crucial. We can't afford to lose the Celina account, and you know Harrison Perlmutter can be a viper."

Sarah nodded. "I know." How well she knew! "Is there anything else, chief?"

He shook his head. "I have to fly to Montreal tomorrow and I'll stay the weekend, I think. I'll call you tomorrow afternoon. Good luck.''

Sarah smiled. She would not let him know how discouraged she felt. "Have a good trip, and don't worry." He nodded, and as she closed the door the thought came to her that she just might lose the Celina account. She knew there was a possibility, even though everything had been signed, sealed and delivered two weeks ago. But if Jelda Celina was unhappy, her Italian temper was not to be contemplated.

Gail met her back in her office. "Boss, Della Morris just called to remind you about cocktails tonight. She especially asked that you not be too late. She said a quarter to six would be just fine."

"Oh, blast!" Sarah muttered. "I'd forgotten Della's bash was this evening." She made a face. "This just hasn't been my day. Call her, Gail, and beg off for me." Then sighing, she added, "No, I'll do it. I can't expect you to do all my dirty work."

"Can I go now?" Gail asked. "It's five after five, and I'm supposed to meet my new Mr. Wonderful for a drink in half an hour."

"Of course," said Sarah, slightly jealous and therefore replying with more warmth than she felt. "Go and have fun." As she watched Gail almost run out the door to her own office, Sarah remembered how it used to be when *she* was meeting Peter after work, her own "Mr. Wonderful." Was that what was bothering her today? Could Webb Jackson possibly be right about her needing a man? She scoffed at the idea, but allowed her thoughts to drift to what it would be like to have someone to count on, to share life's laughter and tears with. A special man who'd understand that her need for the stimulation of a Manhattan career was just as strong as her need for the peace and solitude of Samsqua. But how could she expect someone else to understand it when she didn't herself?

She was about to dial Della's number when Gail buzzed on the intercom. "Boss, your sister's on the line!"

Johanna! She picked up the phone and spoke hurriedly. "Johanna, where are you? In Boothbay?"

"Nope. Still on the island. Else Sanchez is letting me talk ship to shore from the *Griffin*."

Sarah could picture her sister's dark head against the salt-sprayed window of the boat. She'd probably be wearing a tattered old ceramic firing smock and a tam that had seen better days. Else, the wiry little captain of the *Griffin*, would be bent over the radio dials, counting the seconds of the phone call. A wave of homesickness washed over Sarah, along with a deep longing to see Johanna again. It must have been months. "It's good to hear your voice, Jo. I miss you, and I really miss the island."

"Since when?" Johanna's laugh was sarcastic, though not unkind. "I don't believe you! You wouldn't trade places with me for anything in the world."

Today she certainly would, Sarah thought, and changed the subject. "How are you? And how's your Mr. Farraday?"

"Fine. His restoration work on the Running Mallow is progressing very well. When he gets through with the design it'll be the most beautiful and comfortable inn on the island."

"Which isn't saying a great deal," Sarah teased, "considering the fact that the Cricket Hearth's plumbing is ridiculous and the Iron Donkey isn't insulated for winter. . . ."

"Go ahead, big-city sister, make fun of us!" Johanna replied lightly, then said, "Okay, enough chitchat. When will you be coming up? Can you get the whole week off?"

"When?" Sarah was confused.

"Didn't you get my letter?"

Sarah stared guiltily at Johanna's paperweight on her desk, then at her top drawer. She suddenly remembered the letter that had come two weeks ago, which she had hurriedly pushed into the drawer and forgotten. The day it had arrived had been incredibly hectic, and she had planned to read the epistle later.

"You *are* coming, aren't you?" Johanna asked. "Grandlady is seventy-five only once, and it's a Saturday."

Of course, Sarah realized with a pang. October 9 was grandlady's birthday! Her head swam. "Oh, Johanna, Madame Celina's new campaign has just blown up in my face and—"

"I shouldn't have bothered you!" Johanna's voice dripped ice. "I just didn't realize that your life is filled with so many *important* matters that you can't even take a weekend off—"

"It's not that," Sarah soothed, looking hurriedly at her desk calendar. October 9 and 10 were marked down for the Grays in Connecticut. She would see them another time. She hadn't been home for three months! Where had the time gone?

Her sister broke in on her thoughts. "You're not coming—is that what you're trying to say?"

"No, no, I really want to get away."

"As usual, you're only thinking about your career. You've got to be a smashing success or you'll go up in smoke!"

"Oh, Jo," Sarah said, her eyes stinging. Couldn't Johanna see the pressure...? "You don't understand...."

"Yes, I do," Johanna replied dryly. "Madame Celina's account is, of course, terribly important. I'm sure that grandlady will understand." Her voice was arch. She paused and went on wearily, "I suppose you're too busy to write to her, so I'll make up some excuse."

"Johanna! Listen to me." Sarah's voice was sharp. "You don't understand anything!" She was close to tears. "I do need to get away, and of course I'll come home for grandlady's birthday. I promise. I'll drive up to Boothbay on Saturday, the ninth."

"Great! Be early. You know the *Griffin* embarks

promptly at ten o'clock during off-season. You could fly to Portland and rent a car. It would save about three hours.''

"No, no, the drive will do me good. I'll see you then, okay? Take care.'' They said goodbye and she heard the circuits switch. Else Sanchez, who never patched calls through that weren't emergencies, was probably pacing up and down on the deck. Lord only knew what she would charge Johanna for the call!

Sarah slumped in her chair and placed her palms against her temples. Resignedly, she dialed Della's number, and when the butler answered she could hear the background din of party noise. She glanced at her watch. It was five-thirty!

"Sydney, this is Sarah Mackenzie. . . .''

A moment later Della was on the line. "Ducks,'' she was saying in that breathless way, as if they had been talking for hours, "please don't be late—not tonight. I've got half of Bel Air here, and I need someone to keep them sober.''

Sarah knew very well that the party was proceeding at a very proper pace—probably on the dull side. But even if Della's parties were inclined to be rather stuffy affairs, she was still a very famous hostess. Out of towners could get acquainted at her gatherings in a matter of minutes, and she brought some of the most powerful people in Manhattan together. People that Sarah could well do without tonight.

"Della, I've had a perfectly miserable day. . . ."

"You might as well come over here and be miserable." She laughed shrilly. "No, I didn't mean that. I seldom ask favors, but I do need help tonight. You've never let me down before in an emergency. I don't have anyone from advertising, while all the other 'arts' are covered. Besides, Sir Basil Northcombe is dropping by on his way to the airport. He asked me to go skiing in Switzerland. He's dear, but you know me, I couldn't get a ski suit big enough! I hear through the grapevine that he's bored with the Flannel agency. I need not remind you, dear, that he's a multimillion-dollar account."

"But we already represent Madame Jelda Celina, Della, and I couldn't very well take on an active competitor, even if he does market only men's toiletries."

"Come for just an hour."

Sarah paused. "Peter Schaeffer won't be there, will he?"

"My dear, what kind of monster do you think I am? Of course I wouldn't invite you and Peter to the same party! And if it's a choice you come out the winner every time."

"Okay, Della, I'll come—but only for a little while. See you soon." Sarah sighed and hung up the phone. She felt rather sorry for Della. At forty—a very comfortable plump forty, because she took her frustrations out on food—Della lived in a luxurious Central Park South condominium, courtesy of a rich unknown aunt who had died without any other heirs.

But while Della might be financially secure, Sarah suspected she was terribly lonely. The woman still believed, after ten long years, that the wife of the man she'd been seeing would grant him a divorce any time now. Perhaps, Sarah thought, she was being cynical, but after her experience of a few months ago with Peter Schaeffer she was wary of men in general.

She had lived in New York long enough to know that many executives who lived on Long Island had sleeping arrangements in Manhattan. She was certain that there was a legion of smartly attired, nubile young girls who kept their weeknights free for married lovers. Every weekend, en masse, this cloud of beautiful butterflies, alone or sometimes in pairs, queued up for Broadway shows, descended on the museums or walked through the park feeding pigeons, while their men barbecued steaks in their own backyards or mixed cocktails for their married friends. It was humiliating to realize she'd almost become one of those women herself....

The small pain was building in the middle of her forehead. Going to her private bathroom, Sarah shook a packet of headache powder into a glass of water and grimaced as she swallowed the mixture. Then she removed her lipstick, washed her face with castile soap until her skin glowed and went to the closet where her emergency supplies were. She viewed the six outfits, kept there for such occasions as tonight's party when she didn't have time to go home to change. She never wore an outfit to even a casual party that she had worn during working hours. Placing her appearance firmly in the hands of fate, she closed her eyes and reached blindly into the closet. She opened one eye. Her hand had come to rest on a red silk Anne Klein number. *Very well,* she said to herself. *I need the boost that red always gives me. Tonight I'll be the scarlet woman!*

She pulled off her suit, slipped the dress over her head and adjusted the tight bodice. Then going into the bathroom again, she removed the shine from her face with pressed powder, added a bit of taupe eye shadow and a light coating of Madame Celina's Deeply Red lipstick. What was the banner headline she had given the advertisement featuring the pale blond model that Marial had photographed all in white? The only touch of color had been the glowing red of her lips.... "Create the perfect afterglow before you go out, with Deeply Red, the inspired new fall shade by Madame Celina...." Well, tonight she could certainly use some of that celebrated inspiration!

Just before leaving the office she selected a black-and-silver shawl, which grandlady had crocheted for her when Sarah left Samsqua. One last check in the mirror told her she was probably overdressed. Then, turning her desk lamp off, she left for the party.

"GOOD EVENING, MISS MACKENZIE," the butler said formally as he opened the door to Della's suite. Sydney had been working for Della for years and was as firm a fixture in her world as her married lover.

Sarah smoothed the silky red material over her slim but curving hips and glanced over the gathering of some of New York's elite. She recognized several faces, and was about to plunge dutifully into the crowd when a waiter approached.

"Good evening, Scotty," she said with a genuine smile, appreciating the familiar dark good looks of New York's most popular waiter for hire. Scotty was forty but looked thirty, and was so popular that he was booked every afternoon and evening six weeks in advance.

He sidled up to her peculiarly, and she looked at him quizzically. But instead of facing her he turned toward the door and whispered, "Peter Schaeffer and his wife are on the terrace."

At that moment Della, looking slimmer than usual in flowing russet chiffon, rushed up and planted a kiss on her cheek, and was about to murmur something in her ear when Sarah hissed, "Traitor!"

"I called you right back when I learned someone was bringing them, but you'd already left the office."

There had never been a day like today! Sarah said a hasty goodbye to Della and headed for the door, pulling the black-and-silver shawl around her slim shoulders. The last person in the world she wanted to see tonight was Peter Schaeffer. She would go home and go to bed, and she just might never get up!

She reached the crowded hallway, eager for the peace and quiet of the outdoors. But the battle had just begun. As the elevator opened a throng of merrymakers spilled out, apparently on their way to another party on Della's floor. The doors stayed open until most of them were out—and suddenly they were closing. From inside the elevator an arm intervened, and when the doors sprang open again a bronzed hand held them there. Before the rest of the partygoers could get out, Sarah felt herself swept along with another crowd crushing *into* the elevator.

Panicking a little, Sarah tried to relax and move with the flow. She didn't have much choice anyway. Her slender body was shoved unceremoniously into the elevator—and a broad, male, rock-hard chest.

She instinctively tried to bring up her hands to brace herself, but they were pinioned at her sides. She lifted her gaze and it was all she could do to raise her head to see what kind of head was attached to such a magnificent body. Her gaze traveled the length of the small-dotted silk tie to where the white crispness of the shirt met a sun-bronzed chin, but she couldn't arch her neck any farther. Nor did she wish to; her only thought now was to get out of the elevator and its stuffy claustrophobic air.

They finally reached the main floor. People spilled out just as Sarah began to feel her panic rising again, her brow sweating with the intense heat generated by the closeness and noise.

She was so light-headed she thought she might sway, but the bronzed hand gripped her elbow and turned her to face the open doors. The touch seemed to give her an odd kind of strength, and squaring her shoulders, she walked out into the air-conditioned lobby.

"Whew! What a crush!" she gasped, turning to look up at the man beside her, at the same time trying to extract her arm from his grip. "Thanks for your support, but I'm all right now." She looked into his face then, and was conscious only of magnetic deep brown eyes, flickering with unusual highlights.

She was suspended in time for a moment, thinking of nothing, unaware of her surroundings. It occurred to her, somewhere in the far recesses of her mind, that this moment was, of all her life's moments, very special—as if she'd waited twenty-eight years to arrive at this place, this time. She saw in those eyes an understanding, a strange familiarity, and it frightened and amazed her.

A deep silky voice cut through her mesmerized state. "You look as if you've just seen a ghost. Let's get some fresh air." And the hand that had grasped her elbow slid across her shoulders, holding the shawl around her. He was pulling her across the shiny marble floor when her senses fully returned, and she stopped dead in her tracks, wriggling out of his possessive hold.

"Just a minute, please!" she said indignantly, and

at his questioning annoyed look added, "I don't even know you." This was said somewhat triumphantly, for she was pleased that she'd arrived at this perfectly good reason not to be led outside by this disturbingly handsome man. But as her vivid green eyes were raised to his face, they took in the whole picture: dark blond hair curling slightly over the jacket collar; the high forehead and thick dark eyebrows; piercing eyes; and tanned, weathered, impossibly handsome features. "Just a minute!" she repeated, to his apparent amusement. "Yes, I do!"

Steven Burke! How could she have been pressed so intimately against a star like Steven Burke and not have known him? No wonder her initial reaction to him had been so devastating. Those brown eyes had captivated thousands—millions, probably—of women around the world, and no doubt he was adept at using them to his full advantage.

But now those eyes were looking at her with nothing short of derision. "Look, miss—whoever you are—if you're over your stupefaction could you manage to stop gaping? If you've fully convinced yourself that I'm human, of course. Rest assured actors have all the regular needs and desires of other people." There was a hint of amusement now and his voice was softening seductively. "The only difference is that we can usually have them satisfied more easily."

She ignored this provocative remark, for her head was spinning again. She had to sit down, and she

headed for one of the sofas lining the plush apartment lobby, trying to ignore the suggestive gaze she
felt boring into her back as she left his side. It was
too much to handle! Meeting a movie star like Steven
Burke was surprising enough, but the range of emotions he'd evoked in just a few short minutes was
more than disturbing. She'd thought he was someone
special.... Special enough, she now thought ruefully. A movie star! She was behaving ridiculously,
of course; she knew that. But one didn't meet Steven
Burke every day.

He was standing in front of her now, his thigh
muscles straining against the fine black material of
his slacks, his hands holding his jacket apart as they
rested on narrow hips.

Lord, is he attractive, she thought wildly. "Did
you come from Della's party?" he continued, and at
her nod asked, "Then why leave so early, and all
alone? In that outfit I'm sure you could find at least a
dozen takers."

She flushed at this, remembering her choice of
dress. Angry and exasperated, she said in her frost-
iest voice, "Mr. Burke, I don't know what your
problem is, but I don't wish it to become mine.
You've obviously gained an unfavorable impression.
If you dislike women swooning over you, then I
would suggest you're in the wrong business. Besides,
I hope it shatters your apparently oversized ego to
learn that my weakness came not from meeting the
great Steven Burke but from having had one hell of a

terrible day, seeing a particularly nasty ghost at the party and being nearly crushed to death in an airless elevator!''

Something indefinable sparkled in his eyes, and he sat down beside her on the sofa. She edged away slightly; he seemed to give off an extremely unsettling aura when in proximity. "Forgive my manners. We've not even introduced ourselves properly. I'm Steven Burke, and you are. . .?''

"Sarah. . . Mackenzie,'' she added reluctantly.

"Well, Sarah Mackenzie, I've no excuse for my rudeness, I'm afraid. I can only tell you that I find you a very appealing woman, and you rather caught my interest until you recognized me. I have no patience or need for awesome looks just because I've acted in a few popular pictures—even if the looks come from a gorgeous creature such as yourself.''

To her amazement Sarah blushed. She'd heard compliments from men before; what was it about him that made them so different? Was it simply because he was famous? At any rate, she had to admit to herself that her reaction to him hadn't been simply because he was Steven Burke, the actor. But she wasn't about to tell him this. "Okay, Mr. Burke, truce. It seems we both jumped to a few conclusions. Now if you'll excuse me, I think I'll grab a cab and go home. It *has* been an exhausting day.''

"But we can't let that dress go to waste, and I do have to give my regards to Della. Come back to the party with me. I take it your 'ghost' is a former boyfriend?" he asked, his brown eyes mischievous.

"Yes, but—"

"You don't strike me as a woman who would let a man chase you from somewhere you wanted to be, Miss Mackenzie, and I happen to know you want to be at that party with me."

The arrogance of him, she thought, but then caught the amused gleam in his eye. Well, arrogant or not, he was certainly the most intriguing man she'd ever met, she admitted to herself. And the look on Peter Schaeffer's face would be worth it. . . .

"All right, Mr. Burke, I'm game."

Smiling inwardly, she thought this encounter must be part of a fantasy—the topper to an unreal day. As unresisting as an opening umbrella, she had allowed herself to be picked up in an elevator by a man with a formidable reputation—if one believed the gossip columnists, and she had been around the Fourth Estate long enough to know that there was usually some grain of truth in even the most far-fetched item. But if she were going to carry out this folly she might as well do it in style—on the arm of a movie star.

It gave Sarah a glow of satisfaction to see Della's shocked expression as she came back into the room holding Burke's arm. Around the room a very short and delicious pause greeted their entrance. Della frowned before she flashed a brilliant smile and came toward them, fleshy arms outstretched. Steven Burke was obviously the first real celebrity of the evening. Della expertly guided him through the crowd to the bar, leaving Sarah wedged in between an off-Broadway actor with little talent and a novelist who was more than a little drunk. Her triumphant entrance, as welcome as it had been after her catastrophic day, was short-lived indeed. Sarah suddenly felt bereft, alone, and as she watched Burke become surrounded by surely every female at the party, more lost than ever before.

CHAPTER TWO

"SARAH DEAR," Della put in at her elbow, "I didn't know that you knew Burke."

Sarah turned. "Really?"

"You're so strange tonight. I don't think I've ever seen you so. . . well, so subdued."

"Really?"

Della's eyes glittered in her plump, overly made-up face. "Can't you say anything except 'really'? Remember, I've known you ever since you left Samsqua, but you're showing a new side of yourself tonight. What's come over you?"

"I'm just awash with men tonight." Sarah replied suddenly, thinking of Burke, and was immediately sorry she had made the statement.

"And what is that supposed to mean? You're talking like someone out of the Sunday funnies."

The younger woman smiled mirthlessly and sighed. "I do rather feel like Little Orphan Annie, and I'm going home to bed."

"Not before you meet Basil Northcombe. You may not have the opportunity again soon. . . ."

Sarah took her hand. "Della, thank you, but I'm

not in the mood for English royalty." Or, she almost added, movie-star royalty, either, as she saw that Burke was still besieged by female attention.

"Oh, for heaven's sake, Sarah," Della exclaimed. "Come down off your high horse! Basil isn't at all stuffy. Besides, he hates to be called 'sir.'"

"Did I hear my name being bruited about?" a voice said out of the crowd.

They turned simultaneously, almost bumping into the man standing behind them. He was tall and dignified-looking with dark hair shot with silver and gray green eyes. But he wasn't as old as Sarah had thought. He looked a young forty. As he fired a long black cigarette from a platinum lighter, Sarah thought that he also looked as if he had just stepped from the magazine pages of the Sunday *Times*. Wasn't there a Basil somewhere in Little Orphan Annie's past?

"Sarah Mackenzie, I'd like you to meet Basil Northcombe."

If he kisses my hand, Sarah thought, *in my present mood I'll burst out laughing!* He held out a ringed hand and said, "It's a pleasure to meet you, Miss Mackenzie."

"How do you do?" His eyes were the first thing she noticed about his face: green as mottled jade but not as cold. Unlike Steven Burke, he was *less* attractive than his photographs. But he was elegant in a manner that even the best-tailored New York male could never attain. Surprisingly Sarah found that she liked him, despite the way he openly admired her red-encased body, lingering far too long on the slight swell of breast the gown exposed.

"Della tells me that you handle Madame Celina's advertising account. Your campaign for After Nine was a rather tidy bit of business...."

"You're being very polite."

"I mean it," he said, examining her face, "and I'm not talking as a competitor, because I'm not really, since as you know we do only men's toiletries."

It must have been partly her mood of the evening, or Sarah would never have looked at him quizzically and said, "Oh, but the underground story is that you're working on a line of women's cosmetics."

He glanced casually around the room but did not lose his composure. "In our business, I suppose, there are really no secrets," he said evenly. His tone had not changed; it was still friendly. "The underground also says that Madame Celina is scrapping your *Vogue* ads." He appraised her quickly. "Is that true?"

Sarah felt clammy and cold but she did not become confused, or change color, or stammer unintelligibly. Thank God, she told herself, she was meeting the test. She smiled and went on in a conversational tone, "Since that decision was only arrived at today, news does travel fast."

"Yes, otherwise you wouldn't be aware of what we've been up to at the plant in Switzerland...." He studied her again for a moment. "I need something really special to launch the line—something fabulous."

"What are you going to call your product?" Sarah asked, throwing caution to the winds, fully expecting him to turn frosty.

"Truthfully, we haven't decided," he replied calmly. "We obviously can't call the line Basil. I'm too much identified with a masculine image to turn effete at this juncture."

"You have qualms about the new line?"

He held up his hand and laughed. "Not at all, Miss Mackenzie. On the contrary, I think that you'll be pleasantly surprised." He smiled and went on conversationally, "In fact, Jelda should be prepared to put up the fight of her life."

With difficulty Sarah smiled, too. "She's very tough, you know."

"I know." He lifted an eyebrow. "She may look fragile, but she has the bite of a hammerhead shark."

"Shark?" Suddenly Della joined them. One of the beautiful things about Della was that she instinctively knew when, and when not, to break into a conversation. "Are you discussing deep-sea fishing?"

"Yes," Basil Northcombe said, "in a way." He turned to Sarah. "I've enjoyed meeting you. If you're ever in Switzerland, you must come to Klosters. We'll have tea or a drink—or both, perhaps."

Sarah held out her hand. "Thank you, *Sir* Basil," she said, feeling impish, then gave him a genuine smile to show she meant no offense. When he had disappeared into the crowd Sarah thanked Della. "You just saved my life. The conversation was getting sticky."

"Oh?" Della sighed. "I had a feeling you'd be friends or something." Then she glanced at Sarah sharply. "I don't know what there is about you that's different tonight, but you've just ensnared two of the most divine men in town, and you act as if you don't give a damn."

"Frankly, my dear, I don't," she said, half-jokingly. Then, spying a dark blond head across the room, she sighed. "Della, say goodbye to... to Steve for me. I certainly didn't ensnare *him*."

"You can't desert him!"

"*He's* deserted *me*! Anyway, let's you and I get together one day next week for lunch." She touched Della's hand lightly. "I promise I'll be better company then."

Della's plump face broke into a smile. "There's nothing wrong with your company now. But I think you're becoming jaded, dear."

Sarah had just reached the door when she felt a tap on her shoulder. "And where do you think you're going?" The smooth voice was unmistakable. She turned, her heart beating a little faster. He had pursued her! Suddenly her spirits felt immeasurably lighter.

"I thought you were quite happy with one of Della's little Long Island society girls. They thrive on these occasions—'' She stopped short, surprised at her own nastiness.

He laughed. "I got cornered by someone trying to sell me insurance. Aren't you beginning to feel claustrophobic? Let's get some air." He led her through the crowd. People shifted, creating a small path for them as they made their way to the terrace. At that moment Scotty came by with drinks on a tray. "Scotch and soda, Mr. Burke, and a very dry martini with a twist for you, Miss Mackenzie."

"Thank you," Burke said, and turned to Sarah. "How did he know what I like to drink?" he asked. "Do you have psychic waiters in New York?"

She gave him an amused look. "Scotty can tell you what every celebrity in Manhattan drinks!" She glanced over Burke's shoulder. Not ten feet away on the terrace stood Peter Schaeffer, talking to some Madison Avenue types whom Sarah knew only casually. By his side a very blond woman was nervously sipping a cocktail and fiddling with a cigarette. She had pale blue eyes and a tanned skin that was beginning to turn leathery. She wore a particularly vacuous expression, and even the soft, expensive, sea-green gown did not add an air of distinction, Sarah thought. She knew she was being catty, and it surprised her to realize how deeply she still resented Peter's deception. But it was all too human, she supposed, to project anger onto the innocent person, which Mrs. Schaeffer certainly was in this case.

Someone had opened the door to the terrace, and an old advertising man was saying, "The wet suit did flatter her. When you turned the page all you saw was that come-hither look and the caption: 'Off Catalina or the Azores, Hermes swimsuits say it all....'"

At that moment Peter Schaeffer looked up, a re-signed blank look in his eyes. He saw Sarah and glanced quickly away, flushing. Obviously she was the last person in the world he had expected to see. He tried to control his expression—hard to do with a little-boy face that mirrored his thoughts so exactly. He glanced at her again, and this time did not look away. When he nodded, Sarah unconsciously nodded back, suddenly realizing that what she had felt for Peter Schaeffer had been nothing more than infatuation.

"There's Della!" Burke said, taking Sarah's arm. "Let's say our goodbyes." He guided her toward the door of the apartment where their hostess stood.

Basil Northcombe came up behind her while Burke chatted with Della. "Going so soon?" he whispered, his tanned face crinkling in a smile. "I was hoping you'd introduce me to your boyfriend."

Sarah muttered, "Which one?" before she could stop herself. She was slightly embarrassed by the remark, but her companion laughed appreciatively, unaware that her sarcasm hadn't been intended as humor.

"I've always wanted to meet Steven Burke," Basil

went on. "I almost bought a Chinese junk after I saw *The Refugees*."

Sarah gave a hollow little laugh. "If there's a man in this room who doesn't identify with Steven Burke, I'd like to meet him," she said, and held out her hand. "It was enjoyable talking to you, Mr. Northcombe."

This time he did bend down and kiss her hand. Out of the corner of her eye she saw that both Steve and Peter were watching the performance—just part of an evening that could only be called an impossible fantasy. Surely she was living a dream. She had never before been involved in so many plots at the same time. But instead of feeling giddy Sarah experienced only a certain numbness. She was like an actress with three leading men, she thought. And everyone else in the room, including Della and Scotty, was the audience.

Basil left her then, but before she could turn around a hard voice spoke into her ear. "You seem to know everyone—every man at any rate," Burke said. "More ghosts?"

Sarah ignored his tone and shook her head, hoping his mood wasn't changing again. "No, just people I run into all the time at parties. It's a kind of clique, I guess."

"I think it's time to get the hell out of here!" he whispered. "We'll go have dinner."

"I'm very tired. . . ."

He looked at his watch. "It's early—only seven-fifteen. You can be in bed by nine."

She glanced at him quickly, trying to ascertain if he had made a pass. Had he meant *they* could be in bed by nine? His eyes held a hint of amusement rather like a predator sizing up its prey. Then they widened innocently, as if to say, "Me? Make lewd suggestions to you? Never!"

She had to smile then, but wouldn't relent. "I'm really not very hungry, Mr. Burke. I...had a late lunch."

"All right," he replied. "I know just the place—a little restaurant near Sky Rink. The soup is superb and the salads are almost as good as the ones in California."

He smiled then, showing even white teeth; it was a smile that lifted her heart. Throwing caution to the winds, she nodded.

They said goodbye to Della, whose motherly glance at Sarah plainly said, "Don't do anything foolish, my dear—not a one-night stand with a man you've just met, even if he *is* a movie star."

Outside the weather had turned even warmer. The rain had stopped, but the air was still damp and heavy with the August heat. Men were walking down Central Park South in their shirt-sleeves, and women did not even bother to carry shawls or sweaters. The gray-haired doorman nodded pleasantly and whistled for a cab, obviously proud of his savoir faire. Sarah knew that he had recognized Burke instantly. He had opened doors for presidents and kings, and it was his business to know who was who in *Who's Who*.

She expected him to be haughty, but he stepped forward solicitously. "Ah, Mr. Burke, is it a cab you want?"

Burke nodded. "Jamie's Restaurant."

The cabbie was a wholly different type. He kept up a steady stream of conversation down Central Park South and Fifth Avenue. He recited the name of surely every film in which Steven Burke had ever appeared. "When he runs out of pictures he'll start on my affairs," Burke whispered with a grin.

"Have there been many?" she asked casually.

"What do you think?"

She didn't want to answer that, so without considering the consequences she asked, "Are you married, or have you ever been?"

"I've never found it necessary." He shrugged. "I like my own company—most of the time," he said, leaving no doubt in Sarah's mind just when he *did* require female "companions."

"Don't you ever get lonely?"

He took her hand. "Not when I have a lovely lady like you by my side."

He *was* in good form, Sarah thought cynically. The lines! Earlier, she had thought that they shared the same sort of attraction—not just a physical one, but also a desire to get to know each other better. But obviously she had been wrong, and Della's warning look had been right. He was handing her every cliché in the book. "I know a line when I hear one, Mr.

Burke,'' she said coldly, drawing away from him in the cab.

"That wasn't a line," he said. "Sarah, half of my life has been devoted to spouting bad dialogue, and if you've heard some of it, I'm sorry." He looked out the window. "I've never married because, frankly, I've never found a woman that I could take on a long-term basis, both physically and intellectually. Most of the women I meet are in show business, naturally, and there's professional competition. Or they think I'm an easy way to get to the top." He sounded suddenly very bitter.

"Then what you need, Mr. Burke," Sarah replied laconically, "is a *hausfrau* type, who'll never poke her head out-of-doors, who'll bow when you come home at night and perhaps even drop into a little curtsy—unless, of course, you'd think that was competitive, too!"

He paused and said in a very low, very even voice, "We seem to have got off on the wrong foot again. I do like you, Sarah, but you've got to meet me halfway. Now, if you can suffer my company for the next few hours or so—" he took her hand, and her pulse began to race "—let's start again."

She looked at him, trying to piece together this moody stranger who wasn't really a stranger. "All right. I guess I have been rather on the defensive tonight."

His hand reached out, his warm palm flat against her cheek in the darkness of the cab. "Ah...she's wise as well as beautiful." Then he took out his wallet, and Sarah was conscious for the first time that the taxi had stopped and the driver was listening intently to their conversation.

The cabbie actually opened the taxi door himself. Sarah was impressed. It had been years, it seemed, since a New York hackie had opened a door for her. Usually she was left at the curb stuffing bills and change back into her purse. "Say," the man was saying to Burke, "didn't you once date Karen Black?"

"No, she was one I missed," Burke quipped, then handed him a large tip and murmured to Sarah, "What did I tell you?" He winked at the cabbie and accepted the man's little bow with a smile. Apparently he was accustomed to hero worship.

The door of the restaurant held a Closed sign. "Damn," Burke muttered. "C'mon. Maybe we can get a back table across the street at the garden restaurant at Rockefeller Center."

But the place featured a long motley queue of what looked to be tourists. "Any ideas?" Burke asked, and Sarah shook her head. It was on the tip of her tongue to say, "I scramble a mean egg," and invite him up to her apartment. Under other circumstances, with a different sort of man, she would have unhesitatingly done so. But this was physical attraction such as she'd never dreamed of, and she did not intend to set herself up for a situation she could not handle. Thank God for her New England conscience, which usually kept her treading the straight-and-narrow path. It had never steered her wrong before.

"I'm not really hungry anyway," she said as they leaned over the rail and watched the diners below munching on crisp salads and sipping wine.

Burke took her arm, and she felt electricity flow between them as if he had touched her more intimately. What was going on here, she wondered. She looked up into his face, and again a shiver of excitement tingled down her spine. He must have mistook it for a chill, for his arm slid around her shoulders and she was pressed against him. She must become accustomed to the fact that she was with Steven Burke. When they were walking side by side, her strides matching his, a sensual current seemed to pass between their separate bodies. But when she looked at him it was a totally different sensation. The famous face that she had seen so often on the screen in close-up now took on another dimension, because it was only part of the entire package. *This* Steven Burke was alive, vital, warm.

But genuine?

Suddenly Burke swung her around to face him. "Hey," he exclaimed, his face lighting up like a little boy's, "do you skate?"

"Why. . . yes," she replied, trying to avoid staring at him. "My sister has a private pond on Samsqua."

"Samsqua?"

She smiled up at him. "I was born on an island off

the coast of Maine." She sighed. "Grandlady taught me to skate when I was six."

"Grandlady?"

She laughed. "We call my grandmother 'grandlady,' because she certainly is grand, and a lady besides!"

"I was brought up on a farm in Nebraska, but I didn't learn to skate until I was twenty. That was eighteen years ago—and a far cry from what I had to do in my second picture. I played a Swiss skater and had to perform a devil's dance on ice. Ricky Bartell, the Olympic champion, actually worked in the long shots, but I had to learn to skate well enough to do the medium shots. Since then skating has become a great pleasure. Come on, let's burn up that ice!"

Sarah looked down at her red gown. "I can't skate in this, Steve! Besides, where would we ice skate in summer?"

"Well, there's an indoor rink I know of fairly close by that offers year-round skating. And I don't think this suit was made for sports, either, but I'm willing if you are."

"All right!" She laughed. And as they returned to Fifth Avenue to hail a cab for West Thirty-third Street, she thought how extraordinary it was to be with a man who took charge, who was accustomed to leading. On most of her dates she'd chosen the stage play or restaurant, even the wine sometimes. But Burke had a mind of his own, and if it was folly to go skating in an Anne Klein dress it was at least a departure from the ordinary. When was the last time she'd been asked to go skating?

After Sarah and Burke had been fitted with skates at the Sky Rink they waited a moment until the last phrase of the disco number was finished. The next recording, the "Blue Danube" made her look up at him and laugh. "Wouldn't you know?"

He nodded and took her arm. "Numbers like this should have been outlawed years ago." Yet the impossibly romantic music stirred them both into action as he expertly guided her out into the middle of the half-empty rink. They completed the first turn, and she was surprised at his expertise. "Why, you're a marvelous skater," she exclaimed. "I bet you could be a professional anytime."

He grinned in a captivatingly boyish way. "You're not so bad yourself, babe."

No one had ever called Sarah "babe" before, and she giggled at his teasing manner. He swung her to the right and executed a difficult turn, which she followed exactly, knowing from the pressure of his hand on her waist how he wanted her to react. Each moment held a breathless excitement as she obeyed his unspoken commands. Then in the middle of the rink, after an ambitious whirl that took her breath away, her full red skirt spread out in a perfect circle, he turned her to the right and guided her into a European-style waltz. Whistling with pleasure, he drew her out at arm's length as they skated side by side in perfect time to the music.

She glanced at him out of the corner of her eye. The dance was coming to an end; the music building to a crescendo. His well-shaped head was held high, and she was spellbound for a moment. But then, as they should have arced to the left, Sarah's head spun and she stumbled, dragging Burke down with her as they collapsed together against the railing, laughing and out of breath. It was then they heard scattered applause. At the edge of the arena two small children clung to the rail, their mother's hands on both their heads. Burke took Sarah by the waist and led her forward. They nodded to each other solemnly and then bowed low to the children.

Filled with more self-confidence than she had felt in years, Sarah slipped into a curtsy, but her left skate slid out at an angle and she pulled Burke down with her onto the ice. It was like a slow-motion divertissement, studied and programmed into their act. The children applauded again and laughed with delight before their mother waved and propelled her charges up the aisle.

Burke rose effortlessly, helping Sarah to her feet. "Are you hurt?" he asked anxiously.

"Only my vanity—and my derriere!"

When she had regained breath as well as composure they skated to the entrance of the rink. Other couples were now on the ice, skating to another Strauss recording even more romantic than the last.

"Shall we have another go?" Burke asked, looking into her face with such—was it admiration—that she thought surely she could fly over the ice without the aid of skates. She felt elated, but shook her head. "I'd better not press my luck."

They had sat down on the bench and started to remove their skates when two teenagers asked for autographs. Burke complied in a friendly manner, and then caught sight of a small crowd near the entrance to the rink. "I was wondering how long it would take," he said conversationally, then asked a rink man if there was a back entrance.

"Are you bothered very much?" Sarah asked as they headed down the long corridor to the exit sign that the man had pointed out, after he, too, had received an autograph.

"Not much. But—" he laughed, his brown eyes twinkling with amusement "—you get used to entering and leaving through the back entrances of hotels and restaurants. I spend a lot of time in alleyways."

"Doesn't *that* bother you?" she asked with wide eyes. "I guard my privacy with a vengeance!"

"Not particularly." She thought he sighed, but then he changed the subject. "I know a tiny little place in the village that has great spaghetti."

She shook her head regretfully. "I really have to go home." The unwilling thought came to her that if she were to deal effectively with Madame Celina in the morning, she'd have to be sharp.

"Where do you live?"

"Up Fifth Avenue, across from Central Park. It's not really that far."

"Shall we take a cab partway, then walk?"

"If you like."

"We don't walk much in California," he said, guiding her up the street to where a taxi waited. "There are no sidewalks in Malibu. If you walk you're stopped by the police."

"But how do you get exercise?"

"A health club usually, or jogging along the beach. That's why I like New York. Everyone walks."

They took a cab a few blocks and after tipping the driver generously, Burke took her arm possessively as they strolled up the Avenue in the falling darkness. Scattered along the way were a few other couples, smiling and talking and holding hands. Together, Sarah thought—just as she and Burke seemed to have formed an unspoken alliance.

Sarah's sense of contentment was cut short by the knowledge that this would undoubtedly be a "one-night stand"—but without the usual connotations. A California movie star would not have the slightest intention of seeing someone like her again—an over-worked New York advertising executive. She knew she was merely a mild distraction while he was in town. She was sure he had numerous girl friends in many ports of call—probably star-studded and glamorous, well versed in easing his tensions after a difficult day's shooting....

"Steve calling Sarah. Come in, Sarah."

"Sorry. I was thinking about how I'm going to approach *madame* tomorrow," she lied, hiding, as she often did, behind the guise of the cool business-woman. Was it self-protection that warned her to keep her distance from men? Usually she wanted to discourage unwanted suitors, but tonight she wondered. There seemed to be something special about this man.... Oh, what did it matter anyway, she asked herself angrily. He'd be gone tomorrow, no matter what she said or didn't say.

As they walked she told him about her job and her life in New York, trying to maintain a reasonably objective tone. If she'd been mixed up about her life *before* tonight, now she was in total turmoil! Gradually, though, she relaxed, and conversation came more easily to both of them. Once again she sensed an under-the-surface closeness to him. She felt she knew more about Burke within a few short hours of meeting him than she'd learned about Peter Schaeffer in months. Or was there simply not that much to know about someone like Peter?

"I'm starving," said Burke, and stopped at a peanut stand. "Don't you New Yorkers ever *eat*?" Munching on the redskins, they continued down Fifth Avenue, and Burke took her hand as a flower seller hobbled out of a restaurant. The old lady, face dappled and withered, rummaged in a wicker basket and produced a gardenia, which she coyly thrust forward. She might have stepped out of an old etching displayed at the Whitney Museum of Modern Art on this side of the park.

"It's me last one," she trilled with a faint Irish brogue. "And it's only because I want to get home early that it'll be goin' for a bargain price."

A bill was dutifully exchanged, and Burke came back to Sarah holding out the lone flower as if he were a little boy giving a present to his teacher. "An orchid to grace your beauty."

A simple flower, yet it was Sarah's prize possession at that moment. Ridiculous tears stung her eyes as she said, "Orchids make me sneeze."

He bent down and kissed her cheek. It was probably because this public show of affection was so unexpected that she found herself blushing. To hide her confusion, she brought the gardenia up to her nose and inhaled the heady fragrance. She had never been especially fond of the aroma, but tonight it was the most precious scent in the world.

The moon still shone brightly, casting shadows from the skyscrapers over the street. When Burke and Sarah reached the fountain in front of the Plaza Hotel he squeezed her hand, and they paused to take deep breaths of air. Then they crossed the street and strolled along the sidewalk nearest the park.

"I wish we could go for a stroll down the path to the sheep's meadow," Burke said, "but it's not safe and I don't feel like a fight tonight. Make love, not war—remember that slogan?"

Sarah ignored this latest attempt to ruffle her. "At

home it's such a pleasure to walk on the paths that crisscross the island. When it's a full moon, like tonight, you can clearly see every rock, bush and stone." She pointed to a tall building across the street. "That's where I live, on the fourteenth floor. My terrace looks down on where we're standing now. I have to live where I can see greenery; then I don't feel so cooped up and caged."

Steve slipped his arm around her shoulders as they crossed the street and approached her building. "Well, let's see if we can let you out of your cage tonight," he drawled.

Sarah drew back slightly. "I must go in, Steve— alone. It's late and I have to get to the office very early in the morning."

"You're rather special to me, you know. Aren't you going to at least offer me a nightcap?"

"Steve, it's been pleasant this evening, but let's not fool anyone, okay? You know as well as I do that we'll never see each other again. Our lives are simply too separate and important to us to ever merge in any way—and if they want to call me Miss Professional Virgin they can go right ahead!"

Oh, God, Sarah, she thought miserably as she caught a passerby's curious stare. Her voice had risen almost hysterically, and now she was mortified at her melodramatic outburst. She stared into fierce brown eyes, wondering at this man who seemed to have changed her entire personality in a few short hours.

Suddenly she felt very sad and very tired, and she

turned away from him to hide her weakness. Immediately his lips were at her ear, commanding her to face him. She did.

His face looked menacingly dark, the light mood of most of the evening replaced by an almost tangible tension. "I accept you for what you are, Sarah. You should try it, too, someday." He shrugged. "We're both adults, but it's your choice. We have tonight. Why don't we just enjoy it?"

She'd heard it all before from the smooth-talking executives she'd had dates with. Live for the moment. Sex without love. The utter casualness of it. . . . That kind of shallow arrangement had always puzzled her, but the thought of it with Steve disgusted her. With him, *nothing* could be casual. . . .

"I leave for England tomorrow, Sarah," he announced flatly.

"Picture business, of course," she said rather cattily.

"*The Refugees* is giving a command performance."

"You mean for the queen and all?" She hoped he had missed the awe in her voice.

"For the queen and all." His strong brown hands were on either side of her face, tucking a few strands of hair back behind her ears. Then, as his lips descended toward her, touching her warm mouth, Sarah felt a curious dizziness overcome her. But in an instant the kiss had ended, and she saw his mouth form the words, "I'll be gone for three weeks, but I'll call you, Sarah. I promise. Then we'll continue the exploration of Sarah Mackenzie. Okay?''

She stared at him, still amazed at her own reaction to his touch, his kiss, his voice, his words. She nodded slowly.

He leaned over and kissed her cheek, and for one wild emotional moment, as her heart beat in three-quarter time, she almost blurted out the magical forbidden words, ''Come upstairs.'' But she gathered her strength and stood back. ''Good night,'' she said softly.

Sighing, Sarah watched him cross the street and stride down Fifth Avenue toward Fifty-ninth Street. He had walked down a long deserted thoroughfare at the end of one of his pictures. She couldn't remember which one, but she recalled that he had worn a white trench coat, and his broad shoulders had looked daunting to any potential threat.

She turned abruptly under the canopy to the building. Eric, the doorman, had discreetly disappeared inside during those last few minutes with Steve, but he now resumed his outpost at the door, which he opened with a little bow. ''It's a beautiful night, Miss Mackenzie,'' he said.

She looked up and smiled. ''Yes, it is, Eric. A very beautiful night indeed.''

UPSTAIRS Sarah undressed slowly, then pulled on her ruby-colored velour bathrobe, tying it loosely around her waist. Although she was tired she was not yet sleepy. She went out on the terrace and looked down over Central Park, then shifted her gaze directly below to the sidewalk where she had said goodbye to Steven Burke. She hugged the soft material around her shoulders and sighed. The warm mist had cleared, and once again the humid August heat filtered up from the wide sheets of concrete that surrounded and crisscrossed the park.

The image of Burke's rugged smiling face came up before her eyes, and she felt a new surge of excitement. He might be annoying at times, but at last she had to admit that here was a man who intrigued her. She'd thought that scrambling to the top of her profession was the only thing that mattered, but she was somewhat surprised to realize that Steve Burke mattered, too. She was, and always had been, a self-sufficient sort of person. She prided herself on the fact that she could work rings around most men she knew in the advertising game. But was it so important? Certainly she was proud of her achievements, but lately the drive just hadn't been there. She did miss the life on Samsqua; she'd missed it for years if she was honest with herself. What else in life had she missed in her relentless struggle to prove her business expertise?

Now, when she was least prepared to deal with him, Burke had entered her life—exactly the kind of man, she suspected, who could hone in on a person's weak spots and use them to his own advantage. And Sarah knew only too well that she was vulnerable to him, to his overwhelming sensuousness. Never had she felt such desire as when he'd held her. Never had she acknowledged she needed a man. . . .

Lord, Sarah, if grandlady could hear your thoughts. . . . Then *she'd have something to scoff about.* Whenever Sarah had been outraged by either her grandmother's or Johanna's outmoded attitudes toward male and female roles, her indignant, feminist-oriented opinions had been met with amused tolerant glances. Certainly the older woman hadn't had much choice in her day and age—but Johanna! Even though her boyfriend, Luis, seemed a good, kind man, Sarah thought Johanna was far too wrapped up in him for any healthy relationship. If "love" meant the kind of servile mentality that Johanna seemed to exhibit toward Luis, then love wasn't for Sarah. She'd been independent for most of her life, and she had no wish to change that now. In one respect she was lucky, she supposed. Her work paid her far more than she needed, so that she'd had no cause to worry about financial security for several years now.

Her eyes swept over her comfortable apartment with its deep green broadloom, low-slung, champagne-colored love seat and gold-and-green striped wing chairs. The rest of the room was fresh and light—modern like herself, in most ways, she mused wryly.

Wandering into the light blue bedroom, she thought about a friend's comment that blue was not a color for a bedroom. "Too cool, Sarah," she'd said. "There's absolutely no passion in blue."

No passion. . . like me?

Unbidden, her thoughts sprang to a lean muscular body and a tanned, perfectly carved face. A face and a body that had seduced dozens of women on screen—and how many "off duty"?

She shook herself mentally. If she were wise she would run back to her safe little office at Duncan-Fairchild and slam and bolt the door. If there was one element that she didn't need in her well-ordered existence it was a man—and an actor at that! Yet she was drawn to him as a person, not as a performer. On the screen she could take or leave him; he had never made that much of an impression on her. Yet in person, in the flesh, he had an appeal that came close to being irresistible.

A thought suddenly struck her: what if he didn't call her when he returned from England? He would be traveling in glamorous society during the next three weeks. How many females of the species would he meet—females who were enthralled with his movie-star image? How many of these same women would quite blatantly offer themselves to him? Her competition was enormous.... She chuckled at an image of herself as the conniving seductress, complete with claws to ward off any threats to her and "her man."

The telephone interrupted Sarah's daydreaming, and she was still smiling as she picked up the receiver.

"Yes?" She made her voice sound bright and professional, as she always did. She disliked people who answered the phone in an uninterested way; it was one of her pet peeves.

"It's Webb," said the voice, "and I apologize for ringing you so late. Are you sitting down? Well, please do so and prepare yourself for a shock. Are you comfy?" He paused. "I thought you should know that you've been named Advertising Woman of the Year by *Advertising People* magazine. I just got the word and I'm writing the story for *Women's Wear Daily*." He paused. "You're the lead column!"

It took a moment for the importance of his announcement to sink in, and then Sarah didn't know what to say. It was all too new. "That's very... nice," she managed to sputter at last.

"Nice?" His voice was incredulous. "The top award of the year—and all you have to say is *nice*! Good God, girl. Now settle down and give me a good quote."

Amazingly, her mind was still taken up with her companion of the evening. "I can't right now. Think of one for me...."

"I will *not*!" he replied peevishly. "By the way, is it true that you worked your feminine wiles on Steven Burke and whisked him away from Della's party?"

"As a matter of fact, Webby, we came to the party together."

"But I didn't even know that you knew him!"

Sarah's head was swimming. "If you must know the truth, we met in the elevator."

"He *picked you up*?"

"Well, as a matter of fact—" she was growing impatient "—if you want to look at it that way—yes, he did pick me up. We ended up ice skating at the Sky Rink."

"Steven Burke on a public ice rink? Really, Miss Sarah!"

"It's true. It was great fun. He's really a very nice man."

"Nice! Everything is *nice* with you tonight!" He paused. "Is he there with you now? Is that why you sound so guarded?"

She laughed. "You should know me better than that, Webby. I'm alone."

"I thought you might have invited him up for a drink. Now get your brains together and give me a good reaction to the award."

"I'm thinking, truly, I'm thinking. But today has been so...strange, and I'm overly tired and.... I don't know anything anymore."

"Sarah, what *is* the matter with you? I can't tell my readers that you were *confused* when you heard about the award. It doesn't go with your image...."

"It's not the award," she hedged. "I'm just worn out." Then magically her brain cleared, and she responded angrily to Webb's question. "You can say that as a charter member of the Professional Virgins' Society...."

"You're not throwing that up at me!" he objected. "What *is* wrong with you? I thought I knew you fairly well, Sarah, but—"

She was immediately contrite. "All right. Sorry. I guess I need a vacation. I'm all fuzzy inside."

"I wish I had tape-recorded this conversation to play back to you when you're sober or sane—or preferably both!"

She paused, knitting her delicately arched brows together. Drawing a deep breath she said, "Here's the quote: 'I'm very grateful to the board of directors of *Advertising People* for their confidence in me, and I shall do everything in my power to live up to the meaning of the award. It's a distinction that I will always cherish.'"

"That's fine, Ms. Mackenzie, but it doesn't have much heart."

"Neither do I at the moment," Sarah replied—not for *Advertising People*, anyway, she added to herself. "Now go make your deadline."

"Okay, this'll do. Forget the interview tomorrow. Oh, can I mention Burke?"

She thought she'd read that Steve was a relatively private person. "No, Webby, please don't." She went on quickly. "We're just good friends." Then she laughed. Besides, he probably wouldn't even call her again, and then all she'd have was her humiliation.

"Have a good sleep, Sarah," Webb said, and hung up.

Sarah poured a small sherry, sat down on the sofa and rested her slender legs on the coffee table. Sleep was impossible now. Too much had happened in the past twenty-four hours. Any other time she would have waltzed around the room at the news of the *Advertising People* award, but not tonight.

She shivered. With that statuette on the mantel she would have to work even harder to keep her special niche, and for the first time in her life she wondered if she could stand the pace. Suddenly she wished fervently that she was a little girl back on Samsqua, running barefoot over the flat rocky ledge of High Mountain....

When she finally went to bed sleep escaped her as she tossed and turned. The mattress felt like five acres of hard cement, and she could not find a comfortable spot or a relaxing position. Finally she dropped off into a fretful sleep and dreamed.

She was wearing a gossamer-thin, white gown and she was floating over an enormous sheet of ice. The music was very loud, a hauntingly beautiful classical piece. A strong arm gripped her waist and it seemed to scorch her skin. She was propelled into impossible steps and attitudes far beyond her expertise, and though she tried to hold back, was forced into an elaborate dizzying whirl as insistent hands constantly guided her into more intricate turns. She was breathless and exhausted, but the demon at her side was insistent; she was incapable of refusing him control of her body.

The more she protested, the tighter his hold became, bending her low in a wide circle over the ice—so low that her hair became covered with hoarfrost. She was completely in his power as the silent dance consumed her. She was fighting for her life. If he let her go she would fall and break into a thousand icy splinters.... Then the music stopped and the hands loosened, and she was careering dangerously over the ice, alone. Applause that resembled terrible thunder echoed down from the gallery. She turned her head. Burke was skating off into the distance, into a mist that covered the far side of the rink. He was being swallowed up. Then he turned, and brown eyes pierced her soul. With a terrible sort of finality he waved and bowed to her; and then he was gone....

Sarah awakened with a sob, her heart pounding, fists tightly clenched. It felt as though she had been crying for a long time; she was completely drained, exhausted. Gradually she became calmer. "It's only a dream!" she said aloud, suddenly feeling foolish. She lay back on the damp sheets and glanced at the clock. She started, then jerked upright. She had overslept! It was eight-fifteen, and she was due at Madame Celina's at nine!

Still shaken by the dream, she welcomed the warm spray of the shower and its soothing yet exhilarating effect on her jangled nerves. She thought about what she should wear. It had to be fresh, bright and reasonably sophisticated.

Towel-drying her wet curls, she went to the mirror

and peeked at her face under the towel. Her heart sank as she noted her pale skin was even paler than usual—even a little blotchy—and her eyes were puffy and red from crying. She usually wore only the subtlest of makeup during the daytime, but obviously more groundwork was necessary today! She selected one of Madame Celina's liquid foundations. Perhaps her distressful night would pass undetected if she did not sit too near *madame*.

Twenty minutes later, dressed in a pale blue dressmaker suit set off by beige pumps and purse, Sarah stood in the air-conditioned lobby, breathing very evenly in order to calm herself. The doorman was attempting to hail a taxi, and she hoped fervently that it would come soon. Her heart was still beating rapidly; she was still a bit concerned about the dream.

Although it was not yet nine o'clock the thermometer read ninety-two degrees. She wanted to look as cool and as unruffled as possible, and the crisp blue suit would help nurture the illusion. Her nerves were raw, but outwardly she looked poised and commanding.

"Your taxi's waiting, Miss Mackenzie."

"Thank you, Eric," she replied graciously, and suddenly she felt in control once more. She stepped out onto the steamy-hot sidewalk and into the air-conditioned cab.

She was on her way to see the queen of the American cosmetics industry, a title conferred on her by her colleagues. How would their meeting go, *madame* unhappy with Sarah's ad campaign and Sarah feeling her life had been turned upside down last night? Suddenly she thought of flowers for Jelda Celina. Yes, she would have the cab driver stop at a florist's. Violets. She would bring violets to sweeten her up. Flowers did that to a woman, didn't they? She smiled to herself and remembered the scent of a gardenia on a hot summer's night. . . .

CHAPTER THREE

MADAME CELINA lived in a fourteen-room town house that overlooked the East River. Sarah always felt a surge of excitement when she walked up the red-bricked entranceway to the carved mahogany double doors of Sutton Place. She was stepping back in time, into a world that few people outside an intimate circle of Middle Europeans knew anything about. Exuding an aura of youthful vitality, Jelda Celina waged a continual effort at gracious living that had nothing to do with the bored jaded social scene of the nouveau riche. Her business and social activities were financed by a family fortune amassed two hundred years ago. A Sorbonne education lent her a self-assured air of breeding.

Sarah still had her hand on the doorbell as Sebastian, the butler, answered the chimes. "Good morning, Miss Mackenzie," he said with a nod of his silver head. If a Broadway producer were casting the role of a distinguished diplomat in one of his hit plays, he could not have chosen a better type than Sebastian, who looked upon his profession as if he were president of American Airlines. "*She* will see you in the study," he said quietly, and then added sotto voce, "and *he* is in the drawing room." A swift subtle look passed between them.

"Thank you, Sebastian," she replied, her heart sinking. If that viperish vice-president Harrison Perlmutter was on the sidelines, then this was no ordinary hand-holding meeting, where Sarah could usually appease Jelda without drastically altering her own ideas. She was not prepared for a caustic exchange of wits—or subtle insults—with him this morning. Burke seemed to have chipped away some of her armor; she knew she would be more sensitive and vulnerable to criticism today.

She willed herself to be calm, trying to collect her thoughts as she followed Sebastian down the black-and-white corridor that displayed contemporary bronze statues and Chinese museum pieces of the Ch'ing period. Under *madame*'s deft touch the seemingly incongruous combination of the old and the new did not look at all out of place. They passed by the drawing room, where Harrison was no doubt pacing back and forth in front of the gallery that housed three original Picassos.

The butler announced Sarah as if she were Princess Grace of Monaco.

Madame Celina, her back to Sarah, was seated at the Louis Quatorze desk, ostensibly looking at the river traffic below, which was probably typical of New York's rush hour—terrible. "Good morning, my dear," she said, and quickly swiveled the chair, somehow giving the impression of a grand stage entrance. She was full of wiles. "You're two minutes early. I adore promptness—and violets, too, but not necessarily in that order." She took the proffered nosegay and arranged it into a small empty Florentine vase on her desk, as if she had fully expected the tribute.

Madame Celina was a tiny woman, just about five feet. Her hundred-pound, birdlike frame was swathed in a flowing emerald silk caftan. The fabric had the sheen and texture of the last century, but the design of the robe did not conceal a faint dowager's hump, which, Sarah decided, made the old lady look even more fragile. No one even knew how old she was; the *Blue Book* and *Who's Who* differed by as much as ten years as to her actual birth date.

The queen of the American cosmetics industry wore no makeup other than lipstick, but Sarah saw that her weary eyes were edged with false eyelashes, meticulously applied. Madame Celina resembled an exotic rapacious bird as she swooped down on the stack of layouts at her elbow, expertly separating the proofs with brilliant red talons.

"I apologize for asking you to come at such an ungodly hour," she was saying. Obviously, to Madame Celina anytime before luncheon was obscene. She patted her high, expertly dyed blond pompadour, which was as much a part of her image as her pursed lips, and which also added a good five inches to her height. "I might as well come out with it," she announced not unkindly. "But sit down, Sarah; you're making me nervous. No, not there—here, by me." She indicated a chair next to the desk, a position Sarah did not relish. "We'll have to change my campaign."

Sarah quietly breathed her relief. At least Duncan-Fairchild still *had* the account!

"I'm sorry that you don't like the layout, *madame*," Sarah said gently, "but if you remember, I've always felt we should have gone with a more personal approach. It's served you well in the past."

The expression on *madame*'s face softened somewhat as she looked down at her, and her green eyes sparkled momentarily before clouding over. "I agree with you." She raised her voice. "Harrison, come in please."

"Yes, ma'am?" was the instant reply. Madame Celina's nephew stood in the doorway—a tall, gaunt, graying figure dressed impeccably in a gray Italian raw-silk suit and managing to look almost as old as his aunt. All his costume lacked, Sarah thought, were spats. Harrison Perlmutter was the only man over nineteen whom she had ever heard address a close relative as "ma'am."

"Hello, Harrison," Sarah said coolly, not pretending cordiality since there was no love lost between them. For *madame*'s sake they had to be civil to each other, but some of the most vitriolic—and ridiculous—disputes she had ever participated in had also involved Harrison Perlmutter. They disagreed, as a

matter of principle, on everything. In the four years
that they had been forced to work together on the
Celina cosmetics account they had never ever seen
eye-to-eye. *Madame*'s pretense that they were close
associates—even friends—was a further source of ir-
ritation to them both.

"Good morning, Sarah," he replied icily, taking in
every article of clothing that she wore in one sweeping glance. He also gave the impression that he was
disdainfully aware of her swollen eyes.

"I'm changing the whole After Nine campaign,"
his aunt announced firmly.

"But ma'am, I thought you had agreed that the institutionalized approach was the best!"

"You must have caught me at a weak moment,"
she replied, sitting down primly behind the desk. "I
can't understand why you want to keep on emphasiz-
ing the company, when all of my great campaigns
were based on the personal touch. After all—" she
turned to Sarah "—I *am* the company!"

Harrison managed a small tight smile. "Of course,
ma'am, but I do feel that a photograph of you in a
lab coat is a bit. . . unethical."

"Why? I work there at least two hours every day."

"But you're not a chemist, ma'am."

"Of course not," she snapped, "but neither are
you for that matter, and you'll take over the company one day!" She paused. "What was your suggestion for the caption of the lab photo, Sarah?"

"If memory serves, I think it went something like

this: 'For my new After Nine liquid makeup, I have carefully combined the best European ingredients with American computer know-how to create the most perfect flattering shades for After Nine.' "

"That computer bit," Harrison said peevishly, "may sound modern, but isn't it stretching the truth?"

Madame Celina sighed gently, and the sound was like the rustling of dry leaves. "Perhaps. But technically—"

"Yes," he interrupted, "it's true that we *do* use computers in accounting. . . . "

"If you feel strange about the wording," Sarah put in quietly, trying to keep the peace, "we can come up with another line that will give the impression of the space age without directly mentioning computers."

"Nonsense!" Madame Celina scoffed. "The computer idea is the crux of the entire statement." She turned to her nephew. "If authenticity is what's bothering you, Harrison, bring a minicomputer into my lab. We'll feed it some statistical material on the American female and some color samples and—"

"You don't understand, ma'am; it's not that simple. We're saddled with something called 'truth in advertising.' "

"I'm not ashamed of anything that goes into my creams and powders. My face cream is mainly glycerine and rosewater—'pure as pure can be,' as grandfather used to say. As for After Nine, it is, as you well know, only a liquefied version of our pressed powder.''

"But the American female. . . .'' he put in lamely.

"If the American female took proper care of herself as to diet and proper sleep,'' Madame Celina replied tartly, ''she wouldn't need After Nine—or any other cosmetic for that matter! I create makeup to cover bad complexions; a woman with good skin would be a fool to wear any face product. The skin should be allowed to breathe, not be masked by any coating, even if it is After Nine.''

Harrison paced around the room. "You're beginning to sound like someone from the Food and Drug Administration!''

"Get me a good photographer, Sarah, and give me a day's notice,'' *madame* said.

"It may be tomorrow. We're on deadline with the *Vogue* ad as it is.''

"Oh, very well.'' She sighed. "At my age what difference does one day make? I could sleep for twenty-four hours and still wake up looking decrepit. When one reaches the stage where one's *wrinkles* have wrinkles, nothing helps!'' She leaned forward confidentially. "Everyone wanted me to have a face-lift years ago. I suppose I should have, but I didn't want to look 'pulled.' I'd seen so many ladies of sixty who looked like porcelain dolls. That wasn't for me, especially in my business. I've got to look natural.''

Madame Celina shrugged her thin shoulders. "Later, when plastic surgeons perfected their craft and tied sutures up into the hair so that their clients no longer looked glacial, I was too old. Well, I never had very good bone structure, even when I was young." She sighed and looked up quickly. "Now before you leave, Sarah, wash your face. Get rid of that stuff around your eyes. And while you're at it, use some of my pore cleanser and a toner."

Sarah colored and shifted her position in the chair. Harrison Perlmutter, his mouth turned up at the corners, left the room with an airy little gesture. "I don't ordinarily use foundation," Sarah confided, "but.... Well, I had a bad dream last night and I woke up crying."

"Do you want to tell me about it?"

A wave of affection for the old lady washed over her. "I met a most unusual man last evening and we went skating—of all things—at the Sky Rink. It was one of those strange encounters...."

Madame Celina leaned forward. "Is this the beginning of what we used to call a 'romance'?"

Sarah shrugged her shoulders. "If it is it's going to be a one-sided romance. I think I amuse him, and that's about all." She sighed. "I didn't think I'd ever feel this way, especially at my age."

"*Your* age!" Madame Celina looked toward the ceiling. "How old are you—twenty-eight?" Sarah nodded. "My dear, in Europe a woman isn't even considered *interesting* until she reaches thirty. I had the most passionate relationship of my entire life at forty-two! Americans make such a to-do about this age thing. The media concentrates solely on youth, and that's not fair. Last year's census reveals that the average age of the U.S. population is thirty.'' She paused. ''My dear, you are just learning now what it's like to be a woman.''

''Well, this man is...extraordinary, I must say. But in my dream he left me and walked off into the mist. I was alone, and I knew with a terrible certainty that I had lost my one chance for happiness.'' She paused. ''Isn't that silly in this day and age?''

''And you woke up crying as if your heart would break.'' Madame Celina paused. ''You remind me of myself at your age. Oh, if only I were young again!'' She looked down at her hand, which had begun to tremble slightly. She held up her fingers before her face and examined the meticulous manicure. ''It's started again,'' she said, almost inaudibly, and swiveled her chair so that her back was turned once more to Sarah. She looked down at the river view. ''I've been under medication for almost a year, but the doctor says the condition will only worsen. If...if I begin to...to shake all the time, I won't leave this house to conduct even one seminar. I won't have the public see me trembling like some leaf in the wind.'' She paused, and her voice grew so faint that Sarah had to lean forward to hear. ''I've really had it all, my dear, so when that time comes I'll just close up shop.''

She turned back to Sarah with a soft smile. ''I'll be eighty-eight next March. But if a man came into my life just now, as feeble as I am, I certainly wouldn't send him away!'' She laughed hollowly, her dark-fringed eyes luminous and watery. ''When I was your age I had equal amounts of ambition and sex appeal. Like a fool I stimulated the first and discredited the latter. I was forty-four before I married. I wanted to be *sure*, you see. Before then, when a young man came along who wanted to marry me, I ran because I wanted to avoid a crisis.'' She looked up quickly and said firmly, ''Sarah, my dear, don't wrap yourself up in a cocoon the way I did. Be open, ready to experience.... A career for a woman of your talent is only part of the game. In my day, a woman with ambition was considered a romantic outcast.'' She sighed again. ''What I mean is, I hope that you don't end up like me—a shaky old toad on the borderline of senility....''

''But, Madame Celina! I can't think of anyone less—''

''Do you think that you could fall in love with him?''

Sarah hesitated but nodded, biting her lip.

''Then don't fight your heart.'' She paused, then grinned. ''Now clean that stuff off your face and give me a call a bit later.''

Five minutes later Sebastian met Sarah in the corridor. ''*She* left word that *he* is to drop you off at your office, Miss Mackenzie,'' Sebastian whispered, avoiding her eyes. ''*He* is waiting in the limousine.''

Carl, the chauffeur, was standing at the door of

the silver gray Rolls-Royce, the dove gray of his
uniform unrelieved by even a bit of colored piping
around collar or cuffs. She nodded; he opened the
door and helped her into the pewter-toned interior.
Everything about Harrison, it appeared, was gray.
She had never been invited to either his apartment on
East Fifty-seventh Street or his house at Sands Point,
but she presumed they were decorated in variations
of that color.

Harrison, his face scarlet, turned to her furiously.
"How *dare* you side with her against me!" He
paused a moment, his complexion gradually losing its
vivid color, to be replaced by its natural grayish
tinge. "You've deliberately turned her against me to
feather your own nest!"

Sarah, who was unprepared for his outburst,
nevertheless realized that this was no time to be glib.
"Look, Harrison—" she turned in the plush seat to
face him "—you know that all this is untrue. Both
campaigns were concepts of mine. Your aunt first
agreed that the institutionalized approach was best,
which made you happy. I accepted all of your suggestions, some of which were, frankly, against my better
judgment."

"Such as?"

"Such as insisting on a brunet model when
blondes photograph better against a dark background. But I went along with you." She leaned
forward slightly. "But I did *not* know that she had
changed her mind until this morning. I was as sur-

prised as you were when she decided on the personal approach."

"I don't believe you."

She wanted to lash out at him, but quieted the temper that was quickening her pulse. She paused a moment and summoned a tolerant tone. "I'm sorry she went against your wishes, but after all she's the queen pin and the ultimate boss. Harrison, let's be frank. You and I have never cared very much for each other, but I have always respected your position, and you have respected mine. Kindly look at my point of view. I am blessed, I think, with some creative spirit. I was pleased about the campaigns because they were my babies and both effective. It wouldn't matter *what* approach *madame* wanted. I never, ever, take sides in a controversy—especially where family members are concerned." She paused, and then added, "If we can't be friends, at least, Harrison, let's not be enemies. I'll help you in any way that I can—but not against *madame*."

"You were on the phone with her last night for over an hour. One of the servants heard part of the conversation!"

"You're wrong. It wasn't me. Whoever passed that along was mistaken."

"Now you're also a liar!" Harrison's lizard eyes were mere slits. "Tread warily, Miss Mackenzie. You'll regret you ever crossed me."

The limousine stopped in front of the Duncan-Fairchild building. As Sarah was being helped out of the car, she could almost feel the knife between her shoulder blades. She thanked Carl, then bent down so that she was in Harrison's line of vision. "I'll ignore this conversation, if you will. We've an important campaign to sell to the public, and it's going to take both of us to do it." She held out her hand, but he had turned away.

Carl, his face a closed mask, shut the Rolls door, and Sarah turned swiftly and walked into the building. She could hardly call the morning a triumph, and it wasn't even eleven o'clock.

CHAPTER FOUR

GAIL LOOKED UP from her desk as Sarah approached. "Good morning, boss—and congratulations!" she said cheerfully, handing Sarah a long list of names. "I think everyone in New York has called you this morning about the award." She thrust a folded-back newspaper over the sheet of paper. "You're on page one of *Women's Wear Daily*. They used a photo taken last year at the Waldorf at the Halston party— you know, the one with you holding the champagne glass? Makes you look like a party girl."

Sarah looked down at the shot. "Well," she said wryly, "why not? I think my image is too uptight anyway!" Not seeing Gail's look of surprise, she went into her office and shook her head at the desk, which contained a backlog of work. Her day had begun.

"How'd it go, boss?" Gail was right behind her.

"All right, I suppose, considering the fact that the old dear scrapped the entire *Vogue* layout. Now she wants to go along with my original premise. That lab campaign took six weeks of hard work. Harrison is livid, of course. Thank God the stuff's still in the file.

Run down to the art department and pick up the mechanicals. Then call Marial, our temperamental photographer friend, and see if he's free tomorrow for a Madame Celina session. When's the deadline on the *Vogue* ad?''

"The twenty-seventh."

Sarah rubbed her forehead. "And Gail, could you please bring me some black coffee?"

"Need an aspirin, boss?"

"No, this is one headache I can get over myself. And don't call me boss."

"Okay, boss," Gail replied cheerfully, and headed toward her office.

Somehow she got through the morning. Ethan Fairchild phoned to say he was delighted with the approach they were using in the Madame Celina ads. "The old girl has been around so long, she's practically the last of her line. Helena Rubinstein held first position until she passed away, but Jelda Celina has inherited her mantle. Who needs or wants institutional ads when you've got the real thing?"

She did not even have time for lunch. It seemed like everyone Sarah had ever met on the Eastern seaboard called. Mail dictation took an hour and a half, and she was not at all sure that she was even making sense. Then, when she was about to go home, Marial called. Yes, he could photograph Madame Celina, but not until Saturday morning. He'd have finished proofs by Monday afternoon, but his fee was phenomenal.

"The shots must be very fundamental," Sarah told him. "Take a dozen or so in her little laboratory, and make sure she wears a white coat. . . ." She paused. "I want the sterile look of a lab, but I don't want to imply that she's a chemist—that's too dry an approach. You might have her mixing powder in one of those little blending machines, or possibly weighing musk oil for perfume or something. We don't want to give the impression that she's merely puttering around. What? No, I won't come to the photo session. You've been around long enough to know what we want. She trusts you and will respond to any suggestions.

"Oh, and after you've finished with the lab stuff, ask her to change into one of her hostess gowns and shoot her in front of those fabulous Picassos in her drawing room. You'll have to retouch her face, neck, arms—any flesh that's showing. She's lost a lot of weight since you last photographed her. But don't airbrush everything out. *Madame* has to look old— but *good*. Shoot some of the drawing-room stuff in color in case *Paris Match* or any of the slick magazines want to do an interview." She hung up the phone wearily. Her feet ached, her head whirled and she was faintly nauseated.

Gail was on the intercom. "Who do you know with the initials S.B.?"

"What do you mean?"

"Well, a messenger just dropped off the longest florist's box I've ever seen—it's as big as a freight car—and the card just says S.B."

When the white box was resting on her desk she untied the satin ribbon, and paused a moment before removing the top of the carton. It had been a long time indeed since she had received flowers at her apartment, and the first time ever at the office. For a moment Sarah saw Burke's face looming above hers, his head silhouetted by the streetlight as he said good-night. She parted the cloud of white tissue and drew in her breath. There lay two dozen long-stemmed white roses—at this time of year, the most difficult rose to obtain. The tightly curled buds were as perfect as gleaming porcelain. She flushed as the night came back to her. If she had invited Burke up for a drink and the scene had progressed as he had obviously wanted it to, would they have been red?

Gail burst into the room and exclaimed, "S.B. is Steven Burke!"

"You'd make an excellent sleuth, Gail." Sarah laughed.

"But why didn't you tell me?"

"Why should I?" She removed the roses, which she placed on her desk, one by one, careful not to disturb the tiny tubes of nourishment attached to each stem.

"I've worked for you for two years, boss, and I thought I was your confidante."

Sarah nodded. "Well, so you are."

"Well," Gail expostulated, her eyes bluer than ever, "if I had a date with a movie star as 'big' as

Steven Burke, I couldn't keep the news to myself. I'd take advertisements out in the *Times*."

"Everyone knows that you're undisciplined," Sarah retorted with a laugh. "Now, I have to find a vase that will do these posies justice."

Gail sighed. "What's he like?"

"What's *who* like?"

Gail sighed again, louder this time. "All right, I won't pester you. Obviously your lips are sealed. Was it with a kiss?"

Sarah turned crimson and knew it, cursing her fair complexion. It wasn't just embarrassment at Gail's teasing; she was remembering all too vividly her own surprising response to Steven's kiss. Why had he sent the flowers? To leave her with fond memories of Steven Burke's gentlemanly manners? It wasn't his manners she was remembering, though. Would he call? He *had* to call!

At five o'clock Sarah looked at the list of people she was to call back, shook her head and pushed the intercom. "Gail, I'm going home. Can you come in at eight tomorrow morning? And I'll expect you to be bright and efficient, so see that Mr. Wonderful doesn't keep you out until all hours. We've got work to do."

"Okay. Miss Morris is on the line."

"Well, ducks," Della exclaimed breathlessly, "you're the talk of the town, what with the announcement of the award *and* Steven Burke. Your stars must be in the right place."

"For a change!" Sarah laughed.

"Now take a bit of advice from someone who's been around. Handle Burke with kid gloves. Be nice to him. When I was a girl—long before the American Revolution—we used to have a saying that someone was 'gone' on someone else. Well, Burke is gone on you."

"Della, you're ridiculous. We've known each other all of one night!" Sarah replied cautiously, and then went on lightly, "He's an interesting man."

"*Interesting?* The man is devastating to all females of the species!"

Sarah laughed. "That may be so, but so what? He's just a normal human being, Della." *Who are you kidding, Mackenzie. . . . ?*

"I received a dozen long-stemmed American beauties not half an hour ago, and the card just said, 'Thanks.'" Della paused meaningfully. "He wasn't thanking me for the party."

"You're speculating."

Della's voice dropped an octave. Gone was the speech pattern of the twittery hostess; she was serious. "Sarah, I've known you for a long time, but I've known Burke longer—since he was a kid. Success really hasn't changed him—not the way it's changed you."

"What do you mean?" Sarah was piqued. "Essentially I'm still the same girl who came from Samsqua eight years ago."

"Yes and no. You're used to being in charge now,

and you *can* be hard on people. You're an efficient and creative executive—"

"So what's wrong with that?" Sarah broke in, angered somewhat at Della's criticism. "I've found my professional niche. I'm happier than I've ever been in my life."

"Of course you are. You're twenty-eight years old and at the top of the mountain."

"And I'm going to *stay* on top of the mountain!"

"Which is just fine, but it's going to get increasingly lonely up there although I realize that's a cliché. Oh, you may not realize quite yet, but thirty is just around the corner, and forty comes up awfully fast. I know. I've been there. If you pass up Burke...."

"I'm not passing up anything, because he's not offering anything!" Sarah exclaimed. "I wish people would leave me alone!" Her voice softened. "I know you mean well, Della, and you're a dear person, but I've just met the man. He's got his world and I've got mine. He has an excellent reputation as a womanizer, in case you've forgotten."

"Well, you can't expect him to sit at home staring into the fire, Sarah. The public always overestimates the lives of movie people. They're far more lonely than they appear. How many times can you date someone who looks up to you as some sort of sex symbol? I daresay that Burke has known very few women who consider him an equal. Being that high on a pedestal must be a bore."

"But what has all this to do with me?"

"Don't be dense," Della said. "One of the reasons he was drawn to you, I think, was because you saw him as a person above all else. I was watching you at the party—and remember, I've seen you with other men and Burke with other women. But the two of you together struck up some kind of flame."

"I'm so glad that you know my feelings, Della," Sarah replied tartly, "because I don't, really. Now can we change the subject?" She paused. "I need your advice. Grandlady is having her seventy-fifth birthday, and I want a very special gift—a topaz ring. Where did you get that beautiful topaz necklace you have?"

"Sorry, I simply can't remember," she returned rather haughtily. "Mark my words about Steven. Bye," Della said, and hung up the phone.

Sarah looked at the receiver in her hand for a long moment, then sighed. Della, she decided, was one person she should definitely talk to early in the day, when her cloak of diplomacy was firmly in place, not at five o'clock in the afternoon with a tough workday behind her. She resolutely put all thoughts of matchmakers and their victims out of her mind.

Now about that topaz. . . .

ONE MORNING three weeks later, feeling rested and refreshed after nine hours' sleep, Sarah had just sat down at her desk when the intercom buzzed.

"Steven Burke is on the wire from London. I can't *wait* to meet him! Is it true that he's seven feet tall, or does he just look that way on the screen?"

"Stop wasting his money and put him on." Sarah waited, holding her breath, so that when his deep actor's voice came on the line and said, "Sarah?" she burst out breathlessly, "Burke? The connection is so clear!"

"I'm standing by the window of my suite at the Savoy. You'd like it, I think. We'd have dinner by the fireplace. It's cold as hell here in London."

"I'm sure you didn't make a transatlantic call to talk about the weather," she replied, trying to stop herself from imagining his brown eyes lit with firelight.... "How was the command performance?"

"Actually, I'm calling because I'm taking the Concorde back on Tuesday, and I want you to have dinner with me."

"Tuesday?" Sarah ran through the pages of her appointment book. *Tuesday... Tuesday.... Please let it be something I can change.* "Oh Steve, I'm sorry, but I've got to see Harrison Perlmutter on Tuesday evening."

"Another ghost?"

She laughed. "Hardly. He's a client—Madame Celina's nephew. Fussy as an old maid—and nasty. But he runs the business."

"How about an after-dinner drink, then?"

"Judging by the way this account is progressing, the session will probably drag on till all hours."

"And I have to go to the Coast on Wednesday." He clicked his tongue. "Look, if I come back on Monday can I see you?"

Sarah turned back a page. "I must attend a banquet."

"Can you miss it?"

"Can't—picking up an award." For some reason she avoided telling him just *what* award.

"Do you have a date?"

"No."

"Then I'll take you."

"Oh, Burke, you'd be mobbed by passersby! And all advertising executives aren't necessarily immune to the appeal of a movie star, either."

"I'll wear a bald wig."

"Be serious!"

"I am. I'll bring a big stick and beat off the hungry hordes." He paused and then went on quietly, "I *do* want to see you. I may not be back in New York for months. I've just signed to do a James Bond-type secret-agent flick for Sir Lew Grade."

Wonderful, she thought. *I'll never see him.* Aloud, she said, "That's great!"

"Is it black tie?"

"Afraid so."

"See you then." And he was gone.

THE INTENSITY OF HER REACTION at first sight of him on Tuesday evening frightened her a little. He *was* devastating, but she knew that to him she was no different than any of his fans.

He stood looking down at her, brown eyes meeting the brilliant green of hers, his face reflecting a range of emotions. "You look beautiful, Sarah Mackenzie."

She turned away to hide her pleased flush. Beautiful? He certainly was a practiced charmer, smooth as the sherry she was pouring from her limited bar selection. In contrast, her own movements were jerky and unnatural, and she felt overly conscious of the low-cut front and back of her dress. Why wouldn't he look somewhere else?

"I hope sherry's fine with you...Steve. I'm afraid it's all I keep on hand."

"Why didn't you tell me, Sarah?"

"Tell you? About only having sherry?"

"About only being the Advertising Woman of the Year," he said.

"Oh. I didn't think you'd care," she said simply.

"If I didn't *care* would I fly over three thousand miles to take you to your damned banquet?"

This was confusing and not a little upsetting. Why was he going on so? Shouldn't he be a little *happy* for her?

"Forget it," he said, tossing back most of his drink and setting the glass on a nearby coffee table. "Let us go and present you to your public."

As she was donning the simple matching jacket of the dress, he came up behind her, and their eyes met in the hall mirror. "Here," he said, placing a small, perfectly wrapped box in front of her. "Congratulations," he added dryly.

In spite of the strange way in which he gave the

present, Sarah was delighted and couldn't help but show it. A brilliant emerald lay nestled in a white velvet box, and as she lifted it a delicate gold chain revealed itself. She gasped and turned to face him, eyes shining. "Thank you, Steve. It's gorgeous!"

"Turn around now." And his hands held her hips and made her do an about-face. "Let's see if I was right." He held the necklace against her slender white throat, and she watched in the mirror as his lips came down to her nape, his warm breath on the delicate spot sending a rush of adrenaline throughout her tensed body. He brushed the delicate hairs maddeningly with his tongue before he peeked around at her, smiling at her expression and gently kissing her right temple before securing the clasp of the necklace.

"I was right, it seems. It matches your eyes perfectly."

She was sure he could see the naked longing in those eyes, and had to agree with him on one score—they were as brilliant and fiery at that moment as the jewel between her breasts.

Raw desire, she mused as she turned off the lights before following him out, did strange things to a person. It seemed as though even her physical appearance was changing. But the glow in her eyes merely echoed the warmth in her heart, and that more than anything convinced Sarah she was in trouble.

THE GRAND BALLROOM at the Waldorf-Astoria contained four hundred dressed-up versions of the top product of Madison Avenue. "The agencies might as well have moved all the office personnel over en masse," Sarah muttered to Burke as they came into the enormous room.

The maître d' recognized Sarah and smiled broadly. "Congratulations, Miss Mackenzie." Then his smile widened, if possible, as he acknowledged her escort. "Good evening, Mr. Burke." He straightened his spine and led them to the Duncan-Fairchild table, over which Ethan presided like the kindly grandfather he was not. His eyes gleamed as Sarah made the introductions, and he looked at her with something more than mere admiration. He was practically openmouthed. Sarah enjoyed his momentary lack of composure, one of the few times when he had been unable to conceal his feelings. She knew that Burke was a favorite of his, and his wife, Janet, grand in a dress that made the best of her rather stout figure, was obviously in a state of shock.

During the elaborate dinner—pâté, vichyssoise, and stuffed leg of lamb—at least two dozen people made their way to the Duncan-Fairchild table, ostensibly to pay homage to Sarah. But since she had only a nodding acquaintance with most of them, it was obvious the main purpose of their visit was to get a close-up view of Steven Burke. Their table companions were lively and interesting, and Burke and Ethan especially seemed to like each other.

But this was her night, and Sarah wished her parents could be with her. They'd have been so proud, she knew. They'd both been very "old-world"—her father a Scottish Presbyterian, her mother a native of Samsqua. When they were killed in a boating accident the tragedy had deeply affected the young Sarah. Theirs had been a loving home. They hadn't been wealthy, but her father's charter-boat business in Boothbay had provided all the comforts they could have wished. How she longed for them to see her tonight....

Sarah realized that she was in a relaxed nostalgic mood. The glow of the evening diminished only over the chocolate mousse, when she saw Peter Schaeffer gazing in her direction from a far-off table. His wife was again by his side, dressed in a blue floral-print gown. Peter's glance turned into a stare as their eyes met. She nodded, and he waved back rather uncertainly. Her gaze drifted back to Burke, so poised and at ease, so self-assured and strong. The contrast between the two men could not have been more pronounced. How happy she was at that moment; how proud that it was Steve sitting at her table.

The lights dimmed and a spotlight followed Tristam Elliott, the editor of *Advertising People*, to the podium. There was a brief staccato round of applause. Known throughout the industry for his endless speeches, Elliott, whom she had known casually for years, was possibly one of the most boring men alive. Sarah settled down with a fresh cup of coffee, expecting a long involved speech that would put the most ambitious junior account executive peacefully to sleep.

A few moments later Sarah was startled to hear Peter Schaeffer's name being announced. When she had regained her composure, she saw that Peter was standing at the podium, nervously fingering the lapel of his tuxedo, his boyish face looking twice as young in the glare of the spotlights.

"For the single most imaginative advertisement of the year in the industrial division," Elliott was saying, "I'm pleased to present this engraved plaque to Peter Schaeffer of Dolin-Parks Advertising, for his brilliant Firefly spark plug concept. This season everyone will be talking about his banner caption: "The combined light of ten thousand fireflies can't hold a candle to the performance of one Firefly spark plug.""

There was a brief round of applause. Sarah sat dazed in her straight-backed chair, face white under her Celina Number Six. Obviously Peter was as surprised as she was, because he was blushing furiously. His usual glibness vanished as he managed to stammer a hurried "Thank you." Then he clutched the plaque awkwardly to his chest and returned to his table, his face still mottled red and pink.

While the other plaques were handed out for concepts in various divisions, Sarah kept her face composed. Burke, sensing something was wrong, regarded her with narrowed eyes. She couldn't look at him. If he guessed that Peter's award-winning slogan was actually *her* idea, mentioned casually during a date, he would also guess about her involvement with Peter. He mustn't know how she had been used, how stupid she'd been. Peter Schaeffer, in the end, had meant nothing to her. And yet she had allowed him access to her creative bank—and, temporarily, her heart.

Looking back, Sarah now realized that where men were concerned, she was far from cool and sophisticated. Even a man like Peter, with his lack of perception, had seen her vulnerability and used it to his own purpose. What on earth could a man like Steve do to her?

She had to keep her composure, but under Steve's penetrating gaze she felt that the best she could do was look pleased at Peter's success. She even tried to smile at him as he passed their table on his way back from the stage. But one thought predominated: Peter Schaeffer was a worm.

She knew more eyes were on her than Peter; too many people had known of her presumed affair with him. She thought it funny that she had fancied herself in love with such a man and had never even been tempted to sleep with him. While a man like Steven Burke.... Well, she didn't even need to *think* about it. He acted like a tidal wave on her emotions, obliterating all reason....

Tristam Elliott was onstage again and holding up the gold statue of a woman with a laurel wreath.

There was utter silence in the room. "Ladies and gentlemen," he intoned unctuously—as if he were reciting the Lord's Prayer, Sarah thought—"it gives me singular pleasure and personal gratification to now present *Advertising People*'s Woman of the Year trophy. This majestic award is not given for a single advertising concept, as all of you know, but for a body of superlative work in past years." He held up his hand and indicated the Duncan-Fairchild table. "This year's recipient: Miss Sarah Mackenzie."

As Sarah made her way through the labyrinth of tables there were tears at the back of her eyes, but she masked her feelings with a tight smile. It seemed to take years to reach the outer rim of the spotlight, then years more before she finally stood at the podium. This was her moment, her supreme moment. She smiled confidently, outwardly totally at ease, a credit to her achievements and her reputation.

Flashbulbs were exploding in the darkened ballroom as she accepted the award, and she caught a glimpse of Steve's face. It was emotionless, and she suddenly felt as though the situation were totally unreal.

She was the commodity of the moment, a salable asset that *Advertising People* would successfully market for the next twelve months, when her throne would be usurped by another executive who might be her strongest foe.

The gold figure, which looked diminutive at a

distance, weighed at least fifteen pounds! Sarah could picture herself staggering back to the Duncan-Fairchild table under the weight of it.

She paused a long moment, and a hush spread over the room. She looked up squarely into the spotlight, and the speech that she had so carefully memorized slipped from her mind. Yet, as the stillness seemed to intensify, she was in complete command. "I'm very grateful to *Advertising People* for naming me the Advertising Woman of the Year, my first professional recognition." She smiled and went on clearly. "My last award is still on my mantel—a nickel-plated statue presented to me in high school, as the Girl Most Likely to Succeed—in basketball!"

There was a wave of laughter and applause, and she went on lightly. "Ten years later I still find myself making one-handed passes, but this time the court is located on the corner of Madison Avenue and Fifty-eighth Street.

"I hope to continue to learn from all of you—especially Ethan Fairchild, who surely shares this with me," she said, holding the statue high. "If I have ever entertained doubts about my choice of a profession I'm very happy tonight that I had the good sense not to listen to myself. Thank you, Mr. Elliott and *Advertising People*, for this superlative accolade." Impulsively she kissed the editor's cheek, and then it was over.

IN THE CAB going back to her apartment, Burke was silent for a long time. Then suddenly he turned fiercely gleaming eyes on her. "So we wish to continue to learn from our colleagues, do we?" he mocked harshly, and she drew back physically from his anger. "I suppose Peter Schaeffer knows many tricks of the trade, so to speak. How many campaigns has he helped *you* with?"

The irony of his absurdly unfair accusation almost made Sarah erupt in hysterical laughter, but the look on his face was dangerously serious, and she quickly sobered.

"Just what in the hell are you implying, Steve? Peter Schaeffer, help me? Have you gone out of your mind? Do you think that because I'm a woman I can't write copy for a million-dollar account? That I can't delegate work to professionals and subordinates? Just watch me sometime, Burke. You'll be surprised at what I can do."

He grasped her chin swiftly in a viselike grip, his lips taut and thin. In the flickering darkness of the cab, the shadows cast by New York's towering slabs of concrete passed over his lean face, lending him a positively sinister air.

"And just watch what I can do," Steve said as his mouth crushed hers in a searing possessive kiss, the weight of his body pressing her into the seat corner. Still his mouth held hers, while his hand rested lightly on her throat.

Not like this, her mind screamed. She was vaguely

aware of her hands clutching his hair, trying to pull his head up. But at precisely what moment her fingers relaxed against his finely-shaped head, she didn't know. His lips were soft now, hovering above hers tempting her to close the gap between them. His flicking tongue made her lightheaded, overwhelmed by desire. His hand began to trail down her neck, then curved to hold a softly swelling breast, partly exposed by the cut of her gown. When she gasped with pure delight at the feel of his warm palm, he claimed her lips again.

Oh, this is bliss, to be touched by this man, to know he wants me and I want him. Oh, God, how I want him!

Suddenly he pulled away from her, and she was left shivering with reaction, as though she'd been doused with cold water.

"Very nice, Miss Mackenzie, but a trifle restrained," Steve said nastily, appearing not at all shaken or in the slightest way affected by the contact. "Did Peter Schaeffer teach you how to make love, too? Was he the first? If it *was* him you'd better go back for a few more lessons."

His words stung, and to Sarah's horror tears sprang to her eyes. But before she crumpled completely she summoned enough strength for a satisfying slap across his face.

The violence of her action and the apparent hostility in his brown eyes when he had spoken shocked her. She stared at him now, wide-eyed. Never in her life had she purposely hit anyone; she abhorred violence. What was this man doing to her?

"Very sophisticated, Sarah. Very dramatic. Ever thought of becoming an actress?"

At last the cab reached his hotel. Sarah hadn't even been aware Burke had given his address.

"Get out!" she cried on a choked sob. "Never let me see your face again. Leave me alone!"

"Surely," he said patronizingly, and shrugged as though she were some crazed irrational woman off the street. He bent down for something on the floor of the cab and handed her her gold statue, the symbol of her success.

"It wouldn't do to forget this now, would it? I'm sure you've more than earned it. Goodbye, Sarah." Burke stepped into the street and soon vanished through the hotel's revolving doors.

THE NEXT FEW DAYS were, thankfully, overly busy for Sarah and her team on the Celina account. She would take refuge in the routine of the day: rising, a few exercises, a light breakfast, then work until all hours of the night. But more often than not her movements were mechanical, and she knew her work was not the best.

She was back in the world in which she felt most comfortable, yet something had changed. She knew some dormant part of herself had awakened, for she experienced an awareness, a new sense of...freedom, she supposed. Yet she was oddly frightened.

For the first time in a long time she felt that another person could be important to her—though Burke was probably the last person she should choose to be the recipient of such a feeling.

Indeed, she marveled that it had taken someone like Steven Burke to transform her way of thinking. She supposed it was his enormous sex appeal that had weakened her resistance. She admitted to herself for the hundredth time since the night of the banquet— after which she supposed he had flown home to the Coast—that he was a desirable, enormously attractive male.

He was also the cruelest, most unfeeling cretin she'd ever met! How *dare* he accuse her of using Peter Schaeffer to get ahead! If only he knew the real story.... The shock of his attack in the cab had been too unnerving for her to reason with him, and it was beneath her dignity anyway to defend herself against something she hadn't done.

Returning home one evening about nine-thirty, Sarah had a quick omelet and was just relaxing in a warm bubbly bath when the telephone rang. Her startled reaction surprised her; she'd always been a reasonably calm steady person. But she picked up the receiver and said, "Hello" in what she hoped was a pleasant voice.

"Sarah." The sound of his voice shook her all over again, and she sank into the comfort of the love seat. Then anger and sarcasm surfaced.

"Burke, how very nice of you to ring me. Are you

in New York for something special, or does the
studio send you across the country to keep you in
touch with the masses, the rest of us lesser mortals?''
She hated herself for her cattiness, but the hurt he'd
inflicted was still bitter within her.

"Claws in, Ms. Mackenzie, please." He paused
for what seemed interminable seconds before saying
quietly, "I wish I *were* in New York, seeing someone
very special."

She clutched the phone more tightly and hugged
her midriff with her right arm. The warm glow his
words had set alight reached her face in a smile. But
she only said in a stern voice, "So?"

"Sarah, look, I'm sorry for what I said the other
night. It was unforgivable, and I'll explain one day,
but for now just, please, give me another chance,
okay?" There was silence on the other end, so he
continued. "I'm still in L.A., but I have to see you
soon. You've been on my mind and—" he hesitated
"—I just have to see you. Is that possible?"

She was immediately suspicious of his humility—
Burke was not a humble person—but before she had
time to think she was saying, "Yes. Yes of course you
may." *What's wrong with me,* she thought. *Have I
lost all my New England pride?*

"I have this damned airtight shooting schedule until next Thursday. How's Friday morning? Can you
possibly tear yourself away from Madame Celina?"

If there was sarcasm in his voice she chose to ignore it, and merely said, "Friday afternoon, and

you've got a deal." Then a thought struck her. "Oh,
no, wait! That's the weekend I go home. To Samsqua, you know. It's my grandmother's birthday,"
she added lamely.

Then on a wild impulse that she was to regret immediately, she said, "Why don't you come? Johanna
has room. It would be good for you to get away."
She remembered Johanna saying the same thing to
her.

"Love to. That was one of the things I wanted to
ask you about, in fact."

"What—Samsqua?" Why should he want to know
about her tiny island home?

"Yes. Tell me about it."

"Well, what do you want to know? Samsqua's located about twenty miles out of Boothbay Harbor
and covers three square miles. Technically, it's
owned by grandlady, but the villagers have ninety-
nine-year leases."

"Is it wild?"

She laughed. "I suppose they kick up their heels
once in a while."

"Come on, that's not what I mean and you know
it. What's the terrain like?"

She mused a moment. "Off islanders would call it
'picturesque,' I suppose—and yet that's not the right
word. It's beautiful in a primitive kind of way. In
fact some areas aren't very accessible. There are no
real roads on the island, and we have only one car, an
old Model T Ford that's used to transport luggage.

When it breaks down—which is often—we use a goat cart. Get the picture? There's not even electric lights.''

"Sounds great!''

"We'll drive up to Boothbay and take the *Griffin* from there.''

"Which hotel would you recommend?''

"We only have three. The Running Mallow's being restored, the Iron Donkey's plumbing is out of the Middle Ages, and the Cricket Hearth's always booked. But it will be all right. My sister has a cottage with an extra room.'' Stupidly, she added, "I'll bunk with her.''

"I don't want to be a bother,'' he said.' "I'm hardly a friend of the family.''

She shook her head. "You're my friend; that's enough.'' Then she thought to herself, *I'm out of my mind! This man is used to hotels with superb accommodations and amenities, and Johanna isn't even a good housekeeper!* Aloud she said, "You must remember, Burke, when I said the island was primitive, I meant primitive. They live very simply.''

He chuckled. "The simpler the better, Sarah. Remember, I was born on a farm in Nebraska, and location jaunts like Taiwan or Mindanao aren't exactly picnics. I bend with the wind. I'm sure Samsqua is luxurious compared to some places I've seen.''

"We can't stay at the logical place, unfortunately. Grandlady lives in a huge Victorian home called Needlepoint House, but it's all closed up now except for four rooms downstairs, where she lives with an old housekeeper, Edna—who's almost as ancient.''

They made arrangements to meet on the next Friday and said goodbye. Sarah was left wondering just what she'd let herself in for. A weekend in Samsqua with Steve might be wonderful fun, but more than likely it would be dangerous, too. After all, couples who went away for weekends together were usually either having an affair or were very serious about each other. Which category would Steve put her in?

She couldn't let him see how much she already cared for him. It was ridiculous, of course. Naturally she'd be attracted to him; he was the epitome of male magnetism. But beyond his physical appeal she knew very little about him apart from what she'd read in the press—and most of that was hardly in-depth. Apparently he was rude to reporters and photographers, brooked no flattery and gave nothing of himself away. His secrecy had only added to his box-office appeal.

So what were her motives for inviting a movie star away for a weekend? Perhaps because Steve was able to stir her dulled senses. His presence seemed to have rejuvenated her, given her fresh lifeblood. She would—*had* to—explore his magic further.

She would tap Steve's energy the way Peter Schaeffer had tapped hers. Maybe that was the most one could expect from a relationship these days.

At the very least, it might improve her copy!

CHAPTER FIVE

FIVE MINUTES TO 3:00 P.M. on Friday the *Griffin*, bound for Samsqua, slipped noiselessly into berth No. 4 at Boothbay Harbor.

Sarah watched Else Sanchez, the robust, swarthy-faced captain who wore an old seaman's jumper and a blue-billed cap. Standing on deck she brought a whistle to her lips. As the piercing jabs of sound sliced the air, insistent as Fifth Avenue traffic, the habitués of the wharf went about their usual business, paying not the slightest bit of attention to the tourists forming a loose queue on the dock.

Glancing around, Sarah saw Steve under the awning of a souvenir stall. He was holding a miniature match-stick schooner—encased in an even tinier bottle—up to the sunlight streaming into the stall. Sarah drank in his lean length: the faded blue jeans and low Western boots; the light brown calf-leather jacket fitting snugly over his denim shirt, hinting at the strength of the muscles beneath. She smiled at his fascination with the souvenir. Then she sighed and thought how impossibly attractive he was, though he never seemed to show that he was aware of it. She would have to be careful; she'd never been so attracted to a man. . . .

The repeated blasts from Else's whistle must have jarred him, for he turned and caught Sarah's admiring gaze. Flashing a smile that devastated her, he then lowered one eyelid in an absurdly flirtatious wink, and Sarah's embarrassment at being caught staring at him was lost in the fun.

"Show you a good time, sailor?" she drawled, then sidled up to slip an arm through his, pulling him away from the stall. "Come on, now. We'd better not keep the captain waiting. She's apt to get nasty, especially if a wind is blowing up. This is the time of year for sudden squalls. Else has been known to leave half the passengers browsing among the seashells."

"She won't go, I'm sure," Burke answered. "Surely she wouldn't leave a native behind!"

"It wouldn't make any difference. There's no love lost between our families. She resents us still. Her father used to be grandfather's manservant—if you could call him that. Really, he stayed in the house and helped out with odd jobs, but to hear Else talk you'd think grandad had kept him in chains. Besides," she continued, "I'm an off islander now. To be in her good graces one must live and breathe Samsqua. I'm a traitor."

As they made their way across the rough, sea-whitened planking, Sarah hugged her camel's-hair coat around her, thankful that she had also worn her dark brown wool slacks. The autumn chill presaged a cold windy crossing. They lined up at the end of a small chattering queue largely comprised of enthusiastic young couples holding cameras, fishing gear, field packs and an assortment of carryon luggage. Steve checked to be sure that their own small suitcases were on board.

The autumn sun peeked out suddenly from behind a dark cloud. Sarah felt the stirring of a familiar and poignant nostalgia as she observed the Boothbay wharf transformed into varying and startling shades of gloom and brilliant color. Breathing in the misty, salt-tanged air, she reveled in the bustle of humanity on the wooden platform. She knew in her bones that she was headed home.

"Look," a preteen girl cried, "there's Steven Burke!" Suddenly the queue disintegrated, and he was surrounded by a loose knot of people. Sarah, thrust aside by the gathering, looked around frantically for a policeman. But apparently Burke did not require help; he was talking animatedly to the group and signing slips of paper. The crowd was friendly and well behaved; there was no pushing or shoving.

Momentarily deserted, Else Sanchez, not understanding why one of her passengers was causing so much trouble, clapped her hands smartly. Receiving no response, she once again resorted to the whistle. "We leave for Samsqua in two minutes flat!" she shouted angrily. Burke, at the head of the new line, motioned for Sarah to join him.

"Are you vacationing on Samsqua, Mr. Burke?"

asked a young dark-haired boy, eyes full of hero worship.

"No, just going over for a couple of days."

The boy's companion, a freckled-face girl with a small pinched chin, stammered, "I—I just can't wait—to see *The Refugees*. I bet it's great!"

Burke laughed easily. "I hope you like it. We had a lot of fun making it."

"What's your next picture about?" a jean-clad woman in her twenties demanded, thrusting forward a grimy piece of paper and a stubby pencil.

He signed his name with as much of a flourish as he could manage, considering the quality of the paper and the length of the pencil. "It's called *Devil's Dare*, and I play a secret agent."

"I'd sure like to have some money in that!" a garrulous redheaded sailor exclaimed. He laughed, showing an array of enormous white teeth. "Might be able to raise a couple of thousand."

Burke grinned. "Thanks."

"What's your budget?"

"Six million."

The crowd laughed, the sailor shrugged, Else blew her whistle and order was restored.

"Else Sanchez," Sarah said when they were on board, "I'd like you to meet Steven Burke."

The captain nodded. "Howdy-doo," she replied with a polite smile that showed no recognition. Apparently she never went to movies.

The ancient open deck of the *Griffin* sported worn,

sea-washed benches of gray planking, but the rails had been recently painted red. When all the passengers were seated Else Sanchez looked briefly seaward and then back to the group. "So far we've got pretty fair weather," she said huskily, "and I don't expect any problem in crossing. When we arrive on Samsqua, a Model T will transfer your luggage to your hotels." She paused, then cautioned, "I want to remind you that I'll be leaving at 3:00 P.M. sharp on Sunday, and since I won't be coming back till next Friday be sure you're at the wharf on time. If some of you want to stay over, let me know. Remember, weather is changeable at this time of year. You all might want to come back in season next year—anytime between the fourth of July and Labor Day. I cross every day then."

. As the captain continued her spiel Sarah guided Burke around the starboard side of the *Griffin*, away from the seated passengers. "You were very nice to those people," she said quietly. "Don't you ever get flustered?"

He shook his head. "Not often. It's part of the business." His brown eyes sparkled as he paused. "Oh, once in a while a guy in a restaurant who's had too much to drink will want to pick a fight with me, or I'll get propositioned by some lady. But on the whole the public is usually quite considerate— although I'm often asked very personal questions." He smiled. "It's not unusual for someone to want to know how much money I make."

"I know how you feel. I resent *any* prying into my life, which Lord knows, isn't the most fascinating in the world."

He looked sharply at her. "I thought you loved New York."

"Oh, I do, I guess. It casts a spell, you know? But it can turn you into a different person—if you're not careful," she added pointedly.

"And you, Sarah Mackenzie, have been careful? Is the woman I saw when we were skating, or back there on the wharf looking homeward, the real Sarah, or is she the dazzler who accepted the award for Advertising Woman of the Year? Who does she *want* to be?"

His brown eyes were holding hers, rooting her and forcing her to watch his face. Like a magnet he was drawing her closer to him, willing her to see nothing but him, hear nothing but his voice....

"I...I don't know."

"I do, little Sarah." And he drew her to his warmth, held her head against his chest. For a few unreal moments she stayed there in his arms, drawing strength from him. Then she remembered where they were.

"I *have* to work, Steve. It's my lifeline, my ticket to being myself—whoever that is," she said as she stepped away from him.

"I know, Sarah, I know." She thought she saw his eyes cloud with something—was it sadness—before he turned to rest his elbows on the rail. "So do I."

FOR SEVERAL MINUTES there was only the sound of the *Griffin*'s motor as the boat cut through the bottle-green, frothing water. Then Sarah shaded her eyes with her hand and pointed toward Boothbay, now a tiny sliver of land on the horizon.

"Look—see the sea gulls riding the thermal air currents? Else says the same ones follow the boat over and back. They're like pets. Outside of gulls we don't have much birdlife on Samsqua."

"How did the island get its name?" he asked.

"Let me see if I can capsulize it for you.... The island was first charted by a man called Samuel Fordyce in 1774. The first thing he did—he was a merchant seaman—was to sink a well; the second was to marry Uneema, an Indian maiden of the Mohegan tribe. She became part of his legend, and the island became known as Sam's Island. She bore him four sons, strange wild boys who led a kind of Robinson Crusoe existence.

"One day in the year 1815, Fordyce—who was an old man by this time—and his boys sailed to Portland for foodstuffs. They ran into a hurricane on the way back and got lost. For months Uneema, as the story goes, watched for their return from the ledge on High Mountain. For her remaining years she lived alone with her grief, and gradually the place came to be known by the residents as Sam's Squaw's Island." She paused. "My great-grandfather knew her because he ran rum to all the islands from Nova Scotia." Sarah glanced back over her shoulder at the

Griffin's captain. "Else's grandfather was first mate on his rum boat."

He grinned. "She's the perfect picture of a liberated woman—independent, self-satisfied and apparently bringing in good money."

"Yes, I think she's quite happy in her own world. I've talked to her many times about what I do in New York City—my campaigns and so on, but she's really not interested.

"Else doesn't seem to give a damn for anyone since her husband, Raoul, was washed overboard during Hurricane Belle. He was an old-fashioned sort of man. Always came to see grandlady once a week. Grandlady believed—and still does—in a world in which the rich take care of the poor, and Raoul's pride sometimes had to take a back seat to necessity. So that's why Else's forebears were little more than slaves to my family—to hear her talk about it! But those were hard days."

At that moment Else Sanchez blew her whistle. "Look, Burke," Sarah cried, "we're almost there!"

In the near distance the island loomed, its gray rocky edges bordering a few marks of civilization and, farther inland, green hillsides dotted with lines of burnt orange, gold and crimson. Sarah, still clutching Burke's arm, took in the scene as they drew nearer.

"You're home, babe," his deep voice whispered in her ear.

The *Griffin* headed into the harbor with an enormous burst of speed. Then twenty-five feet from the dock the captain cut the engine, and the boat glided serenely into its slip. An old man with a huge red nose, dressed in a rough woolen jacket, expertly caught the rope and made it fast around a whitish weather-beaten stack pole.

A motley group of people, deeply suntanned faces showing above faded orange and brown Windbreakers, stood on either side of the gangplank. Both men and women were attired in a variety of overalls and jeans, but all sported what Sarah deemed essential—heavy boots. In contrast, the half dozen tourists waiting to go back to the mainland, ever present instamatics in hand, wore everything from designer jeans to clingy sweater dresses. One disgruntled barefoot teenager was carrying her scuffed and broken high heels in her hand. "Tourists never learn," Sarah said, "and the islanders are very concerned. There's no doctor here, although first-aid kits are plentiful."

"Everyone looks so *modern*," Burke exclaimed. "I expected berets, beards and handloomed sweaters." He sounded disappointed.

"What did you expect—a model of an eighteenth-century fishing village? What you're seeing, my friend," Sarah went on laconically, "is the *real* islander. During the season you'll get your berets and smocks and Vandykes. It's all part of the act the islanders put on for the summer people—not that we—they—want to be phony. But Samsqua needs the income the tourists bring in, even if it's just for a day's outing and lunch at the inn. There's so little else on the island. Besides, we don't have to worry about their moving here for good. It's far too rugged.'' She laughed, and continued confidentially, "You know, when Johanna and I were little girls mother made us wear peasant dresses down to our ankles all summer long.'' She raised her eyes skyward at the memory. "Our 'job' was to greet the women off the *Griffin* with dainty curtsies, and then present little nosegays of fresh wild flowers. How *they* loved it, and how *we* hated it!''

"I don't even see any children,'' Burke said, looking over the group.

"I shouldn't wonder. They're all probably hiding under the beds!''

"The whole scene looks like a painting that we've just stepped into,'' Burke said slowly, raking his fingers through sun-bleached hair. "I like it already.''

"I'm glad,'' Sarah replied seriously. When the men smiled and tipped their hats to her, she briefly acknowledged their salutes. They ignored Burke.

"They don't know who I am,'' he whispered. "What a pleasure!''

She laughed. "Don't kid yourself. They know, but islanders are peculiar. They'd never let *you* know they know!''

"Mornin', cap'n,'' a brown-skinned old man in overalls said to Else Sanchez.

"Good morning, Pete.''

"Got what I come for?''

"*¿Quién sabe?*" She laughed raucously and handed him a small bottle-shaped paper bag. With a familiar air of camaraderie he patted her affectionately on her backside and slipped the parcel up his wide threadbare sleeve.

From the winding, packed-earth road, down past a row of old paint-peeled stores, a 1927 Model T Ford thundered, shooting a fine cloud of dust into the air. A grinning lad of not more than fourteen jumped lightly out of the vehicle and intoned nasally, "I'm Georgie. First stop—the Cricket Hearth. Then, ah, the Iron Donkey." He saw Sarah, and his mouth opened in a wide smile of pure pleasure. "Hello, Miss Sarah! Miss Jo said you were coming, but I wouldn't believe it till I saw you. In for the whole week?"

"Three days to be exact. You must have grown about a foot since I last saw you, Georgie."

He flushed. "Yes, ma'am, I'm gettin' up there." Then he noticed Steve for the first time and shyly ducked his head around the stack of luggage that Pete had piled on the wharf. When his face reappeared above a bright red vinyl suitcase there was little in color to distinguish one from the other.

Sarah pressed Steve's arm. "Obviously a die-hard fan."

Georgie piled the luggage into the Model T, jumped into the cab and sped up the hill, awkwardly negotiating the turn at the apex. The preteen girl they had met earlier was taking a photograph of the old man with the giant red nose, who was making a great show of casting his fishing pole, minus bait or hook, into the shallow water.

"I hope she's using color film," Burke said with a grin, "because it would be a pity to record that magnificent proboscis in black and white. The old codger's probably paid by the mayor to contribute local color."

Sarah laughed. "Every islander's supposed to provide a certain amount of charm. It's part of the image. We cater to tourists, remember." She paused. "He must be a newcomer; could be a judge or engineer who'd suddenly had it and copped out."

Burke's next words were softly spoken. "Probably retired here to keep his sanity."

"Oh, Johanna," Sarah called suddenly. "Hello!" She waved at the figure of a slim, dark-haired young woman scurrying down a path by the side of an uneven line of gray weather-beaten buildings. She turned to Burke. "There's my sister! I was wondering if she'd remember to come down, although meeting the boat is an island tradition." The woman ran up, quite out of breath, and flew into Sarah's outstretched arms, kissing her first on one cheek and then on the other.

"Steven Burke, I'd like you to meet my sister, Johanna."

Watching them being so polite to each other, shaking hands and exchanging pleasantries, Sarah sighed inwardly. Johanna really was so cute, with her black curls and pert nose. And so petite! Suddenly Sarah felt lumbering and oversized. With face flushed from the run down the hill, her large lovely brown eyes looking up at Burke and a half smile playing around her generous mouth, Johanna was beautiful in a way that she herself could never be, Sarah thought.

Johanna, noticing Sarah's scrutiny, laughed nervously. "Please don't pay any attention to the way I look. I've been working most of the day. Somehow time just slipped away, and then I heard Else's whistle.... " She took Sarah's arm. "I do hope that you've explained to Mr. Burke that life's very casual here, and not to expect gas, lights, radio, television— or most modern comforts, really."

"By the way, just call me Steve. Could I use the name that Georgie calls you, Miss Jo?"

"That's my professional name. All my pieces are signed that way." She laughed. "It's a holdover from childhood. Grandlady used to call us Miss Sarah and Miss Jo, but I've forgotten why."

"I haven't," Sarah replied. "We *were* little misses. You were six and I was five. We were so prissy, dressed in identical white dresses with blue bows in our hair and Mary Jane sandals with white lisle stockings. Don't you remember that one Sunday— probably Easter—when we'd been reading *Little Women*. You were pretending to be Jo, who coughed a lot."

"We were always doing fantasy plays, weren't

we?'' Johanna giggled. "It all comes back, but it wasn't Jo who had consumption; it was Beth!''

Sarah smiled softly. "Strange how memory plays tricks. I do know, though, that it was because of *Little Women* that grandlady gave us those nicknames.''

"We were such brats,'' Johanna exclaimed. "Does anyone ever call you Miss Sarah anymore?''

"Only a columnist I know in New York. He spent a weekend here last year, remember? Researching a piece on me.''

"Oh, yes, Mr. Webb. He's quite nice.''

"One of your ghosts, Sarah?'' Burke asked, his voice betraying an almost imperceptible tension.

"Webby?'' She burst into a peal of laughter. "My heavens, no! He's a dear, but you'd have to meet him to know what I mean.''

At that moment there was a loud buzzing sound, and Burke looked around expectantly. "What's that?'' he asked.

Johanna reached into her large pocket and extracted a timer, which she turned off. "I've had the charcoal kiln going all morning,'' she explained. "In five minutes it'll be time to take out the ears.''

"Ears?'' he asked.

She nodded solemnly. "Yes, ears! I'm firing a ceramic lamb in several pieces, which I'll assemble and put together with resin. The ears, which are very tiny and delicate, have broken four times. I think it's the glaze I'm using. Anyway, I hope they didn't break this morning. Shall we take the side path? I know it's the long way around, but the ocean view is spectacular. Do you know, on a clear day you can see Boothbay?'' Johanna and Sarah started up a little traveled path to the right that led behind a series of old barns gray with fungus and pitted and aged by harsh sea winds.

They had reached the top of the small hill, which veered sharply to the left. "Look," Sarah said softly, pointing toward the ocean. The shallow and deep currents shimmered in awesome, ever changing kaleidoscopic patterns that seemed to fade into a mottled buttermilk sky, now overcast with dark menacing clouds. The contrast of the deep green sea, the splashes of red and gold on the trees and the purple and silver of the shrubbery was strange, even unreal.

Burke took a deep breath. "It's almost ghostly."

Johanna nodded. "The changing of the seasons is the most moving," she said quietly. "After a few hours I think you'll find the mainland very foreign. Everyone cheating everyone else because money is king. Billboards and rock music—all that hubbub. Everyone running frantically back and forth, breathing air that's unfit for—"

Sarah forced a laugh. Johanna's voice of doom was perilously close to her own these days. "This is no time for soapbox speeches, dear. I could give a similar dissertation on the beauty of New York and how exciting it is to walk down Fifth Avenue, or explore the Village, where change is constant, or...."

She paused and looked skyward. "We'd better hurry or the rain will catch us." She turned to Burke. "After a while you get used to the sudden changes of weather."

Burke nodded and looked down at the pale green trailing yew at his feet and the huge maple trees, ablaze with fiery hues. "I could live here permanently, I think, and be relatively happy."

"You're joking!" Sarah rejoined, her voice too hard even to her own ears. "I can't picture you stuck here on Samsqua the rest of your life. You belong... out there." She pointed vaguely toward the Maine coastline.

"Yes, I suppose I do. It was an interesting thought anyway." The cynical tone was back, and she hated it—though she knew her tone had goaded him to some extent. She was afraid a man like Steven Burke could never settle down, especially on Samsqua. He'd miss the glamour and the nightlife—and resent the woman who'd made him give it up.

Johanna glanced at the dark sky and shivered. "Shall we take Pride Path home?"

"What?" he asked.

"Samsqua is crosscrossed by paths," Sarah explained, "each with the name of a pioneer lady. There's Faith, Hope and Charity. There's also Lucia—that's named for grandlady—and many more. You'll have them all memorized in a day. All of them meander back to a starting point at the wharf, so it's impossible to get lost."

"On second thought let's take Patience home," Johanna said. "It's not quite so rough."

Burke grinned. "Could there also be a Primrose?"

Johanna pressed his arm. "Wouldn't you know that I live two feet off Primrose Path?"

The terrain became wilder when Patience Path veered sharply to the right by a huge boulder, shadowed by a giant willow tree so ancient that it could barely support its greenish attire. The branches of the tree hung down in such profusion that the trunk was completely obscured. Sarah almost slipped on the moist grass underfoot, but Steve caught her arm and held it, whispering, "Can't have my leading lady spraining an ankle, can I?"

The dark clouds were boiling overhead, and splashes of rain began to hit the path. Since lightning did not seem imminent the trio drew back under the abundant foliage, dodging a sudden deluge that sprayed their cheeks and hair.

They took up the path again after a few moments and paused on the summit of the hill. Although the sky was dark immediately overhead, the harbor below was lighted intermittently by sun rays that sliced through the gray clouds, displaying constantly shifting moods over the ocean's surface.

"There's the house," Johanna pointed out to Steve.

Built of stone and brick, Glass Cottage was nestled in a patch of green amid rocky terrain. It had white-

gabled turrets—two of them—on each side of the
main structure, and looked just like a fairy-tale castle
set among stands of maple and birch. A number of
tiny leaded windows dotting the house were inlaid
with stained glass, and a wrought-iron fence surrounded an immaculately groomed garden.

Sarah's heart contracted at the sight of Steve looking down upon her childhood home. Her past had remained locked away in that part of her that was pure
island girl—far removed from the New York career
woman Steve knew. She was comfortable with that
veneer, but this setting would reveal a Sarah without
that coat of sophistication, and she wondered how he
would react to it.

Somewhere deep in the recesses of her mind she
feared Steve's seeing her in her natural habitat. If
there was only a faint hope that a slightly feminist
advertising executive could find happiness with a
famous star like Steven Burke, there was even less
chance for love between him and a woman who
longed for the simple joys of life on Samsqua. Sarah
doubted that he could make that kind of life his. And
she now knew she couldn't live here alone. She'd
want a man, a man to walk with and just be with. She
didn't *need* one, she assured herself, but life would
be complete with one.

Ironically, she was certain that man would have to
be Steve.

"It's like the witch's house in Hansel and
Gretel," Steve was saying. "All icing and ginger-
bread."

A spattering of rain cascaded down over the garden. Johanna looked up at the dark sky and shook her head. "It's really going to pour. Come inside. Samsqua's dry, Steve, except for rum, or I'd offer you some warming brandy. On second thought, however," she grinned, "you look like a whiskey sort of man."

The rain began to pour out of the sky in a veritable torrent then. As they stepped into the informal intimate New England parlor they realized that a sharp chill had crept into the room with the dying sun. Exquisite antique furniture and paintings hung against flowered wallpaper gave the room an elegant yet cozy look, and Sarah was enchanted all over again. On one wall was a floor-to-ceiling fireplace with kindling at the ready, its dark oak mantel a match for the heavy beam striping the ceiling.

"Will you light the fire, Steve, while I fix us some hot-rum toddies?" Johanna said. "It's going to be a long cold night. When the weather suddenly turns like this I wish I had a wireless."

"Wireless?" Burke asked, amazed.

Johanna grinned. "Sorry, we're very 'old country' here. I mean a radio. You'll have to get used to our island ways, Steve. Everything here is ancient." She looked around the room. "I sometimes think antiques are like spouses," she went on softly. "I imagine you have to live with them a while before appreciation truly sets in."

He looked about the room. "This Quakerish setting calls for a cat."

Sarah's eyes glittered. "You haven't met Mustapha, who is not Quaker at all, but will do until one comes along." A pale furry ball, which had blended in perfectly with the beige cushions on the horsehair sofa, raised its head and mewed feebly.

"Mustapha hides under a masculine name," Johanna explained, "but she's quite feminine. She came scratching at my door one frightful midnight last year, half-frozen and scared out of her wits. She'd been bitten by some wild animal. I nursed her back to health, but sometimes at midnight a wild beast of some sort will cry out from High Mountain, and she'll crawl under the covers of my bed and nuzzle against my cheek. Otherwise, I'm afraid she's rather independent."

They drank the delicious toddies in silence, and Sarah, her head resting against the back of the ancient creaking rocking chair, thought in amazement that she was truly relaxed. After a while Burke peered out one of the stained-glass windows through scattered panes of pale amber grisaille, and turned to Sarah. "How about going for a walk? The rain has stopped."

"There are slickers in the hall closet, just in case," Johanna offered.

They dutifully slipped on the yellow oilskins, so huge that they both looked as if they were wearing ponchos. Sarah struck a pose. "Yves Saint-Laurent was never like this!"

Burke laughed. "We look like we're going spear-fishing!"

Outside the air carried a musty odor that was very much like the smell of dried leaves that had turned damp in the forest. Burke hugged his slicker around his shoulders and guided Sarah down Primrose Path. She had the peculiar feeling that she was being taken into unknown territory, although it was she who knew the island and Burke who did not. It was his strength—the fact that he was by her side—that made her feel secure, yet a little apprehensive. She had never before felt as out of control as she did when in his company. He was a type of man as far removed as possible from her business acquaintances in New York, and he was more exciting than she'd ever dreamed a man could be. She checked herself, telling herself it would end—that their worlds were thousands of miles apart. But for almost the first time in her life she wanted to live for the moment, not plan five years in advance. Shyly she slipped her hand into his, and his warm grasp returned the pressure.

The wind had died down now. The air was clean and smelled of the sea. There was no rain—only misty gray clouds that jealously hugged the top of High Mountain. She thrived on this kind of weather. The air in Manhattan was somewhat less than fresh, she reflected, and for the hundredth time she wondered how she could stand living there.

"I've become accustomed to the hot dry air of Southern California with its smoggy haze," Burke said, taking a deep breath of the sweet damp air. "I'd forgotten the joy of walking along a quiet deserted beach. The vastness of it reminds me of Nebraska."

Sarah nodded. "I can imagine." She paused. "This is one reason Johanna can never leave Samsqua. She can't stand the congestion of city life."

She almost lost her footing on the wet grass as they picked their way over several large boulders strewed across the beach. He looked to the horizon and breathed deeply again. The purple-and-blue sea matched the twilit sky above. Such a ghostly silence pervaded that Sarah thought she could hear her heart beating beneath her sweater.

The beach spread before them, rocky coves poking long fat fingers into the coarse sand. It was hard packed after the rain, and the holes made by crabs or other sea life were black pinpoints in the cementlike grayness.

Suddenly she felt a resounding thwack on her bottom, and Steve was grinning as he ran backward away from her. "Race you!" Then he turned and was off, sprinting into the twilight sun.

"Unfair!" she cried as she gave all her strength to the task.

The wind whipped her face and sent her auburn hair flying behind her, and she thought for one second how silly she must look in the huge yellow slicker. But the exhilaration of the chase gave her face a rosy-cheeked hue. When she finally caught up to him, puffing and breathless, she was naturally lovely in a way that no Givenchy gown could have made her.

They laughed and tried to catch their breath as Steve drew her into the shelter of a massive rock formation, yards from the ocean. She was still chuckling at their childishness when he pulled the absurdly big hood of her oilskin down over her face.

"Hey!" she cried as she flung her head back to free herself, laughing infectiously.

But when she saw the odd seriousness in his brown eyes, her laughter died away.

"Sarah," he said, holding her head between his hands, "you know, I've never met anyone quite like you. I wish somehow...." His was almost an anguished look now, and Sarah held fast to his strong shoulders, confused yet unable to break away. She only knew that Steve was deeply troubled, and her heart lurched in her breast, feeling his pain as if it were her own.

"It's okay, Steve. Don't tell me anything you don't want to. I ask nothing. You don't have to give me anything...." Her hand came up involuntarily, and she stroked his dark face with tender fingers.

"Sarah, my darling Sarah, if you knew.... I *want* to give you everything that's in me, but—"

"Don't say it, please," was her distressed cry, because now *she* hurt. She was aching in the region of her heart, for she guessed he was saying a lasting relationship between them could never be. His work, his home, his entire life—it could never include Sarah, no matter where she lived or who she was. He was an actor above all else, and she knew he was driven by a need that easily matched her own compulsion to work in the jungle that was New York.

The tide was coming in, the waves crashing against the rocks nearby, and the sound echoed the thunder in her brain. Never be, never. . . .

"It's okay, Steve. I understand. If anyone understands, I do." She smiled, then, to ease the moment but also to let him know she was strong. He must think her capable of taking it. She knew him well enough now to know that he would not see her again if she were to start crying pitifully or making the situation uncomfortable. . . .

And she *must* continue to see him.

They walked on in silence until, a hundred feet ahead, an old wooden sailing vessel lying half-buried in the sand came into view. Its hull was covered with blue moss. Slick, deep green seaweed was wrapped around the rotting mast and shattered rail, mottled with age. The sea had hit the boat with such force over the years that the wooden planks were worn down; the grain in the wood showed through, as if sandblasted by modern machinery.

"This is perfect!" Burke exclaimed.

"Mmm, I know what you mean," Sarah sighed, letting the sense of history and tradition and timelessness she'd always felt on her island home impress itself upon her.

Burke was circling the old wreck, nodding somberly then looking around him to the flatness of the beach to the east and the increasingly rocky hillsides farther away from the vessel. The tide continued to rise, now sending huge green foamy waves crashing against the jutting rocks. The reddening sun twinkled between the spray, making it appear as though a million tiny pieces of glass had just been shattered. As the waves receded they carved rivers into the craggy stone in an age-old pattern.

Catching Sarah's wistful gaze Steve smiled and grasped her hand. "C'mon, babe, I've got some phoning to do."

"Phoning on Samsqua? You've got to be kidding. You'd have to use Else's ship to shore on the *Griffin*, and she's probably already gone. Besides, who do you want to telephone? I thought this weekend was for both of us to get away."

"Babe, this setting is perfect for the chase scene at the climax of *Devil's Dare*: that old wreck, the fabulous rock formations, the hills. If we can complete filming before the snow comes—"

"Steve, what are you talking about? You can't *film* anything here on Samsqua!" Her heart had begun racing, and she fought for an explanation that would quell her sudden attack of fear.

"Of course we can. Why not?"

"Well, you—you just c-can't!" she sputtered indignantly. "This beach, this lovely old boat— Well, they're mine. Not mine—I mean, they're part of my childhood, my life, and you can't put them on show for millions of gawking movie patrons to see. I just can't allow that," she ended on what she hoped was an authoritative note. In the back of her mind she realized that Steve could—and would—do anything he damned well pleased.

He appeared to know this, too. He was calculating now, his eyes still busy with his surroundings. "There'll be problems for the sound crew, and we could lose days by the weather—but to hell with all that. This is where I'll play my final scene."

"Haven't you heard one word I've said?" Her voice was rising, and she told herself sternly to keep calm. They were business people now, and she had just as much savvy as he did. This was *her* territory, and he would not infringe on it. She glared at him defiantly.

"I heard, Sarah, and I'm afraid I'm not convinced. You talk about motion-picture making as though it were something evil or crass. What the hell do you think I do for a living?" He was angry now, his voice still low but carrying an edge of pure steel. "I'm an actor and I have the respect of millions of people. I have never done any picture that I didn't believe was important enough to spend the money on. Each picture means something—to me and, I hope, to moviegoers. And *Devil's Dare* is just that—a great picture. God knows it's more 'socially significant'—if that's what you're worried about—than some of those ridiculous advertising campaigns Madison Avenue comes up with."

His tone told her just what he thought of *her* career, and being hurt herself she in turn set out to hurt him. "I will not have a Hollywood movie filmed on Samsqua. It *is* crass and will cheapen the place immeasurably. Hordes of people who care nothing for the island itself will invade it just to catch a glimpse of macho-man Steve Burke doing his thing," she taunted. "Go somewhere where your little groupies can scream and drool without upsetting the people who live here. They're *my* people, and this is *my* home, so take your cameras and microphones elsewhere. Why don't you go to Martha's Vineyard? It's already ruined since *Jaws* got hold of it."

"It is not 'ruined,'" he said in exasperation. "Sarah, you're being absurd. You care more for New York than for this island or anyone who lives here, except for Johanna, and I bet she would welcome the publicity. She seems infinitely more in tune with the world than you are—for all your years in the Big Apple."

"Don't even compare me with Johanna again, Burke," she said quietly, and turned away. What was she fighting for anyway? What he had said was basically true. If she loved the island then why had she scorned it all this time, visiting Johanna and grand-lady perhaps twenty times in the past four years?

Was Johanna wiser than she was? Wearily Sarah thought of her efforts to "make it," and the virtual tunnel vision she'd found it necessary to adopt as she climbed the ladder. Why should keeping Samsqua unspoiled mean anything to her when she worked in a business that exhorted masses of television viewers and magazine readers to, in effect, "Buy this and stay young forever," or "Use our product and be happy!"?

"Steve, please don't bring a crew onto Samsqua. I know I must seem like a hypocrite, but this is something I feel very strongly about, and if you care anything about me at all you'll try to understand."

His eyes narrowed, whether from cynicism or some other emotion she couldn't tell. "And you, Sarah Mackenzie, should try to understand that *this*—" a toss of his head indicated the scene before them "—is important to *me*."

Sarah could only plead with her eyes, but the coldness she found in his handsome face defied and finally defeated her struggles. Then anger came to her, renewing her strength. "What I understand, Mr. Burke, is that your bloody movie is about the only thing you care about in this world." She paused. Not bothering to choose her words carefully, she lashed out, "My childhood was a happy and loving one, and I want to preserve those memories in my mind. They are not for public viewing! I'll not— Let *go* of me," she hissed as his hand tightly grasped her wrist.

"Listen, you spoiled little rich— You wouldn't fight me on this if you knew me at all." He tossed her arm aside as though he were disgusted with it. Then he smiled a half smile. "And don't waste your time trying to hurt me, because it's impossible. All the hurt went out of me a long time ago."

But she'd seen his eyes flicker briefly with something mysterious, before the steely glint took over again. Her heart leaped into her throat and tears pricked her eyes. Confusion subdued her angry thoughts. She didn't want to fight—didn't even want to hurt him. But something within her welled up forcefully, something she'd never felt before. It was desire, she knew as she gazed at the man opposite. But it was something more, too. Something almost too much to bear at times, and she wondered if she could possibly be losing her mind. Never had an individual affected her so deeply; never had she felt such...oneness before. It frightened her because it was the unknown—and contradictory—because someone who was in many ways a stranger had the power to make her feel this way. She must keep at least her brain functioning. It was her only defense against being completely swept away.

"I have to, Steve. I have to fight you," she whispered, and prayed that he didn't see in her expression just why that was so.

For a moment they stood motionless, neither of them aware of the gold red orb finally disappearing below the horizon, washing their figures in a soft pink light. Then, as one, each moved toward the other, drawn by a force impossible to resist. Sarah's face was pressed against his chest, exposed by the gap in his oilskin. The warmth of his body, the clean male scent of his skin, the heavy beating of his heart were overwhelming. She wanted to stay there forever, his strong arms encircling her, his hands now moving to caress the nape of her neck. Then he was pulling her coat apart to look down at her face, then lower to the outline of her breasts. She felt naked under his gaze, and even before his hands began to caress and stroke her she knew her desire was apparent. His lips met hers, warm and moist, moving sensuously in an exploration that she was eager to accommodate. They clung to each other as the ocean winds lashed around them. . . .

Finally they broke apart, but slowly, breathing deeply of the fresh salt air while still holding each other with their eyes. Then they exchanged tender smiles, and Steve encircled her slim shoulders to guide Sarah away from the angry swirling ocean, holding her close to him as they started up the beach.

They walked aimlessly for a half hour, each lost in thought and unwilling to break their fragile truce. As they reached Primrose Path, they found Johanna running up a yellow-and-red flag on a tall pole.

"What on earth is she doing?" Steve asked.

Sarah laughed. "We're without communication, so the islanders have worked out a code—a flagging system. For instance, if we want to visit grandlady, who lives on the windward side of the island, we don't just drop in, but check with binoculars first. If she's home she'll be flying her own personal flag. A blue flag tells us she's gone for a ride; an orange flag means she doesn't want visitors, like now. The system may seem rather pagan to a civilized person, but it works."

"What are the other flags?"

"When we go to the mainland we fly a red flag. If we're ill or in need of help we fly our personal flag upside down, as captains do at sea."

Burke just shook his head.

Johanna smiled. "Don't make fun of our local customs. If you think this is strange wait until you find out some of the others!" She paused. "Excuse me. I've got to start dinner. It's very simple—flannel hash." She waved and hurried into the house.

"What is flannel hash?" he asked.

Sarah raised an eyebrow. "You'll see!" Her gaze traveled upward to the darkening purple sky, where a brilliant shade of blue, washed by the rain, cast a silver blue mist on the opposite mountain. "Look at the mountain, Steve. It matches the color of the sea. Also, the tides have changed. There may be a freeze, after all."

When they came into the kitchen, Johanna looked up from the stove. "Your luggage arrived while you were out," she said. "I had Georgie put Steve's case in the upstairs bedroom." She busied herself with the pots. "Miss Sarah will be bunking with me down here, I presume." She looked at Sarah.

"You presume rightly," Sarah said quickly.

"Okay. If Mustapha bothers you during the night, Steve, just toss her out into the hall. I rather think she likes men."

After Johanna had filled the thermos with more rum tea she invited Sarah and Burke to accompany her to visit Luis Farraday at the Running Mallow. As they emerged from the perimeter of the huge rock below Patience Path, a cold damp wind rustled the nearby maple trees, creating an eerie sense of another presence observing their progress. A sweetish smell permeated the air, an odor at once pleasant and sharp. Eventually Johanna pointed to the silhouette of a building that leaned against the protective shoulder of a rising glen. A half-buried sign proclaimed: The Running Mallow Inn, for Ladies and Gentlemen.

A relic of the Queen Anne period of architecture, white with age and gray with deterioration, the old place seemed to infuse the immediate surroundings with an almost overwhelming aura of the past. The structure, in spite of its tumbledown state, would give no quarter to the present.

It was as if the original architect had seen such a house in a dream, and while the image was still fresh in his mind had drawn the blueprints, indiscriminately incorporating Gothic roofs, Roman lintels, stained-glass windows, cupolas and a widow's walk. But the pièce de résistance was the sight of a dozen lovely, fragile nineteenth-century caryatids, immodestly draped wooden ladies who held up the graceful second-story facade.

"Doesn't it remind you of *The Hunchback of Notre Dame*, and that dwarfish little man swinging around the parapets?" Sarah asked.

"It looks like something a Hollywood art director might design," Burke agreed, "after a drunken night on the town."

Johanna scoffed at their jokes. "It was built in 1880," she said proudly.

"Tell me, Johanna, about that old wreck on Taylor's Beach," Burke said, ignoring Sarah's piercing angry look. She turned away from them as Johanna began the story.

"Yes, tell him about it, Johanna; you're the island historian." Neither seemed to catch the sarcasm in her voice.

"Only because grandlady refuses to remember anything anymore."

"Which reminds me," Burke said, "when am I going to meet her?"

Johanna sighed softly. "Her birthday's tomorrow. We'd go up now, but she's still flying an orange flag. She may be tired after her ride this morning." She paused. "Now, let's see...the old boat. Well, years ago when Sar and I were little, a man called Brood and his two sons sailed the boat down from Nova Scotia. Would you believe they didn't even have a lantern on board?"

"Or a wireless," Sarah couldn't help interjecting. She was getting caught up in the story of the boat, as she always did.

"But the weather was good, and they thought they could reach Portland without any trouble. Then a squall blew up suddenly—as they do in these waters—and the ship was wrecked."

"What happened to Mr. Brood and his brood?" Steve asked.

"Thankfully," Johanna went on quickly, "they had a modern inflatable lifeboat that saved them. Later, when the wreck was in danger of being swept out to sea, some of the villagers towed her into the cove. It's really a great tourist attraction."

"Exactly," drawled Steve, obviously for Sarah's benefit.

They were at the rusty ancient wrought-iron gate that surrounded what was left of the lawn in front of the Running Mallow. A rising wind whistled about the caryatids, their wooden body scarves seeming to move. "In a way," Steve remarked, "it's too bad that it's being modernized."

Johanna laughed. "Please...*restored*. There's a difference, you know. When it's finished it'll be the most comfortable inn on Samsqua. We hope to attract a lot of rich old ladies who'll come here for the entire season. Can't you see them all lined up on the porch—a rocking-chair brigade?"

Sarah giggled, all thoughts of moviemaking forgotten. "Considering the quality of the competition from the Iron Donkey and the Cricket Hearth, it should do well.''

"The Cricket Hearth?'' Burke said. "I can see the advertisement now in the *Saturday Review*.

Paying guests taken at small quaint hotel. Simple atmosphere: home cooking, relaxing beach, old rocks, historic site. Bring walking shoes.''

"You're not far wrong,'' Johanna put in, "except that the Cricket Hearth used to be a bordello that was closed, I think, during the flu epidemic of 1918. They say that even now, on All Hallows' Eve, the old sailors can be heard pounding on the door. There's also supposed to be sounds of women laughing and the clink of glasses. . . .''

"Toasting with your grandfather's rum, no doubt!'' Burke replied.

They walked single file down the curved stone path that was infested with pale green moss, and made their way up the creaking steps onto the porch and into the lobby. The foyer appeared to be the model for innumerable old summer homes. The only accessory left over from its former grandeur was a giant tarnished copper chandelier, which held dozens of candles.

Two sets of scaffolding were placed against the north and west walls of the entrance, and four men in white overalls were tracing with templates elaborate designs on the ceiling. Pale ivory, powder blue and soft pink swirled in an intricate paisley pattern. "Oh," Sarah said, examining the repainted columns and the colored stenciling. "It's going to be quite lovely!"

"Yes," a male voice called from the top of the north scaffold. "Wait until the painting's finished, the windows washed and the brass polished. The carpet's going to be green—the color of that moss outside." The man, redheaded and tall with powerful muscles molded by the thin T-shirt he wore, looked down and waved a paintbrush, grinning. "Hi, Sarah. I'm Luis Farraday." He was younger than she'd imagined—perhaps twenty-eight, she decided.

"Hello," Sarah called, "and this is my friend, Steven Burke."

The men exchanged greetings, then Farraday climbed carefully down the scaffolding and picked his way over the floor cluttered with broken plaster. He kissed Sarah on the cheek and shook Burke's hand. "I admire your work," he said simply to Steven.

"Thank you. I admire yours, too," Burke said, looking around him, and Sarah felt a surge of pride. Steven Burke might be arrogant and high-handed, but he was definitely not self-centered.

"Well, thank you, Mr. Burke. You're kind to say that." Luis smiled. "I know they say making movies is hard work, but think about all those beautiful girls you get to make love to! That's when I envy you!" A wink in Johanna's direction assured them all that he was teasing her.

Burke laughed. "It's not all that easy. You have to worry about such things as lights, camera angles and not squashing noses. And once you've kissed your leading lady about twenty times and wiped the lipstick off that's smeared all over you, it's not fun anymore. Remember, too, there are about sixty-five technicians looking on all the time. Kissing can get very technical." He slanted a sideways glance at Sarah. "I prefer my lovemaking spontaneous."

"I know what you mean," Luis Farraday said with a laugh, putting his arm around Johanna. "I just wish we had more of it!"

Sarah laughed, too. She liked him. She had never seen a person as freckled as Luis Farraday; there was not one square inch of visible flesh that was not covered with golden brown spots. His dark eyes were piercing, and he had a peculiar amused twist to his thin lips. Sarah could also see, with pleasure, that he liked her sister. Yet he and Johanna made such an incongruous pair that Sarah wondered what had been their initial point of attraction.

"What's for dinner?" Luis asked. "I'm starved."

"Flannel hash," Johanna replied smugly. "And if I get home in time I'll throw an apple pie in the oven. Meanwhile let's have rum tea." She placed the large thermos on an ancient table, and removing four tin cups from the top poured out generous servings of the dark fragrant liquid.

Burke held up his cup. "Here's to all our ambitions. May we all live to see them materialize."

Career ambitions, money, fame. The important things in Burke's life. Sarah's heart felt heavy.

"I'll drink to that," Luis said, taking a long drink. His face went red. "Man, that's choice!" he exclaimed. "Grandfather Concannon sure knew what he was doing when he ran in this batch of rum!"

Sarah nodded. "The age helps," she said dryly.

"When do you start on the restoration of the exterior, Luis?" Burke asked after taking a good pull of the rum tea. "If you keep enough of this firewater around the place may paint itself!"

"We'll be here all winter. Else has brought almost all the interior materials over on the *Griffin*, but she'll soon be cutting her trips down, and then with bad weather and all it'll probably be March before we can start on the facade. They wanted it finished by the fourth of July, but I said no way. The guests will just have to put up with the mess a little while longer. The interior will be finished sometime this winter, though, and quite habitable."

There was a sudden clap of thunder; then flashes of lightning illuminated the old lobby. "It's going to pour again," Johanna said. "We'd better be going. Aren't you going to knock off early, Luis?"

He looked at his watch. "It's six o'clock. I'd better stick around for another hour." He glanced at Sarah. "I'm not a finish painter, but I fill in after the boys up there do the outline work. No plush office for *this* architect, I'm afraid. On a job like this I work alone—keeps me on my toes.'' He saluted. ''See you later.''

Lightning flashed again as Johanna called from the doorway, ''Better hurry. It'll be raining pitch-forks and mermaids in a minute.''

A FEW HOURS LATER, after they had consumed the flannel hash, a simple but delicious mixture of chopped canned corned beef, a few onions and fresh-ly boiled beets from Johanna's garden, they topped the meal off with slices of hot apple pie. Johanna then pulled the cretonne curtains over the windows in the parlor and lighted the coal-oil lamps. The small room, its collection of antiques gleaming in the glow from the lamps, didn't smell so musty because a pun-gent cedarwood fire also crackled in the fireplace, courtesy of the men.

''I wish there were some entertainment,'' Johanna reflected, taking up an embroidery hoop and easing herself down into the wing-back chair by the fire-place. ''But there isn't, unless we row over to Booth-bay through the rough seas!''

''Don't apologize, Johanna,'' Burke said, lighting a cigarette. ''Some of us love the simple life—occa-sionally.''

''Well, I imagine poor Sarah's dying of bore-dom,'' she said, and gave her sister a teasing grin.

''Even geniuses have to give their brains a rest once

in a while," Sarah retorted with a smile and a cocky flip of her head. "Are you becoming a confirmed islander, Luis?" she asked.

"My God, no!" Luis came up behind Johanna and grasped the wings of the chair with his big hands. "I like the big city too much. Besides, that's where the money is. New York's gone wild with building. But this spring I came up to sail for a weekend and get some sun, met Johanna and found out that Mr. Drury was ripe for a restoration job on the Running Mallow. My price was right, so here I am. It's a challenge, I can tell you! And I don't mean the restoration job!" He laughed heartily as Johanna threw a cushion up behind her, catching him on the side of the head.

As the men spoke about materials and craftsmanship, Sarah sat on a stool in front of the fire and shelled fall peas into a large wooden bowl, glancing now and then at Johanna and Luis Farraday. Their attraction for each other was a gratifying thing to see. She had begun to think that her sister might not find a man to love, a man who would give her the kind of artistic approval that she needed without feeling threatened himself. That type of man was rare, even in these days of dawning awareness of women's capabilities. But *this* man, although he wasn't handsome in the same sense that Burke was, had a certain quality that seemed to complement Johanna's personality.

If only Steve were the type of man who could accept a woman's need to be independent— But no, never, she thought. Steve would demand a woman's every attention, would require her to pander to his enormous ego, produce little Burkes— It grabbed hold of her, that thought, like a revelation. To have Steve's children. . . . They bewildered her, the urges she was feeling now. She'd never pictured herself as the motherly type, and yet suddenly she couldn't imagine anything more fulfilling. She chided herself for the direction her thoughts were taking, for the natural events that would have to precede childbearing were mysterious and a little frightening to her. His kisses had set her on fire, telling her what desire truly meant—nothing like her lukewarm response to Peter. But beyond that an intimate relationship with him was too much to bear thinking about.

Steve looked as handsome as ever in the firelight, but Sarah thought she now detected another quality in him. His guard was down—perhaps that was it. Whatever it was, his rugged features bespoke such inner peace and acceptance of himself and his world that a new rush of respect coursed through Sarah. He was a man who had faced the challenge of a small-town boy from the Midwest adapting to a high-profile career in Tinsel Town. He had come out a winner, and she thought how exciting it would be to be the woman who helped him meet future challenges.

The odor of vanilla wafted strongly into the room, and Johanna was saying, "Gosh, I'd better peek at grandlady's birthday cake. If I let it bake too long, it'll get crusty around the edges and I'll never hear the end of it!''

"The cake would fall for sure if I baked it," Sarah added. "I've cooked with gas so long in New York that I don't think I could manage a wood stove." She turned to Luis. "How do you feel about primitive living?''

"It's a relief from the Big Apple. It seems to me that I'm on a long vacation—and getting paid for it, too!" He glanced at his watch. "I've got to get back to the Running Mallow. There are blueprints to check before I go to bed.''

"But I thought you were staying here?" Sarah rejoined, then realized the implications.

Johanna came in from the kitchen and stood by Luis. "You should know better than that!" Smiling, she took his hand in hers. "What would the islanders think? It wouldn't be proper with so many vacant rooms at the inn. People would talk—especially since we're so often seen together.''

Burke gave Sarah a sardonic smile. "Looks as though you'll be a fallen woman in the islanders' eyes. But then, I guess they'd hardly expect a city woman to be as pure as snow.''

Sarah glared at him, fury rising up in her. But a wish to keep the peace this weekend, especially in front of Johanna and Luis, forbade her venting her anger. "Yes, Steve," she said sweetly, "but we don't have to live here day-to-day. Besides, they don't think of me as an islander anymore. And don't forget we're chaperoned by Johanna!''

They said good-night to Luis. Then Burke stood up and stretched his six-foot frame toward the ceiling. He turned to Sarah. "Another walk? I'd like to see what that old sailing vessel looks like by moonlight."

Well, she couldn't stop him, she supposed, but she certainly wasn't going to go with him and give him the idea she condoned his plans to use the island in his film. Secretly, though, she had to admit to herself that she was glad he appreciated the beauty and mystery of the old wreck, even if he did want to tell the world it was there and have people start carving their initials in it, or taking endless photographs of little Bobby or Sue perched on the ancient hull—"Look, Betty, here's a shot of that famous old boat— Brood's or something. You know, the one in *Devil's Dare.* . . . '' She could just hear them now.

"I'm tired, Steve," she said now. "I've had a busy day, what with the drive up here this morning and all. But we'll give you a flashlight. It's easy to lose your way at night."

He laughed at that. "I wouldn't want to lose my way," he mocked with feigned fear. "Especially on Primrose Path!"

While Johanna searched for the flashlight in the hall cupboard Sarah started to clear the dessert dishes from the table; Burke's critical scrutiny was becoming increasingly hard to bear.

She had often viewed Brood's old shipwreck in the moonlight when a full round disk hung in the sky and the Milky Way lighted up the heavens. Her heart beat faster as she thought of she and Steve gazing at the roaring tides worrying the broken old ship, the moonlight sculpting every crag and bit of moss in sharp bas-relief. He would surely take her hand and draw her close, and his mouth would seek out her own and all resistance would be lost. She was strong, but she doubted if she could withstand the combination of the most romantic scenery possible and Steve's blatant sexuality.

She knew herself well enough to know her limits— or did she? When she was with Steve all rational thought seemed to leave her.

After the door had slammed behind him the cottage seemed suddenly cold and empty. She almost ran after him then. He would have reached Patience Path by now and would be watching the tides coming in, slapping gently against the rotted hull. Perversely, she longed to be there, too. How quickly her moods shifted since she'd met him! Temptation would lead to submission, she warned herself. And submitting to a man like Steve would bring a heartbreak greater than any she'd experienced with Peter. He'd implied as much.

Sarah sighed again and went into the kitchen. Under control now, she stacked the plates in the sink and hunted for the detergent. There was something about doing the dishes that was safe and sound—and somehow far removed from temptation.

CHAPTER SIX

SARAH DIDN'T KNOW whether it was the acrid smoke or the blinding blue white light that awakened her. A burning odor that she finally identified as charcoal permeated the room through her half-open window. Why would Johanna be building a fire in the hearth at—she looked at the luminous clockface on the bureau—four o'clock in the morning?

Another flash of light outside the window, which vanished before Sarah's gaze. Lightning? It started up again, but this time the stream was unyielding... lasting. She looked at the empty twin bed on the other side of the room. Getting up quickly, she opened the rain-streaked window and peered out. The illuminating source was shining in a slanting pattern from a tiny room across the courtyard. The leaded windows jutted out to face directly into Sarah's room. Of course. She was an idiot! Johanna was working in her studio. She'd forgotten about her sister's strange working habits.

Fully awake now, and with little hope of getting back to sleep without much tossing and turning, she got up and pulled on her bathrobe, running swift hands through her curls. She thrust her feet into mules and headed across the expanse of hallway leading to Johanna's workroom. A shaft of light fanned out in a crescent from under the door.

Just as Sarah was about to turn the knob a deep voice arrested her, and she turned to catch Burke's question. "Hello, what *is* that smell?"

"Johanna's charcoal-burning kiln. I couldn't sleep, either." She looked up at him, thinking that even at this ungodly hour he looked healthy and dynamic. Wearing nothing but his jeans, he casually displayed a lean muscled torso, tanned and covered with black hair that formed a T on his chest and trailed down to the buckle of his belt. She forced her eyes up to meet his face, and found his lips were twitching in amusement at her obvious embarrassment. "I, uh, should have told you not to take any notice of anything that seems peculiar around here."

"I'm a light sleeper."

"Do you want coffee?"

"Sure," he said.

"I'll make it. Why don't you join Johanna?" she asked, feigning unconcern and almost backing into the kitchen. Suddenly she was all too aware of the figure-hugging velour wrapped tightly around her nude body. Damn his attractiveness! It made her feel like a twittering teenager again, the blushing schoolgirl awed by the football hero. As she prepared the coffee she willed her pulse to slow down to a normal pace.

"I'd rather stay with you, thanks," Burke said, and she whirled around, a false smile planted on her face.

"Sure. Want to grab three cups from the shelf there? I bet Johanna would love a cup of coffee. Honestly, I don't know how she does it—up this early, working already. . . ."

Her words died away as Steve turned her to face him. Why did she always lose her voice when he got within two feet of her?

"Do I *scare* you, babe?"

She gave a short nervous laugh. "Steve, really. Please don't call me 'babe.' It's so. . . so. . . sixties. No one calls anyone 'babe' anymore."

"I do."

"The kettle's boiling," she said stupidly, and continued to stand there, although she managed to drag her eyes away from his face to stare earnestly at her slippers. *They're ridiculous slippers,* she thought absently. *Little pom-poms on the top. . , . Snap to it, girl. Don't let him do it again. Think!* And she grabbed at the kettle and made the coffee.

"Come on, let's go downstairs," she said. As she led him out of the kitchen to the studio she could feel his gaze running down her spine and over her bottom to her shapely legs only partially covered by the soft robe.

The acetylene torch died, and the place took focus and shape. In the middle of the room stood Johanna, black gloved and silver goggled, looking like a surrealistic character from outer space. She placed the torch on the table, pulled off her gloves, pushed the goggles up on her forehead and laughed. "Welcome to my dungeon. I'm sorry if I woke you up. Oh, thanks for the coffee," she added as she saw the extra cup.

"Is this the way you spend your nights?" Burke asked. "It looks like you're engaged in some kind of pagan ritual."

"I am!" Johanna's mouth, wiped clean of lipstick, tilted mockingly as she removed the goggles and shook out her dark hair.

Sarah looked around the cluttered interior. It was garretlike, certainly, with small windows and stone walls; it might have been an attic in Paris. She hadn't been in here in years. Many small tabletops affixed to sawhorses held innumerable white-swathed objects.

Glass tubes were stacked oddly in small groups, each pile a different color. She had seen such supplies at country bazaars, where men practicing the ancient art of glassblowing fashioned little boats with sails, minute animals and tiny pianos as fragile as the wings of a butterfly.

Burke shook his head. "The mystery deepens."

"A maiden lady working in her cellar in the wee hours of the morning should not be so overwhelming," Johanna said cryptically. "Perhaps if I were canning fruit or putting up preserves...."

"I still don't know what you *do* do here." He picked up a tube. "Are you a glassblower?"

"No." She went to a nearby table, where she whisked away a cloth from a tall object. She darted from one table to another until all the figures were unveiled. Then she stood back and waited, a proud but apprehensive look in her eyes.

Sarah saw that she had turned the room into a Byzantine gallery. Figures, busts, vases, obelisks and even caryatids holding up urns were arranged in a cacophony of color—all fashioned of glass, but glass unlike any other that she had ever seen.

The front table held a drunken Bacchus, the god of wine, that was all the more unusual because it rested on only one hairy hoof. The other hoof was stretched out at an angle, as if he were executing a figure eight on a sheet of ice—in this case a sheet of opalescent glass. The horned head, the beard and even the furry body were made up of hundreds of pieces of fine, subtly curled wire, inserted into the glass body. But the face, ears, chest and hands were as smooth as a piece of fine marble. The piece, shot with light yellow, dark red and burnt orange, sent shivers up Sarah's spine. The way in which Johanna had caught the movement of the Bacchus was phenomenal.

"You like my Dionysus?" she asked softly.

"I'm overwhelmed!" Sarah exclaimed when she could find her tongue. To her, Johanna's "art" had always been suspect. Of course, the only object that she had seen for years was the paperweight of Samsqua's wharf, which even Johanna admitted was far from her best work. But these pieces on display, Sarah realized to her astonishment, were very good— No, more than that. Some of them, like the Bacchus, were brilliant. She could not believe her eyes.

"How in the world do you do them?" Burke asked.

"Well, first I make the stand—sometimes metal, sometimes glass or a combination of the two. Like Dionysus here. The smooth parts are achieved by what we call 'flashing'—heating then cooling the material in order to soften it and meld the different colors. The hairs, as you see, are made of copper wires that are individually inserted with pliers into the glass while it's still molten and manageable. I have to work very quickly. See?" She took a drawing from a drawer and held it up. "This is the cartoon and the plan for Dionysus. It's very detailed."

"It looks like you've worked it out with trigonometry!" Steve studied the drawing carefully.

"It has to be all mathematics at first," Johanna replied, "or I'd lose contact. The figure would get away from me, and there'd only be a blob of glass and wire left."

Steve turned to the bust of an ancient mariner made up of sea and earth colors, so realistic that the beard seemed to take on the salt-washed stain of seaweed. There was also a young Dutch boy, a masterpiece of ingenuity fashioned from bits of blue. The resemblance to Georgie, the young island boy, was unmistakable.

There were also vases of purple and gold, a pair of hands in shades of gray and a pink Victorian lady whose myriad wires made her ostrich-plumed hat seem to come alive.

"I can see grandlady posed for that in one of her mother's old hats," Sarah said. "It's quite effective."

"Essentially I work with vitreous pigments," said Johanna. "Powdered glass and metallic oxides like copper, iron or manganese." She held up a taped finger. "I got this from fluoric acid. An hour or so ago I stained some small pieces of glass a deep purple. But I wanted a pattern of light to shine through, so I painted a design with acid. Unfortunately it also burned my skin. *Fortunately* my skin has been somewhat hardened by this type of work."

"Where did you get the idea of working with glass?" Burke asked.

"I don't really know." Johanna smiled as her eyes roved around the room. "I guess it was when Georgie found some pitted broken bottles washed up by the sea. I incorporated the bits in a clay vase that I was forming on the potter's wheel. It turned out so well I thought of inserting copper wire. Then I began working in glass."

"I can't get over the results," Burke said, looking around at the figures. "They're extraordinary."

"The leaded effect is really difficult and takes an

eternity," Johanna explained. "At first I used pastel-colored grisaille glass, but it was too expensive. Now I buy from a firm in West Germany that'll fill my rather small orders. Or I make 'pot metal' in that charcoal fire chamber over there. I've got a batch going now. It's awfully complex because the formula must be exact and has to be watched intently until the melting point is reached. And the torch is always a problem for me. As a craftsman, I'm still a baby. And as a craft, glasswork is still a child, too. Believe it or not, it's the only trade in the world that has progressed very little since the thirteenth century!"

Burke ran his hand around the smooth mouth of a massive orange-and-red vase that was made up of numerous tiny oblong pieces of glass joined only by thin wires. "Sarah, feel this. It has the texture of soft cool silk." He looked at Johanna and asked, "Have you ever had an exhibition?"

"Heaven's no," she laughed. "I'd be scared to death. I've never even sold very much. My work is for me alone, I guess. It's so personal."

Suddenly a timer buzzed.

"That's the small kiln. I'm doing a pure ceramic piece. Take a look." She pointed to a table and a design for a lamb to be made up of hundreds of tiny glazed ceramic jigsaw-puzzle pieces.

She drew on a glove, turned a dial on the kiln, opened the door and brought out a tiny pink leaf-shaped object. "This is that dratted ear I was telling you about yesterday. It's broken about a dozen times in the firing. It gets impossibly hot in there, you know. But the ceramic cools very quickly.''

Fascinated, Sarah and Burke watched her paint glue on the underside of the ear, then dexterously fit it into the ceramic puzzle. She slipped her goggles over her head as if by habit.

"There," she said proudly, standing back. "It'll be finished when I pour over the epoxy resin, which I prefer to use instead of ordinary grout.''

Burke looked at the figure again and shook his head. "I'm not much of a critic, but what you're doing here is all line and balance, isn't it? You're really an expert at construction.''

"I've never thought of my work that way, Burke, but I can see what you mean." She brought her hand up to her temple and brushed away a few strands of dark hair, then went on with a thoughtful vague air. "Artists, I think, basically please themselves; it's a solitary life, really. I've always loved Samsqua, and it has many advantages, but occasionally—like now— when I want so badly to talk about my art. . . . Well, talking is. . . like feasting." She paused, then abruptly changed her tone. "I am boring you both silly." She looked out the studio window. A rosy glow was replacing the darkness. "It's also time for me to get back to bed, but I'll make breakfast first. How about scrambled eggs, bacon and toasted homemade bread?''

"Mmm, you bake bread, too?" Burke asked.

She laughed. "I'll make someone a good wife

someday—if I can find a man who'll put up with all this." She gestured around the studio. "Sar, would you make some more coffee?" She took quick steps toward the door then abruptly turned around. "Oh, I've forgotten to take off my goggles!" She came back to them. "You see, I'm not used to having company—you know, showing my work...." She whipped off the glasses, shook out her hair and looked down at her soiled smock. "Sarah, you always look bandbox fresh—no matter what the hour or circumstance. Who did your dressing gown?"

"Well...Christian Dior," Sarah replied. Why should she suddenly feel guilty?

Johanna swung around, the same wide felt skirt she had worn the day before twirling around her trim figure. "My skirt," she said in falsetto, "is by F.W. Woolworth." She fluttered her eyelashes. "And my firing smock was designed for me by J.C. Penney!"

Sarah laughed then. "Well you *do* have certain privileges, Miss Jo. After all, you're older than I—"

"Only eighteen months!"

"Which can sometimes be an eternity...."

"Now, girls," Burke grinned, holding up his hands as if he were demarcating the battle lines. "It's too early in the day for a cat fight."

Johanna grasped Sarah around the waist and twirled around with her. "Don't pay any attention to us. We haven't had a serious spat in years!"

"True. Not since you pulled the ears off Murgatroyd," Sarah said. "That was real cruelty."

"Murgatroyd?" Burke asked skeptically.

"My pink stuffed rabbit."

"And," Johanna replied gravely, "do you remember what happened next?"

"I think I cried."

"Yes," Johanna replied softly, "you did that, but not before you pulled the cotton wadding out of Geraldine." She looked up at Burke. "She was my stuffed turtle, and I loved her more than anything in the world."

Suddenly the girls looked at each other and burst into peals of laughter. Then Johanna said, "The bacon's in the cooler outside the kitchen door—remember?"

"Of course. I'd forgotten that you still used that old thing. Come on, Burke. I'll start cooking breakfast." She started up the stairs. "See how she is?" Sarah remarked humorously. "First *she* was going to do breakfast, and I was going to make the coffee."

"Artistic temperament!" Johanna shouted laughingly from her workbench. "It lets me get away with murder!"

THAT AFTERNOON Sarah and Burke took Primrose Path to the apex of High Mountain. The sky had emptied itself of rain and it was still quite cold, although the sun was bright enough in the cloudless sky to cast shadows. "Look, it's so clear you can see Boothbay," she cried, and going to the ledge pointed to the mainland.

"You mean that little speck over there is civilization?"

She nodded. "So near, and yet so far." She faced him, tucking her hands into the pockets of her jeans. "I'm beginning to get anxious. Two days on Samsqua is about all I can take these days. I'd like to be over there, getting into my car. I'd drive back right now. It's crazy; one minute I never want to see New York again, but then I really miss it."

"That's too bad." His tone was serious as he turned to her. "You're much more at home here. You look even more beautiful, in fact. Why don't you give up the rat race, Sarah? It's not for you. Live here on Samsqua."

"*Live* here? What on earth would I do here? What do you suggest—build tiny ships in bottles? Or knit and sell cardigans?" She knew she was over-reacting and wondered why. She'd had the same idea herself.

"Okay, okay," Steve said lightly. "Just a suggestion. But I do think you'd be happier."

As he spoke Burke stooped to pick up a rock to throw, and stopped dead when he caught sight of a stone tablet caked in moss and dirt. Sarah dropped beside him to help brush it off and cried, "Look, Steve, we've found it. It's been lost all these years, and we've found it!" She smoothed the old stone with her hand. "Oh, God, Steve," she said reverently. With a tremor in her voice she read:

"Here lie the remains of
UNEEMA
Beloved wife of
Capt. Samuel Fordyce.
Himself, retired from the sea,
a respectable landowner and
father of four sons: Matthew,
Lorne, Jacob and Phillip.
Uneema, being of the Mohegan tribe
of Connecticut, entered life's travail
January 9, 1752 and passed into Heaven
March 6, 1855 of old age
and sorrow for her husband and sons
lost at sea."

"Imagine living for over a hundred years...." Steve said quietly. "It's true, then—the story, I mean. I thought you were just reciting an old wives' tale coming over on the *Griffin*." He moved beside her and placed his arm loosely around her waist.

"I'm glad we found her resting place," Sarah said, sentimental tears glistening in the corners of her eyes. "Is it a premonition, Steve?"

"Of what?"

"Oh, I don't know. Maybe you and me," she ventured.

"I don't believe in superstitions," he said flatly.

She turned toward him. "Neither do I. Yet I have this eerie feeling, with her so close and...."

"I thought you didn't have any emotional ties to the island except Johanna and grandlady."

She pulled away from him, walked to the ledge and looked through the gathering mist that was slowly obliterating the Jonesport lobster boats anchored in the cove below. "I did say that, didn't I?" She paused and took a deep breath of stinging fresh air. "I meant it at the time, but now I'm not quite so sure." She glanced down at the roughly chiseled words on the slate gravestone and shivered. Suddenly she felt very confused about where her life was heading. She knew that she didn't want to lead it alone. "Oh, hold me, Steve. I need to feel you holding me...."

He drew her against him and searched her face. "Sarah, love, I need to hold you, too." And slowly his lips came down to meet hers. A thrill ran through her and she clung to him for support. The emotionally charged moment, heady with promise, threatened to overwhelm her....

The moment was shattered when from far beneath them came the sound of pounding hooves and the playful snort of a horse. "Haw! Haw!" the rider shrieked.

Burke broke their kiss, and they turned simultaneously to look below. An enormous black stallion was galloping down the path, missing overhanging trees and bushes by mere inches. A green apparition in a matching hat covering a mass of elaborate curls reined in the horse at her gate.

Sarah laughed and waved. "Hello, grandlady!" she yelled.

The figure waved, and alighting gracefully tied the reins loosely around the newel post before disappearing into an impressive house.

"Come on, Burke," Sarah said. "I'll show you the quick way down." She took his hand and led him to an unused path that was almost obliterated by trailing yew. "Johanna and I used to come up this way," she explained. They were only halfway down the hill when they heard an exclamation, followed by another "Haw!" Heavy hooves sounded, and a shower of pebbles was shaken loose from the path.

"My God," Burke cried, "I'd hate to get in her way. She rides that stallion like a bat out of hell!"

Sarah laughed. "That's Magnifique. He's part Arabian. She's always ridden him that way. She says that if she falls and breaks her neck it's a good way to go." She paused and grew serious. "That used to sound funny when Johanna and I were younger. Now it's not funny at all. The way she rides it could happen."

"I wonder why she didn't wait for us," Burke mused, helping her down to Primrose Path.

"You'd have to know grandlady to understand. She doesn't like to meet new people—especially men—unless she's all gussied up—" Sarah stopped in midsentence. "I haven't thought of that expression in years—'all gussied up.' Anyway, when we go calling at Needlepoint House she'll be presiding like a grande dame over her birthday cake. You'll see!"

"I'd like a few shots of Brood's boat to send to Sir Lew Grade. He has to see how perfect this is. C'mon, let's go down."

Sarah stiffened. Did everything have an angle to him? The unwelcome thought struck her that the only reason he'd come on this weekend jaunt at all was to scout out the island as a possible film location. The vitality drained out of her as she remembered the urgency of his words: "I have to see you." Why—to get an "in" on Samsqua? She supposed the few kisses they'd shared were his way of thanking her.... Her heart ached, and anger at her own stupidity compounded the hurt. He was using her, just as Peter had used her. And she'd fallen for the ploy hook, line and sinker.

She resolved to get through the weekend as civilly as possible. But after that Mr. Steven Burke had better watch himself! Two could play his little deceitful game.

Sarah shook her head as if to dispel her unsavory thoughts. "Let's go home." She pointed to the cove, where, like a small flotilla, the Jonesports were all putting in for shore. "They're all being brought in. Their skippers are in radio contact with the coast guard. It means a storm's brewing—coming in on the windward side. We can't see it from here; we're protected by High Mountain. We'd better get home, though, just in case."

MUSTAPHA WAS DOZING peacefully by the fire when a sudden draft shot down the chimney, spreading sparks over the hearthstone. She howled, jumped into the firewood box and cowered in the corner, the hairs on her back standing on end. Johanna ran in from the kitchen, calling softly to the cat, reaching down and smoothing her fur. The barometer on the mantel indicated the pressure had dropped to 30.60! She looked out the window at the ominous gray sky. "We're going to catch it!" she said flatly, looking out again apprehensively.

Burke took the binoculars from the kitchen table, went out on the patio and trained the lenses below. "Everything's up tight in the cove now. All the boats are moored." He moved the glasses over to the windward side of the island. "Sarah," he called, "what does a blue flag mean?"

She came up behind him. "It means someone's not at home. Why?"

"Take a look." He handed the glasses to her.

"My God," she cried, "that's the roof of Needlepoint House. Is grandlady still out with Magnifique? She could be lying hurt anywhere if he's thrown her!"

Johanna threw down the dish towel. "Damn," she muttered. "Wouldn't you know! Well, we've got to find her before the storm hits." Going quickly to the hall closet she took out three yellow slickers. "You and Burke had better go down Patience Path. She rides home that way sometimes. I'll take Hannah Path, and we'll meet at Needlepoint House. Say a prayer that we find her unharmed."

As Sarah put on a slicker, her beautiful face frowning and concerned, she looked to Johanna for reassurance. "Grandlady's an old island hand. Surely she'll know a storm's brewing, won't she?"

Burke shot Sarah a look that plainly said, "I hope you're right."

"If she's tethered Magnifique somewhere and is taking a walk through the woods she may not realize anything's amiss. She's an old woman, Sarah," he reminded her. "She's not necessarily as sharp as she once was."

"Or she might be down among those boulders that protect the Sea of Spiders," Johanna added evenly. "If she's daydreaming, as she does at times, she won't realize she's in danger until the winds strike."

Scurrying outside, Johanna proceeding north and Sarah and Burke south, they braved a bone-chilling breeze that set their teeth chattering. Sarah huddled closer to Burke as the wind whipped about them. The gray clouds were shifting across the sky in vaporous patches, uniting here and there into dark clots before disintegrating again. Another cloud layer above the first was purple and swollen with rain.

Sarah and Burke bowed their heads against the pelting rain as the wind howled wildly. At one point

Sarah was hurled against a large boulder, dropping to her knees at the impact before Burke could reach her. Only his "It's all right, babe, I'm here" prevented her from giving way to tears. In the comparatively quiet wood they paused for breath—but not for long, taking advantage of the lull to set out on the path with renewed energy. But their frantic calls were futile, snatched away by the wind. Lucia Concannon and Magnifique were nowhere to be seen.

By the time Johanna reached Hannah Path the dark blue horizon was streaked with pink and amber. But for once she did not stop to view the magnificent display; her grandmother could be lying hurt among the rocks below.

The Running Mallow shuddered forlornly in the wind. Storm windows had been put up, and a single chink of light glowed through the many-paned windows in the huge boarded-up dining room. Johanna held back an impulse to yell to Luis Farraday, to assure herself that he, at least, was safe. Then, dismissing her reaction as paranoid, she ran on down the incline to Charity Path.

As Sarah and Burke came out into a small clearing by a spreading cypress, huge drops of rain pelted down forcefully, causing the sand at their feet to dance. They followed Hope Path, which veered right and crept along a mountainous ledge. A sudden icy blast hit and they almost slipped, treading over some sweet wanda.

There were no footprints or hoofprints anywhere on the path.

The ice-cold rain turned to sleet as they quickly surveyed the boulders that protected the estuary of the Sea of Spiders. They made good time up Hannah Path, protected by the trees that Grandfather Concannon had planted eighty years before. As the wind increased the sleet turned to hail. Grasping each other firmly, Sarah and Burke stepped back under a knot of trees to regain their breath, and were joined a few moments later by Johanna, who shouted, "She's nowhere!"

"Not a trace," Sarah agreed. "Does she ever ride down to the private World War II beach?"

Johanna shook her head. "No, she never goes off the paths, thank God! Come on, let's go!" Holding her head down she rushed out of the woods and picked her way down the familiar embankment. She held Burke's hand, and with Sarah in tow the threesome continued their frightful journey, pelted by hail and whipped by wind. The yellow slickers, stiff and unyielding, protected their bodies from the increasing dampness.

At last they dodged under the eaves of the stable at Needlepoint House for a brief respite. Sarah turned at a sudden snorting sound—and behind them, warm and undisturbed, Magnifique gently pawed the straw fodder. Lifting up his head to the open space above the door, he eyed the storm contemptuously, his soft muzzle vibrating in the wind.

"Thank God!" Johanna cried. She leaned back on the sea-whitened planking, gasping with relief. Then she removed a cube of sugar from her inner pocket, which she gave to the horse. Magnifique nibbled the sweet gratefully. The world had returned to normal.

Sarah leaned her head against Burke's shoulder. "I could see her dashed to pieces over the rocks," she said tremulously, then became indignant. "Honestly, I don't know how you put up with her, Johanna!"

A soft slurring echo separated itself from the whipping sound of ice pellets smashing against the rocks. Instinctively they gazed up at Needlepoint House, which looked forlorn and incredibly ancient stuck to the side of the cliff like the mud nest of a bird. The whispery sounds, they realized, were roof shingles being lifted upward, dozen upon dozen. They were tossed in the air like sets of playing cards. Turning into little gliders, they rose on the frigid currents.

Fighting for breath, the trio zigzagged up the path against the wind and finally reached the house. They leaned, panting, against the massive doors. Burke clanged the salt-pitted brass bell again and again. Then finally, after what seemed like hours, the door swung open and a huge gust of wind mixed with hail propelled them forward into the middle of a Spanish-tiled entrance. Burke closed the door against the elements.

In serene contrast to the chaos outside, the house was strangely quiet. Except for an occasional banging shutter an occupant might not know that a storm raged outside. Edna Lowery, the rotund little house-keeper, her back as stoutly erect in her black bombazine as her boned corset would permit, helped them off with their rain gear, clucking like a disturbed hen.

"Edna," Johanna bit out furiously, "will you please take down that damned blue flag?"

"Oh, we forgot!" Edna wailed, her face scarlet. "I'll need some assistance."

"I'll do it," Burke volunteered.

Her composure regained, Johanna introduced Burke to Edna, who appraised him with a quick backward glance, then led him up the stairs to the mezzanine. She guided him to the window ledge that held the steel pole, opening the window so that he could disengage the flag from its moorings.

"You needn't have come," a musical voice reverberated from the beamed ceiling in the living room to the tiled floor in the foyer. Lucia Concannon, dressed in a formfitting lace peignoir, swept into the room. Burke, flag in hand, stood on the landing looking below. She was as perfectly made up and groomed as if she had stepped out of an elegant 1940s magazine illustration. Her platinum white hair was swept up off her temples and parted in the middle of the crown—a popular style, circa World War II. Bright vermilion lipstick made a bold slash in her marvelously sculptured face. She looked as if she had been frozen in time somewhere between 1941 and 1945.

Sarah glared at the trim figure. "We almost killed ourselves getting up here," she cried, "expecting both you and Magnifique to be crushed on the rocks."

Lucia Concannon laughed merrily. "Sorry not to accommodate you!" Her frosty blue eyes rested on Burke, who was folding the flag with Edna's help. Her gaze lingered on his broad shoulders. "Well, aren't you going to introduce us?"

Disconcerted, Sarah looked up at Steve. "Steven Burke," she said formally, feeling like a little girl again, "this is my grandmother, Lucia Concannon."

He descended the stairs, and coming quickly forward kissed her cheek. She drew back and surveyed him with amusement. "I'm told that you're in talking pictures, and that you want to make use of our island in one. Is that true?"

He grinned at her. "First I have to have your permission." He paused. "It's a spy movie."

"I love intrigue. I think the last talking picture I saw was called *A Yank in the R.A.F.*, with that good-looking Tyrone Power. Do you know him?"

Steve looked at the old lady kindly. "I always liked his work, but he's been gone now for some time."

"Pity," she sighed gently. "He was so *beautiful!*" She turned to the living room. "I like beautiful men." She glanced back at him, surveying his face coquettishly. "Samsqua was barricaded during the war, you know. All the beaches were covered with rolls of barbed wire, and there were patrols of marines and Seabees. The villagers used to laugh because we had hives of real bees on the island in those days, and Samsqua's sea-bee honey was highly prized. We lost all of them—the real bees, I mean—during one of those terrible winters...." She laughed without humor, a dry chuckle.

She turned and appraised Burke again. "Well, as long as we're all here let's have some tea." She raised her voice to say, "Edna, put on the kettle."

Sarah exchanged looks with Johanna, and they clasped hands and went into the living room. Lucia Concannon sighed. "There they are," she said. "Miss Sarah and Miss Jo, all grown-up and still behaving as if they were eight years old." A smile hovered over her vivid red mouth. "I think we should put some of my husband's rum in the tea. You all look chilled to the bone." She went to the window. The sky was still filled with flying shingles. "I needed a new roof anyway, and this storm will provide a perfect excuse for the insurance company." She whirled around. "Well, do sit down, even if you're all damp."

Sarah scrutinized the room. Nothing had been changed; the same antiques were arranged meticulously, and the windows were still covered by the raw-silk draperies brought from Paris in 1935. Several Chinese chests were arranged around a Louis Quatorze settee, and on the opposite wall a large seventeenth-century brass sword kept company with a series of small gilded chairs that might have come from the Waldorf-Astoria ballroom. A collection of threadbare tapestries hung on the east wall, and the Empire sofa upon which grandlady had seated herself had been upholstered in a garish hibiscus- patterned brocade that reminded her of the wallpaper in Johanna's living room.

Lucia Concannon lighted a long black cigarette with a kitchen match, inhaled deeply, then blew the smoke out straight and smooth. She opened her blue eyes as wide as possible. "Do you have a lot of money, Mr. Burke?"

"Oh, for heaven's sake, grandlady," Sarah said quickly. "What a question!"

"I have enough, Mrs. Concannon," Burke drawled.

"Good!" The old lady looked peevishly at Sarah. "It's about time that we added a new fortune to the family's holdings! I like Johanna's Luis Farraday. He's a talented architect, but he'll never earn worthy commissions if he undertakes such jobs as restoring the Running Mallow! There's no real money there. He should be in New York designing skyscrapers."

Johanna glanced at Sarah quickly, then turned to her grandmother. "You keep referring to Luis as 'mine'...."

"What's wrong with that? He *is* your man, isn't he?"

"Not in the sense that you mean. I don't own him."

Lucia Concannon looked exasperated. "Well are you or are you not having a romance?"

Johanna flushed and looked helplessly from Sarah to Burke.

"After all, Johanna, you're almost thirty years old and still unmarried."

"I'll help Edna with the tea," Johanna said stiffly, and left the room.

"What's wrong with her?" Lucia Concannon asked suddenly. "Luis obviously adores her, and she seems devoted to him...."

"Grandlady," Sarah said, hoping to distract her, "do you know what day this is?"

"Of course," she snapped. "It's my birthday! Seventy-five years ago today I came into the world in this very house. It was storming—like today—and mama was up there at the window in the master suite watching papa and the midwife fight their way up the path." She laughed tonelessly. "They almost didn't get here in time. The midwife helped deliver me, still dressed in her raincoat and galoshes." She sighed gently, then turned back to Sarah.

"As we were saying, Miss Jo should catch Luis as catch can. And you, Mr. Actor Man, do you have designs on our Miss Sarah?"

"Well, actually...."

"You can call me grandlady, if you like. Everyone else does, but I'm not really grand—or even a lady for that matter. Now, go on, explain your position!"

"It's true that I have designs on Sarah, grandlady," he said meaningly, assuming the pose of a Spanish grandee, twirling an imaginary mustache in exaggerated fashion. "But I don't think she has designs on me!"

The old woman laughed appreciatively. "And you, Miss Sarah?"

Sarah was saved from answering by the clanging of the door knocker. "Now who can that be?" Lucia Concannon cried, calling for Edna to put on more water. She shook her head as she turned to say to Burke, "Apparently we have other guests. I wouldn't be surprised if we were entertaining the whole village by nightfall!"

Burke opened the door to Luis Farraday, who stood panting on the threshold, his raincoat dripping water over the tiled floor. "The staircase windows at the Running Mallow were just blown in," he fumed. "All of Tiffany's beautiful stained glass has been broken to bits. There's nothing left except a gigantic hole in the wall!"

LATER, after the hot-rum tea had been served and the hail had vanished with the wind, a coldness crept into the living room of Needlepoint House. Burke, assisted by Luis, lighted a fire in the giant brass-faced fireplace.

Luis turned to Johanna. "Before I came up here I asked Mr. Drury about replacing the stained glass. He wants you to execute a new design, Johanna."

She looked at him incredulously. "But I've never

been involved in anything so major! I wouldn't know where to start!" She shook her head. "I'll have to refuse, of course. That's a job for a professional."

"Nonsense," Lucia Concannon interjected. "You're not an amateur. You've been working in glass since you were eighteen! The windows at Glass Cottage were beautifully done."

"My windows are small potatoes compared to the Mallow's. I don't have enough room to work in my basement and no real equipment, and I don't think I'm strong enough to...."

"Balderdash!" her grandmother retorted, lighting another cigarette. "*You're* always going on about women's rights, Sarah. Tell her! She won't accept a commission because she feels physically incapable. That's ridiculous! And heavens, Jo, if old Drury is willing to employ you you can hire all kinds of help. The man's not a fool!"

Johanna held up her hands. "We can discuss this later." Obviously angry, she went to the window and looked out at the fast-darkening landscape. "The wind has died down," she said quietly, "but a heavy mist is rolling in." She turned back to the group. "If you'll all chat over another cup of tea, Luis and I will go back to Glass Cottage and fetch the goodies, grandlady."

The old woman chuckled deep in her throat. "I assume," she said with a gleam in her eyes, "that by goodies you're referring to my birthday cake and presents? With what we've already been through today I think that would be anticlimactic." She looked from one face to another. "Let's call off this so-called celebration until tomorrow. All of you come up at noontime, and we'll eat ourselves sick and I'll open my gifts."

"But grandlady," Johanna objected, "your birthday is today."

"So what?" the old lady said, mashing her cigarette into a hollowed-out lion's-tooth ashtray. "I think the older one becomes, the less should be made of it." Just then the door knocker clanged again. "Are we to have no peace?" she exclaimed. "Who can it be this time?"

"I'm beginning to feel like a majordomo," Burke said with a laugh, and opened the door. Else Sanchez, closely resembling a damp and bedraggled cat, stood on the threshold. Her seaman's cap had slipped halfway down over her eyes.

Sarah stared at the stocky figure. It was the first time she could recall that the little captain had ever made the journey up the hill to Needlepoint House.

Lucia Concannon rose stiffly, then came forward. "Do come in, Else," she said warmly. "Come in and have some rum tea with us."

Else shook her head and pulled the bill of her cap. "No thanks, Mrs. Concannon. I must get back to the *Griffin*." She shifted her weight from one foot to the other. "I was just listenin' to the small-craft warnings on the radio, and while I was shiftin' dials, tryin' to get Portland, I came across a commercial station and the news...."

"Surely a big blow isn't coming in? Hurricane weather is over," the old lady said nervously.

"Oh, no, the worst of the storm is over. According to the coast guard the satellite pictures show the weather front has already moved out to sea. There'll be sunshine tomorrow for sure." She paused uncomfortably and looked at Sarah. "There was so much interference that I couldn't get all the details, but just before the set conked out altogether I got the information that Madame Celina died of a heart attack about four this morning."

CHAPTER SEVEN

On THE WAY BACK to Glass Cottage, Burke hugged Sarah comfortingly. The silence between them grew as they made their way slowly down Hannah Path. But there was no need for words, for the silence was filled with understanding. For once his presence wasn't disturbing to her. More so now than ever before, she wanted him by her side. His sympathy for her enveloped her, emanating from his body like a smoldering torch.

"Do you want to talk about it?" he asked quietly. "About Madame Celina?"

She shook her head. "Not necessarily. At least, not very much. I don't want to grieve for her, because she wouldn't have wanted to go on much longer even if she had a choice." She turned to him. "She had palsy, and although she was under medication she was afraid that she would start to shake uncontrollably. You see, she was a very vain woman. The past few years she lived for her seminars, little gatherings where she gave her own views on beauty. Those were her times to shine, to be the expert everyone believed her to be...."

Sarah smiled. "She would have made a marvelous actress. Her timing was superb. You should have seen her give an interview!" She paused then as they walked on. "Oh, no!" she cried suddenly. "I forgot about the campaign! All of it will have to be scrapped, I guess. I do have an alternative plan—not nearly as good—that we'll have to use. Time is of the essence, but I can't get back to New York before tomorrow. This is one time I wish that we had good transportation to Boothbay. But the *Griffin* is our only boat."

Her worries followed her back to the cottage.

The smell of frying ham wafted out the back door of Glass Cottage as Sarah and Burke came up the walk. Johanna was at the stove and Luis was setting the table. "This is certainly a domestic scene," Sarah said lightly as they came into the kitchen.

Luis looked up and grinned, his face turning so pink that for a moment his freckles disappeared. "I work like a dog all day, and when I come here for dinner in the evening—" he winked and jerked his thumb over his shoulder toward Johanna "—I become a galley slave."

"Poor man!" Johanna said sweetly. "To hear him tell it you'd swear I put him in chains every night and stretch him out on a rack every weekend." She grinned and turned over the slices of ham. "I keep telling him he has to earn his keep!"

Sarah watched Luis and Johanna together, and again she felt slightly jealous. No, Luis certainly wasn't a chauvinist, she thought. They shared a fantastic rapport, and something else besides...a kind of companionship that went beyond a distinction between typically male and female roles.

She glanced sideways at Burke. He would never be amenable to domestic chores and probably wouldn't even want his wife to do them. There were people for hire for that sort of thing. That would be his attitude. His wife would no doubt be a mere showpiece—perhaps a model or an actress. Sarah sighed and turned away.

AFTER THEY HAD EATEN the four of them lolled around the living room, sipping cups of steaming coffee while Burke spoke about *Devil's Dare*. Johanna was obviously excited about the filmmaking process and secretly Sarah was fascinated herself. Something perverse in her didn't want Burke to know that.

"Well, for being stuck out here in the middle of nowhere," Johanna said proudly, "we once had a lot of spy stuff going on ourselves. It was a long time ago, during the war. Grandmother was in her glory."

"Oh," Sarah cried involuntarily, remembering grandlady's stories, "now I know what you're talking about." She turned to Burke. "It wasn't all that much, I'm certain. Grandlady was probably exaggerating."

"Well, President Roosevelt was here! I call that quite a lot!"

"That's just grandlady's story."

Luis leaned forward. "This sounds fascinating. You mean grandlady was a secret agent?"

Johanna laughed. "Oh, I wouldn't go so far as to say that. But apparently she knew a lot."

Burke leaned back in the wing chair and crossed his long legs. "I do know that a lot of sites were utilized on the West Coast. Miles and miles of beach were off limits throughout the entire war. Whole battalions of men received their training there for overseas landings. So I'm sure quite a few sites on the Eastern seaboard were used, as well."

Johanna took a sip of coffee. "Grandlady got rather tipsy one night a couple of years ago and got to reminiscing about old times. She told several stories that were quite hair-raising."

"I think she was leading you on. It sounds like one of her fantasies," Sarah said.

"No, she went into considerable detail. The navy used the windward side of the island to train for a big maneuver in Italy. Apparently the site—the cliffs, the terrain and the ocean below—exactly matched the site of the attack. Grandmother was on Uncle Sam's payroll as a kind of...."

"Den mother to a lot of Seabees and marines?" Burke grimaced and shook his head. "It was, no doubt, the best-kept secret of the war! That would make a marvelous movie, you know...." And Sarah could just see his mind plotting scenario and action for another film.

"It was serious business," Johanna replied, "so don't make light of it. They had chief-of-staff meetings in the ballroom upstairs at Needlepoint House. You see, Burke, Samsqua was almost deserted then. All the men were away at war, and some of the women worked in war plants in New Jersey. There were only about a dozen people left. After all, the island's very isolated. The boats with the generals came over from Portland. Grandlady has some snapshots buried somewhere in one of the trunks in the attic."

Burke leaned forward. "I wasn't kidding about the picture. The plot's all here." He paused. "Do you suppose that's why she dresses and looks the way she does?"

"You mean," Sarah interjected, "that the war was the best time of her life?"

"Could be," Burke replied. "She doesn't want to let go of the past."

Johanna agreed. "We're so used to her that we don't see the signs. Do you really think it would make a movie?"

"No!" Sarah cried vehemently, and was embarrassed at the startled looks she received from Luis and Johanna. But she held her ground and stared defiantly into Burke's eyes. "Grandlady would never approve of it. Her memories are sacred things. They mean a lot to her. She'll never let them—and Samsqua—be exploited in a *movie*." She spoke the last word as though it were obscene, and glared at him.

Burke turned to look at Johanna. "It's certainly a possibility," he answered her, as though Sarah hadn't even spoken. The subject was dropped, though Sarah brooded about it.

Watching him as he lighted a cigarette in his careful studied way, she tried to separate his public image from his private self. Most of the time she was able to forget that he was a celebrity, but at odd moments all she saw was his screen personality. He seemed like a complete stranger. As he puffed on the shaft, snapped his lighter shut and looked up, with the cigarette dangling from his lips, he might have been doing a scene for a picture. Her spine tingled anew, and she wanted to touch him. Then the scene changed before her eyes, because as he got up from his chair and searched for an ashtray he became an ordinary man again. It was an extraordinary shift in persona, and Sarah realized then that she had imagined it.

"What I can't get used to here on Samsqua," Burke remarked casually, "is the silence. It's so quiet that there's almost a ringing in the air."

Luis nodded. "I know, Burke. When I first came here from New York City, for instance, I had a great problem getting to sleep at night. I was used to foot and traffic sounds, and the wail of sirens and honking cars...." He nodded to Johanna. "After I unwound, though, a peaceful feeling came over me, and I began to relax." He hunched his shoulders and went on with new conviction. "I think I could live here year-round—just go into the city on business occasionally and be as happy as the proverbial clam.''

"I see what you mean, in a way," Burke replied with a sigh. "But there's something about city life that's stimulating, too—in quite another way, of course."

"Where do you live?" Johanna asked. She had taken up a piece of fancywork, and in the light of the kerosene lamp her fingers seemed almost automated as her hand flew back and forth with her embroidery needle.

"I live in Malibu, high up on a cliff overlooking the Pacific."

"Do a lot of movie people live near you?" Johanna snipped a thread with a little pair of scissors, then looked up expectantly.

"They used to—some of the stars from the thirties and forties. But now film people tend to live in varied locales. The jet age has brought that about. My nearest neighbor is a banker, and we have some very old, rich *Blue Book* families down the road. Some of my movie friends live in Europe to escape taxes—which is all right, but I believe that if you're part of an American industry that pays you in U.S. dollars, then part of that money should logically go to Uncle Sam." He snuffed out his cigarette in the tiny Spode tray. "And I don't think I'm particularly patriotic."

It was quite an extraordinary experience, Sarah reflected, to see Burke reveal himself, and her respect for him grew. She became aware, once again, of Burke the man, of his sexuality. He was different from any man she had ever met, but somehow she had the feeling that if they were ever to enjoy a more intimate relationship it would have to be strictly on his terms. And as much as she was attracted to him, she was not certain that she could subordinate her own personality to his. . . .

The grandfather clock in the corner chimed eight, and Johanna rose to put her fancywork in her sewing kit. "If you'll all excuse me, it's my bedtime. Four o'clock in the morning comes awfully soon!"

"I've got to get back to the Running Mallow, too," Luis Farraday put in. "I've got some specs to go over." He laughed. "Johanna and I are complete opposites. I'm more creative in the evening, and she can only work early in the morning."

When they were alone the silence grew heavy, laden with unspoken thoughts. Sarah looked at Burke and asked, nervously but politely, "Would you like some rum? I think that's all Miss Jo has in her cupboard."

He shook his head. "No. I've got to the point where I don't drink much anymore. When I was younger a drink after dinner was relaxing, but now it gets my mind working and I can't go to sleep. But you have one if you like."

She grimaced. "Rum is not my thing, and grandfather's rum is potent stuff. After all these years it's practically syrup.''

"Sarah," Burke said, studying her face, "did grandlady raise you girls?''

"Not really. My parents were drowned in a boat accident in the Caribbean about fourteen years ago. Dad ran a fishing boat out of Boothbay, and he'd hurt his leg bringing up some lobster pots shortly before that. So he took a month off to recuperate. They were cruising in hurricane waters.'' She sighed as the memories crowded in on her, and she was silent for some time. "It was a difficult time for Johanna and me. Dad, we discovered, was too kindhearted to be a very good businessman, and he'd left thousands of dollars in debts. He hadn't made a will, so the settling of the estate was further complicated. Grandlady ended up paying all the creditors.'' She looked up. "You would have liked my father. He was rather like some of the characters you've played—or perhaps I mean he was like you yourself.''

"Please don't confuse us. I am not a Method actor. The kinds of roles I've played have not led me to identify with my characters—at least, not usually. That guy on the screen is a phony, a fabrication of some writer's imagination. His feelings are in the script; his reactions are often directed and controlled. And Sarah, my lovely, I am definitely *not* in control when I'm around you.''

His words were light, but she sensed a seriousness behind them that unnerved her. "Really though,

Steve, we don't know each other very well, but at least I know more about you than you do about me. I know how you act anyway, right?" She paused, then plunged in. "There are many sides to me, Steve; I've built up certain walls around me. I've had to, to get where I am. Sometimes I wonder where that is—" she laughed but it was a hollow sound "—and which Sarah Mackenzie I really am." Sarah stopped speaking and looked at him to see if he was laughing—or worse still—bored. "I'm sorry. I got kind of 'heavy' there, didn't I? This is one reason I had serious doubts about bringing you to the island. I didn't want to get this...personal."

He looked at her in wonderment, his eyes almost black in the dim light. "I thought a moment ago that I understood you. Now I'm not quite so sure."

"Well, you see, Steve, I'm used to Samsqua. It has different associations for me than, I'm sure, it does for you." She paused and took a deep breath. "It's the same thing as taking a long sea voyage for some people. I don't think the sea is romantic at all because I've lived with it all around me most of my life." She paused. "But I was afraid that you would think I was setting you up for an affair."

She turned away from him, and going to the front window pulled the cretonne curtains closed.

He came up behind her and held her shoulders. "I'm not some prehistoric type who's going to attack you," he growled into her neck.

She drew away from him. "Don't make fun of me."

"I'm not making fun of you! But you're analyzing us as if we were products that you have to write copy about!"

"That's not true!"

"It *is* true." He paused. "I don't know why you can't just relax and try to not read deep meanings into the simplest of actions. We are having a weekend vacation together, that's all."

"Is that all this is to you?" she asked, the hurt evident in her eyes.

Steve just shook his head in confusion and turned away. She couldn't bear his indifference and hated herself for the tears that stung her eyes. Grasping on to what little control she could muster, Sarah admitted to herself, *he's right, of course. One minute I want to keep him at a distance; the next I want a relationship. But how can I tell him it's impossible for me to be casual when he's around?*

"You're acting strangely here on the island, Sarah. You react differently to me."

Which is exactly why I shouldn't have brought you here, she thought, but only nodded. "I know. I've been 'on the outside' for a long time. Grandlady says that she can't go off the island anymore, because when she comes back she begins to doubt everything that happened to her while she was away. I don't know about that. She's probably dramatizing, which she often does."

Burke laughed dryly. "Do you suppose it runs in the family?"

"Oh, I don't know, now. Johanna—" Sarah stopped short. "But I suppose you meant that for me." The feeling that flowed between Burke and her had altered again; now there was no animosity. "You may be right. Ethan, my boss, is always accusing me of carrying on, and I suppose I do to some extent. Don't you?"

He ran his hands lightly through his sun-bleached hair. "Oh, now and then. But you must admit that I chose the right profession for it!"

She placed her hand on his arm. "Thank you for coming to Samsqua, Burke. You're the first person that I've shared it with, and that's why, I guess, I had doubts. I'm defensive about the island for some reason.... Well, enough. It's coolish in here, don't you think?" she asked, as if making an obscure remark like that would draw the conversation to a close. She didn't want to break the mood by confronting him again about his intentions to exploit the island.

"I'll build up the fire," he said.

"Only if you want to stay up alone and enjoy it. I'm going to bed. It's been an exhausting day—all this exercise and fresh air, looking for grandlady, news of Madame Celina...." She trailed off and chided herself for her excuses. She was going to bed because she couldn't sit here in this wonderfully cozy room with a fire going, and with Burke....

"Well, come and kiss me good-night then," he said, his voice assuming a pleading tone. "I can't sleep without it." He grinned so appealingly she knew she wouldn't refuse.

I'm quite certain you don't very often sleep without it, she thought, but quickly bit her lip to hold back the words. Why did she torment herself with such thoughts? Obediently she went over to his chair and bent to place a swift kiss on his cheek, but he caught her wrist and pulled her down onto his lap.

"Let me up," she said crossly. "You've no right—"

"And you, love, have no right to be so beautiful and sweet. Why aren't you always like this?" His voice was like honey, and he raised her palm to his sensuous lips, sending a kind of shock wave throughout her body. How could a hand be so sensitive, she thought wildly.

He was taking her hand and putting it behind his neck, so that she was forced to lean against him for support. He cradled her, murmuring soothing words which, coupled with her fatigue and troubled mind, sent her into a dreamy state that cushioned any fears. He was raining kisses down her throat as his other hand caressed her now pliant body, following the curves and swells of her slender woman's shape. His touch set her on fire, and she longed to cry out with the ecstasy of being so close to the man she loved....

Somewhere in her subconscious it occurred to her that yes, she loved him. Of course she loved him. Who wouldn't? He was everything, every man—yet he was unique. He had powers no man should have. His kisses were intoxicating, his hands were his weapons. He was conquering her, and she reveled in her submission.

Her checkered cotton blouse had come apart, and she shivered as her breasts were exposed to the chill air, then suddenly covered with a warm palm. "Sarah, darling," he whispered, "you're so lovely.... Do you want me to go on touching you? Here?" as his thumb traced a circle around her hard nipple. "And here?" His hand curved around her hip. "And here?" as his fingers rested on the waistband of her jeans.

No, her mind screamed, but it was as if her body and mind had momentarily separated. Her hands grasped his head as she kissed him, every nerve ending alive, and desire flooded her being. "Oh, Steve," she managed to say, her voice sounding pleading and far-off to her own ears, "please don't do this.... I can't do this. We—we don't love each other."

There was a terrible silence, and his voice was laden with emotion as he said, "Love is a funny word, Sarah. We want each other. Sometimes you have to settle for that."

She brought her hands around to his chest and sat up, drawing her blouse closed. Something in his voice—was it disillusionment—brought her back to reality, and with a supreme effort she cleared her head.

"Well, I don't have to settle for anything!" she declared haughtily, to cover her confusion and shame over what had just happened between them.

She stood up and faced him squarely, clutching her blouse closed. "You may as well know now, Steve, that I don't trust you—not one bit. I realize you probably have several glamour girls at your beck and call—so why don't you take your frustrations out on them?" She almost backed away at the anger in his face as he, too, stood up. But she plunged right in with more destructive words. "I also realize the only reason you came to Samsqua with me was to check it out as a location for *Devil's Dare*. I may have been naive to go along with you on that, and on *that*—" she looked disgustedly at the chair where they had kissed and caressed "—but I'm not stupid. I know you don't give a damn about me!" And she turned away from him to stare at the fireplace until she heard him leave the room. An ominous quiet settled around her, as ominous as Steve's silence had been. He hadn't even bothered to deny her accusations....

Sarah sank down onto the sofa, the tears helping to relieve the pressure behind her eyes and the ache at her temples. She supposed she was crying for a lot of different things, none of which made any sense at all. None of which were attainable.

Finally, she wiped the last of the tears from her reddened eyes and went to the side windows to stare unseeingly out into the night. After a few moments she was able to make her mind a blank. Then she blew out the kerosene lamp and made her way to the room she shared with Johanna.

CHAPTER EIGHT

SARAH WAS CAUGHT in the five o'clock "shop girls'" rain as she inched her way over the crowded Williamsburg Bridge to Manhattan after dropping Burke off at Kennedy International. The drive had been grueling and the tension between them almost palpable in her stuffy damp Rabbit. What a weekend it had been. She badly needed a vacation away from everything familiar, she realized. But she couldn't dream of leaving the city for a long time yet. There was Madame Celina's account still to be worked out with Harrison Perlmutter.

Leaving Johanna and grandlady had been more traumatic than usual. They'd all had a brief birthday party for Lucia on Sunday, and she loved the turquoise earrings Sarah had finally decided on. Johanna had given her an exquisite necklace of fashioned stained glass and copper, and grandlady had even shed a tear when Sarah and Burke had prepared to leave. "Take care of your young man, dear. He's one to hang on to," she'd whispered as they left to catch the *Griffin*. The day had been brilliantly sunny and unseasonably warm, but it did nothing to lift Sarah's sagging spirits.

Burke had extracted what was more or less a promise from grandlady to permit use of the island for certain scenes in *Devil's Dare*, much to Sarah's chagrin. She supposed the old dear was overwhelmed by Steve's charm. Damn. Wasn't anyone immune to him?

Which led her to think again of Burke's flying off to California again, where any number of females were no doubt waiting for him.

She parked the car in the garage, went upstairs to her apartment and immediately poured herself a glass of sherry to sip out on the terrace. The rain had stopped and heat wafted up from the park below. It was that special time between light and darkness that she loved, but tonight the twilight depressed her. She fancied she could hear music from the arena at Sky Rink—a Strauss waltz that brought back painful memories of her and Burke dancing on the ice. She shook the image off. She had an ordeal to face; the next few days would not be easy. Oh, how she missed Burke! After spending the weekend at Samsqua with him constantly at her side, she needed his strength now, in spite of their arguments. "Motivate yourself," she said aloud. "He's in Los Angeles and you, my girl, are here. Face the music."

She slowly finished the sherry, and feeling rather light-headed telephoned Ethan Fairchild at home. Only his recorder answered. She hung up and called

Madame Celina's number, but there was only the buzz-buzz of a busy signal. After five more times it was obvious the phone was off the hook. Then she dialed Harrison Perlmutter's number in South Hampton—but again, there was no answer. She spent a restless night, tossing and turning, her mind racing.

The next morning she was up as usual at seven-thirty, and at eight o'clock the telephone rang. It was Harrison. "I'm so glad you called," she said with relief. "I tried to get you last evening. I spent the weekend on the island, and when I got word about what happened, the ship-to-shore radio had gone on the blink." Her voice broke. "I'm so sorry, Harrison. Your aunt was a marvelous lady, and I loved her very much."

Harrison Perlmutter's voice was pure steel. "I don't wonder at your grief, Sarah. How much of it is for her and how much of it is for your own hide?" He paused to allow the import of his words to sink in, then went on smoothly, "You couldn't get me last night because I was down at the plant, scrapping your publicity and advertising campaign. I've waited a long time to say this. You're fired!"

"What?"

"I said you're *fired*." He hung up, leaving her dazed and trembling. How could he do that was her first thought. She'd worked on the Celina campaign for two years; no one knew the product as well as she did, and her work on it had, after all, won her the

Advertising People award. Harrison was being stupid, but what did it matter? The result was the same. She had been fired from an account, had lost it for Duncan-Fairchild. She felt secure in her job, but the repercussions of losing an account like Celina's didn't bear thinking about. She realized she could find another client to fill that gap without too much trouble, but still, this was a blow to her professional ego.

The thought of calling Burke entered her mind, but she chased it away. She couldn't be forever running to him with her problems. She straightened her spine and gathered courage to face the day. Her world, it seemed, was slowly falling apart.

SARAH, dressed in a classically cut suit of deep rose, arrived at the office at five minutes to nine, and the usually cheerful Gail, her brow furrowed, was taking a note over the telephone. She placed her hand over the mouthpiece and looked up. "Mr. Fairchild wants to see you," she said quickly, and then continued to take down the message.

Without removing her jacket Sarah went down the private hall and knocked twice on the door marked President. She took a deep, deep breath.

"Come," Ethan's voice boomed out from behind the square of mahogany.

"Good morning, chief," Sarah said quietly. "It's really a blue Monday, isn't it?"

With dismay, she saw from his kindly expression

that he was going to play the grandfather. This morning, of all mornings, she could not bear the sympathetic approach.

"How was the island?" he asked conversationally.

"Cold and damp." She paused, then glanced up. "I heard about Madame Celina via ship to shore." She looked away. "It was a personal loss. Lord knows she was a difficult old lady, but she was a genuine person. She *cared*. The quality that I admired about her, I think, was her great strength. To have withstood the pressures all those years. . . ."

"Have you talked to Harrison?" he asked gently.

She nodded. "He phoned me at home this morning." She paused, and tears stung her eyes, so that she had to turn away. "I've been fired off the account."

"I know." Ethan Fairchild's voice was devoid of emotion. "He called me not five minutes after Jelda died. He was absolutely beside himself with glee, and I was appalled. He took great pains to tell me exactly what we could do with the account. I played it very cool and explained that no one is responsible for an act of God, and while it was a pity that Madame Celina's television commercials would have to be dumped, we could go ahead with the alternate campaign." Ethan Fairchild picked up a pencil and began doodling on a yellow pad. "He replied that he'd scratch the whole business and get a fresh approach from another agency." He stopped doodling and looked up. "This morning I heard he'd chosen Dolin-Parks!"

Sarah looked at him incredulously. "But they're a bunch of old-timers. They haven't thought of anything new in years. Harrison is out of his mind!"

"That's not the worst part, Sarah," Ethan Fairchild replied softly. "Harrison was so impressed with that Firefly spark plug award, he's given the account to Peter Schaeffer!"

Sarah laughed, an almost hysterical laugh, but she could not stop. Suddenly all the events of the past eight weeks seemed funny, absurd. Gradually the tension lessened as she gained control of herself again. She went to the window and looked down on the Madison Avenue morning traffic. Most of those people down there would know by noon that she had lost a multimillion-dollar account. But no one would know the inside story. To some it would appear that her incompetence had finally caught up with her, but to others that award on her mantel would seem like the straw that broke the camel's back, bringing nothing but bad luck. . . .

"Snap out of it, Sarah!" Ethan Fairchild said gruffly. "You've been in the business long enough to know that you've got to roll with the punches. No one here at the agency is holding you personally responsible."

Now she was close to tears. "It's just that the whole business is so ironic." Sarah faced him. "Have funeral arrangements been made?"

Ethan Fairchild nodded. "Harrison is taking her back to Milan."

"Milan?"

"Yes, apparently that's what she wanted. I suppose he'll fly over long enough to be photographed at the grave site. You can be sure he'll do everything he can to take advantage of the publicity. Then he'll come back and start the new campaign." He shuffled some papers on his desk. "He told me this morning to have all our invoices in by Wednesday. Therefore, you're excused from the usual Monday morning conference. You'll have to work with accounting to get all the figures together." He paused. "Sarah?"

"Yes, chief?"

"As you know, I've been up to my eyebrows in new projects while you've been busy with Madame Celina. You can take over the William Electronics account."

"*What?*" It was one of their biggest accounts!

"It needs a new shot in the arm—your special touch." He paused and concentrated on his doodling again, not looking up. "That Firefly spark plug ad was quite brilliant. I was most impressed."

She turned away. A hot red flame shot up from her neck until her cheeks were blazing. How could he know...?

"You are, after all, my prize protégée," he answered her thoughts. "Don't you think, by this time, I know your work when I see it?"

THURSDAY NIGHT Sarah curled up on the sofa after dinner and went over the William Electronics portfolio. She was thoroughly sick of reading specifications. Looking at the photographs of the minicomputer that she was supposed to write sparkling copy about, she closed her eyes tightly. Obviously Ethan Fairchild had thought he was doing her a favor by giving her their biggest industrial account, but all she could think about was the wizened woman in those commercials that no one would ever see. Sarah's grief was real, because she had truly cared about Jelda Celina. Yet she found her sadness could find no release in tears.

Damn that minicomputer! There were no ideas floating out in space, and her mind just wouldn't come up with something. The Firefly slogan had come quickly because she was talking off the top of her head. She was having fun, and she conceded that her enthusiasm had been partly motivated by a desire to show Peter Schaeffer how smart she was. That part of it was difficult to admit, but as she looked back, she realized it was perfectly true. Even then, at the height of her infatuation, she had known that he was an inferior ad man. She had wanted to show him up, but she supposed it had also been an act of self-defense against a man her subconscious recognized as essentially weak.

She poured herself another cup of coffee and lit a cigarette. The tobacco tasted raw and bitter on her tongue, and she stubbed out the end of the cigarette thoughtfully, glancing at her watch. It was nine o'clock, which would be six o'clock California time. She made a quick decision; she had to hear his voice.

She took a card out of her purse and dialed the number she had hastily scribbled on the back.

A bored female voice answered, repeating the number she had called, and Sarah gave her name. At that moment Burke's familiar voice came on the line. "I'll take this call," he told the answering service. "Sarah? It's wonderful to hear your voice." He sounded as close as if he were in her living room. "I'm so pleased that you called." He paused for her response, but silence greeted him. He asked, "Are you still there?"

"Yes," she said. "I'm still here." For a moment she had been shy. It was difficult for her to believe, in that split second, that she was calling Steve Burke and that he was answering her back in such an intimate way. Then her self-consciousness vanished. "Oh, Steve, I just feel awful. I've been fired!"

"Good. You're not a career woman now, so you can be my full-time mistress. Hop on the red-eye flight in the morning, and I'll meet you at the L.A. airport."

This was too much. How could he *joke* about it?

"Go to hell! I'm sorry I bothered you!" Sarah slammed the phone down, shaking.

A few seconds later it rang, and after another second's hesitation she lifted the receiver again.

"Oh, babe, I'm sorry. I was trying to cheer you up."

Why had she bothered phoning in the first place? If that was his idea of "cheering her up," she'd rather be alone.

"Now tell me," his deep voice said seriously, "what happened?"

She had to admit she wanted to talk.

"I'm still with the agency," she replied evenly. "But I got fired off the Celina account."

"From what you've told me about Harrison Perlmutter, I think this is the best thing that ever happened to you." Burke's voice was strong and confident, and Sarah held on to every word. "You could never get along with that man. It's best you're out of it."

"I suppose you're right, although it really hurts because I spent so much time on the account. If Madame Celina were still alive—"

"But she's not," Burke put in quickly, "so accept it." He paused. "Ask Fairchild for a vacation. Come on out here and I'll take you to Brussels with me. We start the picture next week."

"I've just been assigned to a new account—a minicomputer thing. What I know about electronics I could put on my baby finger."

"Then tell him to hell with it!" Burke expostulated. "You don't need Ethan Fairchild!"

"Oh, Burke, but I do! I've always risen to challenges," she defended her position, "and maybe it's time I met a few. The Madame Celina account was as smooth as silk. I'd become complacent."

"My advice is to tell the agency to shove it, and come with me on location."

"Burke, I can't. I really can't."

"Well, Lord knows when I'll be able to see you

again. The shooting schedule is eighteen weeks, with
the last week on Samsqua if we shoot the chase
there.''

"Then it will be—" she calculated quickly "—Feb-
ruary before I see you!" she replied weakly.

"Afraid so. I won't be getting any time off. I'm in
almost every scene." He paused, and when he spoke
again his voice was cynical. "Look, if you're so unhappy why don't you call Basil Northcombe? Remember he wanted you to work on a campaign?"

"Mr. Burke," the studied female voice broke in on
the line, "I'm sorry to interrupt, but I have a call
from Paris, France...."

"Take the call, Burke. We can talk later," Sarah
urged.

"Damn." And he hung up.

At four-thirty in the morning Sarah awakened and
could not get back to sleep, so she got up and made
coffee. She was having a second cup when a little cur-
tain in the back of her mind parted. She reached for a
pencil and scribbled on the telephone pad: "While
You're Sound Asleep at Night, the William Mini 508
Is Working Overtime for You...." She hurriedly
drew a man's head on a pillow, then sketched into his
hairline a rough area where the photograph of the
piece of equipment could be brushed in by the art
department. She smiled. The ad would be purely
visual. Nowhere would the word "computer" itself
be mentioned. Yes.... It was good; it was coming....

ETHAN FAIRCHILD looked over the minicomputer layouts and beamed in his grandfatherly way. "We've got full approval to go ahead," he said softly. "Now we can have a big luncheon with the William Electronics people." He rubbed his hands together. "I can hardly wait to see their faces when they discover a *woman* not only designed the new ads but wrote the copy!"

Sarah stared at him in disbelief. "Do you mean to say that they didn't know I had been assigned to the account?"

He saw her flushed face and stammered, "Well, Sarah, you know how industrial people are—not too many female engineers and— Well, these people relate better to men...." He picked up a letter opener, which he turned over and over in his hand. "I thought you surmised what I was doing. You've been around long enough to know about unspoken rules...."

Sarah was furious. "I'm not letting you off the hook on this, chief," Sarah replied angrily. "After all, I'm not exactly unknown in the business. This is prejudice and sexism of the worst sort. If those electronic geniuses loved my ideas and okayed the ads, don't you think I could have handled them? Where was your confidence in me? I was wondering why you didn't let me talk to them. Now I know!"

"Now, Sarah," Ethan Fairchild replied soothingly, "you're making a big issue out of this."

"You're damned right I'm making a big issue out

of this!'' she fumed. "As of this moment you've got my resignation!'' She slammed the door and walked quickly down the private hall to her office, her mind working in three-quarter time. Suddenly she had the answer. She would follow Burke's suggestion. "Gail,'' she called over the intercom, "what time is it in Klosters, Switzerland?''

"Just a moment.'' The reply was so cheerful and pleasant, in sharp and depressing contrast to Sarah's black mood. "It's four-forty-five, boss.''

"A.M. or P.M.?'' Sarah shot back.

Gail giggled. "P.M. Why?''

Sarah was still angry and was in no mood for Gail's fluffiness. "Get me Sir Basil Northcombe—and have the call charged to my home phone.''

"Yes, Sarah.'' Gail replied contritely. She was all business.

Sarah was cleaning out her desk when Gail's voice came over the intercom. "Boss, Sir Basil's not at home, but I managed to wheedle a number where he may be reached in Zermatt, where he's skiing. The overseas operator is trying to get the number now.''

"Thanks, Gail,'' she said. "Let me know.''

Sarah strode to the window and looked down at the familiar view. Very slowly it started to snow, and for a moment she thought of Samsqua and how beautiful High Mountain would be with its sheer cliffs softened by a heavy coat of white. She had just about had it with men and their trickery! First Peter, then Burke, and now kindly old Ethan! They'd all

used her for their own gain, but they wouldn't use
Sarah Mackenzie anymore. If Switzerland wasn't far
enough away, she'd go to China—anywhere to
escape. She had to put all this behind her, she
thought, suddenly realizing she was staring out at the
grayness of New York, not Samsqua. She felt totally
lost, alone, without a home. New York wasn't her
home any more than this office was her home.
They'd both been stepping-stones for her. Through
her success in business she'd gained a sense of herself, Sarah Mackenzie, and she'd done it on her own.
The sheer exhilaration of freedom rushed through
her. She no longer needed this thriving, pulsating—
yes, vibrant city. It didn't matter where she lived, for
environment was only that: day-to-day surroundings.
She felt as though a truth had gradually revealed
itself to her in the past few weeks.

In the same moment that she was mentally thanking Steven Burke for his part in her liberation,
another feeling—one of despair—crept into her and
plummeted her back to earth. Peter she had easily
forgotten, and Ethan Fairchild could keep his job—
she'd find another employer just as good. But
Burke.... She couldn't bear the thought that she
might never see him again. Calculating the sheer
physical distance between them made her realize that.

But it was better this way. The woman who shared
Burke's life could never be independent, autono-
mous. Any career of hers would be an amusement to
keep her busy while he was away on one of his fre-

quent jaunts around the world. He'd never take it seriously. Just as he'd never taken Sarah seriously.

Exhausted by her swift and tumultuous mood changes, she went to her desk, sinking down into a well-worn fabric-covered chair to await a line through to Basil in Switzerland.

"Sir Basil is on the line," Gail announced soberly after a time.

Sarah took a deep breath and picked up the receiver. "Good morning from the Big Apple," she said clearly.

There was a low chuckle on the other end. "Your calling me must be mental telepathy! I've been thinking about you. How did you find my private number?"

Sarah laughed. "My secretary could track down the Abominable Snowman!"

"Don't ever let her go, then. She sounds wonderful." His voice dropped an octave as he went on. "My condolences about Madame Celina. Jelda was one of a kind, and she will be missed in the cosmetics industry."

"You know the details?"

"Yes, probably before you did. Sebastian called me a few moments after she died." There was a long pause and he asked, "Sarah, are you still there?"

"Yes, I'm here. B-but you mean...? So that's how you knew all of *madame*'s business affairs— through *madame*'s butler, Sebastian," she replied incredulously. "I can hardly believe it!" She'd heard of industrial spies, but it just seemed too close to home to be true! So the poor old soul hadn't even found loyalty in her domestic help. Sarah felt ashamed for Sebastian—*and* Basil. What kind of business *was* this?

"He's been in my employ for years. You know very well how these things work."

She ignored the remark. "Although there hasn't been any publicity yet, you also probably know that Harrison is switching the Celina account over to Dolin-Parks?"

"Yes," he said, laughter in his voice. "Now you will be free to take me on."

Sarah laughed. "You—or the account?"

He chuckled. "Now *that's* worth considering! Seriously, I've just bought the world rights to a new perfume from a Dutch chemist. It's the greatest scent since Chanel No. 5, and I think Coco would agree with me if she were still alive. In fact she'd probably have tried to outbid me. I want you to come up with the complete campaign—radio, magazine, and the big one—TV commercials. The works. After we finish talking will you put me through to Ethan Fairchild so we can talk about the financial end of it?"

"There's something you should know, Basil. I've just quit Duncan-Fairchild."

"You've what?"

"I've just given notice."

"Does your leaving have anything to do with Jelda Celina?"

"Oh, no. It's something else entirely. . . ."

"Did it involve money?"

"No, just something that I thought was. . . well, unethical."

"Unethical? Oh, come on, Sarah!" He paused, then went on hurriedly. "Listen, I want you to handle my account, but it must go through a recognized agency. Frankly, I'd set you up in business myself, but there isn't time right now. I want to introduce this new perfume during the second quarter of next year, and this is already October." He paused. "It's none of my business what your disagreement with Ethan Fairchild is about, but you must sort it out!"

"Why couldn't I just come to work for you?"

There was a long pause. "Sarah, politically I want to work through Duncan-Fairchild. I like and admire your boss. I want a responsible agency with a good reputation, but I also want *you*. Now, switch me over to the old boy. If I were you I'd ask for an enormous raise in salary. I promise you'll get it!" He paused. "Good luck." He paused. "This perfume will launch the new line beautifully!"

Sarah pushed the intercom. "Gail, switch this call to Mr. Fairchild."

"Yes, ma'am."

"And Gail, call the overseas operator and have the call charged to Duncan-Fairchild." She smiled, looked at her watch, then calmly continued to clean out her desk. Five minutes later there was a knock on her office door. "Come in," she said brightly, but did not look up from her task.

A discreet cough came from the doorway.

"Yes?" Sarah looked up quickly at Ethan Fairchild. "Yes?"

It was the first time he had been in her office for months. "Basil Northcombe.... I believe he talked to you a few minutes ago?"

"Yes."

"Will you stay and handle his account?" His voice was warm. "It would mean a great deal to me personally, and I need not tell you what a feather it would be in our cap to acquire him as a client so soon after losing Madame Celina. If this perfume goes over we may inherit all of his business, including the men's toiletries."

"I don't know," she parried. "It would require air travel, and you know I don't particularly like flying." She continued shifting papers from the drawer to the top of the desk. "Also, Europe has never really appealed to me. There would be the expense of additional clothing and—"

"Naturally," he said quickly, "I wouldn't expect you to stay on at your present salary."

She looked up casually. Johanna's paperweight depicting Samsqua rested in her hand, giving her the courage to ask the next question. "What kind of money are we talking about?"

He was evasive. "How much are you making an hour now?"

She placed the paperweight on her desk and reached into the drawer for a box of paper clips. "I haven't kept track of what I make per hour since I was promoted from copy writer." Sarah looked at him coolly. It was an appraisal.

He ran his hand through his mane of thick white hair and glanced at her. "Ten percent doesn't seem very much, does it?"

"Not really." She continued to place items on her desk.

"Fifteen percent might be adequate...."

"For someone who didn't need to be dressed in a certain manner."

He glanced at her out of the corner of his eye as she placed a small box on her desk, into which she started to pack personal items. "On the other hand," he said casually, "twenty percent might go a long way toward purchasing a new wardrobe."

"Yes," she agreed, shifting the contents of the box, "it would certainly be an inducement. But with an account of this magnitude, since a great deal of my time is to be billed to the client, mightn't it be fair, also, to let me keep a part of the hourly fee that you're going to bill Basil Northcombe?" She paused. "You usually charge forty dollars an hour." She looked up coldly. "I think I should retain half that amount."

There was a very long pause, and it occurred to Sarah as she searched Ethan Fairchild's red face, that he had dropped the grandfatherly pose the moment that compensation had come up in the conversation.

"It's never been done at this agency—as you know, Sarah," he declared. "And I shouldn't like to establish a precedent."

She closed the desk drawer softly and began to tie the box with a piece of twine. "That's true." She was very formal. "Yet sometimes, when the stakes are high, it pays to relax old outmoded rules." She got up and took her coat from the closet. "I'm tired of being in a penny-ante league, and it's not only money...."

"But," he said, his voice strained and unreal, "it might be far more advantageous for Duncan-Fairchild to have a new vice-president."

Sarah swung around. "What did you say, chief?" she said, then grinned because she knew very well what he'd said. "Do you mean it?"

The moment he heard her call him "chief" he knew he had won. He laughed. "Indeed, I do! It should have been yours when you won the *Advertising People* award." He paused. "You've done more for the agency in the past five years than anyone else. You deserve this." His grandfatherly facade was firmly back in place.

"Oh, thank you, chief!" Before she thought about it she flew into his arms and hugged him tightly. "I'll do a good job—you know I will. I'll work well with Basil Northcombe—and traveling to Europe! I've never seen Europe, you know."

"Hold on." Ethan Fairchild frowned. He was all grandfather again. "Sarah, I know Basil North-combe, and his womanizer reputation is well-founded, let me tell you. You watch yourself, my girl. I feel...responsible for you in a way. You're a funny creature, Sarah. Half child, half business-woman. Keep your cool, dear.''

She stood back and looked at him with wide eyes. "Chief, you're just an old softy," she teased. Then she said more seriously, "Really, Ethan, I appreciate your concern, but Basil's not the dangerous type." She was at that moment, however, picturing someone who definitely *was*. She cleared her throat. "When does the sign go on my door?"

"Better have Gail call the sign painter right now before I change my mind!"

"Did anyone ever tell you that you're a great boss?" she asked. "But don't forget that William Electronics business still rankles!"

He kissed her cheek. "Now take the rest of the afternoon off—but don't go home by Bonwit Teller's, because that raise isn't retroactive."

Going out through the inner office, Sarah met Gail's speculative glance. "You handled that exactly right, boss."

"You listened?"

Gail nodded.

Sarah laughed. "You could be fired for less."

"I know," Gail put in, "but secretaries to new vice-presidents usually get raises...." She held up her hand. "That is, those secretaries who stay in the office. However, those who get to travel with their bosses don't necessarily expect a bonus."

Sarah placed her hands on her hips and nodded. "Start packing. I have a feeling we'll be going to Switzerland soon."

SOMEHOW THE WEEKS SPED BY. One unusually snowy Friday evening in November Sarah sat watching an old romantic comedy on television. The story of two star-crossed lovers seemed terribly corny and old-fashioned, but it was better than another of Della's parties—this one for a newly published author. Sarah had donned her favorite lounging pajamas of emerald green silk jersey, and curled up on the sofa for the movie. But her thoughts weren't with it. She hadn't felt like cooking, so had sent downstairs to the little bistro Les Escargots for veal scallopini and rice, but it lay untouched on the tray in the kitchen. She knew she'd been losing weight, and her already thin face was in danger of looking gaunt. But food held no appeal for her these days. She longed to be on Samsqua, skating on Johanna's pond, breathing the fresh crisp air and growing hungry for a plain New England din-ner. And feeling strong vibrant arms around her, keeping her warm. . . .

At the fade-out of the movie, which featured the standard romantic clinch at the end while the camera panned over the side of the luxury liner to linger on the round full moon, she switched off the set so that the commercial wouldn't disturb the mood the last scene had created. Of course, the film was dated and overly dramatic, but it created a warm feeling all the same. Sarah thought of her own circumstances, and conjured up an absurd image of her playing the leading lady to Burke's hero. Chic New York advertising executive falls in love with famous movie star—with no happy ending in sight. That part at least wasn't her imagination.

IT HAD BEEN three weeks since the telephone-call incident. One day at the office a long white box had arrived with a single red rose inside. The card had said simply, "Call me Thursday at noon EST. Our only chance. S"

Our only chance. That's the problem. She'd known he was leaving the next day for shooting all over Europe and Central Africa. So what was the use in talking when they would be at least three thousand miles apart? She'd weighed the odds and decided: their chances were too slim. She was strong; she was a fighter. But fate had called the shots this time, and she knew when to accept defeat.

She hadn't called.

A week later there had been a flippant letter, addressed simply to "Miss Sarah." "Hi, babe," it started, and she'd winced at the greeting.

Safari scene grim—nothing but torrents, and it's only the so-called short rainy season! Arrived Nairobi four days ago; due to go to another location this morning. Eighty degrees. Some of the crew down with dysentery. I've got mosquito

bites in places no man should have mosquito
bites! Two weeks over schedule. Money's running out; might have to scrap. Producer's having trouble getting funding. I could fund it
privately, but that would mean selling many of
my real-estate holdings, and the market is hide-
ous these days.

Enough of my problems—except one! Why
the hell didn't you call? The lines are impossible
here. Besides, you're never home! Keeping busy
with more ghosts? Don't do anything rash. Save
it for me.

S

How she hated his innuendos sometimes! But
secretly she had to admit she had positively glowed
each and every time she'd read the letter. She'd never
seen his handwriting before; it was bold and firm and
aggressive, like the man himself.

It seemed odd to her that there wasn't enough
money to finish the picture, and for one crazy moment she considered making arrangements to have
her savings invested in the film. But her life savings
were a pittance against what would be required to
finish such a film; *Variety* had said *Devil's Dare*
would be the most expensive film ever made! Why
should she care anyway? It was a crazy business he
was in; let him see how unstable it was. Maybe it
would cure him of some of his arrogance!

Sarah flung the letter down beside her now in a

gesture of impatience, as though removing the letter
from sight would rid her of thoughts of Steve. She
looked around the comfortable apartment, and the
loneliness crept in again. She went to the bedroom
and put her terry robe on, then opened the doors to
the terrace, soaking in the sights and sounds of New
York below her. Christmas lights were dotted every-
where, giving an illusion of festivity. But Central
Park loomed dark and forbidding. For the first time
in her life she wished that she could change places
with Johanna. . . .

This weekend was no time to be alone. She had to
be in old and familiar surroundings. She would weekend on Samsqua.

CHAPTER NINE

SARAH HOISTED UP the Mackenzie "at home" flag and wiped her hands on her jeans. Winter had come early to Samsqua. It had snowed during the night, and the island was encased in a protective white coat. Coming around to the back door of Glass Cottage she noted that a new trellis would have to be constructed over the back windows before the climbing roses started to leaf out in the spring. The old wooden contraption had been patched with string, adhesive tape and wire. It was amazing to her that Johanna could be such a painstaking artist in the studio. Yet something like a broken trellis was carelessly disregarded.

"Good morning, Miss Sarah," Johanna said lightly, coming into the kitchen, a rolled-up piece of butcher paper under her arm.

"Good morning, Miss Jo. How's it coming along?"

"It's the logistics that get me down. I'm not a draftsman."

"But at least you've got patience. I'm afraid mine is running out...."

"I worked all night. I know I look like I'm suffering the aftermath of a demijohn of champagne, but it's always like that when I've completed something really major." A light came into her eyes as she unrolled the butcher paper on the table. "Here is the first detailed rough sketch, complete with plans for the reinforcing bars. If Luis's measurements are correct, each of the three windows will be eighteen feet high and three feet wide...."

At that moment pounding hooves clattered on Primrose Path. "Grandlady's taking Magnifique out early this morning," Johanna remarked, and poured a mug full of coffee, which she brought to the door. A moment later, Lucia Concannon, impeccably dressed in a black riding habit complete with black kid gloves and a bowler hat with a veil and chin strap that pulled back her dewlaps, strode into the room. She took the cup of coffee from Johanna's outstretched hand and nodded to Sarah. Taking a sip, she made a face. "Hannah Path is icy, but the snow is almost gone from the windward side of the island." She finished the coffee, set the mug down with a clatter and sighed impatiently. "Well," she said abruptly, "I assume this is the sketch?" She bent over the drawing. "I can't make head nor tail of it!" she exclaimed.

Johanna smiled. "Now, grandlady, I didn't try to duplicate the Tiffany windows, because that's impossible. So I went for a complete departure."

Lucia Concannon peered at the drawing. "Well,

they only seem like a lot of black lines to me," she complained.

Johanna threw her a quick look. "You're looking at it upside down. Come around the table."

Sarah pointed to the drawing. "Look, grand-lady," she said with wonder. "Johanna's created a series of scenes!"

Johanna nodded. "Yes. The history of Samsqua." She pointed to the design of the first window. "Here, in the lower section, are the first ships that sailed into the cove. Next is old Samuel Fordyce building the dugout where he first lived. Over here is the young Uneema in her native Mohegan dress—and this scene blends into the next section that depicts Fordyce and his sons setting sail for Portland."

"It's. . . wonderful, Jo!" Sarah exclaimed.

Johanna smiled softly. "Wait until you see the full-scale cartoon!" She pointed to the next window. "The main panel shows Uneema, now an old woman, standing on the ledge at High Mountain, which is going to be made up of different shades of blue to show the lupin. Below you can see trawlers in the cove, and beyond—that tiny speck is Boothbay. That figure over there is Grandfather Concannon and his rum boat."

"It didn't have sails, Johanna," Lucia Concannon said. "It was powered by steam."

Johanna made a note. "Thank you, I'll fix that. Now here's the Running Mallow, the way it looked originally and will look again. That's Luis on the porch. Here is the Cricket Hearth when it was a bordello. See the girls posed on the balcony? I got that from an old photograph. There are the Seabees during the war with the barbed-wire beach. Here's Needlepoint House—and there you are, grandlady, on Magnifique, riding down Hannah Path in your green habit.''

Lucia Concannon lifted her thin brows. ''That means I'll look old. I'd much prefer being young, standing next to Augustus on the rum boat.''

''But grandlady,'' Johanna expostulated, ''you told me that you never set foot on that boat.''

''I didn't, but couldn't we have a bit of poetic license? I want to be young and pretty!''

''Grandlady,'' Sarah said gently, ''if the window is going to have significance it must tell the authentic story of Samsqua in as truthful a manner as possible.''

''Well,'' she replied peevishly, ''it's really my island. I should think you'd give me a bit more prominence. Here I'm just a woman on horseback.''

Johanna drew in a deep breath and counted to ten. ''You appear once more in the last panel,'' she said evenly. ''Now in this last section we see the rest of the puzzle. Else Sanchez is bringing the *Griffin* into the cove, and all the villagers are gathered on the wharf: old Pete waiting for his bottle; Mr. Drury and all the others. Hopefully I'll be able to make them all recognizable. I'll work in some tourists, too. Georgie is driving the Model T down Patience Path, and there on the ledge at High Mountain are you, Sarah, with Steve, discovering Uneema's gravestone. Here you are again, grandlady, near the shipwreck."

"Why do you have me standing *there*?"

"It's symbolic!"

"Symbolic of *what*?" she replied tartly. "We're both wrecks—is that what you're saying, Miss Jo?"

"No, grandlady, of course not!" she sighed. "You just fit into the composition, that's all."

"Well, I don't like it one bit!"

"All right, where would you like to be?" Johanna's voice was flat. "On the wharf?"

"Mixing me in with the tourists? No, thank you!" She paused and ran a gloved finger over the third panel. "Why can't you show me picking wild flowers on High Mountain? That might be nice—dressed in a pinafore."

"I don't ever remember you in a pinafore, grandlady!"

Lucia Concannon adjusted the veil a bit more tightly about her chin. "You've only known me as an older woman," she replied defensively. "I used to wear pinafores when I was young, and I did pick flowers...occasionally."

"We'll talk about this later."

"Where are you, Johanna?" Sarah asked.

"Oh, this figure in the bottom of the third panel at Glass Cottage—that's me. See, I've brought the charcoal kiln out onto the patio."

Lucia Concannon stepped back, gazed down at the

drawing and sniffed. "I think it's going to be very nice," she announced grudgingly, smoothing her gloves over her wrists. "Now I must get back. See you later." She turned abruptly, then swung around when she reached the door. "Make my pinafore blue, Miss Jo. Cornflower blue."

Johanna waited until she heard Magnifique on the path, then exclaimed, "Well, we know what she thinks of the design! What are *your* criticisms?"

"Jo, you've got to take Burke out. He—he doesn't belong." She turned away so her sister wouldn't see the pain in her eyes.

"He belongs, Sarah," Jo said firmly, "because he's in your heart. Am I right? Do you love him?"

It was too much, and she turned to Johanna with tears glistening in sad green eyes, spilling over onto long black lashes. "I'm such a fool. Of all the men in the world...!" She fought for control, then managed a small laugh at herself. "Well, I always wanted to make it big! May as well shoot for the top and fall for a man like Steven Burke!"

They laughed together, but Johanna fixed worried eyes on Sarah's taut face. "He loves you, too, Sarah. Yes, he *does*," she said in response to Sarah's vehement shaking of her head. "I can tell. Believe me, he belongs."

LATER, as they ate a simple lunch of cold roast beef and potato salad with crusty rolls, Sarah said thoughtfully, "You know, Jo, this project can make your reputation." She put her slim white hand on Johanna's arm. "I'm very proud of you. This is the best thing you've ever done. You know I'll help you in any way I can."

"Out here on Samsqua no one will ever see the windows except the tourists."

"There is just one small suggestion that I'd like to make." Sarah went to the table, pointed to the Running Mallow, and ran her finger along the drawing until she came to Johanna's figure at Glass Cottage. "That's where Luis belongs—beside you."

Johanna looked up, blushing. "Do you think so?"

"Has he asked you to marry him?"

Johanna shook her head. "No, and I'm not sure he will. How about Burke?"

"What about him?"

"Sarah, what is the problem with you two?"

Sarah sighed and poured herself a cup of coffee from the pot by the kiln. Her face was troubled, and her hand holding the cup shook slightly. "You see, Johanna, I don't know him very well, and there's so little time when we can see each other. He's got a dozen women like me. It's nothing serious for him."

"But surely," Johanna cried, "you *know* him and can trust him."

"I thought I knew Peter, too!" She paused. "I guess I didn't tell you about him." She chose her words very carefully. "He was in the advertising business, too, and he was terribly attractive. We were seeing each other for a few months. One morning I picked up the social page of the *New York Times*, and there was a squib about his wife having an eighth birthday party for their daughter.'' She paused and went to the window. ''I didn't even know he was married. I broke it off, of course. I knew Peter, I thought, better than I know Burke. I don't want to make a mistake again.''

''But everyone knows that Steve's not married!''

Sarah turned to look at her sister. ''Oh, don't be dense!''

''You're scared, that's all,'' Johanna replied quickly. ''For the first time you've met a man who'll take charge. I think, frankly, that you feel threatened.''

Sarah paused, then shook her head. ''He'll rule me from the time I get up in the morning until I go to bed at night. You know I couldn't stand that. He's too strong, Jo. He...overpowers me. And you're right, it frightens me. It's all a big game with him—an act.''

Johanna burst out laughing. ''That's funny, really funny. You're going to have to be more convincing than that! It was no act when I saw him with you. Don't underestimate yourself, little sister. You're beautiful, but you're also brainy. You know the real thing when you see it, and if you'd let yourself see Steve, well....'' She paused. ''When I was in Boothbay the other day I went to the library and read several articles about him in back-issue magazines. He's enormously well liked, and apart from the interviewers saying that he was a slave to work and was a perfectionist on the set, there wasn't a piece of bad news about him. Oh, Sarah, don't let him get away just because Peter was no good...." She paused, her eyes very dark and serious. "When I'm working very hard on one of my pieces, sometimes I have to stop and go on to something else, because I get too involved. I know your job is an important element in your life—Lord knows, you've said it often enough— but maybe you should reevaluate your career."

"I *have* reevaluated my career, Johanna, as recently as when I took on Basil Northcombe's account! I know what I'm doing."

"I hope so." Johanna rinsed out her coffee cup and picked up a dish towel. "But you're so strong. Sometimes men don't like aggressive women!"

"Look, dear," Sarah replied hotly, "*Advertising People* didn't give that award to me for sitting on my derriere crocheting a tea cozy. That statuette, plainly stated, was for my body of work over the past six years. One could say it was acknowledgment for *guts*, because that's what it takes in my business."

There was a burst of mild applause from the doorway, where grandlady stood. "I forgot my gloves."

The girls turned in surprise. "Grandlady, we didn't even hear you riding up Primrose."

"I shouldn't wonder. Going at it hammer-and-tongs! Really, girls, you were brought up in a civilized manner, and now you're quarreling like fishwives."

"We were *not*," Sarah defended herself. "We were just having a quiet little chat."

The old lady smiled mirthlessly. "You can't keep him dangling on a string, Miss Sarah," she stated with a raised eyebrow. "I tried that once with your grandfather and almost lost him. Burke is like Augustus in many ways. He has a lot of quiet strength. You might say that Augustus was an adventurer—somewhat like your fellow."

Sarah smiled wryly. "My 'fellow' is an actor, grandlady."

"Well, I've never seen him act," she retorted, "so I don't know about *that*, but I've seen him in my living room and I've seen him with you, and he certainly doesn't put on airs. He's as natural a man as I've ever laid eyes on, and if I were you I'd grab him before some other woman sets up a plan of attack. He's what we used to call 'the catch of the season.'"

"Oh, grandlady, no man is a 'catch' anymore. Men are men and women are women."

Lucia Concannon sighed gently. "Oh, Sarah, what do you know about men? You can't tell me that you're not in love with him! There are sparks when you're together."

"That's just the trouble—we're not together often enough! Also I'm up to my ears with that damned new perfume, and I can't even find a name for it! It's like there's some kind of conspiracy." She looked at her grandmother. "Why is everything so difficult?"

The old lady patted her black derby. "I'm fifty years old, plus twenty-five more, and life is never

easy." She paused. "But as you'd say, Sarah, I think
it's time you 'got your act together!' "

"As long as you've come back, grandlady,"
Johanna put in, adroitly changing the subject, "how
about taking a peek at my new equipment? Hans and
Henry are down there now."

The studio was ablaze with artificial light. Johanna
had made two full-scale cartoons of the windows,
Sarah noted. One, used for tracing and making templates, had been laid out on the new plywood tables
that had been constructed in the studio, while the second had been tacked along the wall above the tables
so that she could refer to the design as she worked.

New equipment brought over on the *Griffin* included what looked like tons of a wide variety of
colored, hammer-finished rolled glass; a large diesel-
powered generator that provided current for both the
fluorescent lights used to illuminate the work benches
and the large new kilns; glass cutters; soldering guns;
miter boxes; vises and tools of all kinds; and finally,
huge boxes of channeled lead to be used to separate
the pieces of glass that made up the design of the windows.

Hans, Johanna informed them, was an old-time
Viennese glassblower who had worked on some of
the most famous stained-glass windows in Europe
when the devastated countries were rebuilding after
World War II. He'd been hired away from a temperamental New York artist and had brought along
his apprentice, Henry Dorf, a handsome young man

of twenty-five who was an expert in cutting glass to pattern, a procedure that Sarah knew Johanna felt was too difficult and exasperating for her to do.

"This is the first electric light on the island," Lucia Concannon said, regretfully surveying the long tubes that hung over the worktables. "I hope this doesn't catch on, or every house on the island will be as bright as daylight." She sniffed. "Of course, I realize, Johanna, that you need all these modern contraptions in order to create the windows, but you've got to send that generator thing back as soon as you've finished." She glanced into the large mirror, placed at an angle above the door to provide a view of the worktables. She patted her platinum white upswept hairdo. "I must say that one can see clearly with those lights. I do believe I've too much rouge on!"

The girls laughed and reassured her she was as impeccable as ever.

"Why do you look at your work all the time in that mirror?" grandlady asked.

Johanna shrugged. "You can always see mistakes better in a mirror image."

Lucia Concannon glanced at her reflection again. "Yes," she said clearly, "I see what you mean." She paused. "Are you going to make chowder tomorrow?"

"Yes, if Luis will row over to Mercy Island to get some goat's milk." Johanna daubed a bit of hot wax on an oblong piece of ruby glass that Henry had just cut from a template, placing it deftly over its counterpart in the giant cartoon on the table. She pressed the glass down firmly so that it would adhere to the pattern, then surveyed her work. "It's coming along," she said to Hans.

"Ya!" the old man said, removing a blowing tube from his lips. He stood back quickly, allowing the glass to flow into the corners of the mold. Sarah watched, fascinated as she always was by the procedure.

Lucia Concannon sighed. "Well, I'll leave you children to your work," she said, and glanced at Johanna. "I'll come over for a pail of chowder tomorrow afternoon."

As she watched Johanna giving further instructions to the craftsmen, Sarah reflected on the difference between her and her sister's lives. How simple life seemed for Johanna, how happy. Success had brought Sarah its own rewards, and she'd been as fulfilled as she'd thought it possible to be—until a certain dark-eyed actor had intruded. Now the gap in her life was evident, and all the time growing painfully larger....

CHAPTER TEN

THE LULLING MOTION of the small Swiss train, climbing precariously on cogs, had a mesmerizing effect on Sarah, and she dozed. But Gail, with her nose against the window, looking down at snowy Visp Valley, pulled back every now and then to consult the map that was spread out on her knees. She saw they were about to enter a tunnel that was not shown on the map, and nudged Sarah. "I think we're almost there!" she trilled. "Oh, isn't this exciting?"

Sarah opened one eye, then the other, and looked about her at the strange assortment of people. She was certainly used to the sports crowd because there had always been some elementary skiing on Samsqua—and, too, a great many New Englanders cross-country skied. But this group, dressed in everything from parkas to stretch pants, seemed like alien beings. Of course, she reasoned, they *were* foreign, except for a few American students in the rear of the train, who had sung a variety of popular songs until threatend with grave consequences by the rest of the passengers.

Sarah looked down at her own dark blue wool culottes and high tan kid-leather boots. She wore a clas-

sically styled blue-and-beige tweed blazer. Her
cream-colored, thick-knit turtleneck kept her warm
and comfortable. Gail wore a green pantsuit that set
off her blond hair nicely. Together they made a very
attractive pair.

The train crept into the tunnel, and darkness enveloped them. Then suddenly they were on the other
side, and a breathtaking view revealed a little village
nestled between huge slabs of granite covered with ice
and surrounded by snowy mountain peaks. "That's
the Matterhorn," Gail explained, loading her camera
again. "I've got to get a shot the moment we get to
the station."

"Is this Zermatt, then?" Sarah asked as the train
chugged to a stop.

"The end of the line," Gail confirmed, and rushed
out onto the snowy platform before any of the other
passengers could collect their possessions. She ran
headlong into a group of red-coated ski instructors
and their preteen charges. Sarah picked up her purse
and made her way through the crowd of tourists, who
seemed in no hurry to depart. Then at the door she saw
the reason: an anxious tour guide was counting noses.

Gail bent down on one knee and lined up a low-
angle shot of an attractive man holding a pair of skis
over his right shoulder. "Thank you, sir," she giggled.

"*Jawohl!*" he exclaimed. "*Auf Wiedersehen!*"
And he departed with a wide smile and a wave.

"Gail, you're behaving exactly like one of those
tourists on the train!" Sarah muttered.

"But I *am* a tourist!" Gail replied excitedly, pointing to a line of horse-drawn sleighs in front of the station platform. "Oh, look, it's like something out of a fairy tale!" Beyond, the town of Zermatt shimmered in the sun's reflection off the thick snow. The buildings, fashioned of rough-hewn wood and beige native stone and sporting shutters of scarlet, brown and yellow, looked unreal—miniatures set up under a tree on Christmas Eve.

A tall man in a gray uniform approached and bowed. "Miss Mackenzie?" he asked in a strong German accent.

"Yes?"

"Follow me, please." Browned by the sun, the man flashed a smile that showed large white teeth. "Sir Basil is waiting. If you'll give me your stubs I'll collect your luggage."

Gail exchanged glances with her employer and whispered, "He looks divine!"

Sarah quickly whispered back, "I'm going to send you home if you don't behave. We're here on business. Don't go man crazy!"

"Why not, boss? I won't let it interfere. Maybe I'll meet Mr. Right," Gail replied with a perky toss of her blond head. "I guess I should stay away from ski bums, though—like that one who posed for my picture!"

"You ninny! That was Herrman Lippman, the Olympic ski champion!"

Properly chastised, Gail fell in behind Sarah as they found a green sleigh, in which Basil Northcombe was waiting. "Welcome to Zermatt!" he shouted as he waved. He was dressed in brown ski attire, and an orange stocking cap was pulled down over his ears and forehead. With his gray thatch covered he looked no more than thirty-five. Sarah flushed with pleasure as the driver helped her into the fur-covered seat beside Basil. She introduced Gail, who was soon ensconced in the rear.

"Excuse me for not changing to meet you, but I've been up on the Gornergrat until a few moments ago. The skiing is wonderful this year. We've nine inches of new powder over a solid pack. Do you ski?"

Sarah shook her head. "Ice skating is my passion."

He beamed. "Good. You can take your pick of several rinks here. Did you have a pleasant trip?"

"Yes, though it was very tiring. It's fabulous scenery, isn't it? The flight to Zurich was uneventful, but I didn't realize that Zermatt was so far."

"Southern tip of Switzerland," Gail said from the back seat. "We're just a stone's throw from Italy."

"That's true," Basil agreed. "In fact, I often ski from here to Breuil, which is just over the border. It sounds like a long journey, but it's only about ten kilometers each way. Pity you don't ski, or we could have made the trip together."

As the horses pulled the sleigh down the main thoroughfare an old woman in a black babushka led a brace of cattle down the other side of the street and disturbed a few sheep tethered near an alleyway. "I don't see any cars," Sarah said. "It reminds me of Samsqua."

"The cog railway is our connection with the outside world. Zermatt is still essentially unspoiled, considering the state of other ski resorts in the area. As you know, I have a big place in Klosters, but I rent a little chalet when I'm here."

Sarah examined his face. In the snowy outdoors was where he belonged, she decided. He had looked out of place somehow at Della's party. While he was undeniably sophisticated, he also had a certain earthy quality underlying his impeccable manners that she admired. Yet he was quite unlike Burke. It was strange, she reflected, that when she was with other men she always found herself comparing them to Burke. She had a sudden longing to see his face, to see his eyes snap as he asked her an unexpected question. Suddenly she felt very much alone.

She wondered briefly why she had made the long trip. Of course, she had come with her portfolio crammed with hastily penciled ideas. This was to be her biggest coup, a campaign that would solidify her vice-presidency at Duncan-Fairchild. Yet she found her enthusiasm ebbing. She'd begun questioning her goals, and in the advertising game, she knew, that was akin to suicide.

She shook the cobwebs out of her head. *Get a hold of yourself, girl,* she admonished. *You're here for a purpose, and you can't lose your composure now!*

The sleigh drew up before a rambling house with a

slate-tiled roof and vermilion shutters. Basil North-combe nodded. "Welcome to Chalet Weisshorn. It's named after a mountain that's particularly hard to climb. There is a narrow ladder going up to the bed-rooms on the upper floor that requires as much bal-ance as it does to make a difficult turn on the slopes." He laughed. "The original owner, a descen-dant of one of the bourgeoisie families who settled the valley, broke the same leg twice climbing up the ladder after too much Fendant. Overindulgence is hard to avoid. Fendant wine is like a cool mountain stream, and you literally cannot put it down. We shall have to be careful not to have too much or we'll end up sleeping in front of the fireplace downstairs."

The door of the magnificent chalet swung open. "Welcome!" Basil exclaimed flamboyantly.

Standing at the threshold of the beautifully fur-nished room was Sebastian. "Good afternoon, Miss Mackenzie." Bowing his silver gray head, he permit-ted himself a small smile. A long look passed between them. "This is Gail Kraft, my secretary. Sebastian."

"Good afternoon, Gail." He regarded her with disinterest. Sarah was cool toward him. She couldn't forget that Sebastian had spied on Madame Celina.

"If you both would like to freshen up I'll send your luggage up via the dumbwaiter." Basil made a small gesture. "I regret that this house is not fully staffed, so you'll have to do your own unpacking."

Sarah laughed. "Just like home." She paused, looking around her. "Do we dress for dinner?"

Basil shook his head. "No, wear something casual. Slacks might be good. Immediately after we eat we'll go out on the town to do some touristy things. Tomorrow is all work. Your bedchambers are upstairs to the right."

Sarah and Gail carefully climbed the ladder, which was actually a narrow, steep wooden staircase without banisters. The upper story was divided into two spacious sections with a small parlor in the middle; several bedrooms were located on each side of the fireplace.

"Isn't this fabulous?" Gail enthused, and Sarah had to agree. Everything thus far had been simply charming.

"By the way," Gail said slyly, "Mr. Northcombe seems more than slightly interested in you. Should I conjure up a headache tonight?"

"No! Do come along, Gail. I don't want to spend an evening alone with Basil. I want this to be a business relationship only, and you know, I'm sure, all about his reputation! This project must start out right. There's too much at stake!"

"Like a V.P. at Duncan-Fairchild?"

Sarah nodded, but inwardly she admitted the vice-presidency didn't mean everything to her. There were much more uncertain elements in her life at the moment.

If Zermatt was a cold, lazy-looking village during the daytime, there was a drastic change of scene after nightfall. Thousands of skiers fresh off the mountain slopes invaded the tiny streets and crowded into the restaurants, tearooms, and discos in ever increasing numbers until it seemed that the rafters would split. Both men and women sported the skiers' dress code of bulky alpine hand-knit sweaters in many colors, contrasting or matching ski pants and soft boots. Grins and gaiety were the order of the night.

A plethora of languages and accents was orchestrated by musicians plunking, blowing and strumming various instruments. The incessant clinking of glasses accompanied toasts of health, happiness and success delivered in everything from Chinese to Zamindarian. The smells were as intriguing as the sounds: bits of steak sizzling in oil, fondue style; tureens of stew; flambéed desserts; and steaming coffee mingled with the prevailing odor of exotic suntan lotions clinging to tourists from Spain, Italy, France, Germany and the United States. But beneath all the camaraderie was an open sensuousness, a relaxing of inhibitions that heightened the party-loving atmosphere. It was almost decadent, Sarah thought.

Basil Northcombe escorted Sarah and Gail from one watering hole to another. Because it was next to impossible to get the attention of the waiters in every place, they carried their own hot-buttered rums with them. But by the time they finally stopped in the dining room of a quiet family-run hotel, the glasses contained icy globules of congealed butter floating unappetizingly over the top of the rum. They sat at the bar and were eventually served steaming bowls of mulled wine. Somewhere in the background a violinist played sentimental Swiss-German folk songs. The place gradually emptied. The skiers left to be fresh at dawn, when chair lifts started operating.

"On the way back to the chalet let's stop at a rink," Basil suggested, "and have a couple of turns around the ice."

"I'm out of practice," Sarah protested, thinking of Burke and the Sky Rink.

He turned to Gail. "Do you skate, too?"

She shook her head. "No, I gave it up for Lent when I was eight, but I'd love to watch."

They climbed into the green sleigh, and three minutes later were deposited at one of the lighted outdoor rinks, where a fast and furious game of curling had just been completed. The winning team of Austrians, their heads wet with perspiration, sped past them, and Sarah thought how different the natural blue ice looked from that opaque mass manufactured at Sky Rink. Basil Northcombe spoke Swiss to the crusty old man who rented skates, who refused to reply and kept shaking his head. Basil then tried German, French and Italian, but the man just stared at him blankly. Deciding that he was mute, Basil began to converse in elaborate sign language, until Gail piped in, "Maybe he only understands Arabic!"

"Not at all," the old man replied in English with a strong American accent. "I'm from Poughkeepsie." They all laughed, except the old man, who didn't think it was funny at all. It was the end of his day, he

was tired and they were his last customers of the
night. Impatiently he laced up the skates, rented for
four American dollars a pair.

"We'll just skate two recordings' worth," Basil
reassured the old man, handing him a twenty-dollar
bill.

"For that you get three," the old man replied with a
twinkling eye, and cranked up a machine attached to a
small amplifier and speaker. As the harsh scratchy
sounds of a polka blared out woefully across the ice,
Basil took Sarah's hand and sped her awkwardly to
the center of the rink. He was not a very accomplished
skater, and soon Sarah was zooming over the ice
ahead of him, turning in time to the fast music.

The polka was cut off in midphrase and was replaced with a slow fox-trot. Basil took Sarah's hand
and they skated together, Sarah slowing her steps to
his. "You're quite good for being out of practice! I
feel like a novice," he said, holding her tightly
around the waist and guiding her stiffly to the right
and to the left. What had started out to be fun was
now an ordeal for her.

In her mind Sarah tried to replace Basil with
Burke. Once more they were flying over the rink on
West Thirty-third Street, his hand holding her lightly
but firmly as he guided her into an intricate turn.
Then she felt herself being awkwardly pulled to the
left, and she was back in Zermatt with the stalwart
Basil at her side. She smiled at him uncertainly, and
he laughed self-consciously. "I really shouldn't have

attempted this, Sarah. My coordination isn't what it used to be. Skiing is second nature to me, but this! I'll sit down. I don't want to spoil your fun."

She shook her head. "You're really doing very well, Basil."

Again in midphrase, the fox-trot was replaced with the "Blue Danube." Basil skated better to the slow-waltz tempo, and she began to enjoy herself again. Burke temporarily receded into the background.

"You know," he was murmuring, "you're the most attractive woman who's come into my life in a very long time." His hand caressed her waist as they skated.

Determined to keep the conversation light, she scoffed, "I doubt that, Basil. You're one of the most eligible bachelors I know of."

"I'm very difficult to please. The sports ladies aren't my type; I don't want to compete on the slopes. Socialites turn me off, too, because they're always looking over your shoulder for someone who has more money, power or youth."

She smiled. "You don't seem to be one of the ten neediest cases, Basil—let's face it!"

"I like women with brains, and in my business I don't run into them very often. Frankly, most of the ones I encounter have husbands or lovers—not that that disturbs me if the right situation comes along. But at my age I'm looking for something more lasting."

"I understand what you mean, Basil," she answered politely. "But it's a dilemma everyone has to face sooner or later. You're being frank with me, so I'll be frank with you. I think you're one of the most intriguing men I've ever met, and I mean that most sincerely. I admire and respect you. I think we can build an excellent *working* relationship. If you want, or expect, something different, then Gail and I will go back to New York tomorrow."

"Of course," he answered softly, "I don't want you to leave tomorrow. Our business relationship is sound, and thus it shall stay...."

The recording stuck in a groove on the last phrase, and the old man unceremoniously swiped his hand over the needle, causing an abrupt end to the music, which, Sarah thought, was a fitting coda to their conversation. She liked Basil and she wanted to work for him, but there could be no conditions, no strings attached—and especially no emotional ties. She hoped that he would not try to persuade her again.

The streets were quiet now that it was after midnight. It had begun to snow very lightly. Wrapped in lap robes in the green sleigh, the lights of Zermatt dimming in the distance, the trio fell silent. As the chalet came into view the snow stopped, and Sir Basil took a deep breath of fresh air. "I love this atmosphere so much, Sarah. It's intoxicating."

She nodded mutely, but Gail let out a loud exclamation from the back seat. "Yes! Just imagine—we're high on fresh air!"

THE NEXT MORNING Sebastian placed the silver service in the dumbwaiter, climbed up the ladder stair to the sitting room and set up the huge sideboard for breakfast. Chafing dishes contained soft scrambled eggs, a variety of wursts, preserved kippers, sautéed chicken livers and crisp bacon. Under napkins rested buttered rusks, thin slices of pumpernickel, flaky croissants and tiny sweet rolls.

"Good morning, Miss Mackenzie," Sebastian said, inclining his head slightly as she came into the room. "Did you have a good night?"

"Yes, thank you. I haven't slept on eiderdown since I was a little girl." She paused and looked at him obliquely. "Do you miss New York, Sebastian?"

"No, miss. It's very nice working for Sir Basil. Incidentally, he asked that you and Gail have breakfast now. He'll join you in half an hour."

Sarah and Gail ate before the roaring fireplace. "I can't believe I'm actually here," Gail said enthusiastically, chewing on a bit of bratwurst. "Last night was a dream. Did we really ride in a sleigh and visit all those places?"

"Apparently," Sarah laughed, placing her plate on the coffee table and opening a portfolio. She looked at a few drawings and shook her head. "So far all I have is: 'From the laboratories of Sir Basil Northcombe comes....'"

"So far, so good," Basil said, coming up the ladder. He was dressed in a deep blue velvet jacket set off by a gray silk ascot and pewter-toned wool slacks that fitted his trim figure exactly—a masterful tailoring job, Sarah thought. The blue also contrasted neatly with his salt-and-pepper hair and deeply tanned face. "I've never used 'from the laboratories of.' I like that. It may sound a bit clinical, but at this juncture that's all right, too." He removed a small plain bottle from his pocket. "This is the new perfume. I thought you'd like to take a whiff of what you're going to be writing about."

Sarah opened the stopper. Immediately the surrounding area was awash with a subtle fragrance, difficult to identify. "It's sinful!" she exclaimed.

"I can smell it clear over here," Gail said from the window seat where she sat, ready to take shorthand notes of the proceedings.

"Well," Basil said, "what do you think of it?"

Sarah sniffed the air. "It's elusive; one moment you smell it and the next moment you don't."

He nodded. "Exactly. In fact, that might be a good slogan. Until this scent came along I was perfectly content with men's toiletries. I like this because it's not cloying."

"Have you come up with a price yet?" Sarah asked.

"No. That'll depend on the packaging. I assume it will be in the forty dollars one-half-ounce category."

"And how much of that is pure profit?"

He laughed, showing an array of white teeth. "Don't ask!"

"Is the packaging going to be elaborate? Madame Celina's tiny box for After Nine is fabulous. It's constructed rather like a Chinese puzzle. You pull a little tassel, and the box comes apart in your hand. It's easy to reassemble, too. Men are going to love it because of the mechanics."

"So," Basil replied thoughtfully, lighting a pipe, then biting the stem. "Men will be buying the box rather than the perfume! Is my scent really fabulous?"

"Not fabulous, Basil; in fact, it's rather ordinary after the first sniff."

He turned away and stared into the fireplace. "Then we should have a very simple package." He looked up. "Sebastian said that the flask for After Nine looks like a teardrop."

"Yes, it's very elegant." She paused, hands supporting her chin. "We've got to come up with something better."

"Simplicity is fine, Sarah, but we can't present this new scent in a test tube!"

She mused on this, then looked at him with admiration and mischief sparkling in her eyes. "Why *not*?"

He hit the palm of his hand with his fist—a gesture, Sarah thought, more appropriate to Steven Burke than Basil Northcombe. "I think we've hit on something! We'd redesign it so that the bottom is flat, and arrange a decorative cap of some sort."

"Yes! You see, Basil," she went on quickly, "that

would tie in with the 'from the laboratories of' line so well. Then we should do a tall oblong box for the redesigned test tube that would be simplicity itself. How about black with a gold stripe around the top?''

"What's Celina's color for After Nine?''

"Turquoise.''

"We'll think about your idea of black and gold, then.'' He paced up and down in front of the fire-place. "What else can we come up with that would set the industry back on its heels?''

Sarah laughed. "I appreciate your attitude, Basil. May I tell you something? I loved working with Madame Celina because she was so positive, but she didn't have your originality. With most campaigns entire presentations are worked out. Enormous amounts of money are spent on sketches, photos and ordering special logotype before you even *see* the client. Then they either like it immediately, turn it down—or worse yet, criticize it to pieces. They don't usually have an ounce of creativity, and no visualiza-tion. But with you... well, we seem to be on the same wavelength.''

He laughed. "We are, aren't we? The first moment I saw you at Della's party I knew we'd work well to-gether.'' He paused. "I have a confession to make. I asked Della to invite me to the party when I knew you were coming—which wasn't very proper, I suppose. But Della and I go back many years. We had a... a romance once.'' He looked away and then back. "She was so beautiful when she was in her twenties, but she changed, and not only physically...." He sighed. "Well, back to the present. Any other ideas?"

He repeated his habit of hitting his palm with his fist, and again Burke's image sprang up before Sarah's eyes. "Remember all those movies about scientists, where Louis Pasteur or Pierre Curie held a test tube up to the light and proclaimed, 'That's it! I've found it!'—and the background music soared and a heavenly choir sang hallelujah, or a reasonable facsimile thereof?"

Basil Northcombe nodded. "I saw every one of those flicks as a boy. I was fascinated by the heroics." He ran a hand through his gray hair and laughed. "I'll still stay up to see one of those epics on the late show when I'm in the States."

"Exactly." She paused, gathering her courage. "So does everyone else. There's a point of identification. Now, what if in *our* ad—now remember, this is just off the top of my head and there will be many parts missing—but in theory it might work out like this: We photograph a man holding our test-tube bottle casually in his hand. He looks directly into the lens of the camera, and the caption says, 'The scent of a woman....' Then, blah, blah—whatever we decide to call the perfume. Then one more line: 'It's sinful!' "

Basil Northcombe looked at her incredulously, then violently shook his head. "Using a man is the worst possible psychology, Sarah. My God, women would thumb right by the page, not even looking at it, because in their minds an ad of that sort would be pushing after-shave lotion or some such product.''

An inspired thought leaped into Sarah's mind, and her previously frowning brows lifted, a smile working its way over her well-shaped lips. Of course! Why hadn't she thought of this before? She could offer Steve the chance to make enough money to finish the picture—but only if he agreed not to use Samsqua for the chase scene in *Devil's Dare*!

Hastily she imagined how silly Steve might look promoting a woman's perfume. It might have a disastrous effect on his career. But no, the increased visibility could only enhance his appeal, Sarah decided.

She smiled softly. ''Women would not thumb right by the page if the man was Steve Burke!''

''Steve Burke,'' he scoffed, ''posing for a perfume ad! He wouldn't be caught dead in a women's magazine. And besides, Sarah, no money on earth could buy him. He's a multimillionaire.'' He paused and began to pace up and down in front of the fireplace. There was no sound in the room except the crackling of the fire logs and Gail shuffling papers from the window seat.

He stopped in front of Sarah. ''But if we were silly enough to attempt this sort of foolishness Burke is the only man in the world that I would even consider for such a departure. He's got class, that's for sure.'' He shook his head. ''We'd better forget it. Can you imagine my approaching him with a harebrained scheme like this? He'd think I was mad and summon the boys in white coats." His voice rose. "I'm not about to make an ass of myself. . . ."

"Sir Basil!" she said firmly, knowing the "sir" would interrupt his tirade. "There are several things you don't know about Steve Burke. I'm not too far out in left field. I think this ad might fit in very well with his screen image. He's making a film now in which he plays a secret agent—a svelte sophisticated type. It has a decent budget, I gather, but it's being shot all over kingdom come—Brussels, Rome, Paris, Nairobi—and they've run into all sorts of bad weather. They're weeks behind schedule. The big chase that ties the whole thing together has yet to be shot, and they've run out of money. The distributor won't put up any more cash. The companies that are willing to contribute 'finish' money want a huge percentage of the profits, and Burke won't go along with that. He's been trying to raise money himself, but apparently his cash is tied up in other ventures."

She paused. "I don't know anything about your finances, Basil, but *Fortune* magazine once printed that you had an empire encompassing many areas other than toiletries." She glanced casually at her fingernails and went on slowly. "Assuming that some of your assets are liquid, would you consider giving Burke the money he needs to finish the film, in exchange for his services?" When he didn't answer she went on quickly. "This picture means so much to him that he might just go along—television commercials and all.''

He paused. "Burke's never done any television?"

Sarah shook her head. "He's one of the last holdouts."

"How much money does he need for the movie?"

"You'd have to have the lawyers work it out."

"How much did Sir Laurence Olivier get for those Polaroid commercials?"

Sarah shook her head. "I've no idea, but you can bet it was way 'up there' somewhere."

"Assuming we could get an exclusive on Burke's services," Basil mused, "would he do it?"

"He'll do it," Sarah assured him. "Leave it to me."

"Is the movie script any good?"

"I've no idea."

"Well, I don't want to throw good money after bad."

"Well, if you pay Burke it will no longer be your money, right?" she replied sweetly. "And something else just occurs to me, Basil—" she smiled suddenly "—here you're worried about whether the script's good or not, but what happens if he doesn't like the smell of your new perfume?"

AT FOUR O'CLOCK that afternoon, when Basil was taking his usual nap after he had been out on the slopes, and Sarah was writing down ideas for the new television commercial, Sebastian came out on the sunny terrace where she was seated and murmured, "Steve Burke is on the wire, Miss Mackenzie."

She flushed, and with her heart in her mouth followed Sebastian into the living room. She picked up the delicate French phone awkwardly. It seemed like a toy. "Burke? The connection is so clear, you could be around the corner."

He laughed. "As it happens, I am. I'm at Hotel Christiana here in Zermatt!"

CHAPTER ELEVEN

SHE PAUSED, allowing his words to sink in. *Here?* She must work fast! "Oh, Burke, how wonderful, but I thought you were in Rome!"

His voice grew strained. "That's the bad news. The company is shut down. I'm on my way back to Hollywood to try to raise money." He paused, and his tone was flat. "If we don't get some more backing the picture won't make any profit at all."

What a terrible shame, she thought with unwonted waspishness. *You'll only remain a multimillionaire!*

"There may be another way, Burke," she exclaimed. "I can't say any more over the phone. I'll be over in five minutes!"

She asked Sebastian to order the sleigh, told Gail to tell Basil not to expect her for dinner, and then ran up the narrow stairway to the bathroom, almost slipping on the last tread. She stared into the mirror and hurriedly lathered her face with castile soap, rinsing her skin until it shone. Then she ran a comb through her auburn curls and added a bit of gray eye shadow to her upper lids. After changing into plain black jeans and a soft black cashmere sweater, she knew she looked casual but sophisticated. Perfect, she thought, and reached for her camel's-hair coat.

As soon as the sleigh turned the corner of the ice rink her heart started pounding—even before she saw, from a block away, his long lanky form waiting in front of the hotel. It seemed as if she and Burke had been apart for years, as though there were a fragile golden cord drawing them magnetically together. The sleigh stopped, he rushed forward, and suddenly she was in his arms and he was holding her closely. *I can't cry,* she told herself sternly. *I can't break down on the street!* She hugged him tightly until she felt some of her agitation subside. Then she stood back and looked at him. His face under his habitual tan was drawn, and there were circles under his eyes. "Oh," she gasped, "you look exhausted!"

He put his arm around her waist and they walked down the deserted winding terrace that bordered the hotel on the mountainside. The slopes stretched toward the sky, dotted with green and white and topped with misty clouds. This really was the land of fairy tales, Sarah thought idly, taking in the quaint gables of the shops and houses.

What am I doing here, about to blackmail Steve Burke when he's obviously not on top of his form? She shook her head, determined to keep a clear head for her upcoming task.

"I'm beat," Burke sighed heavily. "We shot the train sequence yesterday on a narrow-gauge railway. I was handcuffed and tied up on top of the car, and I had to untie myself, get out of the cuffs and dangle over the edge of the train." He laughed ruefully. "We did it four times."

"But I thought you had a stunt double?"

"He got dysentery. We had to get that particular shot wrapped up yesterday because our permit was running out and so was our money. It was rather fun, actually."

Her hands grew clammy. "It's a wonder you didn't get killed!"

"Apparently I have nine lives!" He increased the pressure on her waist. "Anyway I had a few days off, and I've never seen Switzerland." She looked at him disbelievingly. "Well, not with a gorgeous redhead anyway."

"I am *not* redheaded!" she fumed.

"Not much...." He paused. "Besides, I don't trust Basil Northcombe. He's an old roué. Watch him, Sarah. I wouldn't want you to get hurt."

Get hurt! Did he know what he was saying? Could he possibly be so dense as to believe she would get involved with Basil? That meant, of course, that he hadn't seen any of the love in her eyes—which was not surprising, she thought. She'd camouflaged it well with cool words, words designed to keep him away from her heart.

"You needn't worry about me, Steve. I'm quite capable of taking care of myself. Basil Northcombe's flirtations are the least of my problems...."

Burke threw her a quick glance. "Then he did *try*?"

She didn't like his tone. "Am I to believe that you're jealous?"

He removed his hand from around her waist. "Are you interested?" he countered through tight lips.

"The world is full of attractive men," she replied slowly. "But you should know, for one thing, that I'm not drawn to older men."

"I'm older," he shot back. "Ten years older!"

"Exactly," she snapped. Abruptly she stopped walking. "That's not what I meant, and you know it. Basil is fifty if he's a day!" It was true that she was angry—and yet underneath she was experiencing a new emotion. She, Sarah Mackenzie, for the first time in her life, was discovering what it was like for a man to be jealous of her! It was a strange feeling—half pleasure and half fear. She looked at him again, but all she glimpsed was his strong, stubbornly set profile. She couldn't suppress a smile.

Steve turned away, his gaze sweeping up the Gornergrat. The sun had gone behind the mountain and had left a golden aura, radiating over the summit.

Very calmly she circled around him until she was in his line of vision. "You should know," she said very gently, "that Basil is only my employer. If I wanted an affair, I'd...." She searched for the right words. She felt too vulnerable, as soft as custard inside. She had not meant to defend her position. This was new to her, this business of having to qualify herself. It was, in a way, demeaning. Yet if the shoe were on the other foot, and Burke had gone to visit a glamorous jet-setter in as romantic a setting as Switzerland, she might feel the same way. Yet that wasn't the case at all. *He* had doubted *her*.

"You'd what? Go back home to Peter Schaeffer?" His words stung. He'd assigned her two men, now!

He continued to look up at the mountain, avoiding her stare, his jaw solid and resolute. She didn't know how to react. She had never run into such a situation before. She, who had sat in on tough boards of directors' meetings; she, who had arranged brilliant campaigns that had set the advertising world on its ear; she, who had fearlessly stood up to the strongest men in the business, was at a loss as to how to proceed. The silence between them grew ominous and Sarah turned and took a few steps away from him.

"Where are you going?" he demanded hotly. "Back to Sir Basil?"

She froze, sudden fury rising up in her. Whirling on him, she exclaimed, "Yes, I'm going back to Sir Basil!" She wanted to hurt him. "He's my ideal! He's charming and . . . polite and—and quite sexy!"

He came toward her swiftly and took her hands, holding them down forcibly at her sides as he drew her toward him and kissed her roughly on the lips. She wanted to break away. She wanted to run back to the sleigh, to get on the next plane to New York— back to her creative world that she could easily control. But the fiery passion of his lips stirred her against her will into depths of new feeling, and she felt herself responding wantonly to the pressure of his body.

His lips on hers became less insistent as he kissed her again, tenderly and sweetly. He broke away. "Okay," he said, smiling, "you win, Red. I know now that if there was something between you and Basil you certainly wouldn't have reacted as you did." He sobered, and his deep brown eyes looked somehow saddened. "I don't seem to be able to control these suspicions where you're concerned, and I don't know why that is. Forgive me, Sarah."

She tried to still her erratically beating heart. What a strange man he was! "I was hurt that you didn't believe me," she murmured, tears very near the surface again.

"I was imagining all sorts of things. I was filming the picture on that damned dead continent, with nothing but mosquitoes and bad food. I was tired out of my mind, and I kept seeing you: so cool and beautiful, and so desirable. I kept seeing you and Basil—a man who knows everything there is to know about women—and I thought you would surely succumb. . . ."

"Succumb?"

"It could happen," he said tersely, "if the setting were right."

She sighed. "If you think that I'd be a pushover for some smooth European, you don't know me at all, Burke. I've been around the territory for eight years now, and I've been able to keep my values—

grandlady's values—intact. I deal with men like Sir
Basil every day of my life, and I can read his type like
a book. How can you question...?''

It was her turn to back away as he glared at her. "I
apologized once, and I won't apologize again, dam-
mit." His eyes blazed. "Are we ever together when
we're not fighting?" There was a heavy silence between them, seemingly endless. Then he said,
"You've never really told me how you felt about me.
You've let me dangle...."

"What could I do, Steven?" she asked plaintively.
"We've been together so very little. Two dates in
New York—at Della's party and at the awards. Two
days on Samsqua that we had to cut short because of
Madame Celina's death. You rushed away; then the
picture went on location.... I don't *know* you,
Burke!"

He took her hands in his while his eyes bored into
her soul. "You know me well enough, though, don't
you? Mmm?"

Sarah could only stare in confusion at his enig-
matic words. Then Gail's trilling voice intruded and
Burke grasped her shoulders possessively for a moment before releasing her.

"Boss—" Gail rushed up breathlessly "—Sir Basil
asked me to relay a message. He would like you and
Mr. Burke to come to the chalet for dinner."

"Gail Kraft, I'd like you to meet Steve Burke,"
Sarah said evenly, trying not to sound annoyed that
her secretary had discovered them on the terrace in

the middle of what must look—to her—like a lovers' quarrel.

"How do you do, Miss Kraft," Burke said to Gail, who was looking up at him in such an adoring manner that it appeared she would melt into the cobblestones at any moment. "Please tell Sir Basil that we are engaged for dinner, but we would very much like to have an after-dinner drink with him at the chalet."

"Yes, sir!" Gail exclaimed with a smile, and scurried down the length of the terrace, her flat shoes making a click-clack deadening sound on the stones.

Burke turned to Sarah. "You're having dinner with me. Come inside." As Sarah entered the lobby she noticed that a group of tourists—the same ones who had made the trip up to Zermatt on the cog railway—was milling around the desk, collecting luggage and studying travel brochures. She saw a young girl in a red stocking cap staring intently at Burke. A look of recognition flashed across her face, and she gave a little squeal and ran forward. Burke saw her, too, and quickly guided Sarah to the open elevator. "The fifth floor—and hurry," he said to the startled male operator, but before the doors could close the young girl rushed in, knocking Sarah's purse to the floor.

"I'm Geraldine Barnes and I'm here with my school from Des Moines," she exclaimed, quite out of breath and paying not the slightest attention to Sarah, who was retrieving her purse. "And I'm the editor of our college paper, *The Gladiator*. What do you think about the situation in the Middle East?"

The words came out in a rush as she examined his face closely, perhaps expecting to see his reply written in ink on his forehead.

He glared at her. "Young lady," he replied evenly, "I'm on vacation, and not giving any interviews."

She ignored his statement and went on quickly. "President Reagan—"

"No comment."

"Civil rights—"

"No comment."

"Here's your floor, Mr. Burke," the attendant said quickly, and then turned to the girl. "You must come down to the first floor with me."

She turned angrily. "Oh, buzz off!"

A heavyset, gray-haired lady rushed up from the concierge's desk at the end of the hall, her large key chain dangling at her waist, her ample flesh, encased in stays, swaying rigidly from side to side. She took in the situation at once and quickly opened Burke's door. Once he and Sarah were inside she slammed it and stood guard. "Go below," they heard her shout in broken English, "or I will have you removed."

Sarah leaned up against the door. "Whew!"

Burke laughed. "I was hoping we could have a drink in the bar and then a quiet dinner in the restaurant downstairs. But that's out of the question now." He took her in his arms and kissed her lips lingeringly, so that her knees threatened to collapse as her bones melted. "Mmm," he whispered, "you taste good. I'd forgotten how good."

She clutched him tightly, her arms caressing his broad muscular shoulders. "Oh, Burke, you *feel* so wonderful," she murmured. "I've missed you so much. I'm so glad you're here."

He kissed her again, deeply, and she trembled at the insistent pressure of his body. He looked down into her eyes as she ran her fingers along his strong unshaven jaw. Then he grinned. "I'm not in the habit of running halfway across the world—" The telephone interrupted his sentence. His muttered expletive mildly shocked Sarah.

Breaking away from her gently as the phone continued to ring, he said, "Sorry, babe, but I left word not to be disturbed unless it was an overseas call." He picked up the heavy, old-fashioned receiver. "Yes?" He listened a moment and then scowled. "Very well," he said tersely. "Come up, Sir Basil." He dropped the receiver impatiently into its cradle, whirled around and glared at Sarah. "What in the hell does *he* want?"

She made a helpless little gesture. "In all...the excitement," she stammered, "I forgot...to tell you the news...."

He frowned. "The news?"

She paused, nonplussed. It was an inconvenient moment to bring him up-to-date, but he was looking at her questioningly. He deserved an answer. What would be the most tactful way to explain? "I'll let Basil explain...."

"Explain *what*? I don't understand all this mystery! Downstairs you said that there was nothing between you two, and now—"

"Burke," she broke in quickly, "what Basil is going to talk to you about has nothing to do with him and me. That's a professional relationship, as I told you before." She saw that he was still unconvinced. "This has to do with *business*." There was a knock on the door. "Burke," she said quietly, "be nice, *please*."

He opened the door. "Good afternoon, Sir Basil," he said gravely.

"It's good to see you again, Mr. Burke," Basil replied formally, gazing intently into his face, and Sarah knew that he was coldly evaluating his appearance. Was he seeing Burke holding up the test-tube bottle in the commercial? He nodded at Sarah. "Have you told him?"

She shook her head. They exchanged glances, and she tried to convey to him that he had arrived at an inopportune moment. He was a sensitive man, accustomed to sizing up situations quickly, and he did not disappoint her now. Smiling cordially, he said, "Mr. Burke, I have a business proposition that I hope you'll accept."

Burke, in turn, seemed to size him up in an instant, and apparently decided to be gracious. *He can afford to be gracious,* Sarah thought. A man with no rival.... He actually smiled. "Would you like a drink, Sir Basil?"

"I took the liberty of ordering a bottle of Fendant

downstairs," he replied. "A local wine that is most refreshing. I hope that we will be able to cap our discussion this afternoon with a toast to a successful association."

Brown eyes narrowed, still assessing, Burke indicated a leather chair by the roaring fireplace. "Won't you sit down?"

"Thank you. Could we call each other by our Christian names? I dislike formality between equals. The 'sir' somehow embarrasses me. I suppose it's because my title was conferred rather than inherited."

There was a knock on the door, and a waiter brought in a chilled bottle and three glasses on a tray.

"Now," Basil said, "first of all I'd like to say that I've always had a great appreciation for your work, Steve. The kind of roles you've always played appeals to my inner image of myself." He laughed. "Which contrasts starkly with my actual appearance. Anyway, I understand that the picture-making business is in a state of flux, and I do know something about financing. Before I came over here I made a couple of calls to London. If *Devil's Dare* is to be completed the way the script calls for, presuming there are no more delays, the production company will need an infusion of some five hundred thousand dollars."

Burke nodded briefly. "That's also my understanding."

Basil took a long breath and went on with conviction. "I am willing to present you with the completion money, plus a bit more. Our lawyers will have to work out the conditions and terms.''

"Oh?"

"I am not making this offer out of the goodness of my heart. Naturally I have a proposition—so please hear me out.'' He brought his hands together in a prayerlike attitude; he was all supplication! ''As you know, my main business is men's toiletries. . . .''

And Burke was all sarcasm. ''Your after-shave lotion makes me break out.''

"Me, too,'' Basil laughed. "I use Brut!'' They were cool and prepared, Sarah thought, both of them. "I have wanted to enter the women's cosmetic field for years, but I could never find a product that was revolutionary enough to make the stab. But just recently I've come across a fabulous—and I don't use that word often—perfume that deserves to be put over in an extraordinary manner. Sarah has conceived an unusual concept that I like very much. I hope that you will be agreeable.''

Burke looked coolly at Sarah, then again directed his unnerving gaze at Basil.

"Go on.''

Basil smiled. "Steve, the perfume bottle is going to be shaped like a test tube—but with a flat bottom, of course—and will be black and gold.'' He paused to draw another deep breath. "Your professional image as an adventurer should grow even stronger with this secret-agent role.'' He paused again and leaned forward. When he went on his voice was so persuasive that Sarah marveled at the change that had come over him. A tinge of respect shivered through her as she witnessed Basil Northcombe in action for the first time. He was as polished a performer in the living room as Burke was on the screen. "We want to place a color advertisement in several high-circulation magazines of you with the test tube in your hand. There will be only one caption: "The scent of a woman.... It's sinful."

Burke looked up quizzically. "That's *all*?"

Basil nodded and examined his manicure.

Burke stood up and went to the window. The silence in the room grew until it seemed that the four walls would crumble from sheer tension. Savoring the moment, he turned around slowly, his face grave. "That would be all? Nothing else?"

Basil smiled. "That's all. No couples waltzing in the background or a man playing a violin. Just you— in a big, book-filled library."

Burke paced the room slowly, charging it with his brand of electricity. "What else? A television commercial?"

Basil nodded. "The same lines."

"Sinful.... Is that the name of the perfume?"

Sarah grimaced. "No. Basil neglected to mention that we haven't thought up a name yet."

Burke frowned. "I'll have to know. If I do this damn-fool thing, I tell you right now, I won't push something called Rosepetal or Pansy, or some such...."

Basil held up his hands. "We've got to come up with a name that's unique. I promise it won't be embarrassing."

Burke turned back to the window for a moment. "I'll have to get some input on this from my agent and my lawyer in Hollywood," he mused. "And I'll also have to think about it myself. This is a big step. I've never endorsed anything—and people have been at me for years. I've turned down everything from Scotch to razor blades." He smiled suddenly. "I'll admit this would be a departure for me—very unexpected. Of course, that might be fun! Look what happened to Burt Reynolds when he posed for the *Cosmopolitan* centerfold—complete controversy, which helped his career!" He paused and cleared his throat. "What it all boils down to, I guess, Basil, is that I've got to do this thing—if I want *Devil's Dare* finished. And it *must* be finished." Then he went on, more to himself than to them. "It's good; I know it's good. The footage is just great. We've filmed parts of the world that've never been seen in a motion picture—not even travelogues. It's all fresh. . . ." He paused, then went on quickly. "Basil, I don't see any point in pussyfooting around. If you guarantee that the job will be done in the best of taste, I'll go along with the proposition."

"With Sarah in charge, Steve, I don't think you'll have cause to worry." He scowled at Sarah. "Don't you think you'd better tell Steve your stipulation, love?"

"Stipulation? I thought you were the one with the money, Basil. But I suppose it is Sarah's campaign." Steve waited for her to tell him, his brown eyes boring into her across the opulent room.

"You can have one million dollars for the ads— but only if you agree that Samsqua will not be used in the film."

Her words hung like deadweight. Steve didn't bat an eyelash. "It means that much to you, does it?" he murmured to her alone, ignoring Basil's excited glances between them.

"Yes."

Steve halted his pacing at the window, and looking out at the spectacular view said, "I'm sorry, then."

"You mean you won't do it?" Basil's well-bred calm deserted him; he seemed to be genuinely upset.

Sarah just stared at Burke.

"Of course, I'll do it. That picture will be finished, and it will be finished on Samsqua." He whirled around to fix steely brown eyes on Sarah. "Your grandmother has already promised me her full cooperation. Or have you forgotten that Samsqua belongs to her?"

"You can't mean that!" she cried. "Grandlady wouldn't go against me like this! She must be losing her reason." Sarah's mind groped feebly for a way out, some other way to stop him. But she sensed she had lost.

"Then we withdraw the offer. No deal." Her voice

was hard, but her trembling lips betrayed how upset she was.

"Sarah!" Basil exclaimed sternly. "I want to talk to you—alone." He shot a meaningful glance at Steve.

"I'll be in my bedroom," said the silky-smooth actor's voice. "Do let me know if you need me," he said to Sarah, in a voice that implied more than it stated.

"Sarah," Basil said when Steve's door closed quietly behind him, "we have to make concessions to him. I want him in those ads. I'm sorry to say this, Sarah, but if Burke goes my account goes, too."

Miserably Sarah conceded Burke's victory. She felt betrayed—betrayed by Burke, grandlady, and now even Basil. All right, she thought, let him have the damned island! If grandlady didn't care why should she?

"We have a deal, Mr. Burke," Basil was saying as he walked from Burke's bedroom with him. Steve just smiled at Sarah. "I'm so glad."

His patronizing manner was worse than sarcasm. He was infuriating! Had he no feelings, no compunction? Then the businesswomen took over, and Sarah mentally squared her shoulders, preparing to show her professionalism.

"We have a deal, Mr. Northcombe, *Ms*. Mackenzie." Steve nodded at them each in turn. "Now, I've got a company and crew on hiatus, on their way back to Hollywood. The final chase will take two weeks to shoot—'' he glanced at Sarah ''—which we will do on Samsqua. Can I get this stuff done for you soon—like in the next few days—so that we can use the island while there's still a good snowpack?''

Basil looked questioningly at Sarah, who nodded. ''I can get the same crew that shot Madame Celina's commercial, and Marial will do the still photography for the ad. It can be done very quickly.''

Burke held out his hand to Basil. ''Pleasure dealing with you.''

Basil shook his hand, made a shallow bow, then poured out three glasses of Fendant. ''Here's to all of us. As Confucius says, 'With fire enough, we can cook anything; with money enough, we can do anything.' ''

''Amen,'' Burke said. ''Also, 'Where no money is spent, there is no grace gained.' ''

Sarah shot an angry glance at him. ''It should also not be forgotten that 'An image maker never worships idols.' '' And with more bravado than she felt she tossed back the fiery liquid.

''Now that we've thrown that around,'' Basil said, suddenly all business, ''I have some telephoning to do if we are to get this project off the ground in any kind of fashion!''

Burke nodded. ''I'll call my agent and my business manager.'' He glanced at his watch. ''It will be eight o'clock in the morning in Los Angeles, but that's too bad. It's time both those guys earned their commissions.'' He paused. ''You'll hear from us tomorrow morning, Basil.''

"Not too early now, Steve!" he replied humorously, and they shook hands again. He turned to Sarah. "I'll see you later. We have a great deal to discuss."

After he had made his exit with a characteristic bow, Sarah announced she would get some fresh air on the balcony that overlooked Zermatt. Her head was light from the alcohol, and the stiff, cold breeze should help rid her of that befuddled feeling. She was hardly in the mood for a dinner date with Steve now!

It was quite obvious that he cared little or nothing for her feelings—and, therefore, for Sarah herself, she concluded. She had told him more about herself and her childhood than anyone in the world—about how much Samsqua meant to her—and he had thrown it back in her face. So much for friendship. The lights of the town twinkled against the bluish-tinged snow, and sounds from various nightspots drifted up to Sarah's ears.

If only she could trust him she might be able to understand him. She smiled at the thought, which sounded to her like complete nonsense. But she knew it was true—and that trust was hard to achieve. She still kept her barriers up, still couldn't look into the depths of his brown eyes and give back to him what she saw there. It was *she* who guarded her innermost self, and it would take aeons for any one person to win her trust—and friendship—again. She thought of her life on Samsqua—a rough, isolated life—and she thought of her penthouse in Manhattan—just as isolated but in a different way. She'd never had many friends, and supposed Johanna was the closest thing to a confidante she'd ever known.

She felt a chill run through her, resolving at that moment to strive for a pleasant evening with Steve. She would make the most of their time together; his presence seemed to give her new life. But once he went back to filming, thanks to Sarah's own back-fired plan, she knew she'd need all the support she could get from other sources.

Suddenly she sensed Steve behind her. He put his arms around her waist and stood with his body pressing up against hers. Bending his tall frame to kiss her highly sensitive nape, he then turned her around and met her mouth with his warm lips in a kiss so gentle and fleeting she wondered whether it had really happened. "Thank you," he said quietly, "for saving *Devil's Dare*. If you hadn't come up with this endorsement idea I'd have had to give up...a lot of what I believe in." This was a strange statement. Why didn't he just say he'd lose a lot of *money*?

Taken aback by his method of thanking her, Sarah replied flippantly, "Anything I can do to keep movie stars in their place—I'm talking about California, of course." She breezed back into the hotel suite, holding her arms against a new wave of shivers. "You know, it's going to cost you more privacy in the long run. Your picture will be plastered all over the continent—North America, I mean. But maybe Europe, too. Mmm, I'll have to ask Basil about that...."

"What have I got to lose?" He shrugged, lit a cigarette and settled into one of the plush sofas. "Besides, if Sir Laurence Olivier can do commercials, who am I to refuse?" Strange how Basil had drawn the same comparison.

He poured another two glasses of wine, and Sarah felt the clear pungent liquid gradually warm her insides, although outside she was still chilled despite the thick cashmere sweater. Steve held his glass up for a toast, and as he did so the wine caught the light from the crackling flames leaping in the old stone fireplace. "To us," he said simply. "To what we both want in the world: may they be the same things."

It was said with such seriousness that Sarah's heart gave a terrible lurch, and she almost choked on the wine. But her eyes seemed locked into Steve's brown depths, and at that moment she prayed all her barriers were firmly intact, for the awesome realization came to her that she was truly in love with this man. She longed to settle into his arms and feel his strength again, because she definitely needed it now. A nervous giggle rose in her throat. Tearing her gaze from his penetrating look, she put her wineglass down, mumbling something about getting tipsy. He seemed to find that amusing, and she began to wish fervently that the dinner he'd ordered would arrive.

"Do you realize that in the two months we've known each other this is really the first time we've been alone, without someone hovering nearby?"

She could only nod, then said, "Yes, funny isn't it?"

"I don't think it's in the least bit funny, Sarah Mackenzie." He was coming toward her, his long legs towering over her. She forced herself to look straight ahead, unflinching, and cursed herself for acting so teenagerish. His leg muscles were straining against the faded blue denim of his jeans. His arms were reaching down to lift her from her perch on the sofa to face him.

"You're so beautiful," he murmured as his hands ran over her hair and traced down her neck. "Soft." He caressed her nape and toyed with the hair there before kissing her tenderly on the lips.

To hold anything back in her response would have been the worst kind of torture. She loved him. She loved his caresses and his kisses and the sandy-blond hair through her long fingers. Her back arched of its own volition, and she molded her body to his, feeling his desire and loving the fire that was creeping into her loins.

A sharp knock on the door caused Steve to gradually draw away from her, smiling that boyish smile as if they'd been caught at something. One tanned finger extended to tap her lightly on her nose. Then he went to answer the door.

Sarah, freshening up in the luxurious bathroom, was stunned at her appearance. Her curls were askew, her mascara slightly smudged and her lips ruby red from Steve's kiss. She was flushed, too, and her eyes glowed with a light from deep within. They really did sparkle, she mused. After a quick repair job she hurried back to Burke and their waiting meal, a delicious beef bourguignon with rice pilaf and a tempting Caesar salad.

"I'm absolutely famished," she said, and meant it. She attacked the meal with such gusto that on several occasions she looked up to find Burke smiling curiously at her. "Well, I'm hungry," she would pout, and get back to it.

As they were finishing the telephone rang. While he spoke long distance to Hollywood Sarah had two cups of very strong hot coffee, which she drank while sitting on the hearth. When he joined her his grin was even wider than usual. "My agent is shooting for a million. What do you think? Am I worth it?"

She laughed with him, trying to appear sophisticated and at ease discussing that amount of money. "Seriously, Burke, a million dollars? Sir Basil is agreeing to that?"

"That's for the lawyers to work out. We'll see."

She wanted to ask him about his future plans, but was afraid it might seem prying. Instead she concentrated on trying to find a name for Sir Basil's perfume. It had to be perfect—zingy yet classy, sophisticated yet simple. Foreign sounding or down-home earthiness...?

Once again the telephone interrupted. "That will be my lawyer, grumpy and upset because he's been woken up before business hours, L.A. time." Before he picked up the phone he raised his dark brows and quipped, "He hasn't been up this early since he was cramming for his bar exam!" Steve was back a few moments later, shaking his head. "I was wrong. He's been up for an hour and a half, fighting with Basil's barrister in Zurich." He lowered himself beside her on the hearth and shook his head. "We've got a deal," he said soberly. "Nine hundred thousand dollars for the commercials and the magazine ads." He reached for her hand. "Thanks, Mackenzie. It means a lot."

"I can understand that," she said, a hint of sarcasm adding a frosty layer to her voice. She'd heard that Hollywood people had absolutely no idea of the value of money anymore, and here was living proof. And she thought *her* values were confused! But then, she reminded herself, he *was* using the bulk of the money to finance *Devil's Dare*. She mustn't judge him too harshly, just because she'd lost out personally on the deal.

The telephone rang insistently, and he sighed, got up slowly and picked up the receiver. "Hello.... Yes, Basil?" He paused, and a smile creased his face. "Yes, thank you, I'm very pleased. Now Sarah has to come up with a decent name for the perfume. How about Bold Journey? What? Well, it was a thought anyway...." He turned to Sarah. "He wants to speak to you."

She reached out and placed the receiver to her ear. "Very well. Yes, I understand." She hung up thoughtfully. "The sleigh is outside. I've got to go back to the chalet. Basil's been dictating notes to Gail, and we've loads of paperwork to complete— Oh, yes," she added, "be at the railway station at seven o'clock tomorrow morning. Basil has us booked on an afternoon flight from Zurich to New York." He was coming toward her, and she said quickly as she moved to the doorway, "I'll see you tomorrow, then. Thank you—"

"Damn the sleigh. You're staying here. When will we have another chance?" He perched himself on the sofa arm, looking for all the world like some banal commentator on a TV travelogue, completely without interest in the discussion going on. Perhaps he should call in his agent to negotiate with her to stay the night! Was the man without any...conscience, her weary heart cried.

"Good night," was all she said as she picked up her coat and headed for the door.

It wasn't until she was bundled in the sleigh and halfway to the chalet that she let the tears drop from her eyes. She was being forced to compromise—a few days here, a night there—where no compromise could be made. Her love was full-blown, even though her mind screamed accusations at Steve. He wanted her—that much seemed to be obvious. But like every other man, once he had her she would be cast aside for a fresher newer model. She would not be used again. "Damn!" she muttered as she dashed the tears roughly from her cheeks. All her life she'd been alone and quite happy about it, and then a man had come along to not only cause feverish responses in her body, but also to create total chaos in her mind. She wasn't even sure about her career anymore—and *that* was a miracle in itself.

As the sleigh cut through the solitude of the snowy countryside, Sarah rested her head against the deep red velvet upholstery and sighed wistfully. Nothing short of a miracle would make Steve hers.

Hers. Not for one night, or a year, but forever.

CHAPTER TWELVE

IT SEEMED TO SARAH that she had discarded a thousand names for the new perfume. Finally at midnight, when sleep was impossible, she opened an international dictionary and started with the first word: *Aa*, which she discovered was a Hawaiian word meaning a *bed of solidified lava with a rough surface*. She read further, marking down on a piece of paper the words *abandon, accession, amorous*.... At three o'clock in the morning she had finished adding *dovetail* to the list. Then she found *obelisk*, and later, at dawn, she had reached *zephyr*.

She poured herself a cup of coffee and checked her watch. It was 3:00 P.M. in Zermatt. She put through a call to Basil Northcombe.

"Sarah!" he exclaimed. "Have you come up with a name?"

"No. That's what I'm calling about. I'm so desperate, I've just gone through the entire dictionary. I've found two words that I'm not entirely sure about...."

"Well, don't keep me in suspense."

"Are you sitting down? What image does *obelisk* conjure up for you?"

"Egypt. Tombs. Mummies. Daddies."

"Be serious, Basil. Frankly, I don't like it, either." She cleared her throat. "How does *zephyr* strike you?"

"It's too damned difficult to pronounce. What does it mean?"

"It's the west wind."

"West wind?" He paused. "Maybe the problem is finding one word. Maybe that's what's thrown us off. How about *two* words?"

"How can I come up with two words," she wailed, "when I can't even think of *one*?"

"Now, don't get cross, dear. Maybe the right name will come out of the blue, which I believe is an old American expression."

"That's not bad.... Out of the Blue."

"You're concentrating too hard. Goodbye, Sarah."

"Goodbye, Sir Basil."

THE JOURNEY TO SAMSQUA was very cold. One couple, whom Sarah had known since school days, and an acoustic expert who had been commissioned by Luis Farraday for work on the Running Mallow, were the only other people on board.

"I wouldn't make the trip at all," Else Sanchez groused, pulling the bill of her cap down over her forehead, "except for Thanksgiving. I'd never hear the end of it if I didn't. I've lost money on the last two trips. Oh, I wish Sanchez were alive."

Sarah examined Else's face, and for the first time

saw pain and suffering mirrored in her eyes. Else had always been a part of the *Griffin*, and she'd always seemed like a fixture instead of a human being. How strange that a woman whom she had known all of her life had never been important to her before. Sarah's own selfishness shocked her now. "Else," she said quietly, "if you don't have other plans for dinner tomorrow, come and have turkey with us, will you please?"

Else stared straight ahead, her hands gripping the wheel with more force than necessary to guide the boat. "Why, thank you," she murmured, her husky voice breaking slightly. Then she grabbed for a handkerchief. "I've got this darned cold and...."

Sarah turned away quickly to save the woman any embarrassment, and thought, *this is for you, Sanchez, for all those years that you devoted to grand-lady. How thoughtless we've been to your widow, how uncaring. How selfishly we've all behaved.* When she turned back to the bow Else was still dabbing at her eyes.

Samsqua came into view through the mist. By the time the *Griffin* had reached the wharf the weather had cleared, and the island was revealed in the crisp bright noonday sunshine that illuminated all the crags and crevices on High Mountain, pristine in its snow-clad beauty. For all of the joy of coming home, the moment was marred because she was alone. *Oh, Burke,* she thought, *where are you when I need you so much?*

"PEASE-PORRIDGE HOT, pease-porridge cold, pease-porridge in the pot, nine days old!" Luis Farraday recited at the top of his voice as he opened the door to Glass Cottage.

"It's not pease-porridge and it's not nine days old. It's fish chowder," Johanna cried, coming in from the kitchen in her tattered old blue firing smock, holding floured hands up in the air. "I'm making biscuits," she explained. "Give me a kiss."

"My, you're in a good mood, Miss Jo!" Sarah said, following Johanna into the kitchen.

She laughed. "And why shouldn't I be in a topper frame of mind?" She stood back with the biscuit cutter and curtsied. "The windows are almost finished."

"Great! Aren't you way ahead of schedule?" Sarah asked.

"Yes! All the glass is cut and waxed down on the cartoon. I've only to etch in the faces on the figures, and then Hans and Henry take over and finish the leading."

"Can I go downstairs and take a peek?" Sarah asked.

"Go look. I'll finish my baking." Johanna paused, and then went on with a quaver in her voice. "Besides, I can't bear to see the expression on your face if you... don't like them."

"Silly goose," Sarah said, patting her on the shoulder.

The door to the studio was locked and she knocked lightly.

"Just a moment," came Hans's soft Viennese voice.

The door swung open and he cautioned, "Don't look at the worktable; look up in the mirror above the door." Sarah glanced upward. The reflection revealed all three stained-glass windows illuminated by fluorescent lights. The effect was breathtaking.

"They're magnificent!" she cried. "Truly magnificent!"

Hans nodded. "Now turn around and look at the detail."

She traced the story of Samsqua with her fingers in the air above the glass pieces, and when she came to High Mountain she said, "Look, that's Burke and I discovering Uneema's gravestone!" Tears filled her eyes. "It's very touching to see it all there—my childhood, really."

"That's me in the blue pinafore," Lucia Concannon called from the top of the staircase. "Miss Jo hasn't put my face on yet, but that's me."

"Happy Thanksgiving, grandlady." Sarah flew up the stairs and planted a kiss on her cheek. "But I've got a bone to pick with you...."

At that moment a peculiar sound reverberated over the studio. Grandlady frowned and then exclaimed, "A whirlybird! My God, I haven't heard the sound of one of those since the war! Don't tell me my Seabees are coming back for turkey dinner!" She rushed to the window. Five hundred feet away, beyond Johanna's gate, the helicopter was setting down on a wide patch of sweet wanda. The blades slowly rotated to a standstill, and a dark-clad figure emerged. "Well, I do declare," grandlady muttered. "It's your actor fellow!"

"Oh, this is fantastic!" Sarah cried. "He's come after all!" She pulled on her camel's-hair coat and was out the door a moment later.

Sarah's heart leaped as she rushed toward him. It was like one of those television commercials, she reflected, shot in slow motion with two lovers floating over a field toward each other. Only this scene had just one lover.... Time seemed suspended, but at last she flew into Steve's arms. "Wow," he exclaimed, laughing, "it's good to see you, too." He kissed her and they walked slowly back to Glass Cottage.

"You're so quiet," he said. "Do holidays always affect you this way?"

She shook her head. "I'm just a little dazed, that's all. I had prepared myself for your being in California."

He grinned and pushed back his mop of sun-bleached hair from his forehead. "Well, I'm not!" Then he stopped and turned toward her. "But this is mostly business, babe. I have to get some things cleared up for the chase scene."

Sarah's heart felt like it was being crushed. What a fool she'd made of herself, running to him like that! How could she have thought for one second that he'd come to see her? Business, business, business. There's no business like show business.

She hadn't realized she'd spoken aloud until Steve laughed. "No, there's not—except maybe the crazy advertising world of Madison Avenue. Let's have a truce, okay? I thought we were friends, right?"

Oh, how she hated his rational mundane comments in the face of her emotional turmoil! But she schooled her features and managed to give him a brilliant smile. "Of course, we're friends, Steve. After all, I've helped you and you've helped me. We should be very rich people as a result of this campaign."

"Very rich," Steve said with an odd note in his voice.

They continued walking slowly. "You know," he said in an alarmingly serious voice, "I've decided that certain things in life should take priority. I've always had my fingers into everything to do with my pictures—even areas that didn't really concern me— because I always felt I had to be in charge somehow. It was my overactive sense of responsibility, I guess. Anyway, I find that those kinds of details don't really interest me anymore. I can hire people to do a lot of the work. I think, after *Devil's*, I'll get right out of acting and do mostly producing, maybe some directing. Anyway—" his mood seemed to change again "—I knew I'd missed the *Griffin*, so I rented the helicopter in Boston. And you, Miss Mackenzie, make it all worthwhile." He twirled Sarah around, his gaze roaming hungrily over her.

Sarah looked a vision in high, dark brown boots, a tweedy beige skirt that showed her curves to advantage and a silky blouse in a champagne color.

"Don't be silly," she said, looking down at her simple outfit. "Business is your priority this weekend, right?" She should have held her tongue, immediately regretting the provocative words. "I have priorities, too, I'm afraid—like thinking up a name for Basil's perfume. I'm getting wild. I've got some kind of mental block that I can't get free of! I walk down Fifth Avenue in the evening, and the streetlights flash on and I think, Starry Bright, Heaven's Glow, Night Flame. I get up in the morning and I think, Scarlet Dawn, Pink Morning...." She sighed. "All junky names. I haven't had an original thought since I got back from Zermatt."

He squeezed her around the waist. "It will come," he said. "I know it will...."

Later, when they were having coffee in Johanna's kitchen, grandlady leaned forward. "What does Needlepoint House look like from up in the air?"

"Very beautiful." Burke leaned forward. "If you like, I'll take you up."

She colored and held up her hands. "I couldn't possibly!" She swallowed. "Is it safe?"

"When I flew over from Boston this morning the trip was as smooth as silk. Come on, the outing will do you good."

"You'll be careful?"

"You can't be serious, grandlady," Johanna scoffed. "Don't even consider it at your age."

Lucia Concannon looked at her granddaughter quizzically. "Age has nothing to do with it, Miss Jo! Come on, Sarah, let's do it!"

"But grandlady!" both girls cried.

"Come on, Mr. Burke, let's get cracking!"

Down at the beach Burke strapped Lucia Concannon and Sarah firmly into the bucket seats of the helicopter.

"Easy does it," he said, winking at Sarah. He started the motors, and as the blades began to rotate faster and faster the small craft shimmied and shook. Lucia Concannon gripped the sides of her seat in anticipation of the ordeal ahead, though she continued to stare stoically at the instrument panel. "Let me know...when you're up...young man," she quavered, trying to control her voice and not succeeding.

"We're already up about five hundred feet," Burke yelled over the din. "See, there's nothing to it!"

"We are?"

"Sure," Burke said. "Look, there's the shipwreck."

The old woman continued to stare ahead.

"Oh, look," Burke cried, pointing below. "Needlepoint House!"

Grandlady allowed her gaze to move slowly to the right, then peered below. The newly shingled roof of the old house stood out brightly from the surrounding terrain covered with snow. "Why, it looks so different from up here," she exclaimed breathlessly, and became as excited as a child. "It's huge. Oh, I wish Augustus were still alive to see this!" She gazed out beyond the island, across the expanse of blue green water to the coastline of Maine. "It's so beautiful and so *clear*." She was lost in admiration. "Oh, could we fly over the village?"

"You haven't seen anything yet."

As the craft hovered over the wharf grandlady laughed out loud. "It looks like a picture postcard from up here. Can you get down a bit lower?"

Sarah exchanged glances with Steve. "Sure thing, grandlady," and he dipped to the right. She drew in a fresh breath of air. As they flew over the Sea of Spiders, she examined the estuary carefully. "Oh, I was wondering if you can see the little secret nook from here—and you can! That's where Augustus and I used to have picnics." She colored with remembrance, and for a moment she looked young again. "Lovers always have a way of finding these secret places."

"Look, grandlady," Sarah exclaimed, pointing below, "there's the windward side of the island. You get a different impression of Needlepoint House from here. It looks like a fortress."

She nodded. "It surely does! Would you go around the entire island again? I want to get a bird's-eye view!"

Fifteen minutes later, after they had circled the

island three times, Burke shouted to grandlady, "We'd better head back."

"Oh, must we?"

"It's time for dinner," Sarah said, "and we've got to help Johanna."

Grandlady sighed. "I suppose we must." She turned to Burke. "Can we do this again sometime, young man? This is one of my most memorable experiences."

"Yes, grandlady," he replied with a grin, "we can do it again."

They were nine for Thanksgiving dinner, but the table was set for ten.

"It's an island tradition," Lucia Concannon announced from the head of the table. "Who knows when an uninvited guest may come? All are welcome today."

They were all crowded around Johanna's kitchen table, which had been expanded to its fullest extent. To Lucia Concannon's right were seated Luis, Edna Lowery, Henry and Sarah; to her left were Burke, Else, Hans and Johanna.

The men wore suits and ties, and the women long skirts. Even Johanna, Sarah noted with pride, was suitably dressed in a low-cut gold paisley chiffon, which, although at least five years old, had obviously been worn only once or twice. The material had lost none of its crispness.

Sarah looked down at her own severely tailored, water-green silk suit, and felt horribly overdressed.

The outfit didn't need additional ornamentation, although she could not resist wearing Burke's emerald necklace. Only grandlady, in her electric-blue satin and diamond earrings, looked truly incongruous. But that was to be expected—along with Edna's usual black bombazine.

The only true surprise of the evening was the appearance of Else Sanchez, who wore a maroon wool dress with a high neck. She had curled her short dark hair, and while the result was somewhat frizzled, she managed to look not like a weather-beaten sea captain, but rather a handsome if sedate matron. Of course, her hands were rough and callused, and she did nothing to hide them. She was a very proud woman.

Steve had carved the turkey when Luis confessed that he could passably bone a trout, but knew nothing whatsoever about fowl.

After dinner they all retired to the living room, where Johanna and Sarah served rum and Coca-Cola—not an island tradition, but grandlady's prerequisite for holidays.

After the second round of drinks, when the mood of the group grew livelier, Luis Farraday stood up and raised his glass aloft. "I wish to make a toast. To my bride-to-be, Johanna Mackenzie."

There were gasps of surprise and everyone started to talk at once, until grandlady rose with an air of injured pride. "I'm happy about this announcement, but it seems to me that I, as the oldest member of the

Concannon family, should have been consulted first!"

Johanna laughed. "Grandlady, you've thrown us together from the very beginning. There hasn't been a day that you haven't brought up the subject of marriage in one way or another." She sighed. "We've decided to have a December wedding, so we've got to get the invitations in the mail soon...."

Else Sanchez stood up. "My goodness," she exclaimed. "I forgot your mail, Miss Jo. Something special." She removed a long business envelope from her purse. "It's from the Gate Gallery in Portland," she announced, handing the envelope to Johanna.

Johanna opened the letter with trembling fingers, slowly read the contents, then allowed it to slip to the floor. Her face positively lit up, and she sank down beside Luis. She looked at Steve, who was grinning smugly. "When...?" she stammered. "Why...?"

"Well, what is it?" Lucia Concannon exclaimed. "You look like you've stepped on someone's grave! Give it to me!"

Hans handed the letter to her, and her lips moved as she read the long paragraphs. Then she, too, let the letter slide from her fingers.

"What *is* going on?" Sarah asked.

Grandlady was the first to regain her composure. "It's from the Gate Gallery in Portland. They received the photographs from Mr. Burke along with his description of Johanna's works, and they want to exhibit her entire studio of curios!''

AFTER THEY HAD EACH CONSUMED two slices of pumpkin pie and several cups of coffee, Lucia Concannon looked out the window. "Ah," she said with a sigh, "we must go outdoors. The northern lights are playing over the sky, all the way down from Canada.''

Everyone followed her out to the patio, including Mustapha, who had just come from the studio. They watched the bright sky flames, muted gold and orange mixed in with several shades of deep red, shoot intricate patterns over the horizon.

"I wish there were an orchestra here," Johanna said, drawing close to Luis. "A symphony would be perfect to accompany the lights, don't you think, grandlady?''

"Yes," she replied. "The *Symphonie pathétique* would be wonderfully suitable.''

Hans nodded. "It is a most beautiful sight. I've never seen such colors before.''

"It's like—" the old lady fought for words "—like. . . a winter fire.''

There was a lull in conversation, then Sarah quietly repeated, "Winter fire. Winter fire?" She stood up and shouted, raising her hands above her head in a triumphant gesture, "That's *it*! Winter Fire!''

Everyone looked at her in sudden panic.

"What's got into Miss Sarah? Are you feeling all right?" grandlady asked solicitously.

"Indeed, she *is* all right," Burke announced with a flourish of his hand, bowing low in his best Elizabethan screen manner. "Grandlady, you have just named Sir Basil Northcombe's new perfume. It's Winter Fire!"

CHAPTER THIRTEEN

THE STUDIO where Burke's television commercial was to be shot was located in a huge old building on Fifty-second Street, near the river. It had once been used as horse stables, and on damp rainy days the unmistakable odor of its former inhabitants' mischief wafted to the rafters. However, by November 30 a thick crust of snow had insulated the drafty old place, so that Sarah detected only a certain musty clinging smell. She objected much more strongly to the spicy aroma of the cigar that the director, Vern Halop, was so energetically smoking.

She surveyed the familiar scene. It never ceased to amaze her that it took sixty-five men to shoot a sixty-second piece of film. But the crew was the best Manhattan had to offer, and she was fully confident of the results.

In a tiny corner of the studio the partial set consisted of a very learned-looking library: row upon row of books, purchased "by the yard" from an antique dealer, graced mahogany bookshelves; thick burgundy carpeting complemented a rich, paisley patterned wallpaper; and huge walnut-colored wing chairs were drawn up to a fireplace ablaze with authentic-looking flames that crackled realistically.

Over the set were strung what looked like a hundred lights of all types, shapes and sizes. Yards of spaghetti cable laced the floor.

"Quiet on the set!" the assistant director called.

Halop, a small laconic man, chewed his cigar and drawled, "Let's try a rehearsal, Mr. Burke."

The door opened and Burke strode onto the set. He was dressed in a gray pin-striped suit that accentuated his broad shoulders, along with a pale blue shirt that would look white on screen and a maroon cravat tied in a Windsor knot.

He picked up the test-tube-shaped bottle from the mantel. Looking intently into the camera, he said slowly and distinctly, "The scent of a woman... Winter Fire. It's sinful."

"Thank you," Vern Halop said. "Take five, Mr. Burke. Then let's try it for real." He turned to Sarah. "Good morning. If we're lucky we'll be wrapped up by this afternoon."

"I don't like the way he looks, Vern," she said without preamble.

"Well," Halop replied, "we got the best makeup man in Manhattan." He studied her face carefully. "He did Madame Celina."

She nodded. "He made her look fantastic, but Burke doesn't look rugged enough. He's not a pretty boy!"

Halop sighed softly. "Very well, Miss Mackenzie, but you did say—"

"I know, I'm sorry, but I don't like it."

"Okay." He turned to the gaffer. "Kill the lights!" he shouted.

As the studio went dark Sarah made her way over the cables to Steve's dressing room. He waved when he saw her. "Mornin'," he said lightly. "I'd kiss you, but I'd get some of this goop on you!"

Sarah looked at him closely; then she understood. "Turn around, will you please?"

She saw that the back of his neck was a mass of adhesive tape. The small tabs drew the skin up tightly on each side of his jawbone, which made his chin and neck as smooth as a baby's.

"Oh, God, Steve, what did they do!"

"I didn't realize you wanted this kind of 'look,'" he said, "otherwise I would never have agreed. It's the first time they've used these things on me. I once did a movie with two leading ladies who were a bit past their prime, and they were both tied up like this. They wore wigs and hats and things so the lifts wouldn't show, but they'd go home every night with headaches. I don't know how anyone can act with all this junk on." He patted the tabs on the back of his neck. "And they pull like hell, too." He made a face. "They usually don't start tying up the guys like this unless they're fifty or so."

Sarah shook her head. "I'm so sorry. It's all my fault. My instructions must not have been clear." She couldn't allow such an outrage to Steve. With a heavy sigh, she added, "I'm going to have the make-up man remove everything. I don't even want a base coat; you've got a great tan. I want you to look just the way you do in person." She paused. "You should have raised cain."

He laughed. "I didn't say anything because I assumed you and Basil had got together on this. I'm from the old school, babe, where the director's word is law. Also, I'm being paid a hell of a lot of money to say *nine* words." He grinned. "That's a hundred thou each. Not bad pay, wouldn't you say?" *I think it's disgusting,* she said to herself, reminded once again of how the money was to be used. "For that kind of loot I'd do somersaults," he was saying, then dropped the playful tone. "But seriously, if you want a suggestion...."

"Yes?"

"As it stands I come onto the set, walk to the mantel, pick up the bottle and say my lines." He looked up. "Now I'm not trying to build up my part, but I do think it might be a better introduction if we begin the scene with a close-up of my shoes as I walk down the hall."

"Burke, that's brilliant! I'll tell the director. Anything else?"

"Yes. I'll wash this junk out of my hair."

She paused and kissed his cheek, then grimaced and wiped her lips. "That base coat tastes like Johanna's ceramic glue *smells*!"

He grinned. "That's what you get for getting fresh with an actor!"

"Beast!" she laughed. Then going to the door she

straightened her spine before confronting Vern Halop.

At five-thirty the close-up of Burke's leather shoes was the last shot.

"Okay," the assistant director called wearily, "it's a wrap."

As the commercial union crew dispersed, the photographer, Marial, set up his equipment, which consisted of a four-by-five camera, several lights on stands and a white silk umbrella into which a flashbulb was wired. "This will give me a little diffusion, Sarah," he explained.

"Marial, we've known each other a long time," Sarah replied. "But you don't seem to grasp quite what I want on this assignment. I want you to make Burke look as good as possible—but no diffusion. He must look rugged and natural, the way he looks on the street. I came in this morning to find that the makeup man had plastered five pounds of glop on him, had his hair slicked back and had rigged him up with lifts." She paused. "I think you boys have been shooting too many of those dreamy model types."

Marial winked at her. "You want the macho image, right?"

"He *is* macho, Marial. He doesn't need any help."

"In other words, I shoot the wrinkles?"

She nodded. "All of them!"

"I'm ready if you are, Mr. Burke," Marial called.

Burke was standing in the shadows. "Where?"

"In the chair by the fireplace."

Burke eased himself down into the leather arm-chair, which was bathed in a pool of light. Marial studied him for a moment, then adjusted the camera. "Look right at me, please." He took shot after shot in quick succession, straightened Burke's tie once and twice wiped off beads of perspiration on his fore-head. "Thank you, Mr. Burke."

"You mean that's it?" Steve asked.

"That's it!"

"I'll change and be out in a moment, Sarah!" Burke said. "We'll have time for dinner before I get on the plane."

Marial turned to Sarah. "While he's in the loo, and I'm all set up, how about a shot? You look smashing in that dress. Blue suits you."

She smiled. "Thank you for the compliment, Marial, but I'm not really in the mood."

"Oh, have your picture took," Burke called in a teasing tone. "And later I want him to take us together."

"It's time you were photographed professionally, Sarah," Marial coaxed. "Every time I see one of those candid shots of you in a newspaper, I cringe. You're always worried about clients, but you never think about yourself. Now come over here and sit down!" He quickly arranged several lights in a half circle and posed Sarah before a lowered Austrian drape.

Marial exposed several plates before Burke came in to sit beside her. As Sarah leaned over to kiss his cheek a flashbulb went off.

"You dog," Sarah exclaimed. "Catching us un-aware!"

"Oh, I thought you might like a shot like that to show your grandchildren, that's all," Marial replied casually, sliding another film into the back of the camera.

THAT NIGHT Sarah and Burke stood in the VIP lounge at J.F.K. Airport, drinking sherry and watching the planes land and depart. His plane to Boston was late. "It seems like we're always saying goodbye," Sarah said, trying to smile.

"Can't you come up to Samsqua while we're shooting the chase?"

"I'll try, but I've got the Winter Fire campaign to finalize, and I've been gone from the office so much I'll have tons of paperwork to catch up on."

Inwardly she knew this wasn't the real reason.

He drew her into a sheltered alcove and cupped her face in his hands. "I'll miss you," he murmured as he kissed her tenderly.

"Excuse me, Mr. Burke," an embarrassed airline official put in gently, "but your plane is going to be announced in a few moments."

"Got to go," he whispered. "Avoid the crush, you know. It makes things simpler. See you." Burke kissed her hurriedly again, and was gone.

Sarah found herself waving to a blank wall. Tears stung her eyelids, and she turned away from the mill-ing crowds to the window that overlooked the field.

Her heart ached. Oh, if she could only get on that plane and fly away with him.... She glanced down at the emerald necklace and ran her fingers over the facets of the stone. Then, feeling suddenly alone and very vulnerable indeed, she went out into the hallway and down the ramp to the taxi stand.

"GOOD MORNING, BOSS," Gail said cheerfully as Sarah came into the office.

"Good morning, Gail," she replied, frowning. "And don't call me boss!"

Gail raised her eyebrows. "It's going to be *that* kind of day, eh?"

"I'm afraid so."

Sarah sighed. She didn't feel at all like spending the day cooped up at Duncan-Fairchild. Pausing at the door of her office and counting to ten, she tried hard to think of something pleasant, because she knew that it would take most of the day to read the mail stacked up during her absence. Stoically she opened the door, and then stood back, thunderstruck. Burke's incredibly handsome face stared out at her from every chair and table, and there were additional shots propped up on the floor.

Marial came out from behind the door. "Whad'ya think?" he asked, large brown eyes twinkling brightly in an odd-shaped face.

Sarah zipped around the room, examining each photo in turn. Her dark mood had vanished. "Oh, Marial, they're wonderful." She threw her arms around him and kissed him on the cheek.

"If there's anyone more conceited than an actor, it's a photographer!" he said, basking in the acclaim. "Are you sure they're all right?"

Sarah threw him a long look. "Stop fishing for compliments. You know they're superb! I thought Madame Celina's photos were great—and they were—but you've topped yourself this time, my boy."

"I shouldn't tell you professional secrets, Sarah, but Burke was the easiest person that I've ever found to photograph. I didn't do anything. I just set the camera up and pushed the bulb. People always photograph better when they're either sick or in love." He smiled. "Sarah, I've something to show you." He held up an eleven-by-fourteen-inch color enlargement, and Sarah gazed at her own profile, her lips lightly pressed on Burke's cheek. She was embarrassed that Marial had caught such a personal moment.

"Isn't it gorgeous?" he asked, standing back and admiring his own work.

"It's beautiful, Marial."

He nodded. "The best pictures are never posed," he explained slowly. "Your kiss was spontaneous, and I was all set, ready to shoot, when you leaned over. I just instinctively pressed the bulb in my hand. It really makes a statement, doesn't it?" And the statement was love, Sarah thought. Certainly in Sarah's face. . . and Burke's? Could it possibly be?

"This is a picture for me and me alone," she answered softly. "I don't even want Burke to see it.

I've never been photographed like this before. I look so. . . ."

"Vulnerable?" Gail piped up for her position behind Marial.

Sarah whirled around furiously. "Gail. . .!"

"Oh, boss, don't pay any attention to me. I'm just jealous."

Sarah shook off her sudden displeasure. "What's happened to *your* Mr. Wonderful, Gail?"

"Took one of the neatest powders of the year—and it wasn't Madame Celina's!" She was about to continue when the telephone rang. Gail excused herself, muttering something about actors and photographers and bosses photographed in elegant blue dresses.

Sarah went from one photograph to another, finally selecting three shots of Burke. "These are excellent, Marial. Use whichever has a better negative."

"Now, about retouching. . . ."

"Don't you dare! That's the whole point. This is Steven Burke as he really is." She gazed fondly at the pictures. "Isn't it a crime to be so handsome?"

Marial nodded. "And as a salesman I'll tell you right now, Sarah—he's going to set the cosmetics industry right on its tail!"

THE CHRISTMAS DECORATIONS that trimmed Macy's and Gimbel's department stores in green and red and white were extraordinarily beautiful, Sarah observed from the taxi. It was dusk, and the tiny sparkling colored lights were switching on automatically in store windows as the cab turned up Fifth Avenue.

She had picked up a few presents after work and now felt marvelously relaxed. Shopping always gave her a sense of belonging. There was something about being a part of a large crowd, all engaged in the same kind of "giving" activity, that made her feel humble—especially since she was doing her bit to boost the sagging economy, Sarah thought wryly. She had found the perfect wedding gift for Johanna, an antique cutwork tablecloth with twelve matching napkins, and a pair of eighteenth-century sterling-silver candlesticks.

Her five-day holiday began the next day, and although Ethan Fairchild had grumbled that work was piling up because she had been away so much lately, he had finally waved her out of his office. "All right," he had announced gruffly, "go up to that damned island, but take that William computer manual along so you can at least become familiar with some of those technical terms." He had paused, then laughed. "While arrangements are being made for your sister's wedding, maybe an idea will come out of the blue on how to plan the campaign for that new voice computer."

Sarah had nodded in a cooperative manner, although she had no intention of taking the manual along. This was to be five days of Johanna and Luis and grandlady, and watching Burke film the final chase scene for *Devil's Dare*.

She realized it would probably be the last time she'd ever see him—in the flesh anyway. She hadn't heard from him for three weeks. His check for his part in the Northcombe campaign had gone out over two weeks ago, and she supposed that, money in hand, he would be filming like mad. Though she'd prepared herself for seeing him again on Samsqua while they filmed the final scene, she had no idea how she would endure looking at his picture in magazines and on TV. Perhaps she wouldn't. She would quit and buy a little cottage like Needlepoint House on an island that was not yet spoiled, as Samsqua would surely be with the film's release next spring....

Sarah flew up to Boston on the commuter plane and took a taxi over to the heliport at Boothbay Harbor. Ever since the heavy motion-picture equipment had been brought over on the *Griffin* two weeks before, regular helicopter service had been established between the mainland and the island. Now staples and other supplies were delivered several times each day.

The day was clear, and from her sky view the expanse of water below ran in purplish currents, making a striking design as far as the eye could see. As Samsqua turned from a tiny speck into a lump of land, the pilot slowed the motor. "I have to land a few minutes after twelve o'clock," he announced. "That's when the company breaks for lunch. If I come in earlier, while they're filming, the sound apparatus will pick up the noise of the motor, and I'd really be in dutch.''

He checked his watch, then prepared to land the craft. Sarah noted that the transformation had begun on Samsqua, too. A concrete helipad had been poured over the path of sweet wanda near Glass Cottage. Still, she was entranced at the sight of the snowy island from the air. Apparently they had been filming the shipwreck, because a large platform loaded with gear had been built over the water near the old vessel. As the helicopter descended at a leisurely pace, she saw that Patience Path, leading past the Running Mallow, was congested with bundled-up members of the crew on their way to lunch at the newly opened dining room. A few men looked up and waved as the pilot gently lowered the craft onto the pad. To the right, by the beach, stood a long line of portable buildings, and several large canvas tarpaulins covered literally tons of equipment.

As the pilot helped Sarah from the vehicle she looked around in wonderment. Primrose Path had been widened to allow the passage of vehicles. Shrubs and low-hanging trees had been trimmed on either side of the road. But beyond that nothing else had been touched.

A dark-haired fellow with long sideburns and a mustache, dressed in jeans and red plaid mackinaw, was leaving Patience Path to meet her. He waved, but it was not until she heard the sound of his voice that she recognized Burke. ''This is my makeup for the movie," he said, in response to her astonished look. "I don't want to mess this up," he went on with a grimace, patting his mustache. "It took the makeup man an hour and a half to attach the hairs, one by one!"

She grinned. "I thought you were playing a debonair man of the world. You look like a trapper!"

"Oh, I'm disguised during the first part of the chase," he explained. "But I have to take this stuff off before I swim through the inlet on the windward side of the island with the villain in hot pursuit."

"Swim, Burke? You'll catch your death."

He took her arm and led her up the path to Glass Cottage. "Nonsense," he scoffed. "Come on in. We're having some of Johanna's chowder for lunch." He lowered his voice. "The crew is jealous; they're eating at the Mallow, and the food's pretty ordinary, I gather."

"How are the rooms?"

"Not bad at all. The inside of the inn is all finished. I have what was formerly called the bridal suite. It's got a round bed—one of Luis's follies. Even if I sleep in the middle my feet protrude over the edge."

Sarah noticed several large crates stacked by the gate. "More equipment?" she asked.

Burke shook his head. "No, those are filled with what grandlady calls 'Johanna's curios.' The pilot's going to lift them over to Portland for the exhibit."

"My God," Sarah exclaimed, "I had forgotten the

showing was so soon." She shook her head. "I've been so involved with the Winter Fire campaign that I've forgotten my middle name! If this is Saturday, December 10 and her exhibit opens on the fifteenth— that's next Thursday. And I'm due back in the office on Wednesday." She sighed. "Well, Duncan-Fairchild is just going to be forced to do without their new V.P. for two more days. I wouldn't miss being with her at the exhibit for anything in the world."

"I want to come, too," Burke agreed. "But we'll be doing 'night for night' shooting."

"What?"

"We'll be filming an important part of the chase then. You see, many times in pictures scenes supposed to take place at night are actually shot during the daytime, with a special filter over the camera to make everything look dark. But that's cheating. The audience can always tell because even if it looks like night, there are shadows cast by the sun. *Devil's Dare* is intended to be very realistic, and the director wants the light of the moon shining on the snow—and me and my adversary silhouetted against the sky. There's a scene where I send up flares that fall back on the terrain, so I can aim my gun at the guy who's chasing me. It should be very spooky."

Sarah looked at him strangely. "Speaking of spooky, has Johanna shown you the Sea of Spiders?"

He shook his head. "Why?"

"It's my favorite place on the island, and I want to

share it. After lunch I'll take you over to the spot. It's not far—just below Needlepoint House.''

After they had consumed bowls of delicious chowder Sarah took Burke down Hannah Path and guided him around a huge boulder of pink quartz. "Walk carefully," she cautioned. "The frozen moss is always slippery." They came around the huge trunk of a tree and were greeted by a sudden view of the ocean, framed by giant gaunt trees stripped of autumn finery and covered with ice and snow. The combers, coming in from far out at sea, mixed with the gray water beyond the sandbars, then rushed in over the rocks below.

She took his hand as they picked their way over a pile of stones that looked as if they had been selected by a talented landscape artist—so perfect was the arrangement. "There," she said. "Look below. That's the Sea of Spiders! Years ago the tide came in at this point."

Together they gazed down on an estuary carved out of solid rock and surrounded by several evergreen shrubs. An eerie mist rose from the water, which bubbled like a caldron.

"It's so barren and remote," he said. "You were right; it is spooky."

She shivered, and Burke put his arm around her. "If you weren't here," she said quietly, "I think I'd be afraid. When I was little this place always fascinated me, but frightened me at the same time."

A quicksilver movement in the water below drew

their attention. Very clearly now, as if performing the steps of an intricate ballet, a dozen pink claws reached for a single red leaf floating on top of the water. One creature was quicker than the others, and the leaf disappeared into a frothy mound of bubbles. The calm and beautiful dance suddenly turned into wild primitive movements as the creatures darted to the bottom of the pool.

"This is fascinating—thousands of spiders!" Burke said excitedly. "Are they carnivorous?"

"No, they only feed on the mosses surrounding the pool and the leaves that drop in occasionally. And they're not really spiders—they just look like them. They're really a kind of crab. The sea spiders breed only in this place. There's something about the coastal water that attracts them." She paused. "This terrain suggests buried treasure and evil pirates and square-sailed frigates." She laughed hollowly. "Rather like Madison Avenue!" She smiled. "While we're so near I have something else to show you." She led him up a sandy path, and when a large rock loomed in front of them she let go of his hand and disappeared while Burke's back was turned. There was not a sound.

He called, "Sarah, where are you?"

"Come forward three feet," she answered.

As he walked toward her voice, he saw that the boulder was split in two, and there was just room enough for a human being to slide through the opening. She stood in a protected area, surrounded by rock yet open to the sky. The sweet fragrance of some wild bush that had miraculously survived the snow permeated the air.

"This is where I used to play. Not even Johanna knows about this spot."

"I'm glad you showed it to me." Burke drew her toward him, his strong arms closing around her as he kissed her fervently on the mouth.

She held him tightly, wishing she felt secure in his love, wishing they would never part.... "Oh, Burke, what's going to become of us?"

"You've said that before. All we can do is wait until fate decides." He kissed her more deeply this time, and she responded in the only way she knew—with all her heart. He looked into the depths of her green eyes as if seeing something new there, and a tender smile crinkled his own. "Sarah, love."

He knew she loved him, as surely as if she'd screamed it to the heavens. The relief was immeasurable, but fear crept into her heart. Gail had been right; she had looked vulnerable because she was. Burke would use her for however long he needed her, and she knew now she couldn't refuse him. He was like a magnet, drawing her into his web of male strength and making her want to possess and be possessed. Half of her rejoiced in the thrill of anticipation, but another half cried out in anguish for any sign of love on his part.

"Sarah, would you stay with me tonight at the Running Mallow? Or anywhere. I've got to have you. I've waited so long."

She was lost somewhere in the hands that caressed her windblown hair, the hard maleness that pressed against her pliant body. If she slept with him she *would* be lost—in a far more dangerous way. Steve Burke would be the man she gave her body, herself to, but it was more than that; it would be a commitment, a commitment she couldn't make alone. Along that path was disaster. If he were to leave her after she'd given herself body and soul to him, she couldn't bear it. Couldn't.

"No!" came the involuntary cry from her trembling lips. "I—I'm s-staying with Johanna. All the islanders would know, Steve. I couldn't do that. I could never come home again."

"Damn the islanders and their outmoded morals! What makes it their business anyway? *You love me,* Sarah Mackenzie, and that's my business and yours. No one else's. Not Johanna's, not grandlady's. Stay with me."

"No!" She was crying now, and broke away from him to flee up the path to the safety of Johanna's house. But her mind mocked her flight, racing far ahead of her to the inevitable night when she would sleep with Steven, the night when she would say "yes."

THAT NIGHT Steve asked Sarah to eat at the Running Mallow with the crew. "You won't feel out of place," he kidded, "because we have some other women with us, like the script girl and the wardrobe lady."

"That wasn't what I was thinking about at all," she rejoined. "It's just being there with you...."

"Well, what in God's name is wrong with that?" He was angry again.

She colored. "I mean, everyone will think that... well, you know, one hears about what goes on at movie locations...."

He faced her squarely. "Are you trying to say that you're ashamed to be seen with me? Is that it?"

"No, of course not, Burke! I just don't want all those men, who don't have female companionship here on the island, to think...."

"To think what?" His voice rose.

"Well...." She gestured helplessly.

"To think that we're sleeping together—is that what's bothering you?"

She turned away from him and went to the window overlooking Johanna's patio. He came up behind her, grasped her shoulders and whirled her around. "Answer me!"

"This is not the time, or the place. Johanna will be back with Luis at any moment...." She was flustered and red.

"You brought this up, remember? And if they come in, so what? I'm sure they've had their little fights." He paused and squeezed her shoulders. "I wish I could shake some sense into you. You're behaving like some high-school kid—and don't blame this little episode on that celebrated New England conscience of yours, either!" He let her go and went to the door, then turned back abruptly. His voice was cold, his blustering anger of a moment ago turned frigid. He shook his head. "This is the first serious moment we've had since Zermatt. You know that I'd never embarrass you in front of the crew, and they certainly wouldn't think anything about our being together. And what if they did? I don't know why you're being moralistic all of a sudden...."

Tears were very near the surface, and she did not want him to see her cry. "I just don't want them to think—I mean, it isn't even true!"

He slammed the door, and in the deathly silence Sarah panicked. She couldn't lose him, not now, over such a silly misunderstanding. Flinging the door open, she ran out after him. She looked up Primrose Path, but the bright moonlight showed no moving shadow. Then she turned to the right to the old sailing vessel. There he was, his figure silhouetted against the horizon. She came up behind him slowly, then touched his arm. "We're being silly," she said quietly, paused and then went on with an admission that was very difficult to make. "I...suppose that I was feeling a little guilty when I said I didn't want the crew to think...."

He faced the ocean, giving no indication that he had heard her speak. She swallowed and went on carefully. "Burke, I'm sorry. This is all my fault.... But I wouldn't be in my element. I hate snickers behind my back."

He turned, the moonlight highlighting the deep

furrows in his brow. "Sarah, the first thing you have to realize is that these men are professionals. Each one of them has a job to do—an important job. When we sit down to eat with them tonight—and you're going to be there whether you like it or not— you'll see what I mean. We're not going to be at a head table on a dais. No one will be looking at you. You will simply be my guest." He paused, his voice hoarse. "Frankly they couldn't give one tinker's damn whether we are having an affair or not!"

He took her arm and propelled her up Primrose Path. There was a lengthy silence as they made their way toward the Running Mallow. The tension between them grew until it was an unyielding as a heavy steel band.

A buffet had been set up in the huge dining room decorated in pale green and ivory. Under other circumstances Sarah would have stood back and given her full approval of Luis Farraday's work, enjoying the group's conviviality, but for some reason she felt strange and alienated. The men lined up before the steam table, dressed in comfortable casual clothing, gave her the odd look of approval, but she still felt awkward. Taking small portions of Swiss steak, mashed potatoes and a side dish of coleslaw, she watched Burke heap his plate high with everything from dark buttered bread to string beans with ham.

"We'll eat here by the window," he said in a controlled tone. There was one other person at the table, a tall thin wraith of a man who appeared menacing until he opened his mouth. Then he looked like a rather emaciated version of Santa Claus. His eyes sparkled, and his very white teeth gleamed in the light from the chandeliers.

"Sarah Mackenzie, I'd like you to meet the meanest man in the movies, Johnson Eberle." They shook hands and Sarah was surprised at the warmth in the man's eyes.

"Good to meet you," the man said with a twinkle. "This is a fabulous location. It's going to look great on film. It's more difficult for Burke and me because we've got to cover so much of it on foot—" he laughed, showing his scratched fingers "—and on hand. Burke, isn't this our fourth film together?"

He nodded. "Yep, but this is our first chase on the soles of our feet!" He turned to Sarah. "Johnson is everyone's favorite villain."

Johnson smiled in a friendly way, waving his fork in the air. "You see, while I'm the mildest sort of person in real life—wouldn't hurt a fly—I've got this face that scares the hell out of the toughest dude alive." He leaned forward. "The first thing I learned is to smile all the time when I'm out in public. Otherwise everyone thinks I've got a stiletto up my sleeve or a gun in a chest holster! All the guys want to pick a fight with me, and women always think I'm up to no good."

Sarah smiled at his mock-injured tone and looked around the dining room. She felt foolish for even entertaining the thought that she would seem out of place in such an atmosphere.

"Are you coming down to watch us this evening, Sarah?" Johnson asked.

"I—I hadn't thought about it...." She glanced shyly at Burke, who was paying great attention to his tossed salad. He did not look up. "Why, yes," she found herself saying, "I think I will."

Johnson shrugged. "It's not very exciting really. Burke has to kick me on the shoulder as I'm pursuing him up an icy boulder, and I have to slide down the hill in the snow." He paused and winked. "I'll have body pads under my outer clothing. It won't be so bad."

While the men sipped coffee Sarah finished her meal in a somewhat uneasy silence.

The location for the night scene had been chosen by the director to make use of a huge boulder that appeared stuck to the side of High Mountain, and looked as if it might tumble down on the beach below at any moment. Cleverly placed lights illuminated the huge piece of granite, which seemed to glower starkly against the moon.

Grandlady, Johanna and Luis had already gathered at the site in anticipation of the spectacle, but Sarah, still somewhat upset by her disagreement with Burke, was subdued. "Aren't you feeling well?" grandlady asked.

"Oh, I'm fine," she replied, lapsing into a long silence.

The assistant director appeared with canvas chairs for them and handed out mugs of coffee. The air was bone chillingly cold, and the crew kept flapping their arms and stamping their feet vigorously in order to keep warm. The camera was mounted below the boulder on a huge wooden scaffold. Leaning over to Sarah, grandlady whispered, "They rehearsed this scene all afternoon, all except the slide in the snow." She paused before explaining further. "You see, if they'd practiced the fall the snow would look disturbed, and it's got to appear fresh." She tugged at her gloves. "I rather like this talking-picture business," she sighed. "If I were younger. . . ."

Sarah smiled and took her hand. "I know. You'd become a character actress until you were a hundred years old!"

"Quiet everybody!" the assistant director shouted.

"Camera!" the director said clearly, then waited a moment and cried, "Action!"

Burke suddenly appeared on top of the boulder, kicking violently at something below. Then an arm appeared, and finally the body of a man, clinging precariously to a small bush growing out of the granite. The men maneuvered this way and that while grandlady provided the running commentary. "They'll film that bit of action in close-up later. Now they're shooting the long shot that scans all the action."

"Yes, grandlady," Sarah replied patiently. "I know. We film commercials all the time in New York. It's the same technique."

A quick movement on the boulder caught their attention. Johnson held his hands up in the air for a dramatic moment, then fell back into the snow, rolling over and over, finally coming to rest near a shrub.

"Cut!" the director yelled, adding in a quieter voice, "Thank you, gentlemen. Shall we try it again? This time, Mr. Eberle, when you stop falling land so that you're on your back, please."

While the men were being helped into position, three figures in mackinaws with parkas underneath, began to sweep the snow where Johnson had slipped with long lacy switches.

"That's so the snow will look undisturbed, Sarah," grandlady put in, inordinately proud of her powers of deduction.

"Yes, grandlady, I know!"

For the next hour Burke and Johnson went through their paces, filming the scene four times until the director shouted, "Cut and print," and the assistant director cried, "It's a wrap."

"That means they're through for the night," grandlady explained. Sarah sighed and went to join Burke, who had just climbed down from the top of the boulder.

"That *was* exciting!" Sarah exclaimed.

"It must have looked very rudimentary from here, but on film, it will look quite convincing." He picked up a script from his canvas chair and hurriedly turned the pages. "Johnson and I have to meet the dialogue director back at the inn for a couple of hours' work. We've got some hellish lines for tomorrow that need a lot of work. We've both got a couple of very long monologues." He grimaced and flexed his fingers. "I'm really beat."

"Burke," Sarah said hesitatingly, "I behaved like an infant this evening. I don't know what gets into me sometimes. I guess it's the pressure of the ad campaign, Johanna's wedding and just never seeing you. It's... it's so difficult...."

He looked at her soberly, then said quietly, "Sarah, you've got to learn to trust me completely. I would never do anything to make you feel uncomfortable. But unless you're willing to go along with me on these things I can't see...."

She took his arm. "I'm sorry. I guess it's just that I've lived alone for so long, and I'm so damned self-sufficient, that I rely too much on instinct—intuitive feelings."

"That I understand because I'm the same way—when I'm acting. But when you're with me and you're out of your professional element, I expect you to at least try to understand my point of view." He paused, frowning, his strong jaw and thin lips thrown into sharp relief by the moon's glow. "Also think about what it means to be a wife, because no doubt you'll be one someday to some lucky fool. But if you can't give up some of your stubborn independence, then you'd better become accustomed to being alone for a long time to come." He drew her back under the protection of a maple tree's snowy trunk.

He was in shadow—a dark form that towered above her—while her face was bathed in moonlight. "Do you understand what I mean?"

She nodded numbly. "I understand all that, but I'm not entirely sure I could give up all that's me— not at this stage of the game."

"I'm not suggesting you give yourself up, you little idiot. No man wants a puppet. But you will have to compromise a great deal, and realize that it isn't just Sarah Mackenzie anymore. Sarah What's-Her-Name will be part of a team, and a team works together. You'll have to realize that whatever you do will affect the other half of that team. That's going to restrict your freedom, you know."

Freedom, she thought. *That's ironic! What kind of freedom is this, loving someone to heights and depths that I couldn't conceive of before, and having that love frustrated at every turn? I'd rather feel nothing!*

"You must learn to *trust*, Sarah. I know that Schaeffer gave you a rough time—"

"You know about Peter?" she interrupted. How long had he known? What must he think of her now if he knew how she'd been duped. . . .

"I had a long talk with Ethan Fairchild the day after the awards banquet. He suggested your involvement with Schaeffer wasn't what it appeared. He also—"

"You've been talking to Ethan?" she interrupted again. "You had no right—"

"Where you're concerned, babe, I have every

right. I'd heard some nasty rumors and simply wanted to set the record straight in my own mind. And in Schaeffer's. I paid him a little visit to... well, let's just say we talked. He's a mindless wimp, Sarah, a weakling. How could you have even *dated* him?'' Steve's eyes were stormy, but he was making a strong effort to stay in control.

''I know all that now.'' She sighed wearily, staring out at the white landscape dotted with crewmen and bystanders. ''I made a mistake once; I could make a mistake again,'' she mumbled half to herself, but he heard her and whirled her around to face him.

''You are many things, Mackenzie, but you're no fool. And only a fool doesn't learn from past mistakes.'' Then his face broke into that grin she loved so much, showing the even white teeth so startling against his dark face. His brown eyes twinkled, and she grinned despite herself.

''Besides,'' he added, ''how could you be a fool if you're in love with me?'' And laughing at her outraged gasp, he turned and strode off to the Running Mallow.

CHAPTER FOURTEEN

JOHANNA AND LUIS were married in the little brown shingled Church of the Redeemer, which had witnessed more local history than any other building on Samsqua—including Needlepoint House. All Samsqua christenings, marriages and funerals had taken place in the tiny church.

The pews were crowded with well-wishers, and just before the organ wheezed into "I Love You Truly," Burke counted the house. "Everyone, including the dog, is here," he whispered to Sarah. "Who is that little old lady with the miniature poodle?"

"The Widow Barnes," Sarah whispered back. "She graduated from high school with grandlady. The dog's name is Herman. She never goes anywhere without him!"

The organist segued into "Always," and Georgie, who was at the bellows of the old instrument, was already perspiring, even though it was so cold in the church that by the time the strains of "Here Comes the Bride" floated over the congregation, Sarah was glad she had chosen to wear a heavy wool dress.

There was a flurry of excited chatter, along with

the usual ooh's and aah's, as the congregation turned to watch Johanna walk down the aisle in her grandmother's starched, white lace gown, which Edna Lowery had painstakingly altered.

The chatter, however, had nothing to do with the gown—or even Johanna's dark beauty. The comments were reserved for Lucia Concannon, who accompanied her granddaughter down the aisle. No one could remember such a departure from tradition in Samsqua's history. And when the Reverend Mr. Hallett, almost as ancient as the church itself, asked in stentorian tones, "Who gives the bride in marriage?" that lady announced firmly, "Her grandmother," then stepped back to the left, her thin corseted figure erect, her pale pink ruffled evening gown lending an old-world touch to the occasion.

As Luis kissed Johanna the old organ, pumped up again by Georgie, bleated out the first few bars of "Memories," and tears stung Sarah's eyelids. She glanced at grandlady, who was surely as moved as she, but whose chin was set at a determined angle. Obviously she had no intention of spoiling her makeup by letting even one tear escape her watery blue eyes.

· The reception was held in the newly refurbished lobby of the Running Mallow. As opulent on the inside as it had ever been in its golden years, the old inn was still dilapidated and dreary-looking on the outside, awaiting better weather so that Luis's crew could finish the remodeling job.

The repast, laid out on the Concannon banquet tablecloths, unused since World War II, had been prepared mostly by Johanna. Edna Lowery had contributed an enormous shepherd's pie and had been busy for a week polishing the family silver, black with tarnish from having lain for years in sundry kitchen cabinets at Needlepoint House.

Burke surveyed the long table. "I haven't seen so much crystal and china since I last dropped in at Buckingham Palace," he remarked dryly.

"Yes," Sarah nodded, "this is like the Waldorf-Astoria, except better."

"Sarah," grandlady said, taking her arm, "don't I know that young man over there talking to Johanna?"

"My God, Webb Jackson!" Sarah replied in a low voice. "I wonder what he's doing here? He can't be covering *this* wedding for *Women's Wear Daily!*"

She caught his eye and waved, and he waved back, continuing to talk earnestly with Johanna. He took a notebook from his pocket and began to write in his peculiar shorthand.

"I'd better see what's up," Sarah remarked, and drifted to the buffet, stopping to chat with a couple of high-school friends before wandering over to Webb and Johanna.

"Hi, Miss Sarah," Webb said, kissing her cheek. "I couldn't make it for the wedding, but I was able to hitch a ride on the helicopter from Boston. I'm getting some data from Miss Jo about the Portland exhibit.'' He rolled his eyes. ''I'm doing a piece about the opening, ostensibly covering the fashion aspect. You know—what those rich old biddies who are coming up from Boston are wearing.''

''Do you really think the exhibition will draw those types?''

''Well, after all, the Concannons are in the May-flower registry!'' He grinned and winked at Sarah. ''Naturally I'll write something kind about Johan-na's glass pieces, too.''

''Webb, dear, if you really want to write about something special...have you seen the inn's win-dows?''

''The windows?''

''Come over behind the buffet where you can get the full effect.'' She winked at Johanna and pro-pelled him to the center of the lobby. ''Don't get too close to the túna casserole,'' she murmured. ''Now, Webby, look up!'' As if on cue, the sun came out at that moment, and they were bathed in pools of bril-liantly colored light. She watched his face as he gave the expected ''Ahhhh.''

''Rather nice, don't you think?'' she asked.

''Nice seems to be your favorite word of the year!'' He gazed at the windows openmouthed. ''There's so much color and depth. Who are all the figures?''

''The windows tell a story—the story of Sam-squa.''

''Let Johanna describe it to me,'' Webb said. ''I'll get a quote.''

Sarah stepped back and joined Burke. "He's covering the exhibition in Portland," she whispered with relief, "not the wedding, thank heavens! Webb Jackson is one of the most influential columnists in the country. Something good will come of this!"

Lucia Concannon murmured to Johanna, "The men are fidgeting. It's time to serve the cake."

"We've been looking all over for Georgie. He's taking the wedding pictures," Sarah said. "Oh, there he is! Luis, scout him out...."

"Don't get your sleeve in the icing when you cut the cake," the old woman cautioned.

Johanna threw her a quick look. "I can't wait to get out of this dress. Didn't you find it scratchy?"

"My dear, it's been half a century since I wore that dress. How can I possibly remember? Anyway you're a beautiful bride."

Johanna pressed her arm. "Thank you, grandlady." Then she went to the small, three-tiered cake that she had baked herself, took Luis's hand and looked up smilingly into his face.

"I've never seen you more beautiful," he whispered. "I'm so glad you came into my life."

She smiled. "Correction. *You* came into *my* life!"

Grandlady raised her pale brows. "Which reminds me, dear. Now that you're an upright, forthright married lady, shouldn't you sign your curios *Mrs. Jo?*"

Sarah burst out laughing. "Grandlady, really!"

"Well, someone has to be practical around here!" she retorted. "Now, let's serve the bubbly!"

While Luis was opening the champagne Johanna took Burke's arm. "I appreciate all your help, Steven, really, but I don't know why I allowed the gallery people to talk me into this exhibition. I'll just die if no one likes my work."

Burke pressed her hand. "Johanna, how can anyone *not* like all those beautiful pieces?"

"You're in the public eye, Burke. What do you do when you get a bad review?"

He laughed softly. "You learn to live with them after a while. One thing in your favor one hundred percent is that you're a 'homegrown' girl! Your work is fresh, original and new."

"Oh, I hope the critics think so, too. That Webb Jackson can be cruel. I've seen some of *his* work!"

"Do you know," Burke said slowly as Sarah moved up beside him, "I've had a credo all of my life that's helped me more than anything. If people for some reason don't like my work, I think, *to hell with 'em! As long as I please me, that's all that's important!*"

Sarah looked at him with added respect. "Is that what you really feel?"

"Of course!"

Then grandlady rapped a glass with a spoon, and everyone turned to look at her. "My dears," she said huskily, "I propose a toast to the bride and groom.... Success, prosperity, and may they produce a great-grandchild for me to enjoy before I take to my wheelchair!'' She laughed as the guests all raised their glasses.

"No one can say that this isn't grandlady's party,'' Burke said in an undertone as he took a sip of champagne.

"Amen,'' Sarah replied softly.

SARAH, JOHANNA, LUIS AND GRANDLADY were strapped unceremoniously into the bucket seats of the helicopter, and the pilot waited patiently, watching for the assistant director's red flare to shoot up the windward side of the island so that he could take off for Portland. The company was filming Burke's climb up the sheer cliff below Needlepoint House, and if the craft took to the air while the cameras were turning the helicopter would be seen in the shot. Five minutes later the red flare went off over the top of High Mountain, and the pilot started the motors.

Once they were ensconced in the Jefferson Suite at the Portland Hotel, which housed the Gate Gallery on the first floor, grandlady scurried away to the hairdresser's. When they were alone Sarah took Johanna by the hand. "I've a surprise. We're going shopping for a proper gown for you tonight.''

"But I brought along my ankle-length paisley skirt and that yellow silk blouse that you gave me for Christmas two years ago. . . .''

"Johanna, don't you think you should wear some-

thing more...sophisticated? You've got to wear a
long dress—something chic and grand.'' She grinned.
"This will be my Christmas present *this* year.'' Then
sighing, she added, "I've also got to pick up something for myself—something stark and simple. You're
the star tonight!''

In the designer collection at Harolds Sarah found
a dark blue jersey shift for herself and a burgundy-
colored gown with three-quarter sleeves and a deep
V neckline for Johanna. "It's perfect!'' she exclaimed as Johanna stood reluctantly before the pier
glass.

"The dress looks strange,'' Johanna said uncertainly. "There's something wrong with *me*!''

"What you need is a good bra, and for heaven's
sake stand up straight!'' Sarah announced, guiding
her into the lingerie department.

A half hour later, back at the hotel, Sarah sham-
pooed Johanna's hair carefully twice, added an egg
rinse, then wound up her long hair on jumbo
rollers.

Luis had retired to the bedroom to watch a local
football game, coming out only long enough to have
lunch with them. He was strangely silent. Painstakingly Sarah applied a set of long false fingernails over
Johanna's chipped moonless nails, then added two
coats of deep red polish. "Now,'' she announced,
"go into my bedroom and take a nap.''

"But I never sleep in the daytime!''

"Well, you don't have to *sleep*, just rest. You've

got to look absolutely smashing tonight, Miss Jo!''

Johanna did not come out of the bedroom until four o'clock. "I did sleep," she said incredulously. "But I've got a headache coming on."

"Then take two aspirin!" Sarah retorted, combing out her own hair, then deftly applying a brush. She made herself up expertly before smoothing a thin coat of Madame Celina's Translucent Gold liquid makeup over Johanna's pale face, working the color into her hairline. She added beige eye shadow and brown highlighter, then combed out her hair and stood back. "Now," Sarah said triumphantly, "step into your gown and I'll zip you up."

"I feel so funny," Johanna complained. "My face itches and I can't breathe."

"It's your new bra. Honestly, Johanna, I know why you don't wear anything under your firing smocks. But you do need support, and you're also slouching again!"

"I feel like a clown with all of this stuff on my face," Johanna complained.

"After a while you won't even know you've got it on." Sarah helped her into the dress, zipped up the back and examined her carefully. Something else was needed. Rummaging in her luggage she came back with tiny garnet earrings, which she attached to Johanna's earlobes. "Now," she said with a little push, "go look at yourself."

Timidly Johanna turned toward the full-length mirror in the dressing room, and confronted a creature that she didn't recognize at first. She looked at her image in the glass incredulously. Her figure, with its slim waist and breasts brought up firmly over the low bodice of the dress, was rather good, and her face had achieved a new dimension under Sarah's ministrations. "Why, *she's* pretty!" Johanna exclaimed to the mirror. "She's actually pretty." She paused. "But *she's* not *me!*"

"What do you mean she's not you! You've never been more beautiful in your whole life!"

The telephone rang and Sarah answered. Webb Jackson, whose voice sounded even more enthusiastic than Gail's on a good day, greeted her breathlessly. "Miss Sarah, I've got a photographer here in the lobby who wants some shots of Miss Jo before she comes down to the reception. He'll shoot plenty of other stuff with guests later on, but he wants to catch her while she's relaxed and rested."

"Okay, come up in about five minutes, Webby, dear." Everything was going according to plan, she thought. This was *one* campaign that had to go right. No one was going to say that Johanna's exhibit was handled by an amateur. Slithering into the jersey shift, she stood back to look at her reflection, then added a bit of lipstick. She looked understated and elegant, Sarah decided. She went back into the living room and knocked on Johanna's bedroom door. "The photographer will be here any minute. I'll order some coffee. We'd better not have anything alcoholic."

A moment later the bedroom door opened, and Sarah looked up in startled surprise. Johanna was wearing the paisley skirt and yellow blouse, and her face had been cleansed of makeup except for lipstick. She had also combed her hair out into the usual long bob.

"What have you done?" Sarah was furious. "What is the meaning of this?"

"The meaning of this," Johanna replied gently, "is that I can't go down there looking like someone I'm not." She paused, her face strained. "I appreciate what you're trying to do for me, Sarah, but it just won't work. If I wore that getup I'd be unnatural and awkward."

Sarah was exasperated. "You've got to have an *image*, Jo," she replied heatedly.

"Be that as it may. . . ."

"This is the first time in your life you can really shine! You've got to show people you've got what it takes!"

Johanna shook her head sadly. "If I don't have what it takes, Sarah, wearing a two-hundred-dollar dress and garnet earrings, my face covered in a ton of makeup, isn't going to do it!" She gestured feebly. "I'm not some product that you've got to push."

"You are!" Sarah expounded hotly. "You're a commodity, just like Winter Fire or After Nine. The public is going to buy *you*!"

Johanna shook her head vehemently. "No! They're

not going to buy me, they're going to buy my work. There's a big difference."

"*You* are the merchandise." Sarah began to pace back and forth. "If you're colorful and exciting and beautiful, your work will take on that much more stature! You've got to have a fantastic package."

Johanna indicated her cotton skirt and blouse. "This is my 'package,' and if they don't like it, then I can't help that," she said simply, and looked sadly at her sister. "Oh, Sarah, what's happened to your own values? You can't dress me up like a fashion model and expect me to be myself."

"All right," Sarah almost shouted, "go to that reception and sell yourself short! See if I care!"

There was a knock on the door. "Come in," Sarah said evenly, trying to quiet her racing pulse. Johanna looked at her before she moved to answer the door, and said, a melancholy note in her voice, "And you, Sarah. Don't *you* sell yourself short. Don't sell yourself at all."

Sarah blanched, went into her bedroom and shut the door, but sounds drifted in from the next room. Webb Jackson's and another voice—the photographer, undoubtedly. "I've just seen your work, Miss Jo," he was saying quickly, "and it's really stupendous! Now, I want you to stand next to the window so the sunlight will backlight your hair. Maine lass! They'll love you. So fresh, so unique...."

Sarah nervously lit a cigarette, then opened the door to the balcony. It was late afternoon, and the buildings surrounding the hotel were bathed in soft shadows created by the waning sun, which spilled out over the street below and highlighted the skyline. Gradually her heart slowed and she began to feel more composed. What Johanna had said about values had disturbed her. During her eight years in New York, had she exchanged her original set of values for others? Was she still fighting for points that perhaps had never really existed—except in her own mind?

Restlessly she paced up and down the length of the balcony. She was ashamed of herself and her performance with Jo. If she were honest with herself she would have to admit that her attempts to fashion Jo into a glamour girl had been for selfish reasons. She was jealous of Johanna, jealous of her innocent beauty and simple grace. She'd wanted to make her into just another fashionable "classy" lady. She'd been afraid of the possible comparison between them, had Johanna gone in her unmade-up style. Johanna's class had nothing to do with exteriors. She was at peace with herself, and it showed through— along with her devotion to Luis. Tears sprang to Sarah's eyes and she thought vaguely of the red puffiness that would be clearly visible later on. She felt like a misplaced soul, a phony, corrupt in her values and narrow in her vision. And she'd accused Johanna of copping out by staying on Samsqua! A smile came to her tear-stained face as she thought of Burke; his strong handsome face came up before her mentally, somehow haunting her. His eyes seemed to bore into hers, and suddenly she felt like a little girl again. She saw herself at the wharf, greeting the tourists off the *Griffin*, Johanna at her side. They held out flower garlands to the tourists, and it came to Sarah then that Johanna was right. Johanna was only a grown-up version of her childhood self, while she, Sarah, had changed into another sort of person entirely. She had laboriously created that other Sarah Mackenzie—the one who lived on Fifth Avenue in New York City.

The time to face up to reality was now. She had to admit she'd trade her penthouse apartment and her closetful of designer clothes if she could have Steve's love. She'd always need the stimulation of a challenging career, but not at the expense of peace of mind and a loving relationship. She wanted it all, and it seemed to her at that moment, looking out over another bustling city at dusk, that she, Sarah Mackenzie, had nothing.

Half an hour passed before Sarah heard Webb and his photographer leave. Then her door opened, and her sister stood on the threshold for a moment before throwing herself into Sarah's arms. "Can you ever forgive me, Jo?" Sarah asked remorsefully.

Johanna kissed her cheek and hugged her again. "Sarah, I had no right to say those things to you. I didn't mean half—"

Sarah shook her head. "Oh, yes, you did, and you're right," she replied gently. "Somewhere along the way something's happened to me that I didn't know was happening. I haven't thought it all out yet, but I'm going to make some changes...." Sarah looked at her watch. "My God, we've got to go downstairs. You can't be late for your own exhibition!"

"Here, here," Luis Farraday said from the doorway. Then he looked at them both closely. "How come you changed, Johanna?"

Sarah smiled softly. "She decided that she wanted to look like Miss Jo instead of Johanna Concannon Mackenzie Farraday." She said the last in a snobbish highbrow accent. "I do hope you approve."

Luis grinned. "For a moment there, when she was 'all gussied up,' as grandlady would say, I thought the girl I knew on Samsqua was gone. But I see that she isn't. She was in there, inside, all the time."

One of the women's guilds in Portland had sponsored the opening night of the showing, and these well-heeled ladies were dressed in a variety of pastel evening dresses more suitable to summer than winter. Only one old dear wore a black bombazine dress that reminded Sarah of Edna Lowery's regular uniform. Grandlady, she noticed, was talking to a reporter with one hand on the Mayflower registry and the other holding a tall drink that she was sure was rum and Coca-Cola. Grandlady wore her first new dress in years, a pale mauve taffeta with lace edging. Her hair had been washed with mauve rinse, although the hairdresser at the hotel had obviously not been able to convince her to change her forties upswept hairdo. She nodded to the reporter and then stood next to Johanna's piece, *Victorian Lady with the Hat*, so that no one could miss the fact that she had posed for it.

Sarah, who had attended what seemed like hundreds of openings in New York, was accustomed to seeing bored expressions on the faces of husbands who had been dragged along to these events against their wishes. But tonight she was pleasantly surprised to see the men seriously examining the pieces. As she joined Johanna and Luis she heard various comments.

"That little boat with the green sails. . . . Well I've just *got* to have it. . . ."

"I've never seen glass with such color. . . ."

"The wires protruding from the small goat look exactly like hair. . . ."

"This exhibit is as beautiful in its way as the King Tut exhibit was. . . ."

"And to think she's a Maine girl. . . ."

Johanna was beautifully calm, and as she stood by the punch bowl in her yellow blouse and paisley skirt, answering surprisingly intelligent questions, she became slightly more animated and began to speak of her work with great conviction. She was in complete command. Johanna had been right about her clothing and makeup. She would have looked obviously artificial if she had worn the burgundy dress.

Sarah stood alone by the door feeling tired and out

of sorts. Johanna had given her a great deal to think about, and besides, this was not her night. It belonged expressly to Johanna, who at the moment was surrounded by several college art students and their professor, who looked a bit like Albert Einstein. Sarah sipped sherry and tried to keep an interested intelligent look on her face.

"Penny for your thoughts," a voice said, and she turned gratefully to Webb Jackson. "She's something else again, eh?" He raised his eyebrows in Johanna's direction. "She's captured them all, hasn't she?"

Sarah nodded. "I'm so pleased. I think this is the first time that she's said more than a dozen words about her work. Now you can't keep her still."

"Do I detect a bit of jealousy, Miss Sarah?"

She faced him squarely. "Not anymore, Webby. I've come to terms with the fact that I have a beautiful talented sister who puts me to shame." She grinned ruefully, then went on. "No, seriously, if I'm distracted tonight it's because I've got a lot on my mind."

"Like Steven Burke?"

"Maybe."

"And how is the Winter Fire campaign progressing?"

"It's practically finished—at least from my end of the thing."

"Sir Basil is happy?"

"As a clam."

"Is Burke bugging you?"

"Pray tell, about what?"

"Oh, you know how men are."

She gave him a long look. "Is this supposed to be an interview?"

"No." He laughed. "Just a friendly inquiry." Pausing, he asked, "How's *Devil's Dare* coming along?"

"Burke would be here tonight, but they are shooting something called 'night for night.' "

"Well, that's strange, because the hotel just sent a limo to pick him up at the heliport." He shrugged his thin shoulders. "Well, I've got to get a plane for the Big Apple. My piece has to be in by deadline or Miss Jo won't be in *Women's Wear Daily* tomorrow." He laughed again. "I'll type it on the plane—if I can stay away from the champagne."

Burke, here, she wondered as her heart began racing. The rest of the night seemed endless after this revelation.

Then, just before the doors to the exhibit were to close at ten o'clock, an excited murmur rose from the crowd. Steven Burke came into the room. . .with the most stunningly beautiful blond woman Sarah had ever seen. She was dressed in a gold sheath and was smiling dazzlingly at Johanna, ensuring that the photographers would get a good shot of both Johanna and her. Burke was looking around the room and finally settled on Sarah's stricken face, but not before she had time to compose herself and move forward to greet him as professionally as she could.

Her composure left her as she stood beside Steve and was forced to watch as the blond bombshell slipped her arm possessively through his. Steve was smiling openly, obviously enjoying the attentions of two females. *Well,* Sarah thought waspishly, *he can use her if she'll let him, but I won't be around to give him his kicks.*

"Nice seeing you, Steve," she said, and made to move away. She'd go back to her hotel and have a nice hot bath as solace for her wounded feelings.

Steve was extracting the other woman's arm and politely excusing himself as Sarah kissed Johanna goodbye and congratulated her again on the success of the show. She almost ran toward the door, but he was too fast, springing in front of her to block her escape.

"Tsk, tsk, Mackenzie. Is this the greeting I get after braving sleet and snow to come see you?"

"I'm sure you found ways of keeping warm," she said icily, and went to move around him. He side-stepped her again, this time determinedly grasping her wrists. "Steven, this is ridiculous. I'm not going to stand here in the hotel ballroom and fence with you. It's perfectly obvious that you have commitments tonight, so I'll make a gracious exit and we'll call it a night, shall we?" Her head was pounding now, and she was starting to feel the effects of the champagne she'd toasted with all night. "I have nothing more to say to you."

"Well, I have plenty to say to you!" His anger was building, she could see. But instead of warning her it only served to feed her own increasing temper. "You seem to think I sleep with any piece of fluff that comes along. Believe me, Sarah, I could. There's a lot of it around. But Valerie in there isn't my style. Nor is she what my mother would call 'easy.' She's a sweet girl, but she's just that—a child. She needed protection from one of her macho boyfriends, and I can offer that much to her."

"I don't know why you think I'm interested in any of this," she said through clenched teeth, trying to free her hands from his viselike grip.

"Because you love me, damn it! Why the hell can't you admit it?" He was shouting now, and one photographer had come out into the foyer to see what the hubbub was about. "You're scared, and insecure, and confused and you *need* me. And you need this," he ground out as his hard lips came down to her mouth, catching her breath and leaving her dizzy. She clung to his shoulders in what appeared to be a lover's clutch, though in the back of her mind she registered that a photograph was about to be taken. Pushing herself away, and heedless of the now approaching photographer, camera ready, she raised her hand to Steve's handsome face and planted a hard resounding slap on his right cheek.

His face immediately reddened and closed up in anger. She could see that she'd gone too far this time. His powerful body swung around to the photog-

rapher, and grabbing the man's camera he opened
the back of it, exposing the film. "Get out of my
sight!" he spat at the cowering man as he shoved the
camera back at him. Then Steve turned his full attention on Sarah, who shied away from him as though
she were afraid he would hit her.

He ran his hand through his blond hair as he came
slowly toward her. "Sarah, darling, give me your
hand. We're going for a walk." His voice was gentle
now, his palm on hers warm and reassuring, and she
walked with him out into the cool night air.

"I'm so sorry," she pleaded, and she was. She was
deeply disturbed; she wasn't herself.

"Do you remember our talk on Samsqua? About
trust?" He sounded like a teacher, and she recalled
the conversation as though she had been studying it
ever since.

"Yes," she said simply.

"I see it didn't sink in."

"Sorry. I guess I flunk the test, right?"

"You sure flunked it back there."

"You insulted me, treating me like a child in public
like that." Suddenly she was bone tired. She had to
sit down somewhere. "Steve, I've got to sit down.
Can we...can we go somewhere for a drink?"
There, she'd made a positive step. Perhaps then they
could have a talk, a really *good* talk.

He frowned. "I'm afraid not. I'm due back in
Samsqua tonight. The fog rolled in tonight, and we
had to postpone the night shot until six in the morn-

ing. It won't be the same, but it has to be done. And no, little one, Valerie is *not* coming back with me. She was meeting another macho boyfriend at Johanna's opening. Apparently he's not the violent type,'' he added dryly. He paused. ''What's wrong, babe?''

She shook her head. ''Oh, nothing. But I've got to go back to New York on the early plane tomorrow.''

''But it's Friday! Call Ethan Fairchild and tell him you won't be in.''

''I can't do that, Burke. I took today off because of the exhibit, and I shouldn't have. My desk will look like Pikes Peak.'' She thought of the coming weekend. She couldn't keep running back and forth between New York and Samsqua. She made a quick decision. ''I'll call him,'' she said with finality.

''Then at least we'll be able to see each other a bit. We'll probably wrap by Thursday, and I've got to go right back to the Coast for looping.''

''Looping?''

''Rerecording dialogue. When a picture is shot on location a lot of dialogue is lost, so we have to go back to the studio and look at the film and record a new sound track that matches our lip movements on the screen. It's time-consuming and hellish for everyone involved.''

''I'll make that call,'' she said in what she hoped was a confident voice, not at all sure she was doing the right thing. She picked up the house phone and gave Ethan Fairchild's home number.

"I'm so glad that you called," his gruff voice said over the phone. "Get reservations on the plane as soon as you can tonight."

"But chief, I—"

"Sir Basil arrived this afternoon from Switzerland, and we've scheduled an appointment tomorrow morning at ten o'clock. Come in early because we've got to go over his file before he gets here." He paused, and his voice grew more sonorous. "He's only here tomorrow, Sarah. We need you here. We're going to have a real winner with Winter Fire— But all this will keep until tomorrow."

One more time, she thought. Just this once.

"All right, chief. I'll come home tonight." She hung up and rubbed her eyes. Then she looked for Burke, who was standing with his back to her in the corridor, smoking a cigarette. His big broad shoulders were sensuously outlined by the expert cut of his midnight blue tuxedo, and for a moment she thought, *that's* Steven Burke *waiting for me!* Then she sighed regretfully and walked slowly toward him, gathering her courage.

"Burke," she said softly. She was *so* tired. "Of all the luck! I can't go back to Samsqua with you tonight. I've got to go to New York. Basil's in town."

He nodded slowly, soberly. "Oh, *well*," he said exaggeratedly, "mustn't keep Sir *Basil* waiting."

"Burke, that's not fair. I want to be with you, but I've got a job to do." She took his arm. "It's all getting so very complicated."

"So it appears," he replied, crushing out his cigarette on the gray cement with the toe of his gleaming leather shoe. His brown eyes were frosty. "When will I see you?"

"Will the picture be finished on schedule—by Thursday?"

He shrugged his shoulders. "If all goes well."

The pause was awkward, and in that moment Sarah had the feeling that her life was slowly disintegrating, and that she could do nothing to bring it back together. For the first time since her parents' death so many years ago she felt completely helpless. "I've already taken so much time away from the office, that I— Can you come by New York on your way to the Coast?"

"I'm going to take the plane from Boston."

"I could go to Samsqua on Saturday week," she said hesitatingly. "But that wouldn't help, would it?"

"Not if I'm leaving on Friday."

Suddenly her world caved in and she burst into tears. "Oh, Burke," she sobbed, "what's to become of us?"

He did not move to comfort her. "You keep asking that question," he answered softly, "as if I had the answer. I don't, Sarah. You do." He shook his head. "Let's go back and grab a cab. I've got a picture to finish," he went on flatly. "And you've got Sir Basil."

GAIL WAS ALREADY AT HER DESK when Sarah came into the office at five after eight the next morning. She looked up from several magazines spread out over her desk. "Good morning, boss," she said cheerfully. "Have you seen the After Nine ads?"

"You know I haven't," Sarah replied darkly. "I've been away all week."

"Oh, it's going to be that kind of day!" Gail sighed, examining her manicure. Then she thrust out a full-page advertisement. "Well, *this* should brighten it."

Sarah looked at the full-page photograph of the Celina cosmetics plant in New Jersey. Under the Celina sign on the building was the legend:

Throughout the years, the name Celina has been synonymous with the word "excellence." To celebrate our eightieth birthday, Celina is proud to introduce After Nine, the fragrance that's so special, it's already being hailed as the perfume of the year. Remember...it's brought to you by Celina, a firm that stands on its name.

Sarah was stunned. "I can't believe it! They've used every cliché in the book! There isn't even a picture anywhere in the ad of that clever little package that falls apart!"

"They don't show that beautiful teardrop bottle, either," Gail replied smugly. "This is the bomb of the year!"

Sarah shook her head. "I'm glad that the old dragon isn't around to see this," she said sadly, then paused. "Gail, would you run out and get a copy of

Women's Wear Daily? I want to see if Webb Jackson made his deadline with Johanna's story—or if he had too much champagne on the flight.''

"What do you mean, boss?"

"Just go! It's too long a story to explain." Sarah went into her office. The sounds of honking horns and squealing brakes reached her on the twentieth floor through the closed windows, and suddenly she longed for the peace and quiet of Samsqua. She thought of Burke climbing over the sheer cliff below Needlepoint House, the cameras recording every move. Oh, how she missed him!

The office was as stuffy as a broom closet! She turned on the air conditioning, and had just sat down at her desk when the telephone rang several times. She sorted through the piles of correspondence for Basil's file. "Gail!" she called out irritably, but there was no answer. Then she remembered her secretary was not at her desk.

Sarah picked up the instrument. "Yes?"

The voice was one that she had never expected to hear again. "This is Harrison."

"Yes?" She forced her voice to sound calm.

"It's taken me a long time to make this call, Sarah, but it hasn't been easy for me since Aunt Jelda died. I've had time to think things over, and looking back I know that I've behaved badly. I want to apologize to you."

Sarah was shocked. She could think of no reply.

• "I know now that Aunt Jelda knew she was going

to die—a fact borne out by her doctors." He paused, his voice shaking. "But I truly believe that she thought she would live long enough to see the campaign through. Otherwise she wouldn't have spent the money for those ads and that commercial. She was always frugal with the company's money."

There was a pause, which gave Sarah time to collect her wits. "I think you're right about your aunt," she replied guardedly. "Thank you for calling, Harrison." She was about to hang up.

"There's just one thing," he said slowly, his voice very low and husky. "I miss working with you."

Sarah could not believe her ears. Was Harrison Perlmutter on the brink of insanity? She stifled a desire to laugh. "Oh, Harrison, come *on*!" She had nothing to lose by being testy.

"The thing is, Sarah, there's no one around to throw ideas back and forth with. You and I.... Well, we stimulated each other—and what came out was superlative. This Schaeffer fellow was a yesman. I had only to crook my little finger and he'd come running."

Sarah had had enough of the conversation. "Harrison, I really appreciate your calling and giving me all this background information, but I really must go. I've just returned from Samsqua and—"

"Sarah, I...I...want to congratulate you on the Steven Burke Winter Fire campaign. I've just seen some tear sheets. It's brilliant. The best thing you've ever done."

Now she was angry. "Do you realize, Harrison, in all the years we worked together this is the first compliment that you've ever given me, and it's about an ad for a competitor?"

"I thought you knew that I've always appreciated your work!"

"I knew nothing. I would have given up the Celina account numerous times, but I stayed on because of *madame*."

Harrison's voice was so weak it was almost a whisper. "Sarah, I want you to come back."

"You mean you miss your old sparring partner?" She laughed hollowly. "No thank you. Even if I didn't represent Sir Basil Northcombe I'd never work for you again. Never."

"But you owe me something, Sarah."

"Pray tell *what*?"

His voice grew insinuating. "You won last year's *Advertising People* award because of your work on Celina cosmetics." It was a valid statement, as far as it went.

"That is partly true," she conceded. "But those ideas were all mine. You really had nothing to do with those campaigns. I owe you nothing, Harrison."

"But won't you rethink this? I want you to come back, and I'm sure that Aunt Jelda...."

"*Stop it*, Harrison! And don't drag in poor *madame*. I don't like this conversation, but now let me have *my* say." Her voice built. "You really called because you were hoping that I would help you out of a pickle. You'll lose a fortune with the After Nine campaign; it's a complete bust. I think what really hurts you, Harrison, is that it's *your* money going down the drain. But you've no one else to blame but yourself. Thank heavens you don't have to report to stockholders or you'd probably be replaced as president of your own company!''

She was really warming to it now, and stilled his weak protesting ''But...'' with ''I'm not through with you yet, Harrison.'' She went on hurriedly. ''My advice to you would be to part with some more of your precious money and hire a terrific advertising person—one who will help you reclaim some of that prestige Madame Celina was responsible for building all these years. You won't recapture anything, I guarantee you, by featuring a photograph of the laboratory in New Jersey! Goodbye.''

She threw the receiver into its cradle with a clatter that knocked a bud vase to the floor. The sound broke her concentration, and all anger gone, she bent down and picked up the three pieces of glass. Strange, she reflected, how everything was coming together now—in the same way that she would glue the pieces of glass back together to make the vase whole again.

Gail trotted in breathlessly. ''Your sister's made page one!'' she sang, holding out the paper. ''Look!'' On the left-hand corner of the page was a picture of Johanna looking up at the camera expectantly. The headline read: PRINCESS OF GLASS.

There was a small polite rundown of the guests and what they were wearing, and then Jackson had written:

Miss Jo, a Samsqua Island native, was rightly the center of attention during the entire evening, even though Steven Burke shared some of the spotlight during the latter part of the evening. Earlier, the guests moved among the exhibits of unique glass figures, touching, pricing and commenting on the unique technique employed by Miss Jo, who happens to be the sister of Sarah Mackenzie, the vice-president of the Duncan-Fairchild Advertising Agency, who won *Advertising People*'s Woman of the Year award.

Glass sculptress Johanna Farraday works with harmony and balance as well as a critical eye, and the Gate Gallery showing is memorable. This writer especially liked *Victorian Lady with the Hat, Hands, Dutch Boy* and *Bacchus*. It is worth a trip to Portland to look at the exhibit— although that is not to say all of the works of art will still be available. Most of the pieces have already been purchased.

He ended the piece with a memorable line:

The diminutive and peppery artist, looking like an unspoiled vision out of the last century, wore a simple paisley ankle-length cotton skirt and a soft yellow silk blouse tied at the throat. Miss Jo will no doubt do for fused glass what L.C. Tiffany did for lamps. Already there is talk of bringing the collection to Manhattan—the first lap of a national tour.

Tears stung Sarah's eyes. "I'm so proud of her," she said quietly.

Gail nodded and picked up the acrylic paperweight of snowy Samsqua. "She's come a long way from this," she said soberly.

Sarah looked out the window and brushed away the tears. "It's going to be a good day after all," she said brightly, somehow feeling cleansed. She went through the mail, then met with Ethan Fairchild to go over some invoices scheduled to be billed on the Winter Fire layouts.

"We've got to get this paperwork done, chief, but I'm not in the mood."

He glanced at her sharply. "I know. You never are. I don't know why you dislike the financial side of our business."

"I have no head for figures!"

"I would suggest that you should become more involved on all fronts," he snapped, not at all in a grandfatherly manner. "I'm sixty-two and I'd like to start thinking about what I'm going to be doing with my spare time once I'm not coming to the office every day."

She looked at him blankly.

"Sarah," he went on tartly, "I'm only saying that someone has to take my place. Right now the logical person appears to be you."

She paused for a long moment and realized that six months ago she would have been waltzing around the room at such an opportunity. Now she felt nothing but a leaden sense of responsibility. "Why, thank you, chief." She managed a small smile.

He shook his white head. "You don't seem very excited, I must say. I'd think you'd be pleased and flattered that I'm offering such a position to a woman."

"A woman!" Sarah cried. "A woman? Are we back to *that* again? I never realized that you were so chauvinistic."

"I'm not! It's just that you're taking this as lightly as if I'd asked to take you to lunch or some damn thing!" His voice shook. "I've just offered you the presidency of Duncan-Fairchild!"

"Oh, Ethan, it isn't that I'm ungrateful. Please understand. I appreciate your offer, really I do, and I faithfully promise that after the Winter Fire stuff is out I'll really knuckle down to learning more about the financial resources of the company. But right now...."

Gail's high voice, even more excited than usual, came over the intercom. "Sir Basil Northcombe is here."

"Have him come in, please," she replied, relieved to end the conversation. Gail's tone, Sarah reflected, sounded exactly as if she were announcing the arrival of Prince Philip.

Basil extended his arms in an expansive gesture. "Sarah, in all my years in the business I've never encountered anything so special. We shipped a few cases of Winter Fire to selected locations in France, Britain and Italy last week, and they sold out within five days! Apparently it's word of mouth. Just think what will happen when the print ads appear, not to mention the television commercial! I'm putting the factory on three shifts, and the flasks are being manufactured by the gross at the plant in Florence." He paused and took a deep breath. "Now we can't let this momentum falter. We've got to get Steve's commercial out fast—first in the European market, then here. We can't do anything about the magazine advertisements because they're already set...."

"True!" Sarah exclaimed. "But if you'll increase the budget we can take out newspaper ads."

"Capital!" Basil clamped his hands together enthusiastically. "Now, I want to take another look at those commercials!"

Ethan Fairchild turned down the lights in the conference room and inserted the cassette into the television recorder. The large-projection screen, affixed to the wall, turned bright red. Superimposed over the brilliant color was the legend: The laboratories of Sir Basil Northcombe bring you Mr. Steven Burke. The red background dissolved into the interior of a large comfortable library with walnut-colored wing chairs, a beige leather sofa and shaded lamps. The fireplace threw dancing lights over the deep-pile carpeting.

The next shot was a close-up of a pair of polished shoes walking down the hall outside the library and pausing at the door. The camera pulled back quickly and Burke came into the library, dressed in a gray, beautifully tailored pin-striped suit with a white shirt and a maroon cravat. He went directly to the mantel and picked up the black-and-gold test-tube flask. Turning, he held up the bottle as the camera moved in for a medium shot of his craggy face. He seemed to be looking directly at the group in the conference room, and Sarah felt a little shiver of desire spread out from her spine. Burke murmured, "The scent of a woman. . . Winter Fire. It's sinful."

Ethan Fairchild placed another cassette in the machine. "This is the French version."

As the lights came down Gail quietly entered the room and bent down to whisper in Sarah's ear. "Your sister's on ship to shore from Samsqua."

Sarah tiptoed out of the room and followed Gail down the hall to her office. She picked up the phone and was greeted by the expected clatter of interference. The words were unintelligible. "Johanna, I can barely hear you."

The voice on the other end was garbled. Then with a start she realized that Johanna was crying. Gradually the disconnected sounds made sense, and Sarah cried out, "Oh, no!" She leaned back against the desk, her face drained of color.

Faintly, ever so faintly, she heard Johanna repeat tearfully, "It snowed this afternoon.... We'd just got back from Portland.... Grandlady w-went for a ride.... M-Magnifique slipped...."

Sarah's throat tightened, sobs racking her body from deep inside. "I'll take the helicopter from Boston," she said brokenly, then hung up and burst into tears. "Oh, Gail, there's been a horrible accident. Grandlady...." She buried her face in her hands. "She's dead, Gail. She's dead...."

CHAPTER FIFTEEN

THE CHURCH OF THE REDEEMER was filled to capacity. Fifty wooden chairs, borrowed from the Running Mallow, were placed in the rear beyond the last pew.

The entire front wall behind the polished bronze casket was wired to hold the tributes, which ranged from homemade wreaths of sweet wanda and evergreen boughs to a basket of pale green orchids sent from Portland by the Gate Gallery.

Else Sanchez had made two round trips from Boothbay that morning, ferrying over original Samsqua residents and their kin who were now off islanders, plus several historians who had made the trip out of respect for the Concannon Mayflower heritage.

As soon as the seats were filled, Sarah, Johanna, Burke and Luis having taken their places in the front pew, a tearful Georgie pumped up the organ. Played by Edna Lowery, it breathily gave forth with "Always." There was complete silence among those gathered. "Always" at a funeral? It was an intentional choice, for Lucia Concannon had planned her entire service some months before, around the time of her seventy-fifth birthday.

Next came "I'll Be Seeing You," which elicited tears from her old friends, and then the shocker, "The Old Gray Mare, She Ain't What She Used To Be." After that the congregation was prepared for anything. So no one was surprised when Steven Burke, instead of the Reverend Mr. Hallett, climbed to the raised pulpit, his steel-tapped shoes clicking on the butternut planking of the stairs.

Dressed in a pearl-gray suit with his sun-bleached hair combed straight back from his forehead, he looked more like a successful banker than a motion-picture star. "The woman whom all of you knew as Lucia Concannon, and whom I was privileged to call grandlady," he said, "let it be known among family members that she wanted me to say something to all of you today, in lieu of a regular service. This in itself reveals a great deal about this woman to whom convention meant very little."

He gazed somberly out over the gathering of grandlady's mourners. "She lived life with a zest that belied her age in actual years. She gave many of us courage when we needed it most. I like to think that she has inspired all of us to live life in whatever way we choose, regardless of the opinions of others."

He paused. "When she spoke about her late husband, Augustus, who as all of you know—and she was proud to admit—was a rum runner, it was with a respect and affection seldom encountered in today's society. She was an anachronism in her own time. But that is perhaps one of the facets of grandlady's personality that will assure her a place in Samsqua's history—along with her selfless efforts during the war.

"And it's a strangely beguiling fact that the two people who gave this island historical importance happened to be women—women who probably had a great deal in common. Uneema is buried on the ledge on High Mountain, and Lucia Concannon, our beloved grandlady, will rest beside her. They were strong courageous women. God bless them both!"

Tears were streaming down Georgie's face as he pumped up the bellows. Edna Lowery played very softly, "Young at Heart." Until then both Sarah and Johanna had remained stoic, but hearing the words to the romantic forties ballad that grandlady had loved so much, they began to weep. They were crying not for grandlady, who had certainly done everything in life that she had set out to do—which was, in itself, memorable—but for themselves, now forever deprived of her company. Sarah, sitting next to Burke in the crowded pew, took solace from the strength that emanated from him, from the comforting shoulder pressed solidly against hers.

Sarah had been named executrix of the will, the contents of which were well known, since she and Johanna had been present fourteen years before when grandlady had made out her will after their parents' death. Sarah could see her now, standing at the head of the table. "Miss Jo," she had said, looking over the top of her reading glasses, "Glass Cottage is yours, along with four miles of beach and half of High Mountain. Since you don't want to go to college I've set aside eight thousand dollars in a special fund for you to use in your artwork—beginning now, if you wish. I'll also give you six hundred dollars a month, set up in trust for life.''

She had sought out Sarah's face. "To you, Miss Sarah, an education at the college of your choice. After that, since you're the ambitious one in the family, I expect you to earn your own living. So there's no allowance for you. When I go you'll get Needlepoint House and the remainder of the island.''

She had pointed a long bony finger at them. ''Now, as you know, the villagers have leased their land for ninety-nine years, so you both will be landladies, and I expect you to do your duties. You've got a great responsibility.'' She had paused, her eyes growing misty. "There's not much actual cash left," she had added in a very low voice. "Enough for Miss Jo's legacy and that's about it.'' Then she had laughed good-naturedly. "You can fight over my jewels!" Raising her glass, grandlady had saluted them. "And for God's sake, girls, get married soon so the Concannon blood will continue!"

Sarah smiled softly with remembrance and went into the kitchen of Needlepoint House. Edna Lowery was peeling potatoes. Not concentrating on what she was doing, she was paring half of them away. She looked up with a start at Sarah's entrance. "I just feel lost, Miss Sarah. I didn't know how lonely this old house could be without her.''

Sarah patted her shoulder. "I know what you mean." She looked around the room with its antiques and hibiscus-patterned settee, and shivered. "I've got to talk to you, Edna. Naturally I want you to stay on here. It may be lonely because I'll only be coming up infrequently, but we'll work out satisfactory compensation." She paused. "Will you stay?"

The little woman nodded. "I've nowhere else to go." She glanced out the large windows that overlooked the ocean. "I want you to know something, Miss Sarah." She smoothed her black bombazine over the laces of her corset. "About a year or so ago Lucia gave me an envelope that she said not to open until after her death." She reached into her purse and extracted a sheaf of bills. "It's all here—five thousand dollars. I imagine it's for the upkeep of the house."

Sarah shook her head firmly. "No. I assumed you knew that was for you to keep. Grandlady wanted to give it to you tax free. That's why she didn't put it in the will. Now you have enough money to go away, if that's what you want."

The little woman sighed. "Thank you, Miss Sarah, but if you can stand to have an old party around I'll...stay."

For answer Sarah kissed her cheek.

"I suppose you'll want to see upstairs?"

Sarah shrugged. "I don't think so—at least not on

this trip. I imagine the rooms are in a state of neglect. I'm not in the mood for cobwebs and dust. Not now.''

"But there are no cobwebs or dust!" Edna Lowery exclaimed. "All the rooms are spick-and-span, faithfully cleaned and aired out once a week.''

Sarah was shocked. "But we always thought—the family, I mean—that when grandlady moved downstairs years ago, the rooms upstairs had been bolted.''

"No," was the firm answer. "It was just that the stairs were too much for her.''

Sarah was perplexed. "Strange that she never had guests, never entertained." She smiled wryly. "I could have stayed here in comfort, instead of crowding Johanna at Glass Cottage.''

Edna Lowery nodded. "I know. But you know your grandmother. She didn't want to be bothered. She loved her privacy. Why don't you go up and see the rooms?" But Sarah demurred, saying she'd wait for Steve. She wanted him with her; the painful reminders of grandlady would be too strong to take alone.

Edna just lifted one eyebrow, then continued bustling around the room, ensuring that everything grandlady had loved was properly arranged. "I'll make some lunch for us now, Miss Sarah. Then I'll be on my way. You don't mind me takin' a week off? I'll be goin' to Portland. Gonna go see Miss Jo's exhibition, and then on to New York to get some new

clothes.'' She patted her black bombazine. "I've
been wearin' these widow's weeds for fifteen years—
ever since the mister went on to his reward. It's time
for a change. I've got my eye on some of those new
polyester shifts, so that I won't have to wear a foundation.... ''

Sarah smiled. "Why, Edna, I think that's very sen-
sible.'' She paused, then after a moment added idly,
"Oh, could you please put a bottle of that white wine
in the refrigerator? I'm planning to have fish tonight.''

LATER, despite Sarah's outwardly confident manner,
her stomach was churning with raw nerves. Edna had
left and she was alone in the house, waiting for Steve
to finish shooting for the day.

Two weeks had passed since grandlady's funeral,
and the weather was bitterly cold. Sarah had stayed
on Samsqua, presumably to be with Johanna in their
mutual grief, but the opportunity to see Steve almost
every day as they wrapped up the final scenes of
Devil's Dare had been the real motivation. She'd
found out a lot in those two weeks. Grandlady's
will—her most recent one—had changed things
slightly. Needlepoint House had been left to both her
and Steve, the only stipulation being that they marry
and "settle down—the two of them always rushing
around avoiding each other—and carry on the Concannon line, even if my grandchildren's names *will* be
Burke.'' After a few comments on the beautiful chil-

dren the pair of them would be bound to procreate, she had made it clear how much she liked and respected Steve.

In a separate letter to Sarah she told her in confidence how half of the profits from *Devil's Dare*, as well as Steve's salary, would go to aid refugees in specific regions of the Third World. It seemed that Steve's last film, *The Refugees*, had made the world community aware of their desperate plight. But though sympathy was high, the international service organizations involved hadn't been able to raise sufficient funds to help in any lasting way. So Steve had promised the World Relief Fund his share of the profits from his next film. Grandlady had given him permission to film on Samsqua partly because of his charitable intentions. But she was also, she assured Sarah, proud and pleased to have Samsqua immortalized on film, and had sworn to Steve that Sarah wouldn't know about the charity project. He'd also ensured that any damage done to Samsqua would be fully compensated for out of his own money. Although she was curious to know why he hadn't told her all this, Sarah had realized even then that it didn't matter.

Nothing mattered anymore except having Steve close to her. She'd watched each day as he worked, a man obviously well liked by his crew and who excelled in his craft. Every day her respect for him grew, and every day she tried to summon sufficient courage to go to him, to talk to him, to hold him and feel his arms tightly around her. She needed him more than ever now.

She'd spent the week tying up the Winter Fire campaign, after warning Ethan Fairchild that he'd be looking for another vice-president. She'd already rented her apartment and given her clothes to Gail and some other women who could make use of them. She, Sarah Jane Mackenzie, didn't need them anymore. She would inhabit Needlepoint House for at least five days a week, the other two being devoted to any free-lance assignments that Duncan-Fairchild could provide. But they would be few and far between, she hoped. She was going to rest for a while—let her body and her soul get back in touch with the real world, the world of fresh air and simple living. She smiled to herself as the comical image of Sarah Mackenzie as belated "hippie" popped into her mind. *Why not,* she thought. *I'll grow some vegetables, learn to bake bread.... You've got a long way to go, kid.*

She ran upstairs on light feet to check herself in the full-length mirror in grandlady's bedroom—hers now. She'd gained a few pounds and looked healthy and rested. There was a new light in the emerald green eyes, a glow to a complexion so clear it was almost translucent. She ran nervous fingers through her silky auburn curls and smoothed her hands over slim hips clad in rather snug beige corduroys. Satisfied that her Fairisle sweater in tones of green, beige and brown looked just right, Sarah hurried downstairs to await Burke's arrival.

It was dark now, and he still hadn't arrived. Sarah began to wonder if he had received the message, then wondered whether he had and was ignoring it. She decided she couldn't blame him after all. She had avoided being alone with him this past week, but it had been essential. She still had responsibilities toward Winter Fire and Basil Northcombe and had wanted those out of the way before she saw Steve alone again. That done, there was no excuse not to send the dinner invitation. And though she'd rehearsed a million times what she was going to say to him, she still didn't know if she could get the words out.

Footsteps on the path brought her up sharply, and she answered the door to a very weary but still heart-stopping Steve Burke, dressed as usual in blue jeans and denim shirt. Sarah attempted to keep the greeting light, but he kissed her passionately, holding her to him as if he were afraid to let her go.

But she couldn't go; she didn't even want to. *This* was the strength she needed just as she needed oxygen or water. Thoughts of him had been uppermost in her mind all week. But his presence, the feel of him, swamped all other thoughts now. She almost laughed aloud then, remembering how she had once resented the power he had over her.

"It's so right, darling. Darling Steve, I love you," she cried, tears in her eyes, half laughing at her own outburst after all her carefully laid plans. She couldn't control her emotions any longer.

"It's about time," he said roughly, his voice

ragged with emotion as he searched her face. "Sarah, love, are you saying you love me as much as I love you? That you'll be my wife?" His eyes showed Sarah his insecurity, and she realized her erratic behavior had given him cause to doubt her.

"Yes! Yes! I can't live without you! Satisfied?" she teased him.

"Not yet," he growled. And he kissed her roughly again, the impact almost sending her over backward had it not been for his splayed hand supporting her back.

Their kiss was all sweetness to Sarah, even in its urgency. But they had to talk; she wanted to talk. Taking his hand, she led him into the living room, where a crackling fire shot light into the dimness and warmth into the increasing chill.

They talked for what seemed like hours. Steve was somber as he recounted the times he'd said or done something to put further distance between them; admitting that his jealousy had blinded him to his love for her. "You also threatened my way of life, my independence, and I wasn't sure I was ready for it. But I found I couldn't live without you. The problem then was that you seemed perfectly capable of living without *me*. I wanted to hear you say you needed me." His eyes searched her face in the firelight. "I guess my actor's ego isn't so big after all, because I need you desperately, Sarah. I'm not complete without you. You're more important to me than anything else in the world."

There was a long silence, then Sarah in turn confessed her self-doubts, reassuring Steve that much as she had wanted to believe in him, she hadn't allowed herself to open up to that extent.

"Mackenzie, you've wanted to go to bed with me ever since Della's party. Admit it—it's sheer animal instinct."

She threw a crocheted cushion at him across the hearth, and he caught it, laughing. "Oh, pardon me. Did I offend your sensibilities?"

"You certainly used to! Sometimes I felt like a wanton hussy!"

"You do come up with some of the greatest expressions! And don't ever forget I'll attack you however I want, woman." He grinned ever so slightly. "As my wife you'll be there to serve me—cater to my every whim."

"Steve, be serious. Should we talk about that? I mean, you know I'll never be a 'puppet,' as you once put it so succinctly. What if you—or I—can't cope with such a strong personality in our mate? What if one of us just won't give in?"

"Darling," he said, and his handsome face was drawn and serious, "I love you for being you. Just *be* you. We'll grow together and compromise. But we'll be compromising because we want to, because we love each other."

They looked at one another intensely across the firelit room, and their love seemed to crystallize into a tangible thing. Sarah had never felt so happy, so purely, peacefully content.

"Now," SARAH SAID as they stopped at a blue door on the second floor, "I know what this room is. It's the ballroom. It's done in grandlady's favorite color—mauve, and there are matching draperies and little gilt chairs like those in the Waldorf-Astoria ballroom. I remember photographs of this room."

She gaped in surprise as she opened the door to expose the cavernous interior. It was not done in mauve with matching draperies, nor were there any gilt chairs. The room was painted in stark white and carpeted in dark brown plush. In the center of the room a large conference table rested, large enough to accommodate the two dozen wooden captain's chairs that lined the west wall. Venetian blinds covered the windows. But most striking of all were the floor-to-ceiling maps, dotted with hundreds of brightly colored pins placed at obviously strategic positions.

"My God," Burke exclaimed, "Johanna was right. This is a chief of staff's room!" He examined the maps. "Here's Italy. Look at the pins that surround Salerno!"

"I can hardly believe this!" Sarah cried. "Grandlady hadn't changed a thing in almost forty years." She lifted up a pad from the table and read, "There's no alternative but to start the operation at 1200 hours. The fog will be thin then." She looked up. "I've got goose bumps."

Burke nodded. "Me, too." He faced her. "I was kidding earlier when I said I'd like to make a movie about the Seabees and the marines. But now, seeing this room, I'm going to do it, although this time I'll

be on the other side of the camera—directing. I'm
going to do it if I have to sign up for five years of
commercials for Basil Northcombe! This is a story
that's got to be told. Grandlady would love it. It's
pure drama. Maybe President Roosevelt did sit
over there by the window." He pulled up a venetian
blind. "Look down there on the windward side—that
beach strewed with black boulders. That would be
where the men practiced landing their craft. We'll
recreate all of it." He turned to Sarah. "As
soon as we're married—within the month, I'm warning you—I'll get started on the planning. This place
will be the inspiration to do right by grandlady's
story."

Sarah kissed his cheek. "You're a wonder, my
love. Now let's take a look at those other rooms.
Who knows what we'll find?"

But all six bedrooms, each decorated in a different
color and style, were the same as she had remembered
from her childhood. Every artifact was perfectly
preserved, and there was not a speck of dust anywhere. "I can't get over this, Burke." She shivered
again. "It's rather sad really. Grandlady living here,
surrounded by the past. That's why she never invited
anyone to stay. She wanted to be alone here with her
ghosts. But looking back, I don't think she had any
regrets."

After a minute they went downstairs and Sarah's
mood lifted. "Mmm, ghosts always make me hungry. Let's eat!"

AFTER AN ENTREE of fresh-grilled codfish, which Sarah had purchased from old Pete at the wharf, she and Burke drank coffee in front of the fire in the huge living room at Needlepoint House. It had begun to snow, and a chill crept into the room through the huge windows that overlooked the wide expanse of ocean.

Burke lay back on the rug near the hearth, holding Sarah in a loose embrace as the fire warmed them both. His lips nuzzled her hair. "We're getting to the end of the line," he said soberly. "I finish *Devil's Dare* tomorrow and then go back to the Coast the next day. But we've got tonight, my love. At last, we've got tonight."

He kissed her fervently and she returned the kiss, running her fingers lightly over his jaw, feeling his closely shaved chin—those hard jutting lines that caricaturists love to accentuate. She nestled up to him, placing her head on his chest. His hands worked their way under her sweater, sending shivers up her spine. Then his fingertips moved very slowly, tantalizingly to the front until he held the soft swell of her breasts in the palms of his hands. He bent down and kissed her, his tongue gently parting her lips. She reached up to him and the kiss deepened.

As the nerves of her body tightened in anticipation, she sensed that this was the way it should always be. This marvelous feeling...like kindling igniting the logs in the fireplace until the flames shot up, creating an inferno in the grate. His hands were splayed across her back, drawing her more closely to him. Lost in his embrace, she felt him grow taut against her, and she held her lips up once more for his kiss.

Very gently he gathered her into his arms and rose from the carpet. He carried her across the Spanish-tiled foyer toward the stairs as easily as if she were made of air. Confidently she relaxed in his arms as he took the stairs one at a time. Held aloft like this in a warm cocoon, Sarah luxuriated in the memory of a childhood daydream: floating over a great expanse of sky from her perch on the ledge of High Mountain. She had often lain back on the cool moss and given in to her private reveries. The white clouds above would beguile her, and soon she would be traveling through space, her body as light as an aspen leaf.

The strong arms that held her now seemed to impart constant strength as she was transported down the hall and into the master suite. The fire that Edna Lowery had started earlier, after tidying the room, was flickering feebly. Yet the room was warm, and Sarah didn't know if the heat was generated from the fireplace or from the close contact of their bodies.

Burke laid her gently on the huge bed that had given comfort to several generations of Concannons, and looking up at the ornately painted ceiling she shivered. The knowledge came over her that all of the females of her clan had consummated their relationships here, and somehow it was as if all the voices that had ever been heard in this room were whisper-

ing songs of contentment, urging her toward fulfillment.

Very slowly, very tenderly, Burke urged the sweater over her head. She felt his lips graze her throat.
Those same lips that had been so insistent a few
moments earlier were now like gossamer wings, making a kind of tracery over her smooth skin. Circling
each breast in turn with his tongue, Burke took one
hard nipple gently in his teeth, causing exquisite
needles of sensation to shoot through her. Her back
arched toward him. As he deftly removed each article
of her clothing, pausing to plant a kiss here and there
on her warm body, she was drawn down into a hot,
sweet vortex. The experience was totally new. Perhaps she had dreamed of taking such a journey, had
dreamed of a man who could make her feel this
way.... And now that it was happening she let herself relax completely. Shivering, almost overcome by
tactile sensations, she drew his head down to hers
with yearning hands.

Then for a few moments she lay alone on the
coverlet, waiting for Burke to return to her. Her eyes
were closed, her body exposed to the warming atmosphere of the room. Unclothed now, he lay down beside her. His long lean frame was warm and strong,
and as he took her in his arms she felt as if she were
being held by a tight, unyielding force that was as
much mental as physical.

Again his fingertips roamed lightly over her breasts
and thighs, and she moved her curved thumbs in ever

widening circles over his back, tracing from his strong muscular shoulders down his spine to his lower back, and then back up again until she was caressing the hair on the nape of his neck.

He touched her intimately, and she thought she would explode with the rush that flooded her. She knew desire as she'd never before imagined, and ached for the fulfillment that must surely come soon.... Burke drew himself over her lightly and brought his arm under her shoulders until the palm of his hand rested flatly over her lower back. She tensed a moment, and then gave in to the pleasure of his scent and his touch. He bent his head to hers and parted her lips with his own. As he kissed her deeply she knew that this was only the beginning, and desire spread out from her body in warm waves. Never again would she deprive herself of these feelings! Never again would she be content to be alone. This sharing of each other's bodies, this marvelous sense of creating something from nothing, of recreating and recreating the fire, the sheer passion.... "Oh, Burke," she murmured, "I love you so much." She opened her eyes and gazed up into his face. His brown eyes bore into hers, and he kissed her again.

"I've waited what seems like years," he whispered. "I never thought you would come along. The special *you*."

His lips came down on hers demandingly. She felt the guiding palm of his hand under her, and she opened herself to him. She waited one agonizing moment, then another. "Steve, please!" she cried, and then she felt him at last, and it was as if she were being possessed by a force deeper than any she had ever known. When she felt his chest against her breasts she sighed audibly. Oh, the sweetness of that moment. *This* was what made the world out there bearable, *this* was what righted all wrong....

Just as she had been absorbed in her reveries as a child on High Mountain, so was she now carried upward once more. The slight pauses between the spirals of feeling only increased the anticipation.... Quick breaths rose in her throat time after time, only to ebb away as tentacles of fire spread outward from the core of her being, her femininity.

Steve's breathing matched her own now as he increased his movements, and her body lifted up as if to prolong the exquisite agony of the moment. Then, like the shifting colors of the aurora borealis, her body vibrated between pleasure and pain, fulfillment and renewal. She gasped once, then again, and her heartbeats increased until she felt she could no longer stand the exquisite torture. Then she relaxed completely and felt the full weight of his body on hers. She knew that he had reached the same heights of sensation as she had a moment earlier.

"Oh, my darling," he murmured. "Oh, my darling." After a while he shifted his weight to lie beside her, and after a time, while she held him loosely in her arms, she felt his deep even breathing. She knew absolute contentment. He was hers completely. Her dream had come true.

IT WAS A LATE AFTERNOON in March.

Burke had come in from the Coast, having seen a rough cut of *Devil's Dare*, and was as happy as Sarah had ever seen him. "Babe," he exclaimed, "it's awfully good. It'll make hundreds of millions! I can't wait until you see that final chase. It lasts for nine minutes and it's a very exciting piece of film." He laughed. "Samsqua never looked lovelier!" Taking her in his arms he added, "And neither have you, Mrs. Sarah Kathleen Jane Mackenzie Burke." He looked down into her eyes and winked. "How about a whirl around the pond?"

"That would be fun," she agreed. "Spring's almost here and the ice will be melting soon. Then we'll have to wait months to go skating again."

They heard a discreet knock on the door, and Edna came into the living room. She was always warning them of her approach, more to avoid her own embarrassment than theirs. "It's roast duck for dinner," she announced firmly. "And I'm practically burned to a crisp opening that old oven so much." She smiled. "I've been basting that bird with the last of old Augustus's rum."

"We're going down to the pond, Edna, but we won't be long," Burke said.

"I hope not!" Edna replied. "That bird's been giving me fits. It's got to be served within the hour."

"You might chill some of the champagne that Basil Northcombe gave us as a wedding present," Sarah suggested.

The old woman chuckled. "I've got a couple of bottles cooling outside in the snow. Now," she cautioned, "you and the mister be back by six-thirty!"

Sarah patted her shoulder. "Yes, ma'am."

The long eerie twilight was settling in over the island as Burke guided Sarah down Hannah Path to the willow tree, past the refurbished Running Mallow that looked like a painted postcard view, ablaze with light. They took the shortcut to the pond through the back acreage of the inn. "Look, Burke," Sarah said softly. "Look at Johanna's windows!" They paused a moment, their gaze sweeping upward. The windows were brightly lighted from inside, throwing into contrast the deeply jeweled glass tones and the gathering dusk. "I can see grandlady in her blue pinafore from here," Sarah said.

Burke nodded. "And there we are, standing arm in arm above Uneema's gravestone." He gathered her into his strong warm embrace. "We belong here. It's our island now; it's what grandlady wanted," he said, taking a deep breath. "Are you happy—being here, I mean? You don't miss the Big Apple?"

She shook her head. "We've been all through that before, darling," she replied softly. "I've done what I wanted to do, and I left my profession at the top of the heap. That's the way to go out—when you've captured all the glory. I was one of the fortunate ones." She squeezed his hand. "I owe so much to you, Burke. So very much." Sarah paused, and then went on slowly. "If you hadn't agreed to do the perfume ads and commercials, the campaign wouldn't have gone over so well. Do you know what it means to me personally—to have conceived the most successful promotion in the history of the cosmetic industry?''

He squeezed her hand. "The timing was absolutely right. I needed the money to finish *Devil's Dare*." He sighed. "Above all, I needed you."

"Are you happy, then?" Sarah asked in a tremulous voice.

"Need you ask? Are you?"

She nodded. "More than anyone has a right to be...."

He laughed. "Now you're sounding like a B-picture heroine!"

She grinned. "You're right. It's all been said so many times before, but it's still true." She sighed, looking ravishing in her white-and-green ski suit with a white tam on her auburn curls.

Down by the pond he struck a match and lighted the kerosene torches that framed the ice. They sat down on a log and laced up their skates. Then he guided her out to the middle of the pond. Holding her around the waist he turned her this way and that, creating an improvised dance out of the intense feeling of the moment.

As they glided over the ice the dusk deepened until the island was enclosed in a dark blanket, pierced only by the blazing torches. They paused a moment, and he took her in his arms and kissed her tenderly.

Sarah sighed gently, then stood back and pointed to the horizon. "Oh, look, Steve, look!" she exclaimed. "The northern lights!"

Steve faced the horizon where the play of light made ever widening circles in the sky: pale amber mixed with pink and green and the subtle shades of aquamarine that danced as if making their own music.

She grasped his arm. "Oh, Steve, grandlady was right. It *is* like a winter fire. The fire of our love...."

What readers say about SUPERROMANCE

"Bravo! Your SUPERROMANCE [is]... super!"
R.V.,* Montgomery, Illinois

"I am impatiently awaiting the next SUPERROMANCE."
J.D., Sandusky, Ohio

"Delightful... great."
C.B., Fort Wayne, Indiana

"Terrific love stories. Just keep them coming!"
M.G., Toronto, Ontario

SUPERROMANCE

Longer, exciting, sensuous and dramatic!

Fascinating love stories that will hold
you in their magical spell till the last page
is turned!

Now's your chance to discover the earlier
books in this exciting series. Choose from
the great selection on the following page!

Choose from this list of great

SUPERROMANCES!

#1 END OF INNOCENCE   Abra Taylor

#2 LOVE'S EMERALD FLAME   Willa Lambert

#3 THE MUSIC OF PASSION   Lynda Ward

#4 LOVE BEYOND DESIRE   Rachel Palmer

#5 CLOUD OVER PARADISE   Abra Taylor

#6 SWEET SEDUCTION   Maura Mackenzie

#7 THE HEART REMEMBERS   Emma Church

#8 BELOVED INTRUDER   Jocelyn Griffin

#9 SWEET DAWN OF DESIRE   Meg Hudson

#10 HEART'S FURY   Lucy Lee

#11 LOVE WILD AND FREE   Jocelyn Haley

#12 A TASTE OF EDEN   Abra Taylor

#13 CAPTIVE OF DESIRE   Alexandra Sellers

#14 TREASURE OF THE HEART   Pat Louis

#15 CHERISHED DESTINY   Jo Manning

SUPERROMANCE

Complete and mail this coupon today!

- -

Worldwide Reader Service

In the U.S.A.
1440 South Priest Drive
Tempe, AZ 85281

In Canada
649 Ontario Street
Stratford, Ontario N5A 6W2

Please send me the following SUPERROMANCES. I am enclosing m
check or money order for $2.50 for each copy ordered, plus 75¢ t
cover postage and handling.

☐ #1	☐ #6	☐ #11
☐ #2	☐ #7	☐ #12
☐ #3	☐ #8	☐ #13
☐ #4	☐ #9	☐ #14
☐ #5	☐ #10	☐ #15

Number of copies checked @ $2.50 each = $_____
N.Y. and Ariz. residents add appropriate sales tax $_____
Postage and handling $_____.7

TOTAL $_____

I enclose_____.
(Please send check or money order. We cannot be responsible for cas
sent through the mail.)
Prices subject to change without notice.

NAME_____
(Please Print)
ADDRESS_____
CITY_____
STATE/PROV._____
ZIP/POSTAL CODE_____

Offer expires November 30, 1982   2055600000